Two Green Keys

LM Foster

This is a work of fiction. Names, characters, places and incidents are products of the author's imagination. Any resemblance to actual events, locales, organizations, or persons, either living or dead, is entirely coincidental.

9th Street Press
www.9thstreetpress.com

To absent friends

Trident Media Group
Literary Agency
63 Madison Ave, 42th FL
New York, NY 10001

RE: Possible Submission of Non-Fiction Work

Ladies and Gentlemen:

Hi, my name is Carolyn Adyon. If my name is familiar to you, then you're probably a big fan of Alvee Smith-Killem, hot Hollywood ticket and probable shoo-in for *People's* next *Sexiest Man Alive.* That's me that you saw on his arm at the premiere of *Cheyenne Sundown,* the just-barely-made-an-R-Rating-because-he's-just-so-damned-sexy-in-it vehicle that shot him to international stardom.

But you might not be seeing me on his arm anymore. I've been feeling a little tired lately, and I don't think that it's entirely due to our whirlwind Hollywood lifestyle. I think my tiredness might be coming from an entirely different source – a more malevolent one, let's say – and it's just this suspicion that might cause me to lighten fan-girls' hearts everywhere and leave Alvee Smith-Killem.

But first, I've got my tale to tell, how I came to meet Alvee. It's a strange and unusual journey – once upon a time I wanted to be a writer – and that ambition feeds into the story, because if I'd never wanted to write, I definitely never would've met Alvee. If not for Alvee, nothing I've written would've ever seen the light of day.

So, I'll spell it all out, make sure I get the chronologies right. Maybe if you think anybody will believe it, you'll find a publisher for it. You'll have to call it fiction then, put in that disclaimer *about any similarities to people living or dead being purely coincidental,* lest the lawyers that Alvee's money can buy sue me and my discerning publisher back to the Stone Age. Lest I wind up dead myself. Lest this feeling of tiredness just keeps growing and growing until I expire.

So, please find attached, etc.

Sincerely,

Carolyn Adyon

Carolyn Adyon

ONE

It's been awhile now, since the first time I noticed the two green keys hanging off of my roommate's keychain. Ruthanne's prodigious set of keys were the originals that inspired that old warning that too much stuff hanging off your key ring will damage your car's ignition. First she had a big bunch of oversized, plastic baby keys, which she thought was an absolutely adorable, clever idea – baby keys as keychain for real keys! How cute is that?

Attached to the baby keys were perhaps only six or seven metal keys that actually opened things – car doors and apartment doors and office doors. There was a little club card for the grocery store, and one for the drug store.

But in addition to these, Ruthanne had a miniature rendition of the Hollywood sign made out of soft plastic; a large black fob that claimed to be from the Bates Motel; and a pewter deep sea diver's helmet that symbolized I knew not what.

It was a change in the familiar clank of her keys that actually drew my attention to them. We were driving home from work and I noticed a new little rhythmic *tink* among the slapping of all those different bits of plastic, and I looked over at the overtaxed ignition of her car. Two identical metal keys, painted a shiny pistachio green, hung from the very bottom of the assemblage. They clinked together pleasantly.

I could tell that even though these two were metal, they were not there to open things, because the keys that in fact opened things were segregated on a separate part of the structure. For quick access when actual opening had to be accomplished, I imagined.

I asked her, "What's with the green keys?"

Ruthanne looked over at me and smiled, pleased that I'd noticed the addition. "Good luck charm," she said.

"Really," I said. "How's that?"

"It's kind of a long story," she said. "Are you sure you want to hear it?"

Ruthanne had a lot of long stories. She was almost always polite enough to ask if I wanted to hear one of them before holding forth, however. I nodded, and she began.

"There was this actor in the '60s . . ."

I was immediately sure that I was going to be sorry. My friend was what is referred to in the parlance as a fan of movie stars. *A big fan.* She was not just someone who can tell you about where Brad and Angie spent their honeymoon, or why Tom Cruise really isn't gay, or who Bradley Cooper is dating right now – Ruthanne knew that stuff too, but she was primarily a fan of movie stars of yesteryear. She knew thousands of amazing and utterly boring facts about the actors and actresses of the Golden Age of Hollywood right up through about 1979 or so. After that, her encyclopedic knowledge waned a little – stars that were still alive didn't seem to hold as much appeal to her as the old ones and the dead ones did.

Ruthanne's room was decorated with movie posters, and she kept several fat notebooks stuffed with 8 x 10 glossies of all her favorite stars. She added to her collections via the internet, and also made the pilgrimage a couple times a year to buy and trade with the memorabilia shops in downtown LA. Nothing pleased her more than to snag a rare autographed photo, or a hard-to-find copy of some old movie that no one but she and her fellow nutball fans had ever heard of. She would mourn for weeks if someone else beat her to the prize – she called this being *swooped.*

I thought that it was a bizarre hobby for a young woman – while there were many and varied attractive *modern* movie stars, and Ruthanne avidly watched their movies – she only seemed to coo and sigh the most over the ones that had been dead for decades.

It was so weird to me, following movie stars of any kind, dead or alive. I mean, don't get me wrong, I like movies probably more than the next person – but I could never get into movie *stars* the way Ruthanne was into them. Sure, they're all very attractive and watching their movies is entertaining. And maybe they even deserve the millions they make.

But I just couldn't possibly bring myself to care about the opinions, the ups and downs, the triumphs and tragedies, the marriages and divorces and babies and betrayals of fantastically wealthy and beautiful people that I was never, ever going to meet. And if all these triumphs and tragedies, marriages and divorces had occurred in the past, as was the case with the ones my friend liked the best, I cared even less. But these people were real to Ruthanne, like neighbors. She wasted *emotions* on them.

I, on the other hand, was what is commonly referred to as a *movie buff.* Not a *film snob,* mind you – I knew that *The Bicycle Thief* existed, but I'd never seen it. I knew nothing about Fellini, didn't hold Hitchcock as a god. I'd enjoyed *Citizen Kane,* however, long before I heard how amazing it was supposed to be, and Orson Welles' *Othello* was superb.

I could almost hold up my end of the conversation with a film snob, however, if he was talking about some of the old mainstream classics, ones everybody had seen. If he wanted to talk *Casablanca,* or *The Maltese Falcon,* or *Giant,* or *The Wild One* or *On the Waterfront,* I could intelligently discuss characterization and plot. There were a few more of the oldies that I was familiar with – *Gone with the Wind,* or course, or *The African Queen,* or *The Postman Always Rings Twice.* But if he wanted to talk about directors and pacing, camera angles and lighting, I was out. I liked to enjoy movies, not analyze them.

I'd always thought I might like to write them, too, but I'll get to that laughable ambition later.

I'd never seen *It Happened One Night,* or *Breakfast at Tiffany's,* or even *It's a Wonderful Life.* I never watched foreign films if I could possibly help it, especially not old, classic ones. I'd never seen a single thing starring Charlie Chaplin of Mark Pickford or Buster Keaton. In fact, the only silent film I'd ever seen was *The Mystery of the Leaping Fish,* starring Douglas Fairbanks as Coke Ennyday, and that was only because it was outrageously funny and only twenty-five minutes long.

I was a *modern* movie buff – anything from about 1980 or so – if it was made in Hollywood and it had made a little money, if it wasn't too much of a tearjerker or rom-com, then chances are I'd seen it, or at least heard of it. If it was foreign or obscure or too sad or too romantic, then it had probably passed me by. I was a buff, not a snob. And I certainly wasn't a *fan* of movie stars.

"There was this actor in the '60s," Ruthanne was saying. "His name was Franck O'Day. He spelled it F-R-A-N-C-K. His full name was Francis Joseph O'Day." She grinned a little for subjecting me to too much information already. "He disappeared after a plane crash in 1968."

"You mean, he died in a plane crash in 1968?" I asked. "Like Buddy Holly and the Big Bopper?"

"Oh, no," Ruthanne replied emphatically, as we pulled into the driveway of our apartment complex. She put the gate-card into the reader, then looked over at me while the gate slowly clanked open. In all seriousness, she said, "There was never any proof that he died."

"So, if he was in movies in the '60s, and he didn't die in the plane crash, how old would he be now?" I asked.

"I think he was born in . . . ." Ruthanne did some calculations in her head as she pulled into our spot under its rusty awning. I knew that she didn't *think,* she *knew.* As I said, Ruthanne was nothing if not

3

versed in her facts about the lives of ancient movie stars. We got out of the car and I followed her up the steps to our apartment. "He turned eighty. In April." She grinned again. She knew when his birthday was.

"And you think he's still alive?" I asked incredulously. "Like wandering around in the woods somewhere, un-rescued all these years? Like Bigfoot?"

Ruthanne paused on the steps to shoot me a withering, now-that-would-just-be-ridiculous look. "Hold on a minute. I'll show you proof."

She unlocked the door to our apartment with her clinking, clanking keys; the two green ones flashed. I realized that she hadn't even mentioned them and their significance yet – she hadn't even hinted at what was supposed to make them good luck charms. I sighed. This was going to be a long story indeed. But it was all right. Sure, it was Friday night, but it wasn't like I had a date or anything. Ruthanne was a helluva good bartender, and I knew that if I sat still and listened to her story, she'd feed me a couple of good strong drinks, and at least I'd have a nice buzz going by the time she was done with her tale. There were worse ways to spend a Friday night.

Ruthanne set her purse and giant set of keys on the coffee table, and as if reading my mind, she asked me if I wanted a drink. I smiled. "Sure."

Her stories weren't always that bad, I thought. This one even seemed to be going to have a little mystery to it. It wasn't like I had one other thing to do, anyway. I went into my room to change out of my work clothes, then returned to the couch and waited.

A few minutes later, Ruthanne brought me a glass and presented it to me, saying, "In honor of Franck O'Day, I made you a mint julep. I read somewhere that he never drank anything else." Then she said, "To absent friends," and we clinked glasses.

I sipped. The drink was sweet and strong, complete with real mint leaves to make it extra tasty. Ruthie had a whole collection of extra little things to make drinks so that they were *just like they serve 'em in Vegas,* she said. Simple Syrup and mint leaves and limes and olives and cocktail onions, depending on your tastes. It sure beat an ice cube and a shot in a coffee cup, which was how I made a drink. A big fan of old movie stars and a helluva bartender. That was my friend.

Ruthanne set her drink down on the coffee table. "Okay. You wanted proof that Franck O'Day is still alive." She disappeared into her bedroom.

"Sure," I said, and sipped my excellent drink. I could not care less if Franck O'Day was still alive, whoever he was or had been, but I

4

knew that Ruthanne wanted to prove it to me, and after all, I'd made the mistake of telling her that I wanted to hear the long story.

Ruthanne returned with a folded-over magazine. She handed it to me, and sat down in a chair across the coffee table from me and picked up her drink. Already feeling the Kentucky Whiskey warming my synapses, I read aloud, "'1950's and '60's era starlet Jessika Yerdlay passed away December 31, after suffering a stroke. She was 81. She is survived by her daughter, Dolores, who said that her mother passed peacefully a few hours after admission to Cedars-Sinai in Los Angeles.

"'Yerdlay made several movies in the late 1950s and 1960s, but is probably best known for the classic *High Times in Manhattan*, in which she appeared opposite Franck O'Day.'"

I looked up at Ruthanne, who smiled. I continued. "'*Variety* called *High Times in Manhattan* "a delightful comedy about romantic hijinks at an upscale New York hotel during New Year's Eve, 1940," and drew comparisons to *It Happened One Night* and even *Breakfast at Tiffany's*.'"

I looked at Ruthanne. "You know, I've never seen either of those."

Ruthanne nodded, sipped her drink. "Yes, you are a Philistine. Proceed."

I read on. "'*The New York Times* called it "a definite Oscar contender" in 1961. But despite gushing praise from all quarters, it was not happily-ever-after romance but doomed, musically-accompanied romance that was on Oscar's mind that year. Best Picture honors went to *West Side Story*. *High Times in Manhattan* was not even nominated. The picture has since appeared in several Top Ten lists, however. Tragedy and scandal followed Yerdlay and O'Day throughout the 1960s, and they are often remembered more for these events than for their appearance in *Manhattan*.

"'O'Day wed Bridget McSwale while making the film in 1961, but tragedy struck in 1965 when Jessika's brother Roger killed O'Day's wife in an apparent murder-suicide.'" I looked up at Ruthanne in surprise. She sipped her drink, and gestured for me to keep reading.

"'Two years later, on Valentine's Day 1967, Yerdlay announced that she and O'Day were engaged to be married, but rumors swirled that the engagement had been called off when O'Day flew to England alone in July, on the anniversary of his wife's death, to consult with director Robert Ecksmith about a new film. In September of 1967, Yerdlay officially called off their engagement. Long before Roman Polanski would be convicted of similar offenses, Yerdlay stated that she had evidence that O'Day had engaged in criminal improprieties with her daughter Dolores in 1965, when Dolores was only fourteen.'"

5

Again I looked at Ruthanne. This was interesting. Again she gestured for me to continue reading.

"'In January 1968, O'Day planned to leave Japan, where he and Ecksmith had been scouting locations for their film, to return to the United States to answer Yerdlay's charges. O'Day and Ecksmith were declared lost and presumed dead when the small plane they were flying in went missing on January 7th, 1968. Wreckage from a plane believed to be O'Day's was discovered in 1982. However, no remains were recovered, nor was the plane definitively determined to be O'Day's. He and Ecksmith were declared legally dead in 1976. In May of 1968, Jessika Yerdlay was involved in an automobile accident from which she was said to be left "disfigured." She retired from acting that same year.

"'Yerdlay was interred in O'Day's plot in Hollywood Forever Cemetery, which he left to her in his will.'" I looked up at Ruthanne a fourth time. "It says right here that he died in a plane crash."

"No, Carol," she replied, again emphatic. "It says that he was *lost and presumed dead*. Look at the picture!"

Below the article was a black and white photo of a stunning blonde, glaring seductively at the camera, captioned *Jessika Yerdlay, 1961*. Beside this was a grainy color photograph of an old man standing in front of a tombstone. He was wearing a fedora and large sunglasses, obscuring his face; he could be Jimmy Hoffa, for all I could tell from the picture. The caption read, *Lone fan mourns Jessika Yerdlay last week.*

I turned the magazine to its cover and discovered to my surprise that it was *Time* from February of last year. *Must've been a slow news week,* I thought. I flipped back to the article on Jessika Yerdlay and said to my friend, "Don't tell me, Ruthie. Let me guess. You think that this old guy in the picture is Franck O'Day, returned from the wilds of Mt. Fuji to pay his respects."

"Exactly!" she replied. Then she studied me silently before saying, "You know, this could be the story you've been looking for. For your book."

TWO

Allow me to briefly interject a little back story at this juncture. Ruthanne and I met in high school, became inseparable pals. My appreciation for movies and her love of movie stars made our friendship an instant success. After graduation, we landed plum jobs at her uncle's law firm. King Nepot rules all! We were assigned to what was, in another era, called *the typing pool*. There have we stuck for going on ten years now. The pay is good, the work is challenging enough – the volume of documents that need to be typed, executed, and filed at a large law firm is massive.

Ruthanne and I both tried a little college, a little night school, mostly to bone up on our secretarial skills. We each completed legal secretarial certificate programs at the local community college. But somehow, the ambition for an advanced degree never took hold. Ruthie and I settled. Being secretaries was good enough for us. After all, Ruthie had her stable of movie stars to light up her imagination, and I had the not uncommon ambition to be a writer. I aspired to be a novelist, or on my days of more determined dreaming, a screenwriter. I'd even tried to freelance a few movie reviews. But not a single print rag, not one *GoDaddy.com* website, had ever accepted a single one of them.

Ruthanne had suggested that I try my hand at writing about some of her old movie star legends before, but I'd always declined. I'd never heard any that interested me, not even vaguely. The old Hollywood mystery stuff has been done to death – even the Black Dahlia murder has more or less been solved, at least as far as the documentary-watching public is concerned.

But I had to admit that Ruthie was right, this time. This one had everything – a murder-suicide; a sex scandal; a lost-and-presumed-dead actor and director. And if my friend was any example, the guy somehow still had devoted fans. This one did have some interesting elements.

I shrugged. "You could be right, Ruthie. Maybe I could turn it into something." I smiled at her. "Will you be my research assistant?"

"Of course." She smiled back at me. "But you ain't seen nothing yet. Franck wasn't at Jessika's grave to pay his respects. Hold on a second."

Ruthanne disappeared again into her room, then reappeared with her laptop. She sat beside me on the couch this time, and typed. I sipped my drink, then she turned the laptop around and showed me the screen.

There was a series of pictures of the old man and the tombstone, taken from a slightly different angle. The first was similar to the one that had appeared in *Time*, showing him gazing at the grave. But the next one showed him jumping joyously in the air, iron gray hair askew, waving his hat. The third one showed him with his back to the camera, hat replaced, walking away from the grave. The headline beside the pictures asked, *Who can this be, dancing on the grave of Jessika Yerdlay?*

Ruthanne read aloud. "'After a lifetime of ignominy brought on by her cruel, heartless, and patently fatuous allegations, Franck O'Day has now had the last laugh. It looks like he enjoyed it, eh, fans? Keep sending all your good wishes and love energies to Franck. While his health had been faltering a little lately, the death of his enemy and your healing energies have once again put him on the road to recovery. Keep sending in those keys! Watch this space for news of *a personal appearance* in the not too distant future!'" Ruthanne looked at me, blinked solemnly. "See, I told you he wasn't dead."

At last, a mention of keys. Maybe this story wasn't going to be so long after all. I said, "What was that about love energies? And keys?"

Ruthanne sighed, smiled a little sheepishly. "I know you won't believe any of this, Carol. But like I say, it would all make a great book." She picked her drink up from the coffee table, sipped it. "You only believe in things that you can see and touch."

"And sometimes not even then," I said, gesturing at her computer. I surely didn't believe that the old man in the picture was an ancient Hollywood reprobate, returned from a mountainous, snowy death to dance on the grave of his accuser in some sordid sex scandal. And I had to hear a little bit more before I decided if I thought it all was seriously book material or not.

"But you'll give me that there are more things in heaven and earth than are dreamt of in your philosophy?" Ruthanne asked. "You'll give me that?"

Just when I began to think of her as a simple creature, with her unrequitable loves for dead movie stars, Ruthanne reminded me that she was also an erudite, intelligent woman. One must not be too quick to judge the fantasies and obsessions of others, I reminded myself. Because she was right – my philosophy was ill-defined and rough around the edges and there was plenty of room for more things to be added to it. And my fantasies and obsessions revolved around becoming a movie reviewer, a best-selling novelist, an award-winning screenwriter. Even my own mother had laughed at that one.

8

"There's a belief that people can send healing energies to others, Carol," Ruthanne continued. "There are actually several beliefs, several ideas, several names for the process. There's *Reiki*, which is kind of like a laying on of hands –"

"Like faith healing?" I asked.

Ruthanne shook her head. "In faith healing, the people believe that God has a direct influence. God is directing the healing. In *Reiki*, no deity is invoked. It's believed that there can be a transference of the eternal energy from one person to another. If you're sick, your energy is thought to be unbalanced; it can be put back in balance by the transference of energy from others. Some people believe that objects can be imbued with malevolent energy. I know you've heard of that kind of thing – voodoo dolls and cursed objects and haunted houses and so forth." Ruthanne frowned and shook her head. "Some people believe that healing energy can be contained within objects, too; some believe that it can also be supplied telepathically. They believe that it's possible to send love and good feelings to another person simply by meditating. Simply by *sending* these feelings, the other person can receive them and benefit from them. Sometimes it's called *telepathic love therapy.*" Ruthanne paused.

I said, "What does this have to do with keys?"

Again, Ruthanne smiled a little sheepishly. "The keys are a symbol for fans of Franck O'Day. In early 1967, Franck and Jessika started work on a film called *Two Green Keys*. Unfortunately, nothing much is known about it, because it was never completed. It was first shelved in July, when Jessika's brother, Roger, murdered Franck's wife, then killed himself."

"What was that all about?" I asked. I thought again about the as yet unconceived book – this gruesome detail was a lot more interesting than healing love energies and still-unexplained keys.

But Ruthanne shook her head. "I'll get into that later. You wanted to know about the keys."

Indeed. The keys had started this whole thing.

Ruthanne noticed that my mint julep was waning, and continued her story as she went out to the kitchen to make us both another one. "In January of the following year, shooting was slated to resume on *Two Green Keys*. On Valentine's Day, Jessika announced her engagement to Franck. Shooting didn't resume, however, and in July, Franck flew to England with his friend, Robert Ecksmith, who had directed him in his first major feature, a historical biopic about Benedict Arnold."

"Benedict Arnold?" I asked in surprise. "*Really?*"

"It bombed. I have a copy of it though, if you'd like to watch it."

"Perhaps later," I said. I had a sneaking suspicion, as they say, that I'd wind up watching this dog, as well as the aforementioned *High Times in Manhattan*, and probably whatever other epics that had starred Franck O'Day, if I decided to at last really write my book.

Ruthanne returned and handed me a second mint julep. She again toasted, "To absent friends," and we clinked glasses. Then she continued. "Eventually, *Two Green Keys* was shelved permanently." Ruthanne sipped her drink. "There's always been a great deal of speculation and conjecture in the fan community about what it was about, but nobody really knows for sure. Some say that is was probably another rom-com kind of thing, since their first one had done so well. Since there were two keys, maybe somehow things got mixed up, hilarity ensued, et cetera. Others say that it was maybe a more spiritual or magical flick – maybe two keys were needed to unlock some mysterious secret. But no one knows for sure. There are supposed to be a few stills from it, but I've never seen any of them. No clips. Yerdlay never spoke of it, nor did the director. No one has been able to find out who the screenwriter was. The script vanished. It simply became a lost project, a mystery.

"Then Maribeth – that's the lady that runs the website." Ruthanne gestured at the computer. "She decided to create a little symbolism, incorporating the title of this lost work – something that Franck's fans could share. Nobody's ever heard of the movie, unless they've heard of Franck, so it's a little way that we can identify each other, so to speak. Almost like a secret handshake." Ruthanne sipped her drink and grinned. "It works like this. You find two keys. Any two will do – they can be yours or someone else's, it really doesn't matter. You meditate on them – fill them with your good wishes, your love for Franck – then you send them with a self-addressed stamped envelope to the fan club. Franck receives the energy and love from them – and infuses each with a little of his own grateful energy. Maribeth paints them green to complete the symbolism of the movie title, and mails them back."

Ruthanne picked up her voluminous keychain from the coffee table, and looked at the shiny green keys. "No one ever gets back the same keys that they sent in. These keys meant something to somebody at one time, opened some doors somewhere. But they weren't *my* keys, so they don't mean anything to me – I have no personal association with them, so none of my energy is in them. Now they only symbolize my devotion to Franck O'Day." She lightly caressed the pistachio colored metal. "I own something that he actually touched, Carol! Something that's imbued with a little of his energy, a little of *him*. What better good luck charm is there than that?"

10

Not for the first time in our association, the thought crossed my mind that Ruthanne might be certifiable. Sure, she was smart and hip, and sure, my philosophy was lacking on many fronts, but it was obvious that my friend really believed all this stuff she was telling me. She believed that long-forgotten matinee idol Franck O'Day not only wasn't dead – he'd actually touched the green keys that she now gazed at fondly, thereby filling him with his energy, thereby making them lucky.

On the other hand, I figured that Ruthanne was no crazier than all of the autograph hounds in the world, and all the sports memorabilia nuts, people who would spend a fortune on a muddy jersey, just because they believed that their idol had actually worn it during the big game. Some concept of luck, of energy, of a little part of the person being infused into the object, had to play into all that, didn't it?

I asked Ruthanne, "Who is this Maribeth person that runs the website? She's his biggest fan, I'd imagine?"

Ruthanne was simultaneously thrilled that I was asking further questions and miffed that I could suggest that anyone besides herself could be Franck O'Day's biggest fan.

She said, "Maribeth McSwale O'Day is Franck's daughter." When I looked at her in surprise – this was the first mention of any other children besides Jessika Yerdlay's own perhaps-molested daughter – Ruthanne quickly clarified. "She's his stepdaughter, actually. When Franck married Bridget McSwale, she already had a little girl, Maribeth, from a previous marriage. When Bridget was murdered, Maribeth went back to live with her biological father. But she never forgot Franck.

"This fan club has been around for a long time. It used to be a regular snail-mail newsletter thing, but she's been online since 2006 or so. I think she must be pretty technologically savvy for someone in her . . ." Ruthanne did more calculations in her head. She knew how old his daughter was, too. ". . . late fifties."

Okay, that clinched it. Ruthanne was right. Franck O'Day's life story would indeed make a good book.

I'd do a little research, with ever-eager Ruthanne as my assistant. I'd write about this Franck O'Day guy, and Jessika Yerdlay and their soured love affair, and their movies, and their tragedies and scandals. I'd do a little digging into his stepdaughter and her strange requests for healing energy; not to mention the fact that she was putting it out there on the interwebs, that dear old step-dad wasn't dead at all. I'd scare up Jessika's daughter, Dolores, and see what her take on the whole thing was.

11

Yeah, this one would make for a good read, what with the tragedies and scandals – but the crazy, New Age healing energy requests from devoted fans, and those claims of resurrection from the grave – that would put a fresh spin on the whole thing.

Ruthanne could see the cogs and wheels spinning in my head. She smiled. "Where should we begin?"

I held out my glass to her. "I'd like to begin with another drink." I rattled the ice. "If it's not too much trouble."

"No trouble at all."

.

THREE

Early the next morning, I sat in the recliner in my room. It was my favorite place to write. I stared alternately at the laptop on my lap, its blank screen with blinking cursor – and the blank wall of my bedroom. Nothing blinked there, nothing blinked in my head. Nothing yearned to get out and onto the screen. I drummed my fingers on the arm of the recliner (right off the Naugahyde cow) and considered.

I decided that it might be best to start with what I'd already heard about first, so I entered *two green keys* in the Google search box.

The first item in the list was the webpage that Ruthanne had shown me, *TwoGreenKeys.com*. There were no other hits for the phrase. No *Wikipedia* entry – this indicated that Franck's obscure, aborted movie must've been fragmentary indeed. No *IMDb* entry.

No Facebook page, either. Maribeth might be technologically savvy for someone in her fifties, as Ruthanne had suggested, but apparently she was not completely up to date. That was okay with me, however – the idea of a Facebook page devoted to some presumed-dead actor in his eighties and a movie that had never been realized seemed just a little bit creepy to me. How many likes would that attract?

So, I clicked on *TwoGreenKeys.com*. The opening page showed an autographed head shot from *High Times in Manhattan*, next to two giant, antique metal keys, painted the same shade of pistachio green as the little modern ones on Ruthanne's keychain. They looked like something that would open a medieval dungeon: huge and ponderous. Something that would definitely ruin your ignition.

I studied the picture of Franck O'Day, circa 1961. What was it about this guy, dead almost twenty years before my friend was even born, that tickled her fancy so much? The picture was in black and white; he was wearing a tuxedo. He had a high forehead and black, wavy hair. Gray eyes surveyed the viewer from beneath slightly manicured brows. His nose was non-descript, not too big, not too small. He had a large mouth, a nice smile; slightly uneven, slightly crooked teeth.

Overall, a pleasant enough looking fellow, certainly more attractive than your average Joe of the era, perhaps. But surely nothing to get all gushy about. As he was in character as someone from the 1940s, the photo lent him a little of the mystique of stars from that era. But still, I saw nothing spectacular about him.

I had just duly noted these impressions on the blank screen of my laptop, mostly just to make it not blank anymore, when Ruthanne knocked politely at the door. I told her to come in.

"I'm so happy to see you in the writing chair!" She sat on the corner of my bed and looked expectantly at me. "What have you got so far?"

I looked at the vague, one paragraph description of Franck O'Day's picture, and thought that anybody else might be annoyed at my friend's request for results, *already*. I thought that anybody else might be annoyed at the interruption. But not me. Ruthanne was right – it felt good to be in the writing chair again; it felt good to have someone ask to read something I'd written, even if it was only one paragraph. And truth be told, this one was getting off to kind of a slow start, so I was not only not annoyed, I was almost grateful for the interruption.

I knew that I was a little rusty. The last thing I'd written was a sword and sorcery epic, sort of a *Harry Potter* meets *The Lord of the Rings* kind of thing, with a lot of sex and betrayal thrown in. Definitely not for kids. It ran to some four hundred pages of *My Lord's* and *Your Grace's* and other Olde English claptrap. It was execrable, and that was my own opinion of it. Nobody, not even my best friend Ruthanne, had ever made it past the first three pages before suddenly recalling pressing engagements elsewhere. It now served as the necessary weight in the bottom drawer that kept my desk from floating away into orbit.

I knew that the words for this one would come eventually. I just didn't have a clear picture of exactly how this new story should go. Not yet. So I welcomed my friend's interruption. Wordlessly, I turned the laptop in Ruthanne's direction.

She smiled attentively and read the short paragraph. Then she looked up at me, with a not-well-hidden, slightly pained expression. She said simply, "May I?"

Surprised, I nodded, and Ruthanne took the computer from me and set it on her knees. She minimized the page and studied Franck's picture. She tilted her head at the familiar features, smiled fondly. Then she brought up my one paragraph again and began to type. After a few moments she said, "How about this?" The *instead* hung in the air, unsaid. She handed the computer back to me.

Ruthanne had been respectful enough not to delete my short paragraph. Not knowing what to expect – Ruthie had never expressed an interest in writing before – I read what she'd typed below it.

14

Franck considers us smugly in a publicity still from his acclaimed film, High Times in Manhattan. Is there any icon more enduring, more alluring, that a man in a tuxedo? He has the brow of an angel, crowned with glorious wavy hair, as black as midnight. Our fingers itch and ache to run gently through that hair. He has enormous eyes, as dark and as blue and as depthless as an angry, stormy ocean. Poets sing about such eyes. He has the cheekbones of a Greek god, a strong, perfect nose; a manly chin. Franck's subtle, knowing smile tells us that he has peered into our soul — he has kenned our desire, something we are powerless to conceal from him. He has an indescribable, incredible mouth — we would do anything, give anything, for the opportunity to taste that full bottom lip, just once, and Franck knows it. His teeth, just ever so slightly, endearingly crooked, lend an everyman, boy-next-door quality to his otherwise flawless face. The autograph in the corner reads, "To my biggest fan — grateful thanks for all your support — Your friend, Franck O'Day."

I looked up from Ruthanne's glowing, lyrical description, nonplussed. I minimized the window and looked at the picture again. I had to admit that she was right: he did have enormous eyes. But all the rest of it — I just wasn't feeling it. Even if I pretended that this picture was not fifty-some years old, even if I pretended that this man was still alive and that he still looked like this — I felt no stirring desire, like Ruthanne did. If I met him in a bar, I might talk to him, but I certainly would not *do anything* to kiss him.

I was suddenly reminded of the fact that women like different types of men, and your best friends are the ones that like a different type than you. Franck O'Day was so much more than obviously Ruthanne's type — but he didn't do a thing for me.

I could understand Ruthanne's voluntary susceptibility — in real life, she liked dark-haired, blue-eyed white boys, and would look twice at anyone who met those three conditions, even if he was as ugly as homemade sin. And movie stars aren't ugly — I understood how easy it was for Ruthanne to surrender to the same qualities that caught her eye in real life, how easy it was for her to immerse herself completely into fantasies about dark-haired, blue-eyed movie stars — men who were just a little bit more pluperfect than the ones that she actually knew.

Far be it for me to say that I'm immune to attractive actors that are my type — my type being, unlike Ruthanne, ones that are *still alive* — but I can choose to allow myself to be swept along by it or not. Ruthanne was like an alcoholic — she knew full well what triggered her desire, and she not only didn't avoid these things, she reveled in them. She would Google some star's name, hit *Images*, and spend hours just

15

sitting there in the dark looking at pictures. She was addicted to looking at pictures of movie stars as much, if not more, than some people are addicted to looking at porn. And Ruthanne wouldn't have attempted to curb this addiction, even if such an attempt were possible. There was nothing more fun to her than looking at and dreaming about *them*.

I, on the other hand, could handle any attraction I might feel, without sinking into the kind of mire of mindless adoration in which Ruthanne indulged. Sure, I might've felt a little tug when Ryan Gosling looked back at me from the internet, but unlike Ruthanne, I could decide to go with it or not. I could back out at any time; I could just say no to impossible fantasies and immediately get back to reality. After all, these things, these ideas, *are not real*. They're just dirty stories we tell ourselves. We cannot possibly know what these men are like in real life. We only know how *we would like them to be*.

I looked up at my friend's expectant face again. I couldn't think of a single thing to say to her. I appreciated her appreciation – and Franck O'Day's ability to engender such affection from beyond the grave would no doubt be a central theme to the book – but he was no Ryan Gosling, not by a long stretch, and personally, I remained unaffected. I had to admit that Ruthanne's florid description, while no more valid, was certainly more interesting than mine, however.

At last I said lamely, "You can't tell that he has blue eyes from this picture. It's in black and white. And aren't stormy oceans gray instead of blue? And how could you read the autograph? It's too small."

Ruthanne took the computer from me again. Quite familiar with the website, in two clicks, she brought up a full-screen blow-up of the same photograph. This one had been colorized with a loving hand – Franck's eyes were indeed a dark, almost cobalt blue – and the autograph was clearly visible.

Still, I remained speechless, not knowing what further comment to make about Ruthanne's glowing description. She quickly came to my rescue. "Perhaps you can use what I put as a fan perspective."

My eyebrows shot up in surprise and relief. "That's a great idea!" I said.

Ruthanne was not at all taken in. She said, "Too many more fan perspectives, and I'll want my name on the cover next to yours." She rose to leave.

I said genuinely, "I don't have any problem with that, Ruthie. After all, this was your idea."

"You're the writer. I'm just a fan."

"Franck O'Day's biggest fan. Surely that deserves your name on the cover."

Ruthie was tickled that I had recognized her as Franck's biggest fan. "I don't know about all that, Carol. I was just kidding."

"I'll dedicate the book to you. How about that?"

"That'll be great," she replied sincerely. "You just keep on writing, and I'm going to make us some lunch. After that, we can watch *High Times in Manhattan* if you want." She paused, then added, "You know, for research."

"Okay." I figured it was the least I could do.

FOUR

I turned my attention back to *TwoGreenKeys.com*, and clicked on the link marked *Biography*. *Biography*, it said, not simply *Bio*. I shrugged. Whatever.

Francis Joseph O'Day was born at home in Anderson Township, Ohio either April 29th or 30th 1933. Different sources state different days. Franck always maintains that his mother told him that his birthday is April 30th.

Franck's father, Thomas, was killed at the Battle of Normandy, June 6, 1944. The following year, Franck moved with his mother, Louise, to Los Angeles, to live with her brother. In 1946, she remarried. Her husband, Howard Smith, did not adopt the then thirteen-year-old Francis, so he retained his father's last name.

After three films (click here for synopses), Franck met Bridget McSwale at the wrap party for High Times *in Manhattan, in 1961. They were married not long after. Franck was overjoyed by the fact that Bridget already had a six-year-old daughter. He was quoted in* Life, *saying, "It's like having the best, happiest family ever. Instantaneously."*

This wonderful family life was cut tragically short when Bridget was murdered in 1965. Against her will, ten-year-old Maribeth was forced to return to live with her biological father in Kansas. Happily, when she reached her majority in 1976, Maribeth and Franck reconnected. Currently, they live in Los Angeles, California, where Franck is planning his comeback. Watch this space for further news.

I frowned. *Happily reunited.* Pfft. *Planning his comeback.* Right. Nothing about Jessika Yerdlay, nothing about their engagement, nothing about her accusations of molestation. No mention of the identity of Bridget's killer. Nothing about the plane crash.

You're not being entirely forthcoming, Maribeth, I thought. *Time Magazine,* not hardly a bastion of sensationalism and yellow journalism, was more forthcoming than you, and the article wasn't even about Franck O'Day.

I clicked the rotating *Back* icon at the bottom of the page. Beneath *Biography*, I next clicked on the link entitled *Franck's Career Highlights*. I skimmed over the gushing description of *RKO's Sister Sam's Lost Angels*, from 1956 – Sister Samantha and her charges must save orphanage from evil land grabbers. 'Nuff said.

I learned that this was Franck's very first movie role. Even though he was twenty-three at the time, he was youthful-looking enough to be cast in one walk-on scene, in the uncredited role of *prospective teenage adoptee.* No prints existed of the film, but there was a grainy shot of all the child actors, with Franck there in the back, circled in red, looking teenaged indeed.

I read on.

Mistakenly billed as Franck's first film appearance is 1960's George and Benedict, *directed by controversial English director Robert Ecksmith. The film depicted Benedict Arnold in a sympathetic light, as a heroic figure driven to treason by the political machinations of George Washington and other generals on his staff.*

Variety *called it "a dismally ill-timed apology for a universally reviled traitor. While resplendent in period attire, newcomer Frank O'day* (sic) *is horribly miscast as the whiny, thrice wounded Arnold. Forgetting the tiresome plot and predictable dialogue of Ecksmith's sorry re-write of American history, this reviewer instead imagined O'day wooing damsels on the village green."*

The New York Times *said, "Franck O'Day's performance was the only star in the moonless darkness of Robert Ecksmith's dreary attempt at canonizing American traitor Benedict Arnold. Even while hopelessly mired in the atrocious script, O'Day almost made me believe that Arnold could actually have been a dapper gentleman-soldier, wronged by jealous superiors. But not quite. Even the luminous O'Day cannot save this morass of revisionist history. But I see a bright future for O'Day - quick, someone get this man in modern dress and pair him with Julie Christie or Elizabeth Taylor or Jessika Yerdlay!"*

Hollywood *took* The Times' *advice and paired O'Day and Yerdlay the following year in the now legendary* High Times in Manhattan. *The New York Times reviewer, anxious to remind readers that he had foretold Franck's success, wrote, "O'Day has totally left behind the cloud of his initial misstep in last year's forgotten costume drama. He again lights up the screen, and this time he has the ever-effervescent Jessika Yerdlay beside him. Their on-screen chemistry is impeccable. A definite Oscar contender!"*

As we all know, however, West Side Story *won Best Picture for 1961. The New York Times dutifully congratulated the directing team of Wise and Robbins, but in a separate bio article on Franck, they said, "The Academy's snub did not seem to affect O'Day overly, however, because not long after the coveted statuettes were awarded to others, he married Bridget McSwale, age 26. Bridget brings to the marriage her six-year-old daughter, Maribeth."*

The thought struck me that Maribeth liked to talk about herself almost as much as she liked to talk about Franck. She had mentioned herself in his bio, and here she mentioned herself again in a rundown of his career.

There was no mention of the eponymous *Two Green Keys* on this page, which surprised me. But, on the other hand, it had been an aborted project.

I noticed that Jessika Yerdlay's name was linked. So I clicked on it. The page on which I landed was entitled *Jessika, Franck, Bridget, and Roger – Betrayal and Heartbreak.*

Now anyone who has spent any amount of time on the internet can tell you that there is some weird shit out there. Even if you aren't actively seeking out weirdness, even if you are simply *minding your own business on the internet* – as Ruthanne always referred to it – you'll still run across the unanticipated. And I don't mean just porn popping up where you least expect it. That does happen, of course – I once got some filthy photos from a perfectly innocent search for pictures of knights on horseback – *jousting*. I don't recommend a Google search. And of course there is the occasional racist or sexist, epithet-filled, violence-espousing rant, as well as the-aliens-are-from-Sirius-and-they-are-visiting-us crew, the Flat-Earthers, the government conspiracy buffs, and so on.

One of my favorite offerings from the off-the-wall weirdo set was a website put out by a woman from Cincinnati, Ohio, whose overarching theory stated that all the world's ills could be traced back to the disparity in men's penis sizes, and their accompanying awareness of this disparity. I remember raising an eyebrow at that, and thinking, *Go on.*

She posited that it was obvious when otherwise attractive men were under-endowed – these were the ones that were always dating younger and younger women, because, as these men age, they can no longer impress women their own age with their meager equipment. I considered. This made a modicum of sense.

She went on to theorize that all the men with little penises were required by their knowledge of this fact to hide it, and thereby, they became secretive and devious, foisting their secrets and deviousness upon an unsuspecting world. She attributed Napoleon Syndrome not to shortness in height, but to shortness in other regions. Men that are amply endowed exude confidence, she said, not so much from their knowledge that they were big, but more from the knowledge that others were smaller. She lost me a little bit there.

In conclusion, she said, our planet could only advance toward inner peace and tranquility, we could only end war and stuff, etc., if, at the age of majority, men were required to go to an official measuring station, be measured, and then have the result tattooed on their foreheads. She volunteered to found such a station, as soon as she could obtain Federal funding.

These tattoos would allow under endowed men to accept their handicap and work within their means. Women would no longer have to be disappointed once they had reached the point of no return in the first-time-with-a-new-guy arena. Little fellas would no longer hate these women for being disappointed; they would no longer hate themselves for being disappointing. They would adapt to being accepted for what they were, and would thereby no longer feel compelled to lie and deceive.

Eventually, they, and the little-penis problem itself, would both die out anyway, because women would no longer mistakenly pick them to reproduce with. New generations of men would be born with appropriately large members, and we could all live happily ever after. *Right.*

My point is, that after all the weird, crazy, spiteful, and just plain disturbing things I'd seen and read on the internet, I shouldn't have been at all surprised by Maribeth's rambling, hate-filled character assassination of Jessika Yerdlay.

But I have to admit that I was, anyway. In a world filled with denunciations of racism and sexism, it a world where you had best check your facts before posting anything even slightly unkind about anyone, in a world of libel suits and mega-million dollar awards in favor of the libeled, her rant was like a throwback to another age. Neither Dorothy Parker's Constant Reader nor Louella Parsons or Hedda Hopper in their heyday had anything on Maribeth McSwale O'Day's vituperation.

Jessika, Franck, Bridget, and Roger – Betrayal and Heartbreak
Jessica Yerdlay was an ambitious, mediocre, little known actress active during the 1950s and 1960s. She is probably best known for her portrayal of the flighty and self-absorbed Dora in High Times in Manhattan, *a performance which could have served as an autobiographical portrayal. Yet even in a role so suited to her real personality, Yerdlay was lacking. Critics universally agreed that she was carried by Franck O'Day in the film.*

I noticed that Maribeth failed to quote any of these critics, however.

Scenes in which they appear together are memorable because of his presence; scenes in which she appears alone – not so much. Scenes in which he appears alone

21

are all the more luminous because of the absence of her scenery-chewing and over the top histrionics.

Franck has said that Yerdlay's overwhelming affection for him was apparent from their first read-through of the script. And while he admits that he did dally with her during filming – "All that adoration was impossible to ignore," he said – it was most assuredly a one-sided love affair.

Franck met the true love of his life at the wrap party for Manhattan. As fate would have it, Bridget McSwale arrived on the arm of accountant Roger Yerdlay, Jessika's brother. His clients included many of Hollywood's best and brightest of the era, including his sister and Franck himself.

Bridget was originally from Kansas. She had fled a failed marriage, moving to Los Angeles in search of a better life for her and her little girl. She met Roger Yerdlay when she answered a want ad that he had placed for a secretary. Roger hired her the moment she walked in the office, because he'd fallen in love with her on sight. Falling in love with those who can mostly take or leave you was an unfortunate, unwise trait that Roger shared with his older sister. This selfish, delusional habit of theirs would lead to dire consequences for all parties involved.

Roger had been meekly and unsuccessfully pitching his woo to Bridget for about six months. Franck had been seeing the ever-eager and always accommodating Jessika whenever he could pencil her in around his busy schedule. They had appeared regularly in all the gossip columns throughout the filming of Manhattan, and because the movie-going, newspaper-buying public likes to think that the movie stars that fall in love on the screen are also in love in real life, the studio played up the apparent romance. And Jessika went along with the fiction.

In reality, she was nothing more to Franck than a compliant companion for that long 4th of July weekend on the yacht at Catalina, an adequate hostess for Hollywood-insider parties at his house in Malibu, a warm body to thaw him after skiing in Aspen.

The worlds of these four people would collide at the wrap party for High Times in Manhattan on New Year's Eve, 1961.

OMG, I thought. Maribeth could certainly spin a yarn. Her prose was almost as purple as Ruthanne's. I read on.

In a case of life imitating art, Franck was smitten at a party on New Year's Eve, as was the character he played in the legendary film. But unfortunately for Jessika, unfortunately for all of them, it was not she with whom he fell in love, but the tiny vision that appeared at the party on the arm of a lowly accountant. Bridget would later say that she felt self-conscious at the event, adorned as she was in a somewhat ill-fitting frock, one of Jessika's cast-offs, condescendingly lent to her brother's secretary for the occasion.

Franck would later say that he remembered nothing about the party other than Bridget: how they danced and chatted, their chaste kiss at midnight. He didn't notice when Jessika left in a huff, early – about the same time the ball dropped in Times Square. He didn't notice Roger Yerdlay sitting all alone in a dark corner of the room, getting morosely drunk, seemingly resigned to his loss to the better man.

Bridget and Franck were married in June 1962 at his house in Malibu. The clothes for the wedding party, including the adorable gown worn by Maribeth, who acted as flower girl, were designed by Paco Rabanne. An idyllic, month-long honeymoon in Acapulco followed.

Bridget and Maribeth soon settled in at Franck's palatial Malibu home. The three of them were ridiculously happy, the perfect little family, just as Franck had predicted in Life.

Jessika Yerdlay, in an uncharacteristic display of professionalism, did not berate Franck in the press about what she privately considered a monumental jilting. She was quoted in Variety, *saying, "I congratulate Franck on his choice of a gallant bride, and wish them all the happiness in the world."*

Franck would later say confidentially, however, that the first thing that Jessika did upon his return from his honeymoon was attempt to seduce him, the first moment that they were alone together. He was forced to remind her that he was in love with another, married to another. Their previous congress had run its course and was now over. There was no reason that they couldn't remain friends, however. Contractual obligations would force them to make more movies together, so why not make the most of it?

Previous congress? Does anyone still talk like that? Did anyone *ever* talk like that? I tried to picture a little old lady, sitting in front of her computer, writing this garbage. I failed. I read on.

Jessika seemed to accept this friendship arrangement. She remained close to Franck, his new wife, his new daughter. Her own daughter, Dolores, became a beloved playmate of Maribeth's, even though there was almost a five year difference in age between them.

No one interviewed Roger Yerdlay about his thoughts on the loss of his beloved secretary to one of Hollywood's premiere leading men. But it seemed that he, too, had accepted Fate's decree, because he, too, remained close to Franck and his family. He continued to make brilliant investments on Franck's behalf, as well as on behalf of many other Hollywood movers and shakers, making them millions.

In January of 1965, principal shooting began on Two Green Keys, *a film billed as "the reunion of Franck O'Day and Jessika Yerdlay." Little is known about the film. Production stopped when tragedy overtook Franck's wonderful little family on Thursday, July 15th, 1965.*

23

As was later reported in The Los Angeles Times, *Jessika Yerdlay's housekeeper, Cecilia Hernandes, became concerned when Bridget failed to pick up Maribeth from Jessika's house at noon. The little girl and Jessika's daughter Dolores were scheduled to appear in a ballet recital later in the afternoon, and after several calls to the O'Day home went unanswered, Mrs. Hernandes called the studio.*

Franck rushed home immediately. He found his front door standing open, and horror inside. Roger Yerdlay's body sat at the foot of the grand staircase, drenched in blood, his face unrecognizable as a result of a self-inflicted gunshot wound.

Bridget was sprawled face down on the dining room floor, a gunshot wound to her back. Based upon her attire, she had apparently been preparing to leave to pick up the girls for their recital when the murderer struck.

Roger's Corvette was parked in the driveway, and a suicide note was discovered on the dashboard. It was addressed to his sister. The contents of the note were not released to the public at the time. TwoGreenKeys.com *has obtained a copy of the note, however, and we now publish it here:*

"I have been living a lie. Day in and day out, I smile and nod and pretend that my life has meaning, all the while having to watch that smug bastard laughing and cavorting with the woman I love. The only woman I've ever loved, could ever love. I lie awake at night, thinking about what he must be doing to her, and all the pills and booze in the world won't get those images out of my head, won't allow me a night's rest.

"But no more. Today, I'm going to declare myself to Bridget, something I should've done before she ever met that arrogant son-of-a-bitch. I've been a coward, but no more. Today I'll make my love known to Bridget, convince her to run away with me. Why should she stay with him? What has he got that I haven't got? Certainly not money. I'll treat her like the queen she is — she'll want for nothing with me. I'll make her forget about that two-bit actor before we're out of the driveway.

"But if Bridget refuses to run away with me, then I'm going to kill myself. Life is not worth living without her by my side, and the idea of that bastard laughing at me, laughing at my love for her, is more than I can bear.

"But I'll not be the only one going to meet my maker today. If Bridget won't accept me, then I'm honor bound to make her a widow. He said we were friends. What kind of a friend breaks my sister's heart and steals the woman I love?

"If Bridget refuses me, if she chooses him over everything I have to offer her, then neither I nor Franck O'Day will live to see another sunrise.

"If you're reading this, Jessika, please know that I'm sorry. I know that your love for that two-faced son-of-a-bitch never waned, even after he betrayed you utterly. But unlike you, I can neither forgive nor forget. I'm sorry that I took him

from you, but he was never really yours anyway, and after what he did to you and me, I cannot let him live. And after I kill him, I can't live, either.

"Forgive me, Jessika, and never forget how much I loved you."

I paused and squinted at the screen, allowing the import of Roger Yerdlay's suicide note to wash over me. Apparently the killing-Franck thing hadn't materialized. Maybe it had been Bridget that had laughed at him, and he shot her instead.

My next thought was to wonder if the note was even genuine. Where would Franck's step-daughter get a copy of such a thing? I considered that perhaps it was fabricated, perhaps as another jab at Jessika and her tainted love. Perhaps Maribeth had made it all up as a way to spice up her webpage. I shook my head and continued reading.

After the tragedy, Franck was in despair. He immediately sold the house in Malibu. The memories of his happy life there, now gone forever, were too much for him. He took a Spanish cottage at the Chateau Marmont *for himself and Maribeth, and tried to figure out what he was going to do with the rest of his life.*

In the winter of 1965, Peter McSwale, Maribeth's biological father, arrived in Hollywood. He suggested to Franck that he should be granted custody of his daughter, even though he had signed over all parental rights long ago. Franck resisted – Maribeth was all he had to remember Bridget by. He loved the little girl, and knew that her mother would have wanted him to raise her. He knew that he could give her more in life than some country lawyer from Kansas ever could.

Besides, Maribeth didn't want to go. Franck was the only father that she could remember, and she loved him with all her heart. Even though Maribeth was his spitting image, Peter McSwale was a stranger to her.

Still, McSwale insisted. He said that Maribeth would do better in wholesome Kansas – what kind of a life could a little girl have, living in a Hollywood hotel?

In early 1966, Jessika Yerdlay came to the rescue, or at least that's what everyone thought. She offered rooms in her own palatial Beverly Hills estate to Franck and Maribeth, until they could purchase another home of their own, of course. He'd been mulling over the idea of immigrating to England, where his friend Robert Ecksmith had also offered to open up his hearth and home to the bereaved widower.

This relocation had only not occurred because Peter McSwale had filed court papers blocking Franck from taking Maribeth out of the country until the question of custody could be decided.

Jesus, I thought, *this whole story is getting downright byzantine.* Spurned lovers, fairytale romances cut tragically short by murder-suicides,

25

appearances of Kansas lawyers bent on waging custody battles with Hollywood leading men? Curiouser and curiouser. I reminded myself to again thank Ruthanne for turning me on to this convoluted tale. It would indeed make a great book, if I could just get all the chronologies straight, separate the facts from the opinions of one hate-filled little old lady. If I could just decide on the right angle. I foresaw long hours of research yet to come.

So, Franck took Jessika up on her generous offer. He and the little girl he called daughter moved into the grand Beverly Hills home. No more Chateau Marmont, *so there could be no more shadowy accusations that Franck was not raising Maribeth in the best possible atmosphere.*

One can only imagine the grin that must have spread across the Kansas lawyer's face when he read the news in the papers. Because he had thought of an angle that had apparently not occurred to Franck. In his concern over Maribeth's well-being, Franck had seen nothing but good things in their move to Jessika's estate. The place was huge, luxurious, safe. The idea that this move would be construed simply as his shacking up with Jessika had not crossed his mind.

Perhaps Jessika was in collusion with Peter McSwale all along to get rid of Maribeth, the bothersome little girl who was a constant reminder to Franck of the woman that he'd loved, the woman that he'd lost, the woman that had been so brutally taken from him by Jessika's own flesh and blood. How could she ever make Franck fall in love with her, if he was constantly reminded of what he'd lost?

Again I was struck by Maribeth's malice. This loathing of Jessika sounded like the ramblings of a betrayed little girl, a little girl who was now an old woman that had never managed to build a bridge and get over it.

But to be fair, I thought, maybe Jessika had nothing to do with Peter's wish to reclaim his child. Maybe ol' Pete had truly believed that he'd be putting the best interests of his little girl first, by removing her from this den of Hollywood iniquity.

I considered Franck's role in all of it. Maybe he wasn't so reluctant to give Maribeth up after all. He was a young, single, attractive, up-and-comer. His last picture had almost been an Oscar contender. Maybe a little girl that wasn't even his own would be nothing but a burden to him in the future. Perhaps such an albatross around his neck could prove a hindrance to his career? Maybe Franck was not so innocent after all.

But surely, Maribeth couldn't blame Franck, her beloved step-father, *the only father she could remember.* Franck was above reproach in her eyes, a guiltless, well-meaning dupe – nothing but a pawn in Jessika's evil, grasping, possessive game. I shrugged. All that would require quite a bit of sorting out.

The die was cast from the moment Franck and Maribeth moved into Jessika's home. Peter McSwale bided his time. He waited until pictures from a few of Franck and Jessika's parties hit the papers. He must've smiled in glee at the photo that appeared in Life *in August of 1966. It showed a tired and bored eleven-year-old Maribeth, in her party dress, her chin on her hand, sitting alone at a table filled with half empty champagne glasses. The caption read, "The glamorous life continues for Franck O'Day's daughter, barely a year after her mother's murder."*

Not long after, Peter McSwale struck. The powerful studio that employed Franck and Jessika kept the allegations out of the paper: the sinful Hollywood lifestyle that they were subjecting his daughter to could result in nothing but her harm, and Peter McSwale was demanding she be removed from the home immediately. But the studio could not influence the court's decision. A Los Angeles Superior Court judge awarded custody of Maribeth McSwale O'Day to her biological father, and reinstatement of the name she had been given at birth. She would thenceforth be again known as Maribeth McSwale. She was back in Kansas in time for Thanksgiving.

I thought about how sad and mystifying and scary it must've been for little Maribeth, to be torn from her home, to be torn from Franck, to be taken halfway across the country to a strange place by a stranger. And all barely a year after her mother's gruesome death.

But still, I couldn't see that Franck had put up too much of a fight for her. If the studio was powerful enough to keep the public proceedings out of the papers, why hadn't they been powerful enough to quash a custody bid from some Midwestern rube? Why hadn't their expensive, high-powered lawyers been able to beat some country barrister from Kansas?

I shrugged and read on. Now Maribeth veered back from her lengthy digression about her own sad life, and began Jessika's character assassination in earnest.

Jessika now had Franck exactly where she wanted him. He was a broken man – he'd lost his wife and then his child in devastatingly quick succession. He had nothing left. Jessika was there to comfort him, to give him strength. Franck was grateful for her friendship, for her company. But Jessika wanted more. Once she had him completely under her spell, she abandoned all pretense of simple friendship, and lured a lonely and lost man back to her bed.

This resuming of their past relations threw another facet of his life into sharp relief for Franck, however. He realized that he couldn't just remain a sad

27

hermit, locking himself up in Jessika's bedroom forever. Franck realized that he needed to get on with his life, to overcome the tragic cards that Fate had dealt him. He had to get back to work.

In January of 1967, shooting resumed on Two Green Keys. *Earlier footage from 1965 was deemed unusable and was destroyed. That footage, showing a joyful, thirty-two-year-old Franck, blissfully happy in his family life, could not be made to mesh with the footage of an irretrievably sadder, more solemn, thirty-four-year-old Franck.*

On Valentine's Day 1967, Jessika Yerdlay gleefully and exuberantly announced their engagement. As you can see from the picture at left, Franck looks lost and confused, as if he might already be searching for an exit from the hell his life was about to become.

I looked at the photo. Jessika was smiling at the camera. Franck had his right arm lightly draped around her waist, but he was looking off to his left, as if someone had called to him and he was looking that way to see what they wanted. He had a martini glass raised to his lips. I thought he looked not so much lost and confused as bored and unconcerned, perhaps looking to his left at something that he found more interesting than Jessika's announcement of their engagement.

It's all about perception, I thought.

Unbeknownst to the public – it would have caused a scandal, even in free-thinking 1967 – the lash that was spurring Franck on to the altar was Jessika's claim that she was expecting.

In April, Jessika threw a gala birthday party for her fiancé. The guest of honor at the bash would turn out to be Robert Ecksmith, however, and not the surprised birthday boy.

The accompanying picture showed Franck and Ecksmith, facing each other, arms crossed, like that famous picture of Jack and Bobby Kennedy taken around the time of the Cuban missile crisis. Maribeth had captioned it, *Robert Ecksmith advises Franck against marrying Jessika Yerdlay.* Damn. *That went directly to the point,* I thought.

Franck was delighted to see his friend, and invited Ecksmith to stay as long as he liked. This precipitated a huge fight between Franck and Jessika, late on the night of the birthday celebration. Robert Ecksmith had never liked Jessika, and was never reticent about expressing his disdain. He'd never cared for her dubious acting talents – he'd once said privately that if she was the last woman on Earth and he had to film a message for visitors from the future, he still wouldn't cast her. He'd drunkenly toasted Franck at his wedding to Bridget: "Congratulations on your lovely bride, my friend, and kudos to your escape from the sharp and desperate talons of Jessika Yerdlay!"

Franck told Jessika mildly that if she didn't want Ecksmith under her roof, it would be no trouble at all for him to rent a cottage at the Chateau Marmont *for the length of his visit, and it would be even less trouble for Franck to join him there. At this threat, Jessika relented.*

On the afternoon of June 30ᵗ, 1967, Jessika, Franck, and Ecksmith were sitting around the pool at her home. At some point, while Franck was inside taking a phone call, Jessika slipped while climbing out of the pool, twisting her ankle and falling back into the water. From a nearby lounge-chair, Ecksmith lackadaisically extended a hand to help her, but made no actual move to get up and assist her out of the pool.

Hysterically, Jessika screamed for Franck, who ran out of the house and helped her escape the water. He supported her as she limped into the house, but once inside, she assured him that she was all right. She then told him that she felt like she wanted to lie down for a little while, and urged him to return poolside.

Two hours later, a frantic servant again called Franck to the phone. It was Jessika. Without telling her fiancé, she had called a cab and gone to Cedars-Sinai Hospital. She tearfully told Franck that the fall into the pool and Ecksmith's refusal to immediately help her had caused a miscarriage. She told Franck not to bother picking her up at the hospital; she would be staying at the Beverly Hills Hotel until such time as he removed the heartless Englishman from her home.

Jessika's histrionics didn't elicit the response she'd expected from Franck, however. He rushed immediately to neither the hospital nor the hotel. He figured that if the doctors had deemed Jessika well enough to be released, then she was well enough. He didn't feel it necessary to chase her all over town. What could he do about anything now, anyway?

Instead, Franck returned to the pool and told Ecksmith that Jessika had suffered a miscarriage.

"Surprise," Ecksmith returned mildly.

"And she's saying it's your fault," Franck told him.

"Oh, double surprise!" Ecksmith rejoined. He asked Franck if he might use the telephone. Franck nodded, and Ecksmith disappeared into the house.

The 4ᵗʰ of July fell on a Tuesday that year, and Jessika spent the entire week of the holiday recuperating on Catalina Island, without Franck. She believed her continued absence would prompt him to either come to her, or get rid of Ecksmith, or both. She was mistaken. When Jessika returned home the following Monday, she was greeted by an empty house and a housekeeper that would not meet her eyes.

Stung by Jessika's accusations that his actions had caused her to lose Franck's baby, Robert Ecksmith had hired a private detective. While Jessika lounged on Catalina, Ecksmith and the detective presented Franck with the damning evidence. Not only had Jessika not had a miscarriage on June 30th, she'd not even been pregnant. Hospital records indicated that she had been treated for a sprained ankle and released.

A telegram had arrived for Jessika that morning, and had lain in the foyer all day, awaiting her return. It was from Franck, and it wasn't very long. It read: "Two Green Keys shelved indefinitely. Ecksmith on flight back to England by the time you receive this. I'm with him. Return indeterminate."

Oh, snap! I thought. Once again, I wondered how Maribeth was privy to all these private communications, and again I thought she'd probably made up the wording of the telegram, just to lend authenticity.

Throughout the summer, letters and telegrams crossed and crisscrossed the Atlantic Ocean. Franck never accused Jessika of the phony pregnancy/miscarriage scam, so she immediately blamed his departure on Bobby Ecksmith.

It was Ecksmith that had poisoned Franck's mind against her. It was Ecksmith who'd taken Franck away from her. Via telegram, she constantly asked her fiancé, "What have I done? Why are you treating me this way? Why won't you come home to me?"

Franck eventually grew weary of Jessika's transatlantic whining. On August 28th, 1967, he sent the following telegram, the last know communication between them. "Leaving with Ecksmith for Japan tomorrow to scout locations. Forwarding address unknown. Will not be returning to US in the foreseeable future. Don't wait for me. Look for someone else. Best of luck, Franck."

Less than a month after this succinct dismissal, Jessika called a press conference. On the steps of Los Angeles' historic City Hall, she officially called off her engagement to Franck O'Day. She had come to this painful decision, she told stunned reporters, because she had uncovered evidence that Uncle Franck and her daughter Dolores had engaged in improper congress, not long after he and Maribeth had moved into Jessika's house in 1965. Dolores had been only fourteen years old at the time. Jessika demanded that the Los Angeles County District Attorney do something — issue a warrant for Franck's arrest, extradite him from Japan. Something! Some action must be taken to right this terrible wrong!

Jessika had possessed the maternal good grace not to force her daughter to appear at this circus, but she did hold up a photograph of the girl. Gray-eyed and fair like her mother, poor Dolores's picture was splashed all over front pages, nationwide, the next day.

The District Attorney's Office had neither the time, nor the resources, nor the inclination to attempt to hunt down some actor overseas, just because a jilted actress was leveling accusations against him. The whole drama hinged on the testimony of a fourteen-year-old-girl, anyway, and how reliable could that possibly be? The D.A. mollified Jessika with promises of action, but more or less let the whole thing slide. When and if O'Day came back to the states, he would ramp it up again, of course, but in the meantime, he had more pressing crimes to investigate.

But the studio still had Franck under contract – they believed any picture he might make for them in the future would still be a big draw, despite Yerdlay's ridiculous accusations. In fact, the publicity of the scandal might translate into an even bigger box office take. So they dispatched a gentleman named Karl Izona to Japan to persuade Franck to return to the States and face the music.

It took Mr. Izona until New Year's Day 1968 to track Franck and Robert Ecksmith down in the Land of the Rising Sun. It wasn't that they were hiding out – they'd just been spending a lot of time in the Japanese countryside. They were just tourists to the locals – no one had ever heard of the big American movie star and the world-renowned English director in the backwaters of Japan. The language barrier added to Izona's difficulty in locating two unimportant Americans.

When Izona finally found him, Franck gave the studio rep a statement to take back to the American press: "Miss Yerdlay's accusations have wounded me deeply. While I loved Dolores like she was my own daughter during my brief stay at her mother's home, no improprieties ever occurred. Anyone who disputes this is a liar. I look forward to my day in court to answer Miss Yerdlay's sad charges. I have no doubt of my certain exoneration."

Robert Ecksmith said privately to Izona, "Franck would never have even considered such a thing. It would've been wrong on every level. Besides," Ecksmith laughed, "when would Franck have had time to have a go at the daughter, with the mother after him constantly? The woman was insatiable. 'Must I remember?' he quoted Hamlet. 'Why, she would hang on him, as if increase of appetite had grown by what it fed on.'" Ecksmith grinned ruefully at the studio man. "'Frailty, thy name is woman,' indeed. Leave it to Jessika Yerdlay to conjure up such a pathetic and sordid way to get Franck back to the States, to get him back to Los Angeles. To get him back to her. I'll bet she drops the charges as soon as he steps foot on American soil. Just so she can see him again. Just so she can throw herself at him again."

Neither Ecksmith nor Franck were worried in the slightest about Jessika Yerdlay or her accusations.

The picture at left shows Franck and Ecksmith moments before embarking on the trip that was to carry them back to Tokyo. From there they were slated to catch a flight back to the United States, all so Franck could give answer to Jessika's cruel and groundless lies. It would be the last picture of him to surface for more than forty years.

The 1960s were on full display in the photograph. It was in color, with that yellow, always-looks-like-it's-a-summer-afternoon quality of pictures from the era – a feel that you can now easily duplicate on modern pictures with a few clicks. Ecksmith had straight, scraggly, shoulder-length blonde hair, and a full, droopy mustache. Franck's black hair was not as long as his friend's, but shaggier, curlier, covering his ears and reaching to his collar. He sported impressive, mutton-chop sideburns. They both wore Aviator-style shades and heavy coats. They were both smiling widely, obviously not in the least bit concerned with what they were returning to the States to face. The fuselage of a small plane was in the background.

Little did they know that what they were about to face was death. The famous Hollywood duo's last hit would be the side of a Japanese mountain, I reflected.

Franck and Ecksmith's plane went down about an hour after take-off. The pilot was killed on impact and the actor and director both suffered grievous injuries. Franck broke his left arm in two places. Ecksmith broke his leg, also in two places. The pair were rescued by Buddhist monks, who treated their injuries and catered to their every need during their long convalescence. It was while at their monastery that Franck learned the ancient healing art of Reiki, which harnesses the energy of the universe.

OMG, I thought again. Maribeth had lifted this part of her fable almost wholesale from the plot of *Lost Horizon*. The plane crash, the rescuing monks, the healing. The only thing that had changed was the location. James Hilton's novel, as well as the universally panned 1973 movie musical version, take place in Tibet, not Japan.

When Jessika heard of Franck's disappearance and presumed death, she went into seclusion. In March 1968, she attempted suicide, by slitting one wrist and drawing a butcher knife halfway across her throat, starting from below the left ear. As with so many other things in her life, Jessika even failed at this shot at ending it all. While jagged and bloody, her wounds were not close enough to any major arteries to be considered truly life-threatening.

Jessika was left with a thick, uneven white scar from just under her left ear to the center of her swanlike neck. She would never work again, unless her monstrous disfigurement could somehow be worked into the script. That wouldn't work either, because even if Jessika condescended to take the part of some disfigured unfortunate, if the public was ever to see those scars — what they had resulted from was unmistakable. The studio fabricated a story about a car accident, and she retired from the silver screen.

Jessika remained in seclusion, refusing to venture out of the Beverly Hills mansion where she'd spent her happiest times with Franck O'Day. Her daughter Dolores was forced to care for her, to play Max Von Mayerling to her self-pitying Norma Desmond.

32

Franck and Ecksmith lived in complete obscurity in Japan until 1976. Franck knew that his step-daughter had reached her majority in this year, so he at last acted. Through various expatriates in Japan and his old Hollywood contacts in the States, Franck was able to get in touch with Maribeth in Kansas. It goes without saying that Maribeth was beyond ecstatic to hear from him after so many years. In celebration, she immediately formed the Franck O'Day Fan Club, to rekindle the sparks of his memory among his legions of fans. What began as a modest mail-order newsletter grew into this very site.

Franck and Maribeth would correspond for thirty years, and Maribeth would visit him many times in Japan. She was finally able to coax him to quietly return to the United States in 2006, where he has been living in Los Angeles ever since, under an assumed name.

Jessika Yerdlay was ready for her final close-up on December 31, 2011. One wonders if she was aware of the date as she lie dying, if she thought about her only triumph, a movie whose action took place on New Year's Eve. One wonders if she regretted her cruel use of her beloved co-star in that film.

A will Franck had executed in 1967 had left a small fortune in cash and heirlooms to Jessika, as well as a generous amount for Dolores. It was a will that Franck had aimed to have changed when he landed in California to face Jessika's specious charges. But of course, he never had the opportunity. When he was declared dead eight years after his plane disappeared, the will he never got to change was executed, and the holdings that he had left to her reverted to Jessika, including his plot in the Hollywood Forever Cemetery.

Below this entry was the series of three photographs of the old man that Ruthanne had shown me the night before. Maribeth had captioned them, *Who can this be, dancing on the grave of Jessika Yerdlay?*

I re-read the last two paragraphs of *Jessika, Franck, Bridget, and Roger – Betrayal and Heartbreak*.

After a lifetime of ignominy brought on by her cruel, heartless, and patently fatuous allegations, Franck O'Day has now had the last laugh. It looks like he enjoyed it, eh, fans?

Keep sending all your good wishes and love energies to Franck. While his health had been faltering a little lately, the death of his enemy and your healing energies have once again put him on the road to recovery. Keep sending in those keys! Watch this space for news of a personal appearance *in the not too distant future!*

Yeah. This was going to make for an awesome story. So many threads! So many shades of insanity! But I'd had enough of it. Time to let what I'd learned simmer and percolate in my head for a little while. Perhaps an angle would present itself.

Time to see what Ruthanne was making for lunch.

FIVE

When I walked into our living room, I did a classic, clichéd double-take. There was a man sitting on our couch, and for a split-second I thought Franck O'Day had inexplicably stepped out of that 1968 photograph right into our apartment. The one taken just before the plane crash. This guy had the same shaggy, curly, black hair, the same mutton chops. He was wearing Aviator sunglasses. I stopped and stared at him.

Ruthanne, who I hadn't noticed, was sitting in a chair across from him, on the other side of the coffee table. She looked over her shoulder at me and said, "Oh, hi, there, Carol. Have you met Marty?"

Marty smiled at me. He removed his sunglasses and set them on the table, and I was not at all surprised to see that he had big blue eyes. The nose was close, but the chin was all wrong, and his teeth were too straight. But if he didn't smile too widely, and he put those sunglasses back on, he was a dead ringer for Ruthanne's long-dead Hollywood crush. He arose and shook my hand. "So nice to meet you, Carol," he said. "I've seen your name a lot. I'm in charge of the mail room in your building."

"So that's where you met Ruthie?" I asked, looking askance at her. She smiled innocently at me and I looked back at Marty. "In the mail room?" Marty nodded.

I was fascinated. I wouldn't say Ruthanne was a snob . . . well, yes, actually, she *was* a snob. She wouldn't waste her time on any man that made less money than her. She wouldn't waste her time on any man that had less prestige than she did. In other words, I knew that generally, Ruthie wouldn't get caught going to a cat fight with a mail clerk. Not unless he bore a passing resemblance to a circa 1968 Franck O'Day. In that case, I imagined, what he did for a living mattered to her not at all.

"Nice shades, Marty," I commented, then looked again at Ruthanne. "Where ever did you get them?"

Before Marty could open his mouth to speak, Ruthie replied quickly, "Marty called yesterday and asked if the two of us would like to go to the beach with him. When he got here, I noticed that he didn't have any sunglasses. So I gave him this pair." She gestured at the sunglasses on the table. "Which I just happened to have." She grinned at me. "Can't hit the beach without sunglasses, now can he? Do you want to go to the beach with us, Carol?"

"No, thanks," I said. I hated the beach, and Ruthie knew it. She was just being polite. "You kids have fun."

Ruthanne arose, crossed the room and held the front door open. "I'll be down in one minute, Marty," she said.

Marty said to me, "It was nice to meet you."

I said, "So nice to meet you, too." *Just don't change that haircut,* I thought, *and Ruthie might even let you stick around for a while.* He went out the door and Ruthanne shut it behind him.

"Sorry about lunch," she said. "I forgot all about him. He called me yesterday afternoon and asked about the beach." She grinned at me again. "Isn't he adorable? I just discovered him there in the mail room, last week."

"How old is he?" I asked.

"I don't know. Thirty-five, maybe?" Ruthanne was twenty-six. I'd never known her to date anyone a day older than she was. She looked at me. "Who cares how old he is? He looks just like —"

"A thirty-five-year-old mail clerk, Ruthie? Seriously?"

"Oh, pooh," Ruthanne replied. "I'm not going to marry him. I just want to look at him. Pretend a little bit. Have a little fun. I'm sure it won't outlast the weekend."

She put her on own sunglasses, and picked up the pair that she'd given to Marty. *Can't forget the props,* I thought. "If we can't appreciate them just for their looks, what can we appreciate them for?" I asked.

Ruthanne looked over the top of her shades and grinned slyly at me. "If we pass any Ryan Gosling Look-a-Like Contests on our way to the beach, I'll give you a call."

Touché, I thought, and again told her to have a good time. "Just remember, his name's *Marty.*"

"Indeed," she said, and flounced out the door.

Well, hell, I thought. *I guess I'll just have to make my own lunch.*

36

SIX

I made myself a ham sandwich and ate it over the sink. Then I returned to the writing chair. It wasn't like I had anything else to do. I called up *TwoGreenKeys.com* on my computer again, and looked at the list of links on the left-hand side. *Biography* – check. *Franck's Career Highlights* – check. *Photos* – I would come back to that one later. What I was looking for now was more information.

Jessika, Franck, Bridget, and Roger – Betrayal and Heartbreak – yes, we'd been over all that.

How to Send Your Keys – Ruthanne had pretty much explained that one to me.

E-Mail Maribeth – Hmmm. There was an idea. Maybe I could just drive down to LA and interview the crazy lady in person. Or maybe just go right on ahead and talk to Franck himself. Right. I clicked on the link and a blank email popped up.

(I refused to be embarrassed that I still used AOL for email. It tickled Ruthanne to death.

"I've had it since I was a kid," I protested.

She just laughed at me. "My mom still uses AOL," she said.)

I looked at the blank email. It said *francksbiggestfan @twogreenkeys.com* in the *Send To* box. Wow. That left no room for discussion, now did it? I moved the cursor to the *Subject* box, where it remained, blinking. I considered. Just what did I want to say to Maribeth McSwale O'Day, anyway?

Hi, there, how are things in Delusion Land?

I drummed my fingers on the arm of the recliner, then typed *Request for Interview* in the *Subject* box, followed by:

Dear Maribeth, [What else could I call her? Miss McSwale? Miss O'Day?]

My name is Carolyn Adyon. Recently, my friend Ruthanne introduced me to your website. She is a very big fan of Mr. O'Day. [Not his biggest fan, however. That nutball prize obviously goes to you.]

I found your site to be fascinating and delightfully well-written. [If one likes purple prose wielded by a poison pen.] *I, too, am a writer* [among other things], *and would be very interested in writing a non-fiction book, or perhaps even a fictionalized novel, about Mr. O'Day's life.*

I was wondering if it might be possible to interview you, since you are an authority on the subject, and I think that such an interview would be a great jumping-off point for my research. [In other words, I'm going to write this with or without your help.]

I am available to come to Los Angeles at your convenience. [Because I have plenty of vacation days saved up.] *Please share your thoughts with me on this endeavor. Thanks so much for your time!*

I clicked the *Send Now* icon, with its picture of a little flying envelope. I drummed my fingers on the arm of the recliner, wondering what kind of reaction my little, innocent request might engender. I wondered how often she checked her email. Once a week? Once a month? I wondered how long it would take her to write back. Surely, there was not a whole lot of email traffic on *TwoGreenKey.com;* surely, the general public couldn't be burning up *francksbiggestfan's* inbox. The man had been dead since 1968, after all.

I decided to do a little more research on all the parties concerned, and had just finished typing *www.wikipedia.com* into the address bar, when the computer made its little *you've got mail* ding. I clicked on AOL's quaint little mailbox icon. Maribeth had written:

Dear Miss Adyon,

Thank you for your kind email. I think that a book about Franck's life is a wonderful idea, one that has been entirely too long in coming. Before we make arrangements for any interviews, however, I have a question for you.

Have you mailed in your keys yet?

Shit, I thought, *I said I was a writer, not a fan.* I maximized *TwoGreenKeys.com* and clicked on the *How to Send Your Keys* link. I skimmed over all the drivel about the keys' symbolic relationship to Franck's lost movie, skipped all the claptrap about *Reiki* and healing energy, blah, blah, blah, until I came to a neatly numbered list at the bottom of the page:

1. *You can send any two keys you wish — car keys, door keys, padlock keys. The kind of keys, what their purpose was before, doesn't matter in the least, as they are bound for a new purpose. Please try to make them match as much as possible in size and shape, however, as matching keys are much more aesthetically pleasing on your keyring.*
2. *Clear your mind and meditate on the keys for as long as you desire, filling them with your love and energy and warm thoughts for Franck.*
3. *Mail the keys to the P.O. Box listed below. Don't forget to include your self-addressed stamped envelope!*

I got up and located my purse, retrieved my keys. They were nothing as ostentatious as Ruthanne's: just one ring with four or five keys and a soft plastic replica of a California license plate with my name on it, which Ruthie had given me as a gift. No additional fobs, no extra keys.

I texted Ruthanne: *I'm gonna join the fan club. You got any extra keys?*

My friend texted back immediately. Apparently her faux Franck was not consuming her undivided attention. Apparently, she could still look at him and text me at the same time. *That's great! Look in the second drawer of my dresser. There's a bunch of stuff in there. Should be a few old keys.*

Gloria Swanson glared down at me from the *Sunset Boulevard* poster that I had given Ruthie for her birthday, as I rifled through her dresser drawer. Old ticket stubs, a screwdriver. Another pair of Aviator sunglasses, with only one earpiece. An obsolete phone charger. An empty baggie. A solidified bottle of nail polish. A lipstick of a color no longer fashionable. At last, in the back of the drawer, I found a dust-clotted ring with six keys on it. Trying gamely not to break a fingernail, I prised two similarly sized and shaped ones off of it, tossed the ring back into the drawer, and slammed it shut. The annoying things I had to do for my art.

My phone buzzed. Ruthanne had texted: *Don't forget to meditate on them!*

Meditate on this, I thought, and consulted my laptop again. *Mail the keys to the P.O. Box listed below.*

Mail? I tried to remember the last time I'd mailed anything. I failed. I paid all my bills online, corresponded via email. I didn't even send out Christmas cards. Who mailed anything anymore? I texted Ruthie again: *Now I need an envelope.*

You're gonna need 2 envelopes. And 2 stamps. Look in the top drawer of my nightstand.

I crossed the hall again. Gloria Swanson still glared. I located two envelopes, as well as a book of stamps. Mercifully, they were forever stamps, which was great, because I had not a clue as to what postage was running these days. I put two on each envelope, just to be sure, and crossed back to my room. I texted Ruthie: *Thanx. Mission accomplished. How is Marty?*

He is Marty. I'm thinking that it might not even last the whole weekend.

I'm sorry to hear that.

We'll see. TTYL.

SEVEN

I emailed Maribeth: *My keys are in the mailbox as we speak, waiting to be picked up. You should have them by the middle of next week.*

While I waited for her reply, I filled out the envelopes. I dropped the self-addressed one and the keys into the one addressed to Miss Crazy Lady O'Day. I didn't feel like running outside to our communal bank of mailboxes, so I just stuck the envelope in my purse. I was not even sure exactly how to put something in there to go out, anyway. Ruthanne always picked up our correspondence.

I would just drop the envelope in the outgoing mail at work on Monday. Or, I thought, grinning – maybe I could just give it to Mail Clerk Marty, if Ruthie even bothered to invite him back in when they returned from the beach. I'm sure he would know what to do with it.

My computer dinged. I opened Maribeth's email.

> *Dear Miss Adyon,*
> *Franck and I can't wait to receive your keys!*
> *In the meantime, please send a list of questions. Ask anything you like! Franck has been waiting a lifetime to have his story told.*
> *He's been feeling a little under the weather this week, and isn't quite up to a face to face interview at the moment. But he's looking forward to answering your questions, and is looking forward to meeting you in person in the near future. As am I!*
> *I'm very excited at the prospect of your book! Please do not hesitate to tell me anything that I can do to help!*

You could be a little less of a psycho, that might help, I thought. Of course Franck wasn't up for an interview. That was because Franck was *dead*. As dead as disco, as the poets say, something that he hadn't even lived long enough to experience.

I was reminded of a movie called *The Night Listener*, where Toni Collette dupes Robin Williams into believing that she has a sick son, whom he thinks he's talking to on the phone. In the end, we find out that there was no boy at all. We find out that the mother was faking the child's voice, and she is just as nutty as the oft-cited fruitcake.

This whole Franck O'Day bio story was shaping up to be a similarly interesting ride. If Maribeth wanted to pretend she was Franck and answer my questions as him, so be it. I thought maybe that could be the angle for the book: it wouldn't be so much about long-dead, long-forgotten matinee idol Franck O'Day. It would be about his crazy step-daughter and her delusions, her Norman Bates/mother style split personality. That would probably sell better anyway.

EIGHT

For Christmas the year before, Ruthanne and I had pooled our funds and got each other a big screen television. She kicked in half so I could watch *HBO* in HD, and I kicked in the other half so she could watch all her old movies on a seventy-two inch screen. For her birthday, in addition to the *Sunset Boulevard* poster, I'd given her a Blu-Ray player, and for mine, she'd given me a surround-sound system. As far as home entertainment went, we were set.

Deciding I'd done enough research on the as yet ill-defined book for the day, I made a big bowl of popcorn and curled up on the couch, hoping to find something good to watch. I moved the channel guide up and down in vain, however. How many times had I sat through *Pirates of the Caribbean: The Curse of the Black Pearl?* Not even sexy Sam Worthington was going to suck me in to *Wrath of the Titans* again. *Saving Private Ryan* was just too damn depressing, and all the HD in the world couldn't save *Abraham Lincoln: Vampire Hunter.*

I was just about to settle in for the guilty pleasure that is *Judge Dredd* when Ruthanne and her ersatz Franck O'Day returned from their idyllic day at the beach and saved me from myself.

Ruthie looked at the screen, then looked at me. She took a handful of popcorn, and before eating it, said, "Don't we have a rule, Carol? Don't we just say no to Sylvester Stallone?"

I hung my head in mock shame and handed the remote to her.

"In honor of your joining the fan club, in honor of your book, I was thinking that perhaps we might watch *High Times in Manhattan. George and Benedict* is a little . . . heavy. Franck's great in it, but *High Times* is a much better movie, overall."

I looked over at Ruthie's companion, lingering by the door. "What d'ya say, Marty? Are you ready for a little vintage Hollywood?"

The mail clerk smiled, shrugged. "Whatever you ladies would like."

Ruthanne hadn't even looked over her shoulder at him. His opinion didn't matter to her. He was just a pretty face, after all. "Who wants a mint julep?" she asked.

I smiled at Ruthanne. "I would expect nothing less for such a screening. Franck's favorite drink."

Ruthanne looked politely at Marty. He shook his head. She shrugged, and went out to the kitchen.

Marty sat down in a chair across from me. "Would you be interested in smoking some weed, Carol?"

I smiled in surprise. Here was a suggestion that I hadn't heard since high school. I thought about Ruthanne and her snobbishness again. Yeah, thirty-five-year-old mail clerk potheads with anachronistic mutton chops and '60's haircuts? She just didn't bring too many of those home. Generally, they definitely were not her type.

But what did I care? I had no other plans than to sit right here on this couch and endure one of Ruthie's favorite movies. And the novelty of Marty's suggestion had a certain appeal – being stoned for the first time in at least ten years couldn't do anything but help with my enjoyment of *High Times in Manhattan*. I giggled. High times, indeed.

But Marty the stoner was Ruthanne's guest, not mine. She might not appreciate my colluding with him in doing drugs, no matter how harmless and possibly movie-enhancing they might be. So I said, "I'm down, but you should check with Ruth first." Marty nodded, arose and went out to the kitchen to ask permission of his date.

I wondered what they'd talked about during their day at the beach. I couldn't hardly imagine that they'd discussed work, as Marty probably wasn't interested in the tasks of a legal secretary, and I knew that Ruthie couldn't possibly care less about the trials and tribulations of the mail room. Perhaps Ruthie had regaled him with her old Hollywood stories – but I kinda doubted that went too far, either. Unless a person was a fan like she was, Ruthie's stories mostly garnered replies like, "Oh, really?" or "How interesting." Then the conversation usually died. It was a difficult subject in which to feign interest. Either you were a big fan, or you were not.

Music was probably out, too, as Ruthie's tastes ran to stuff as old as or older than the movies she liked. Or if it wasn't old, it was obscure. She also favored modern, somewhat filthy hip-hop. Ruthie was a horse of a different color, let me tell you. Judging by the somewhat hippie look that Marty presented to the world, I guessed that he was probably a Led Zeppelin, Pink Floyd, Rolling Stones, Aerosmith kinda guy. And all that classic rock stuff was lost on Ruthanne.

Other than the fact that the poor guy looked like he'd stepped directly out of a single picture of a dead movie star that Ruthanne favored, it was obvious to me that they had nothing in common.

They returned from the kitchen. Ruthanne handed me a drink, giving me a look that said, *Yes, perhaps this was not the best of ideas.*

I grinned back at her. *I feel ya,* my expression said.

She set her drink down on the coffee table and went to her bedroom. She returned with her prized *Criterion Collection* Blu-Ray

43

edition of 1961's not-even-nominated-for-an-Oscar *High Times in Manhattan*. Even if I didn't know all the other reasons it was prized, I would've known it was prized because she kept in in her room instead of out here beneath the TV with all the rest of the movies. And there was the fact that it was an actual mass-produced disk, something for which she had probably shelled out twenty bucks or more.

Because Ruthie was a fan of obscure and long-forgotten movies and stars (some even more obscure and long-forgotten than Franck O'Day), the films she sought were often not available through traditional retail channels. Ruthie was a gleeful member of a somewhat secretive cabal that traded copies of this old shit, illegally downloaded from God-only-knew-where, all the while bemoaning the fact that they would gladly pay the appropriate copyright holders, if only those same stingy copyright holders would make the films available for purchase.

Yo ho, a pirate's life for Ruthie. In other words, I could be pretty sure that when she drug out *George and Benedict*, it wouldn't be in a shiny plastic case with *The Criterion Collection* written across the top.

But the discerning folks at *Criterion* had deemed *High Times* worthy enough for inclusion in their storied ranks of classics. Ruthanne gingerly extracted the disk and gently loaded it into the Blu-Ray player. She handed the box to Marty, who had sat down on the other end of the couch from me. He looked at the front, then turned it over and gave the back a casual glance. He set the box down on the coffee table without reading it. Ruthie exchanged a glance with me. Oh, he was so out.

Instead of expressing even a cursory interest in one of Ruthanne's favorite movies, Marty removed a large drawstring pouch from his pocket. He took out the accoutrements for smoking weed: a lighter, an elaborate glass pipe, and a fat baggie – again, items I hadn't seen since high school. Yeah, Marty was a pothead, all right. He was so out.

What the hell, I thought again, *it'll be fun.*

Apparently Ruthanne was game for the experience also, because she shrugged and sat down between us on the couch. Marty packed a bowl and lit it, and we passed it back and forth for a few minutes. After waiting an appropriate time for the drug to kick in, Ruthie arose, turned off the lights (we had to have the full theatre ambiance) and started the movie.

At any other time, I would've been uncomfortable to find myself sitting beside Ruth and her date in the dark. That third wheel phenomenon, and all. But before the opening credits were even done, I could see that my friend was completely ensconced in experiencing the film. Her totally disappointing, mail room clerk, pothead, dime store,

44

1968-era, shaggy Franck O'Day knock-off was totally forgotten in favor of the real, circa 1961 Franck in 1940's period dress who was about to walk on-screen. I was forgotten, too. She smiled serenely as the film's title appeared, settled into the couch, and put her feet up on the coffee table. I smiled fondly at her enjoyment, and turned my attention to the movie.

The first scene showed Jessika Yerdlay's Dora checking into the hotel, all a fluster, with too much luggage, sending uniformed bellhops scattering. She was in a hurry. When at last the harried concierge had her squared away and she headed off-screen, Franck's Perry Calibri sauntered up to the front desk, dressed in a tuxedo. He glanced mildly in her direction, and smiled at the concierge.

"Looks like it's going to be a busy night," Perry said.

I started a little at the sound of Franck's voice, a low, rich, amused growl. It was a voice I could listen to all night. Ruthanne had never said anything about his voice; his totally unexpected, melodious, masculine voice. I looked over and watched her close her eyes and smile in pleasure, then slowly open them again.

I wanted to lay the blame on the pot, on the doors of my perception being so uncharacteristically opened. I wanted to blame it on anything else, lest I had to face the fact that Ruthanne was right. Just-a-little-bit-left-of-center Ruthie, with her good luck keys, and her binders full of glossies, and her picking-up-the-mail-clerk-just-so-she-could-look-at-him, was absolutely correct.

From his first appearance onscreen as Perry Calibri, I was forced to admit that Franck O'Day was indeed luminous. Besides his amazing voice, there were his dark-blue eyes, and that crooked smile. *Knowing,* as Ruthanne had worded it in her description of the still from this very movie. He exuded a dark, animal charisma made all the more seductive by the sophisticated evening finery he was wearing. I couldn't help but speculate what he would be like once he was out of that perfectly tailored tux, and my speculations were decidedly NSFW.

I shifted a little bit on the couch. Ruthanne didn't even look over at me, but I stole a glance at her. She sat unblinking, her lips parted a tiny bit, as if she was as surprised and awestruck as I was, as if she was seeing the film for the first time, like me, instead of this being her God-only-knew-how-many screening. Maybe the pot was working on her, too. Or maybe she was always like this while watching *High Times in Manhattan.* She was Franck's biggest fan, after all.

When he spoke, the other actors seemed to dull and blend into the scenery; it was as if he was the only one in color, and it was all because of his persona – his looks, his inescapable charm. Maybe it was just the pot, or maybe it was the Panavision. Or maybe he was just that good. I wanted to believe that there was some additional, outside agent working on me, because I was utterly surprised, completely amazed by my own reaction. Ruthanne was one hundred percent right. Franck O'Day was mesmerizing – the black hair, the blue eyes, the confident smile, that incredible voice – he was devastating.

Too bad this movie is nearly fifty years old, I thought. *Too bad Franck had been dead for almost as long.*

Once they met and fell in love, the onscreen chemistry between Perry and Dora crackled. The longing in her eyes as she attempted, due to the conventions of the plot, to hide her desire for him was a palpable thing. I found her performance riveting, despite myself. I could not help but believe that she loved this man from the bottom of her soul.

When the plot thickened and it seemed as though Perry was destined to lose her forever, the secret, despondent anguish expressed on Franck's face, the suffering woe communicated solely by his eyes, was entirely moving. When they are at last united and reveal their hidden loves to each other, I felt my heart soar ridiculously. No wonder *The New York Times* thought the film deserved an Oscar.

I couldn't believe how not-bad it was. I was absolutely surprised. It was like *knowing* that you were going to be subjected to a lame old movie, dated, probably boring, with bad acting – it was like dreading the experience – it was going to be awful, two hours of your life wasted. Sigh. The things we do for our friends. But then, instead of being forced to withstand such a travail, imagine my surprise – *Manhattan* was smart and funny and witty. The plot engaged my interest; the acting was exceptional.

The biggest surprise was Franck O'Day's completely unexpected sexiness. *Hot damn.* I understood Ruthie's attraction. It was undeniable. *Perhaps I should reevaluate my roommate's taste in film and actors,* I thought in amazement, looking at Ruthanne with new respect. I couldn't believe my own reaction – *High Times in Manhattan* was a *great movie*. Even without singing and dancing and tragedy of Shakespearean proportions, it was *so* much better than *West Side Story*.

The credits rolled, and Ruthanne hopped up and turned on the lights. I watched her enact a theatrical stretch, an entirely fake yawn. "Boy," she said, "am I tired! I think I must've gotten too much sun."

She looked expectantly at Marty, who immediately got the hint and rose. The thought struck me that perhaps they hadn't talked much at all, during the drive to the beach, and at the beach, and during the drive home. Maybe Ruthie had just stared at him a lot. After all, I thought, all the action was taking place inside her head. Perhaps Marty was just a little perplexed over the whole thing – this attractive young woman from the eighth floor had just waltzed in to the mail room one day and started talking him up. They'd gone to the beach, but she hadn't talked much, hadn't been very affectionate. She'd just looked at him a lot. Maybe he didn't know quite what to make of all that.

"Yeah, I'm pretty tired, too," he said. "I guess I'll be taking off now." He gathered up his drug-doing paraphernalia, stuck it in his pocket.

In one fluid motion, Ruthanne took him by the elbow and glided him to the door. If you didn't know her, it might not seem at all like she was giving the mail clerk the bum's rush. "I had a great time, Marty," Ruthanne said, and I wondered if it sounded as clichéd to him as it did to me. He was so gone, so out. I wondered if he had any inkling at all. Marty looked over at me and reiterated that it had been nice meeting me.

I said, "You too, Marty. Thanks for the weed." *I'll be sure to stop by and say hi, the next time Fate finds me in the mail room,* I thought, *though I wouldn't hold my breath waiting for that to happen. It was nice meeting you, and you just go right ahead and have a nice life, because I doubt if our paths will cross again.*

Ruthanne gave him an entirely sisterly hug and opened the door. Then Marty was gone. She looked at the closed door as if she'd shut it on a particularly long and tiresome epoch of her life, instead of just one day spent with someone whom she'd chosen just because of a tenuous resemblance, and thereby had found entirely lacking otherwise. Ruthie sighed and looked sheepishly at me. "He sure is pretty." Then she grinned. "You wanna watch *George and Benedict,* while we still got a little buzz on? I'll make us another drink."

Before I could stop myself, I nodded. "Sure, why not?" While I would've blushed to admit it, I was definitely down for more Franck O'Day. I was curious to find out if it was the marijuana that was making Ruthie's idol seem so deserving of her adoration, or if he really was as charismatic as he seemed.

"Awesome!" Ruthie enthused. She quickly made us another drink, strong and sweet. The Kentucky bourbon laid a nice, warm blanket over my fading high.

Ruthanne went into her bedroom (*a place Marty would never see,* I thought, and giggled) and came back with her laptop. She hooked it up to the TV. As I'd predicted, there was no shiny plastic case; *George and Benedict* was not to be found in *The Criterion Collection;* it was not available from *amazon.com.* Ruthie had downloaded it directly from one of those shady places on the internet. Yo ho.

I knew Ruthanne had an external hard drive and Carbonite and Norton anti-virus, all to protect her precious, unavailable-anywhere-else, pirated movies. The internet was a dangerous place for a fan of old movie stars, I thought. You ran the risk of catching all kinds of viruses and malware and Trojan-horses and other inexplicable system killers when you started downloading feature-length stuff, gratis, from less than reputable sources. My mother always said, you never quit paying for those things you get free. There were some downright mean people out there, people who were definitely not fans, who didn't understand that Ruthie was not out to steal anything, she was just *minding her on business on the internet*, looking for all those impossible to purchase gems. Yo ho, indeed.

Ruthanne dimmed the lights and, with appropriately patriotic drum and fife music, the tale was begun.

All the pot in the world couldn't save *George and Benedict* from being dismal. Everyone was against poor Benedict, right from the start. Washington and all his generals were against him. History herself was against him. Ecksmith had captured the period attire and the stark and panoramic beauty of the New England countryside wonderfully; even in black and white, the cinematography was impeccable.

But while he had aimed to tell the story of America's most famous traitor as a man wronged by the machinations, jealousies, and inadequacies of others, Benedict instead came off as a paranoid, someone who believed everyone was out to get him, whether they were or not. Since he couldn't get the promotions and accolades he felt he deserved, he just decided to take his ball and go over to the other side, like a petulant child.

But even in this dreary vehicle, Franck O'Day was stunning. There was a lot of speechifying, about the nature of liberty and loyalty, and treason and God and Country, and again I was struck by the mesmerizing sound of his voice: its deep, resonant, masculine timbre. His undeniable sexiness shone through the period dress, and seemed to even be played up by it. He was ravishing in the stockings and buckle shoes and many-buttoned uniforms. I found myself wanting to untie the ribbon from his little colonial pig-tail, and free all those masses of curly black hair.

When at last the credits rolled, I was amazed to hear myself say to Ruthanne, "He wasn't in anything else?" I looked at her, feeling like a kid at the end of a too-small banana split. "Just these two?"

Ruthie shook her head sadly. "There's *Sister Sam's Lost Angels*. But I haven't been able to find a copy of that. Besides, he only had a walk-

on in it, anyway. And *Two Green Keys*. That one was never finished."
Ruthie paused, then said, "Y'know great movies really *are* art, Carol."

I blinked at the simplicity of this statement, and looked doubtfully
at its application to *High Times in Manhattan* – she surely couldn't be
referring to *George and Benedict. Manhattan* was good – maybe even great
– but it wasn't *art.*

She shook her head. "I don't mean art in the abstract sense, as in
that which is in the eye of the beholder." Ruthie smiled. "I mean art in
the concrete sense – like a painting. A painting is there, hanging in its
place. Time passes, and different generations discover it. The
personality of the artist that created it is forgotten, but the picture
remains. The picture doesn't age. So it is with great movies. I've been
watching *Manhattan* since I was sixteen. I've got a VHS of it
somewhere. Bought it off EBay." Ruthanne paused. "Sure, there are
other movies in my collection, other paintings. But this one is my
favorite. It has pride of place in my gallery, because it always affects me
the same way – I never get tired of looking at it.

"Different things happen, but this movie will always be a part of
my life – like a painting on the wall. I always come back and look at it
again. It always gives me a thrill." She smiled again. "Perry is always
Perry, young and dashing and sexy. I could still be watching him when
I'm eighty-six, still feeling the same way about him. But unlike with a
painting, you can *see* the artist in a movie – *the artist is the painting.* Do
you see what I'm saying?"

I thought that the pot was making Ruthie metaphysical and me
just stoned. I wasn't sure of anything. Ruthie's movie had turned out to
be worlds better than I had expected it to be, and now she was waxing
philosophical about the nature of art. No, I wasn't sure about anything
right then. When I didn't say anything, she continued.

"I'll get older, but Perry – Franck – he never will. My appreciation
for him will always remain from this one frozen moment in time – just
like a painting. And since there were no other paintings . . ."

Way to go, Franck, I thought. *Always leave 'em wanting more.*

Here was the true tragedy, I thought. Worse than the murder of
his wife, worse than Jessika's horrible accusations, worse even than his
lonely, icy death on a Japanese mountainside. The real tragedy was that
Franck O'Day had only made two movies. Ruthie and I would grow
old. But Franck's immortality would only be contained in these two
movies. It was a damn shame.

But it was not something that I could mourn too deeply. Life goes
on. *Life had gone on:* Franck had been dead since 1968, and he was
forgotten, except by Ruthanne and a handful of others. And of course,

his delusional step-daughter. Perhaps just those few were enough to keep his memory alive and vibrant, at least for each other. But not me. He was great, and it was a shame that he hadn't made more movies. It was a shame that he hadn't garnered a bigger slice of the fame pie, because he'd surely deserved it. It was a shame that he was dead.

But no matter how incandescent he'd been on the silver screen, I couldn't get into him the way Ruthie did. Although maybe I could scare them up for a second, I just couldn't maintain warm feelings for a dead man. I just didn't have her imagination, I guess. Oh, well. Que sera, sera. Next topic.

.

NINE

That night, I dreamed of Franck O'Day. But it wasn't a sex dream, one of those for which the masculine appellation *wet dream* is so much more appropriate when applied to women. No, those kinds of dreams, a girl remembers. I'd had only three or perhaps four of those in my entire life (two about the same person). They were brief, utterly intense, unforgettable; orgasms in one's sleep, usually involving inexplicable, not-necessarily-even-attractive partners. But it wasn't the partner that made them memorable, it was the realness, the concentrated intensity of the physical feelings. Maybe one's mind needed to provide some kind of partner, maybe as a frame of reference for the experience. One might think one was losing one's mind if one just started firing off orgasms without any apparent reason. No, I never forgot a sex dream.

And while still pleasant, this was not one of those. There was Franck, in his tuxedo, and he asked me to dance. We danced a waltz, and a rumba, neither of which I actually know how to do – but I've always wanted to learn how to dance like that, so it was very nice. I listened to his amazing voice, but when I woke up, I couldn't remember what he'd said. Something about loyalty and treachery, perhaps.

While I cooked bacon and eggs for Ruthanne and myself, I again pondered my friend and her depthless affection for old movie stars, but especially her affection for Franck, whom I had so recently left behind in Dreamland in his tux. How *could* she maintain such an absolute love for someone that had been dead for decades before she'd even been born? Someone who'd only made two movies, one really good, and one really bad, and had then disappeared off the face of the earth?

I just didn't have the fertility of imagination to sustain such an impossible fantasy. Ruthanne might as well have had a crush on the real Benedict Arnold, I thought, as far as she was separated in time and mortality from Franck O'Day. When she entered the kitchen, smiling, bright-eyed and bushy-tailed as always, another thought struck me. "Ever have sex dreams, do ya, Ruthie?"

The smile turned into a leer. "All the time. Sometimes about the weirdest people. You?"

I frowned, feeling like I was missing out. "No. Not nearly often enough. I had a dream about Franck last night, though."

She paused with the coffee tipped halfway toward a cup and her grin widened. *"You had a sex dream about Franck?"*

"No. It was just a regular dream. We danced. He talked."

"What did he say?"

"I don't remember." Ruthanne finished pouring herself a cup of coffee and commenced to pouring me one. I scooped some eggs, scrambled, just the way she liked them, onto a plate, followed by a couple of strips of bacon. "Do you have sex dreams about Franck?"

"All the time. Especially since I got my green keys." She grinned at me. "Why do you ask?"

I shrugged. "It's not something that happens to me very often, unfortunately. I was just curious," I added lamely. I didn't want to say that I'd been thinking that maybe her affection for dead movie stars could have some correlation with how lucid her dreams about them were.

"All my dreams are mostly about him anymore, actually," she said, as if confirming my thought. She sipped her coffee and gazed at me attentively. "So what are you doing today?" Perhaps she wanted to change the subject as much as I did.

Now it was my turn to grin. "I got some emails from Maribeth yesterday."

Ruthanne squeaked around a mouthful of eggs. "What did she say?"

"I'll let you read 'em after we eat."

TEN

"Oh, my God, Carol!" Ruthanne could not contain herself. "You're gonna get to *meet* him! Oh! Take me with you! Oh, please, please, Carol! Please take me with you!" I couldn't imagine what she was talking about, and said so. "It says right here, he's *looking forward to meeting you in person in the near future!* You gotta take me with you when you meet Franck O'Day!"

Oh, that's right, I thought. *Ruthanne and Maribeth shared that same delusion, that one where Franck was alive.* "Of course," I said immediately. "I wouldn't dream of going without you." I decided to play along with Ruthanne's craziness. "Are you sure you won't be disappointed, though? What is he, eighty, you said? He's not going to look like he did in *George and Benedict.*"

Ruthanne looked curiously at me. "Why do you think that would matter, Carol? Everyone gets old. We're not hardly sixteen anymore, now are we? But we still remember what it was like. Who cares how old he is? He's still *him.* He's still got those blue eyes, that smile . . . you promise you'll take me with you?"

I held up two fingers, like a Boy Scout. "I promise."

Ruthanne gave me a big hug. "What kind of questions are you going to ask?"

"I was kinda hoping you'd help me with that." Ruthie gave me another hug. I settled into the writing chair, and she sat on the corner of my bed and started firing off questions.

ELEVEN

We went to work on Monday, as usual, Ruthie to her little cubicle, and me to mine, down the hall from her. I typed briefs and writs, copied testimonies from court documents. As always, there was plenty of work to do, and it was not until almost quitting time that I snuck a peek at my AOL account. No email from Maribeth. I was not expecting anything so soon, of course, but maybe she could've sent a little note saying that she'd received our questions and would soon be giving up her mind to the Franck personality that I was sure must live in there, and would be getting back to us soon. But there was nothing.

Ruthanne didn't even mention Franck that day. I guess she knew it was too soon to be expecting anything, also. In addition to more of an imagination, Ruthie was also more patient than me. If I was Ruthanne, I would've been checking my email every five minutes. She really believed that Franck was still alive, that he was going to answer our inquiries, that she was going to eventually get to (OMG!) meet him. If I was her, the suspense would've been killing me. But there was nary an electronic peep from Los Angeles, all week.

Friday rolled around, and we worked, and we lunched, and we went home. I climbed the stairs to our apartment, while Ruthanne paused at the bank of mailboxes. I changed out of my work clothes, and was just about to sit on the couch with my laptop and check to see if we'd heard back from Maribeth yet, when I heard footsteps pounding up the steps. How Ruthanne could run like that in heels, I'll never know. She burst in through the door, breathless, with a small box in her hands.

"Carol! Your keys!" I pointed at my purse on the table. "No! Your *green* keys!" She shook the box, then tossed it to me.

Oh, joy, I thought, *my green keys!* Apparently, Maribeth had been too busy spray-painting keys to put on her Franck personality and answer my interview questions. I frowned.

Ruthanne sat beside me on the couch, fidgeting, waiting with none of her trademark patience while I tore open the little cardboard box. I extracted two sparkling green keys on their own little ring. Wonderful. I handed them to Ruthanne, and she held them up, shook them a little, so they tinked. She reached for my purse, so she could put them on my key ring.

I looked into the box again. There was something else in there, something wrapped in a little piece of bubble wrap. Curious, I took it out. It was a disk, in a little plastic case. Ruthanne was trying gamely to stick the ring with the good luck charms on it onto my keys, without breaking a fingernail. I said her name.

"What?" She said, not looking up, her tongue stuck out with the effort. She paid good money for her nails.

"Ruthanne," I said again.

"What?" The key rings clicked metallically. Success. She shook the green keys so they tinked together again, then looked up at me.

I held up the jewel case. "What do you imagine that this could possibly be?"

She took the case from me. With her pirate's experienced eye, she quickly ascertained that it was a CD, not a DVD; mostly because it said CD-R on the front. So it wasn't a movie.

Franck O'Day Interview 1 was written in red on it. Ruthanne opened the case, and with practiced fingers, she snapped the disk out. (I always, invariably, had difficulty getting them out. I'd even accidentally broken a few in half. One more thing I valued Ruthie for). She handed the disk to me and I popped it into the computer. I clicked on the E: drive. The disk consisted entirely of audio files. I looked at Ruthanne.

She gestured excitedly. "Click the first one!"

I did so, and a woman's voice came out of the tinny laptop speakers.

"Hi, Carolyn! This is Maribeth O'Day. Franck says that I type too slowly, so instead of dictating to me, he's decided that it would be easier just to record his answers to your interview questions. He's still looking forward to a face to face conversation, but he figures that this should tide you over until you're all ready for that."

"Hello, Carolyn. This is Franck O'Day."

"Stop!" Ruthanne screamed. I hit the pause button. "Give it to me." I handed the laptop to her. She arose and unplugged her own laptop from the TV, where she'd been watching more pirated movies from it the night before. She plugged my laptop in instead, and turned the television on. She pushed a couple of buttons on the computer.

"Hello, Carolyn. This is Franck O'Day."

Ruthanne clicked the pause button again. The playback wasn't in stereo, but it was nice and loud, nice and clear, coming through the television. Ruthanne smiled from ear to ear. "Oh. My. God. Carol. *It's him!"*

55

It couldn't be. Franck O'Day was *dead*. There was no way. Maribeth's fairy tale, lifted wholesale from the plot of *Lost Horizon* – that ridiculous fable about the plane crash and the rescuing monks – it just *couldn't* be true. It was just too far-fetched. Franck was dead. He'd been dead for more than forty years. "Play it again, Ruthie," I said.

"Hello, Carolyn. This is Franck O'Day. First of all, I'd like to thank you for this opportunity to tell my story. I think it'll make a great book, if I do say so myself. Mari printed out your questions. My eyesight isn't what it used to be, so I hope you don't mind if she just reads them to me and I'll answer."

Ruthanne stopped the computer again. She said, "It's him, Carol! It's really him!"

I had to admit, it certainly *sounded* like him. His voice was perhaps a shade higher, due to being eighty years old, no doubt. Or maybe it was the recording equipment or maybe I was imagining it. But the timbre was the same, the same masculine melodiousness, the same roguish, ever-so-slightly-mocking tone. It *was* Franck O'Day. There could be no doubt about it. "Well, I'll be a son-of-a-bitch," I said in amazement.

"Don't be," Ruthanne said, still grinning.

I thought back to the questions we'd sent in. Ruthanne had asked simple, fan questions, but I'd been aiming for a little historical perspective – I'd been aiming for some insider, old Hollywood kind of info, stuff that Maribeth couldn't have possibly known. I'd been curious to see how she would try to fake it. It was a little mean of me, I had to admit, but I had to start somewhere. Ruthanne pushed the button, then came over and sat beside me on the couch.

"Ok, let's begin." It was Maribeth's voice, sounding like the little old lady she undoubtedly was. *"Can you share with us how you broke into the film business? What was Hollywood like when you first began making movies?"*

Franck laughed. *"Hollywood was the same then as it is now, I'd imagine. Not every creative mind, not every important director, not every influential reporter is a fag, but most of them are."* Again, he laughed, a low, happy rumble. It wasn't a bitter laugh, or a rueful one. Just a display of amusement.

"I was thirteen when my mom married Howie. His brother was what we called a theatrical agent. He fell in love with me at first sight." Another laugh. *"But you can't be a homophobe in Hollywood, Carol. There's no profit in it."*

I jumped to hear Franck O'Day's dark, silky, mellifluous voice say my name. It was positively surreal, to hear his voice coming through the TV speaker, just like he'd sounded in his movies, just like he'd sounded in that dream I'd had. Saying my name.

"Just because they like you – it's absolutely no reflection on you or your own preferences. But if all the fags' attention unnerves you –"

"They call them gays *now, Franck,"* Maribeth interrupted. *"That other word . . . it's not nice. They don't like it."*

Again, Franck laughed. *"My mother used to call them* flowers. *I don't know if they liked that one, either."* He paused, then said, *"Okay, Mari. I'll use the right word. I wouldn't want to offend any of them. I wouldn't want any of them to have a hissy fit. They have a lot of power.*

"Anyway, like I was saying. You can't be a homophobe in Hollywood. You have to admit to yourself, if the . . . gays' attention unnerves you, then you're probably one of them. And if you're one of them, then you should just go for it, I always say. Why lie to yourself? It's not like you can't hide it in Hollywood. Even today.

"It's all about the face these guys want to give to their audience. Nowadays, it's acceptable. The ones that want to come out, they do. But there's still a bunch of them back there in the closet with the broken tennis rackets and the old board games. They're not sure what coming out would do to their careers, so they just keep it all hidden. It's all about what face they want to show to the public.

"Like I was saying, their attention never bothered me. Attention is attention. Love, adoration. It's all the same. You just acknowledge it, say, 'I'm flattered, but, unfortunately for you, I don't swing that way.' They're usually okay with that.

"So, I didn't mind that Uncle Jesse was a flower, that he had a crush on me. It's not like he ever acted on it. They were a little more apt to hide it in those days, you see, and I was just a kid. But I could tell, nonetheless. It was just the way he looked at me, the way his hand would linger that extra second when he would pat me on the shoulder.

"For ten years, he got me little gigs all over town. Little bit parts, kids in the background. Most of it wound up on the cutting room floor. Once my voice changed all the way, he got me a couple of little one-liners on the radio.

"Then Uncle Jesse, by what luck I'll never know, got me a little casting couch meeting with Patrick Morrison."

"He directed *Sister Sam's Lost Angels!"* Ruthanne squealed. "Oh, my, God, Carol! This is awesome!"

"I was almost twenty-three, certainly no baby, but I was still surprised by Morrison's offer. He was actually very straightforward about it. 'Suck my dick,' he said, 'and I'll give you the lead — '"

"Franck!" Maribeth squeaked in embarrassment.

"What?" Franck laughed again. *"Carol asked about how I got into the business. She wants to know what it was like. I'm sure she's a big girl. She's a writer. She wants to hear how it was. I'm sure that she can take it. Isn't that right, Carol?"*

"Isn't that right, Carol?" Ruthanne echoed gleefully. She leapt up and hit pause. "This is great! It's like he's right here in the room with us! You want a drink? This is all just a little too much for me. I need a drink."

"Yes," I said, "I could definitely use a drink right about now."

"I like to think, maybe he was having one while he was recording this," Ruthanne said from the kitchen. "A mint julep, and maybe a cigar."

I thought that in order to reach the ripe old age of eighty, Franck had probably given up cigars a long time ago. And mint juleps, too.

"I can't quite get my head around it, Carol," Ruthanne called from the kitchen. "Franck O'Day is talking to us!"

Franck O'Day is talking to me, I thought. But I was not sucked in, not the way Ruthanne was. It took me no trouble at all to remember that no matter how smooth and hypnotic his voice was, he was still eighty years old. Ruthanne was hearing Franck O'Day from 1961, from *High Times in Manhattan*, from her fertile sex-dream fueled imagination. I was listening to an old man — someone who, while maybe not dead yet, still had one foot in the grave.

I was wholly fascinated with his story, however, especially the ease with which he was telling it. He was talking to a complete stranger about being propositioned by a male director. He was telling us about it with no compunctions whatsoever, without a trace of self-consciousness.

Ruthanne returned with our drinks, and I wondered suddenly if her illusions were crumbling, what with hearing her idol relating all these sordid homosexual casting couch details. I asked, "How does it feel to hear Franck O'Day say, *'Suck my dick,'* Ruthie?"

As soon as the words left my mouth, I realized that she would take it wrong, and I was not disappointed. She grinned, again from ear to ear. "Are you kidding? Do you think that I haven't imagined, *dreamed* —"

"No, Ruthie, I meant in this context." I gestured at the computer. "He's talking about the director, saying it to him. Another man –"

She shrugged, non-committal. "Well, let's see how the rest of the story goes." She clicked the play button.

"Anyway, I'm going to assume that you're a big girl, Carol," Franck's voice resumed. *"I'm going to assume that you're no goody-two-shoes. I'm sure you've heard enough of my story, already. I'm sure you've already read Mari's website."* He paused, and I could almost see him looking at Maribeth, sitting right there next to him.

"You couldn't want to write a book about my life, if you're a goody-two-shoes. Not after reading all the great details on Mari's website." The note of sarcasm was unmistakable.

Still standing by the computer, Ruthanne paused the recording again. "Are you a goody-two-shoes, Carol?" she asked with a grin.

I grinned back. "Are you?"

"Not on your life." She hit play again, and sat back down next to me on the couch.

"Anyway. I'd read the script for Sister Sam's Lost Angels, *even before Uncle Jesse finagled the face-to-face meeting with Morrison for me. It was not all that, as the kids say. But this was* RKO, *so I didn't just laugh in his face. I told Morrison that I didn't think I was quite up for the lead, and asked him what else was available.*

"'Well,' he said, and smiled at me. 'If you let me suck your dick, there still might be a small part in it for you."

"Franck!" Maribeth squeaked again.

"Maybe I should just do this by myself," Franck said, just a touch of exasperation in his voice. *"If you can't take it. This young woman wants to hear about how it was. I can't help if how it was offends your delicate sensibilities."*

Papers shuffled in the background. *"Must you be so graphic?"* Maribeth asked.

"Kid," Franck said in that low, growling, amused voice, *"it only gets worse from here."* He laughed again. *"That's not entirely true. But Carol asked about my first big break, and I'm getting to that.*

"So, I got a part in Sister Sam's Lost Angels. *I even had a few lines, but they wound up, as such things often do, on the cutting room floor. But the best connection I would ever make came out of my . . . brief association with Patrick Morrison and* RKO. *It was Morrison, you see, who introduced me to Bobby Ecksmith, at the wrap-party for* Sister Sam.

59

"*I remember the two of them were standing by the pool when I walked up with Debbie Sutton.*"

"Oh!" Ruthanne yelped, almost spilling her drink. "Debbie Sutton! She played Sister Sam! She was under contract with *RKO* for years."

"*She was no angel, let me tell you,*" Franck said.

"*The woman's dead, for God's sake, Franck!*" Maribeth said, again shocked. "*Must you speak ill of the dead?*

"*Okay. I was talking about the first time I met Bobby, anyway, not Debbie. Morrison was standing there with Bobby, and they were both watching us from the other side of the pool. As we walked up, Morrison leaned in and whispered something in Bobby's ear, then he glared at Debbie, and she immediately decided that there was someone she needed to talk to back on the other side of the pool.*

"*Bobby smiled at me. He and Morrison both smiled at me, like I was on the menu. I smiled back. Adoration is adoration, as I say, no matter where it comes from, no matter if you don't return it in the least. It's all positive energy.*

"*After a moment of smiling at me, Bobby said, 'Patrick tells me you're quite the up and comer.'*

"*I kid you not, Carol, he actually said that to me, and with a moderately straight face. I looked mildly at Morrison, who perhaps expected me to be shocked or embarrassed or worried. I was none of these things. Even at twenty-three, I knew which secrets were inviolate, and which secrets were shared and with which people. Morrison could say whatever he wanted about me. I knew exactly how far it would go, and was not concerned at all. After all, it wasn't me that was the cocksucker.*"

"*Franck!*" Maribeth squealed.

Franck laughed. "*The next thing Bobby said to me was, 'I've been working on a historical piece, and now that I've met you, I think you'd be perfect for the lead.'*

"*Now I smiled slightly at Bobby. 'Is that a fact?' I said.*

"*'Indeed.' Bobby exchanged glances with Morrison. 'I think you'd be perfect. I have a script in the house, if you'd like to take a look at it.'*

"*'Of course,' I said. Ignoring Morrison, I followed famous English director Robert Ecksmith into the house.*

"*He led me to a little office, there on the first floor of Morrison's giant hacienda. I stood in front of a convenient couch and watched Bobby lock the door behind us. Then he turned and looked at me, in the same way that Uncle Jesse did, the same way that Morrison did. The same way that Debbie Sutton did, for that matter. Only on Bobby, that look was deeper – there was an additional hunger there. I sipped my drink, and smiled in slight surprise when he started to unbutton his shirt. I really wasn't surprised at all. I watched him take off his shirt, fling it on the desk, his eyes never leaving mine, that hungry look only increasing. He took of few steps closer to me.*

"I waited. As he reached out to touch my face, I said, 'I don't know what Mr. Morrison told you about me, Mr. Ecksmith. But I'm just interested in being in your picture. Didn't you say something about a script?'

"Bobby's hand froze in mid-air, inches from my face. He narrowed his eyes, paused. That hungry look never dimmed, even as he realized just how uninterested I was. Then he burst out laughing. He turned and retrieved his shirt from the desk, and threw it on. 'I'm Robert Ecksmith, kid,' he said as he buttoned up his shirt. 'I don't carry scripts around. I thought you looked smarter than that.'

"'I'm Francis Joseph O'Day, Mr. Ecksmith,' I replied, 'and I am smarter than that.' I sipped my drink and smiled at him again. 'But I still bet I'd be perfect for the lead in your picture.'

"Bobby considered me, then smiled wryly. He said, 'That you would, Mr. O'Day. That you would.' He took a pen from Morrison's desk and scribbled something on the blotter, then tore it off and held it out to me. 'Call this number on Monday. Tell them I said to make you an appointment for a screen test.'

"I took the paper from him and stuck it in my pocket without looking at it. 'I will certainly do that. Thank you very much, Mr. Ecksmith.'

"He waved absently and stepped to the door. He put his hand on the knob, then turned and looked at me again. 'Are you sure that you don't want to . . .' I shook my head. 'But Patrick said . . .'

"I sighed. 'I think we'd both regret it, Mr. Ecksmith,' I said. I walked past him and unlocked the door, opened it. I stepped out into the hall, then turned back and smiled at him again. 'After all, we've just met.'

"Bobby smiled at me, then slapped me on the shoulder. 'We're going to be great friends, Francis Joseph O'Day. I just know it. I'm going to make you a star.'

Franck sighed, but there was a smile in his voice when he continued. *"Bobby and I did become great friends, but it wasn't him that made me a star. Not directly, anyway.*

"Ah, George and Benedict. *Where to begin about that one? It was Bobby's vision, to tell the story from the other side, to give Arnold his day in the sun. Bobby thought it would be* revolutionary, *pun completely intended. But nobody wanted to hear Arnold's side. Everyone was happy with knowing him as a traitor; everyone was fine with that. No one wanted to hear anything else.*

"If you showed George and Benedict *to aborigines, or people from another planet, or anyone else who had never heard of Benedict Arnold, then there'd definitely be a positive response to it. It's basically a great film. But to anyone who has even the slightest familiarity with American history, the name* Benedict Arnold *is synonymous with the word* traitor. *No one wants to hear anything else. The whole project was doomed from the start.*

"But I appeared in it anyway, for Bobby's sake. Like I say, we became friends. He introduced me around to all the important people. He was a star in his own right – Robert Ecksmith, the famous English director. George and Benedict *was his one and only flop, did you know that, Carol? Although after it bombed, he did go back to England to make movies. 'Just until the derision dies down,' he said with a laugh.*

"Bobby was the only person in the business that I ever knew that didn't want something from me." Franck laughed again. *"Well, that's not completely accurate. There was that one thing that Bobby wanted from me. That one thing – he wanted it very, very badly. I'd have to say that Bobby wanted that one thing, from me, with the entirety of that part of himself that wanted such things. But above his undeniable – but quite controllable – desire for such physical things from me, we were friends, so he never asked me about it again, except in jest. It was a joke between us.*

"And it was not like he suffered, or carried a torch for me. There were plenty of willing and able young men around for Bobby to do his thing with. And he took advantage of every one that looked his way.

"Even though we both knew that he was in love with me, almost from that first encounter at Morrison's house – Bobby accepted without resentment the unalterable fact that I was just not into all that, that I was never going to do what he so badly wanted me to do.

"I believe he was secretly relieved, actually. Lovers come and go. And when you're famous English director Robert Ecksmith, and you have your choice – they come and go at a little higher volume and maybe at a little quicker rate than average.

"But friendship – that lasts a lifetime. And it's a rare commodity indeed in show business. Sometimes it's entirely too easy to make your friends into just that – commodities – to buy and sell loyalties and confidences.

"Bobby was certainly a good friend to me, my best friend, without asking for one other thing than that I be his friend, too. Like I say, everybody else in the business wanted something from me – financially, physically, emotionally – but not Bobby. I can't tell you how refreshing that was.

"There are echelons in this business – and those in the highest echelons are a closed rank. It doesn't matter how talented you are. It doesn't matter who you know or how you blow, or even how you blow you who you know . . ." Franck paused, waiting for Maribeth to rebuke him again, I imagined. But there was only a quiet rustling of papers.

"It doesn't matter how good you are – or even, really, how bad you are. There are a lot of very wealthy, very famous, very lousy actors. Wouldn't you agree, Carol?

"My point is, good or bad, you only make it into that higher echelon if someone already there reaches down to where you are, and pulls you up there with

62

*them. And that's what Bobby did for me. He introduced me to Donald Sunnerfeld,
talked me up to him. I'd never have gotten anywhere near Sunnerfeld, or even his
assistant, if it hadn't been for Bobby."*

I kinda thought I could guess who this Sunnerfeld guy was, even
though I'd never heard the name before in my life. I glanced over at
Ruthanne. "Donald Sunnerfeld directed *High Times in Manhattan*," she
supplied. "He was also directing *Two Green Keys*, until it got shelved."

Maribeth's voice came out of the television speaker. *"Carolyn's
next set of questions are about* High Times in Manhattan. *Do you want to take
a little break before getting into that?"* There was a pause, but no sound. I
assumed Franck must have nodded. Then Maribeth said, *"Okay,
Carolyn, we're going to end this one right here. Franck will answer your questions
about* High Times *in the next file."*

The faint hiss that came from whatever microphone set-up
Maribeth had used ceased. I looked at Ruthanne and smiled. "Hot
damn!" she said. "Is this awesome or what? Your book's gonna spend
weeks at the top of *The New York Times' Bestseller List!* I can see it
already."

I didn't know about all *that*. I still had to write the damn thing. But
the little tidbit that lost and presumed dead Franck O'Day was still alive
– that was a good start, even if his tales of Hollywood casting couches
from the heterosexual man's perspective were no real revelations.
Trade, after all, was trade.

But on the other hand, I thought, even though people had heard
these kinds of stories before, they hadn't heard them from *him*. I looked
at Ruthanne. "Did you know that this Patrick Morrison was gay? Or
Ecksmith?"

My friend shrugged. "I don't really know too much about
directors. It's never been my thing. I recognize their names from what
they directed, but I never cared enough to find out anything about their
personal lives."

Perhaps *Wikipedia* would take a more personal interest, I thought.
It would be a bombshell indeed, perhaps – at least to people who cared
about these things – if Franck's allegations had not been made before
by others. Maybe no one had ever before intimated that Morrison and
Ecksmith were gay. Such things were not often common knowledge
outside of Hollywood in the old days.

People who cared about these things might rush out to purchase a book in which just such allegations were alleged. I paused and imagined my name at the top of that bestsellers' list, too. Then I came back down to Earth, and asked Ruthanne if she'd make us another drink before we listened to the next recording.

.

TWELVE

It was so bizarre to hear my questions, my *words*, come out of the TV, in Maribeth O'Day's little old lady's voice.

"Can you tell us about filming High Times in Manhattan? *When did you know it was going to be such a big hit? How did you feel when you were passed over by the Academy?"*

"As I mentioned before," Franck said, *"I never would've met Donald Sunnerfeld, had it not been for Bobby. There were a lot of great directors back then, and Bobby knew them all. But I think he steered me toward Sunnerfeld, because he knew that Sunnerfeld wasn't a . . . he knew that Sunnerfeld wasn't gay. Bobby knew that with Sunnerfeld, I wouldn't have to fight all that off again. He knew that if Sunnerfeld cast me, it would be because he thought I had talent, not just because he wanted to . . ."*

I could hear the grin in Franck's voice. He was baiting Maribeth. Papers rustled. When she didn't speak, he concluded with, *"Bobby knew that if Sunnerfeld cast me, it would be because I could act, not because I was just another pretty face."*

"Sunnerfeld not only liked women, he was rather a womanizer, actually. It was a relief to have a director who wanted to chase skirts instead of me for a change. I figured it would be that blonde's problem this time. That's how I thought of her then – that blonde. I'd seen her around, of course, but we'd never been introduced.

"That blonde put Sunnerfeld in his place, before we all even sat down together for the first time. She told him that she was the studio's biggest draw, and if he tried to touch her, she'd have him replaced. I don't know if Sunnerfeld believed her or not, or even if he cared if she could really do it. If he got fired from this movie, it wasn't like he wouldn't be picked up for another one, immediately. He was Donald Sunnerfeld, after all.

"There were far too many available and willing starlets throwing themselves at Sunnerfeld – why should he waste one second of his highly valuable time chasing some high-strung actress who wasn't having any? So he stopped making passes at Jessika and just directed the movie.

"Ah, Jessika. I remember the first time we met, at a little Christmas party before production started. She was there with her brother – I know you've read about him, *Carol.*

"Sunnerfeld said, 'I'd like you to meet your co-star, Miss Jessika Yerdlay,' and I shook her hand.

"She regarded me coldly, I remember that. Yes, the first time Jessika looked at me, her gray eyes were frosty. Positively icy. How I wish that they would've stayed that way.

"'So nice to meet you, Mr. O'Day,' she'd said emotionlessly, then turned on her shapely ankle and walked away. That was it. Roger smiled sheepishly at me, said nothing, and skittered on after her. I don't know what kind of reaction she wanted from me – I don't know if she expected me to run after her, like her lapdog brother did. That wasn't going to happen. Sure, Jessika Yerdlay was beautiful and talented – but she just wasn't all that, like the kids say. At least not to me.

She'd listened to her own press too much, I thought. She believed that she was so talented and sought-after that she could get away with presenting that bitchy, stand-offish attitude to the world. In her defense, I must say that damn near everyone let her get away with it. But I was not impressed – Jessika Yerdlay thought she was a whole lot more wonderful than I thought she was.

"But the ice in her eyes thawed, did it not? Bit by bit she warmed up to me, until by the time we were starting wardrobe, she was quite heated indeed. I just watched her with amusement, as that look in her eyes changed from frosty indifference into that old familiar hungry look, that one I'd seen so many times before.

"I remember the first time she walked into my dressing room and locked the door. You should always beware of Hollywood types that enter a room and lock the door behind them, Carol. It seldom ends well."

Ruthanne giggled hysterically, stamping her feet rapidly on the floor. She leapt up and clicked the pause. "This is just too much, Carol! I love it! It's like he's right here with us! How's your drink?" It was still half full. Ruthanne slammed the rest of hers. "Well, I need another one."

She darted out to the kitchen and the thought struck me that another reason that Ruthanne was enjoying this so much, besides the obvious ones, was that she was already about half loaded. She quickly returned. When she clicked play again, I noticed that she had a mint leaf stuck to her pinkie. I smiled.

"As far as being a hit goes, I knew that the film was going to be big the first time I read the script. It's a love story – a good one, and people love love stories, even the bad ones. I thought it was a shoo-in for the Oscar, the first time I read it.

"But then I heard that West Side Story *was also in production. One problem with this business is that sometimes there are several good stories being shot at the same time. Sometimes these good stories are extremely similar, covering virtually the exact same material. But the studios are in competition – they don't*

care. *No one believes that their movie is not as good as the other studio's almost identical movie. Of course, everyone believes theirs is the best.*

"*West Side Story had been huge on Broadway. But our little film was clever, and it was helmed by a great director. He and the studio believed his movie was the better one, of course.*

"*But when movies are too similar, only one of them is going to come out on top at the Oscars. Two love stories weren't going to get nominated in the same year. And given the choice between two comparable stories, the Academy is always going to choose the sad one. Especially if it's sad and a musical, and had been a big hit on Broadway.*"

Ruthanne stopped the recording again. "I know what he's talking about. Remember when we were kids, when *Robin Hood, Prince of Thieves* came out? With Kevin Costner?"

I nodded and shook my head at the same time. I remembered the movie, but not from when it came out, and I said as much to her.

Ruthanne shook her head. "It doesn't matter. I don't remember it from when it came out probably, either. My point is, it was a big budget movie. Lots of money spent, lots of money made. But there was another Robin Hood movie that came out the exact same year, with Patrick Bergen."

"I haven't seen that one."

"Of course you haven't. It had a little budget." Ruthanne held her thumb and forefinger close together. "No marketing. Nobody's ever heard of it. But it's really a much better film. I remember thinking when I read about it – why would they release two movies about the same thing in the same year? Franck's just explained it. Everybody thinks their movie is the best one.

"And then there was *Tombstone*. Remember that one? It came out in '93. Then came *Wyatt Earp* in '94. It bombed spectacularly. Costner was on the losing side that time. But did it bomb because it was so bad, or because *Tombstone*, from the year before, was so much better? That's what Franck's talking about. Sometimes they make almost the same movie twice, at the same time. And nobody remembers both of them."

How did *Ruthanne know this stuff?* I thought. *And why did she care, or think that I would care?* I stopped myself before I said, *That's interesting.* After this unnecessary extrapolation, now I needed another drink. I held out my nearly empty glass, and Ruthanne quickly ran out to the kitchen and made me another one. When she returned, I said thanks, and she clicked on the play button again.

"*So none of us were truly very surprised when we weren't nominated, except for maybe Sunnerfeld. He took it pretty hard. But even he had to know that we weren't going to beat out* West Side Story. *It just had too much going for it.*"

"*Personally, I couldn't possibly have cared less about an Oscar. I was getting married in June. I wasn't concerned about much else besides that.*"

Maribeth's voice said, "*Carolyn asks if you would talk about your relationship with Jessika. And about Bridget. And about her death – if it's not too painful – she adds that right here.*" Papers rustled.

"*I appreciate your compassion, Carol,*" Franck O'Day said through my television speaker. "*But it's been nearly fifty years since I lost Bridget. I've faced other problems and crises and unusual circumstances since then – so I'd be lying to you, if I gave you the old chestnut – that not a day goes by when I don't think of Bridget. Too many days have already passed. It's not painful to me to talk about her, because I can remember how things were before she was taken from me, how happy we were together. I can remember that as clearly as if it'd all happened yesterday. That old chestnut is accurate. I can remember how it was, even if I've long ago ceased to think about how it could've been.*

"*I suppose that I have to start with Jessika. Even though I'd much rather skip Jessika altogether, and just tell you about Bridget, I know that I've got to start with Jessika, or the story'll be incomplete.*

"*Mari brought me a copy of* Time, *last year, with Jessika's obituary in it. If you've read Mari's website, you know that she doesn't have a lot of love for Jessika. And she's not at all above expressing that lack. But you have no idea, really, Carol, how deeply her hatred goes. But that'll be something we can discuss in person.*"

Franck paused. Papers rustled. He continued. "*Mari brought me a copy of Jessika's obituary, mostly because she wanted me to see my picture in print again. I suspect that Mari took the picture herself and emailed it to them – is* Time *really that desperate for photos? I know she took the ones on the website. They're all terrible – no one can tell it's me.*" Franck paused again, and I imagined him giving his step-daughter a dirty look. "*But for that I'm grateful, mostly because they're such terrible pictures.*

"*Anyway, Mari thought I'd like to see myself in print again, so she showed Jessika's obituary to me. My point in bringing all this up, Carol, is that I remember that it said in the article somewhere that Jessika and I are remembered more for our scandals than for our movies.*

"*I realize that this is unfortunately true. But all of it makes up the sum of my life – and you want to write a book about me. So I guess that, even though she really was never that important to me – no matter how hard she tried – I have to talk about Jessika first.*"

Franck sighed. "*Okay. As I've said, I met Jessika before production started on* Manhattan. *By the time we were in wardrobe, she'd already . . . What's a term I can use, that won't offend Mari, yet'll still convey the correct spirit of the thing?*

"*By the time we were in wardrobe — Bobby would have said, 'she'd already seduced me.' That was a word he liked, a concept that he liked — he always said that about all those young men that caught his eye. 'I invited so-and-so over and allowed him to seduce me.'*

"*Bobby liked to pretend that they were so attracted to him, that he was powerless not to succumb to their desire for him. That was how he liked to pretend it worked. That was his definition of seduction.*

"*His definition of it painted the 'seduced,' if you will, in a submissive light. Bobby, who was one of the post powerful men in the business, longed to be submissive, you see. He wanted someone who wanted him for himself, instead of someone who was just trying to see what they could get.*

"*But his conquests were just that — conquests. Bobby was always in control. He picked, he chose, he initiated. No one ever went home with Robert Ecksmith because they'd picked* him *up. They went home with him because he'd found* them *attractive first, and they swung that way, or they were willing to swing that way, in order to find out what he could do for them, career-wise.*

"*Bobby never did find someone to love that was on an equal footing with him — he never found anybody that didn't want something from him, someone who didn't flatter him just because of what he could do for them. Not in this business, anyway.*

"*But I digress. My point is, Jessika didn't seduce me. She didn't waltz into my dressing room and lock the door behind her and talk me into doing something that I didn't necessarily want to do. That's the definition of seduction to me — when you're unsure about it, and someone talks you into it. When you have to be talked into it, then you have to be seduced.*

"*No one has ever* talked *me into anything, Carol, especially not when it comes to that kind of thing. I've never been unsure about anything — and* especially *not that kind of thing.*

"*Jessika didn't lock the door behind her and confess the overwhelming power of her desire for me, either. Bobby would've laughed at that — who knew better than he did that the power of someone's desire for me doesn't impress me too much? I've been seeing it since I was thirteen years old.*

"*No. Jessika didn't confess her desire, didn't beg me, not at first, anyway. She just walked into my dressing room and locked the door, and told me what she wanted to do, and asked me if I'd like to participate.*

"And I'm not saying that it wasn't sexy as hell — in fact, it was a welcome change. I was tired of the ones that said no — because when I shrugged and said, 'Okay,' that no would invariably turn into a yes. And it made me think — if she's this cagey about something so simple — yes or no — how can she be trustworthy about anything else?*

69

"I'm not saying that I trusted Jessika, either. I like everyone and I get along with everyone, but I've never been much for trusting anyone. I trusted Bobby. And Bridget. And of course, Mari. But that's about it."

Papers rustled again. I came to think of it as the sign that signified Maribeth's presence.

"So Jessika made me an offer and I took her up on it. She was beautiful, and it was her idea. If it hadn't been her suggestion, I would never have pursued her, however.

"I've never been much of a pursuer of anything, really. I've always been an easygoing kind of guy – and invitations of all kinds have always just seemed to flow in my direction.

"'Hey, Franck, do you want to play tennis?' Sure.

"'Do you want to take the yacht to Catalina with us, Franck?' Sure, why not?

"'Nice shoes, Franck. Wanna – '"

"Franck!" Maribeth squeaked a little bit more stridently this time.

Ruthanne giggled again, again stamped her feet on the floor in glee. She paused the recording. "OMG, Carol, he's hilarious! I love him!"

"You already loved him," I said absently. Ol' Franck seemed a little full of himself, in my estimation.

Ruthanne said, "There's nothing better than finding out that someone whom you find attractive, really is *attractive*, in other ways besides just looks."

"Because his looks are gone," I reminded her. It might've been a little bit harsh of me to just say it like that, but it was the truth.

"Probably." But Ruthanne wasn't daunted by my cruel words, no matter how true they were. *Her smile never dimmed,* as the song says. "But so far, his sense of humor is hilarious. And that's current. So who cares how he looks now? I'm just really liking listening to him talk, right now."

"I'm kinda finding him to be an egotistical asshole," I said flatly.

Ruthanne grinned at me. "Really? Because he's sexy and he knows it, and he's telling us about it?"

I opened my mouth to reply to that, but then I abruptly shut it again. I couldn't think of one single argument against the fact that Franck O'Day certainly was sexy, at least at the time that was under discussion, and it was obvious that he and everyone else knew it.

"It seems to me," Ruthanne said, "that so far, Franck's been more of a passive observer than an egotistical asshole. Everybody's been making passes at him – and he's refused or acquiesced as he's seen fit. He hasn't made any demands on anyone. How is that egotistical?"

I shrugged, frowned. I hated it when her arguments were logical. "He just seems a bit full of himself, that's all. Talking about how all these people fell immediately and completely in love with him."

Ruthanne glanced around the living room like she'd lost something. "Wasn't that you that sat through *Manhattan* with me last weekend?"

"Yes, but –"

"But me no buts, Carol. If Franck O'Day was standing right here in front of you, looking like he did then, like he looked to Morrison and Ecksmith and Debbie Sutton and Jessika – you tell me that you wouldn't fall in love with him, too."

"I don't know, Ruthie. It's just like you said, you have to get to know someone before –"

"That's not what I said at all, Carol," Ruthanne countered. "What I said was, it's great to find out that someone that you think you love – "

"Based solely on his looks. You love Franck solely because of his looks. Franck's actually . . ." I almost said *dead*, but even I didn't believe that anymore. "Franck's old now, Ruthanne. I think you're going to be disappointed when the reality of that crashes into your fantasy of *High Times in Manhattan.*"

"That's one of the reasons I love you, Carol. You know everything." She grinned at me. "You think I'm completely shallow – that I'm unable to translate a physical attraction into something else."

"I've got one word for you. *Marty.*" I grinned at her.

"That was an experiment," Ruthanne protested. "It was a failure. Marty was just . . ." She gestured in the air to indicate emptiness, nothingness, ". . . no matter how good he looked."

She paused. "You say I fell for Franck based solely on his looks – I'll give you that. You have to admit that he *looked good* when he was young. If you even *attempt* to dispute that, you're a liar. But you think that I won't still like him now, because now he's a little old man. And I say you're wrong. He's still *him*, even if he's old. Maybe I won't be as physically attracted to the old him, like I am to the young him. Who knows? Maybe he's aged well."

"It would have to be exceptionally well."

Ruthanne shrugged. "You never know. Anyway, no matter how old he is, no matter how old he looks – he's still *him*, and I will still lose my hillbilly mind if I actually get to talk to him in person. Especially

71

after listening to this. We're getting to know him as a person, like you say. So who cares how he looks? He's so funny!"

I shook my head. I didn't agree with her, but there was no sense in arguing with a fan. So far, Franck O'Day was an asshole. Sure, the things he said were funny, but the humor was at the expense of others. He was laughing at the feelings of others. He was immune to the passions and desires that others felt for him — and he found that funny. For reasons I couldn't have wholly explained, I found it offensive.

Ruthanne clicked the play button.

"Anyway, you get the point, Carol. Jessika made me an offer and I took her up on it.

"At first she would drop by my house at her whim, because she was the undeniable Jessika Yerdlay, and nations prostrated themselves before her. At least that's how she felt.

"This just dropping by behavior was okay with me. I wasn't doing anything else, most evenings. But Jessika soon found that her laissez-faire attitude toward common politeness and courtesy left her sitting alone in her Jag out in front of my house on more than one occasion. All dressed up with nowhere to go.

"Sure, I'd see her if I was home. But if I wasn't going to be home, I certainly didn't check in with her first. Why should I check in with someone that just dropped by whenever she felt like it? Sometimes I didn't come home at all, and that's when jealousy turned Jessika Yerdlay polite.

"She started calling before she came over, calling to let me know if she wouldn't be coming over, calling to ask if I wanted to come over to her house.

"And after a while, I just fell into the habit of it, Carol. That's my irredeemable sin, I guess. Jessika was always there, and she was attentive, so I gave her what she wanted. I gave her my company, let her host my parties, squired her around town, slept with her. But it was just because it was easy. It was just because she was there.

"I didn't love Jessika, Carol. I didn't dislike her, but I didn't particularly like her, either. I could never quite bring myself to trust her, and I certainly didn't love her. She loved herself more than anyone else could, anyway.

"But I guess perhaps I shouldn't have kept company with her as much as I did, eh? When I didn't love her? But it's not like I lied to her. It's not like I made her any promises, not one single one.

"Jessika was always telling me how much she loved me, how completely she loved me. I would always say, 'I know you do, Jessika,' and I'd hug her back or kiss her back or whatever it was she wanted at the moment.

"But I didn't love her, and she knew it. I never told her that I did. Not one single time."

"Oh, turn it off, Ruthie," I said in disgust. Surprised, she complied. I visited the bathroom, and when I returned, I said, "What a bastard he is."

Ruthanne looked at me curiously. "You mean, because he didn't love Jessika? He never told her that he loved her."

"So what?" I flopped back down on the couch and recovered my drink. "If he didn't love her, he shouldn't have stayed with her."

"Oh, that's just bullshit," Ruthanne said, dismissing my comment with a wave of her hand.

I was getting sucked into the trials and tribulations of Ruthie's ancient movie stars, despite myself, and book or no book, I wasn't sure I liked it. Not sure one bit. Her beloved Franck O'Day was a bastard.

When I continued to frown, she said, "Haven't you ever had one of those?" She gestured at the television, displaying its list of files from Maribeth's CD, writ large and in HD. When I looked perplexed, she said, "Remember Danny? From high school?"

I nodded slowly. Danny from high school. Danny Tripplewhite, star quarterback, walking, talking, smiling embodiment of Big Man on Campus. Yeah, I remembered Danny. Tall, muscular, sexy, blonde and blue-eyed, he was perfect, every school girl's dream. I also remember thinking that he was an arrogant asshole. He didn't do a thing for me, either. But not Ruthie. Ruthie had a crush on Danny that was larger and more all-encompassing even than the one she had on Franck O'Day, whom she'd never met. After all, she'd actually known Danny, had classes with him, talked to him. Dated him.

"You remember what I used to say, even then?" Ruthanne asked. "That life is filled with beautiful men, and the most wonderful thing about it is that, every now and then, you get to have one of them?"

Yes, I remembered her saying that, remembered thinking that it was damned philosophical for a sixteen-year-old girl.

"I lost my virginity to Danny."

Yes, I remembered that, too. I remembered being appalled that my friend would allow that shallow cretin to touch her. No matter how cute he was. There was nothing more to him than cute. I couldn't have verbalized just who I would've chosen at the time – but I knew he would've had more going for him than just cute.

"I also remember you crying your eyes out when he dumped you." I said. So distraught had she been, I reflected now, that immediately afterwards, Ruthanne's tastes had migrated from blondes to dark-haired boys.

Again, she made that dismissive gesture with her hand. "Yeah, Danny was a son-of-a-bitch. And I knew it all along. That's just my

73

point, Carol. Danny was a son-of-a-bitch, but I didn't care. *I wanted him.* He was flawless. I loved everything about him, even the fact that he was a bastard. He never loved me back. I might've tried to delude myself that he did, but I really knew he didn't. Still, I didn't care. All I wanted to do was look at him, to hold his hand, to kiss him, *to be with him.* Do you understand what I'm saying?"

I closed one eye and squinted at her. "You're saying that you lost all your self-esteem the moment you saw Danny Tripplewhite? Is that what you're saying?"

I expected Ruthie to get angry at that remark. No one had more self-esteem that she did. Witness her complete self-control in the face of the temptation posed by Marty, her Franck O'Day look-alike. I knew she'd wanted to try that one out – he was a dead ringer for that one snapshot out of time, and, hell, her imagination alone would have made it good for her. But in the end, she just couldn't go through with it – her sense of her reputation at our place of employ, her self-esteem – they just wouldn't let her sleep with a mail clerk, no matter who he looked like.

But to my surprise, Ruthanne wasn't offended. She clapped her hands together and said, "Exactly! I lost all my self-esteem, I lost my self, *itself,* when I saw Danny Tripplewhite. All that was left was my desire. I just had to have him, no matter what. It didn't matter that he was a no-good son-of-a-bitch, it didn't matter that he didn't love me. All that mattered was that I got to be with him."

I continued to squint at her. "And all this is healthy?"

"Of course it's not healthy! I'm not saying that it's healthy, I'm saying that *it happens!*" She gestured at the television again. "Jessika obviously felt the same way for Franck as I felt for Danny."

"And therefore," I replied, "I reiterate: Franck was just as much of a bastard as Danny was. He shouldn't have stayed with Jessika if he didn't love her."

Ruthanne shook her head. "You're not picking up what I'm putting down, here, Carol. Jessika didn't care that Franck didn't love her. I read somewhere that someone famous once said to someone else famous, 'I'm not here because I love you. I'm here because you *want me to love you.*'" Ruthanne took a sip from her drink to let me digest that slightly drunken mouthful.

"I'm telling you, Carol. Jessika didn't care that Franck didn't love her. She no doubt wanted him to, I'm not disputing that. *But she didn't care that he didn't.* Just his physical presence in her life, just being around him, that was enough for her."

"And he knew all this." Now I gestured at the television. "He's told us so, *ad nauseam*. And as such, I say again, he was a bastard. He shouldn't have led her on —"

"Oh, no. Now you're just making shit up. If we believe what he's told us so far, he didn't lead her on. He never once told her that he loved her."

"But —"

"But me no buts," Ruthanne repeated. "What was he supposed to do? Lock himself away from all these adoring people? Jessika? Ecksmith? Franck wasn't pathological, Carol. He didn't lie to them, just because he could. Just because he knew that they'd believe him, because they'd *want* so badly to believe him. He didn't make promises to them and then break their hearts. It wasn't his fault that they fell in love with him."

There was a flaw in her argument, somewhere. *I knew there was.* But I couldn't quite put my finger on it.

"Even if he'd turned Jessika down, she'd still have chased him." Ruthanne paused and sipped her drink thoughtfully. "There's no cure for wanting a man like that. It's like a disease. The only cure is to grow some self-esteem, like you said. The only cure is to find a man that you might not love as much, who you might not *desire* as much, but who loves you back. And sometimes you don't even want to settle for that."

"You're nuts," I told her.

Ruthanne arched an eyebrow at me. "Perhaps. But it doesn't make what I said any less true." She paused, sipped her drink. "Are you over your people-are-evil-for-not-saving-other-people-from-themselves hissy fit? Shall we see what else Franck has to say? Or should I put *Manhattan* in again, and remind you just how inescapably desirable he was?"

I threw one hand up. "Proceed."

Ruthanne clicked play, and again Franck O'Day's voice filled our living room.

"So there we were, Jessika and I. She had her house, I had my house — but mostly I stayed at her house, because I didn't want her getting too comfortable at mine. I was at least smart enough to know better than to let that happen.

"And then it was New Year's Eve, 1961. I remember Jessika bitching — she didn't want to go to Sunnerfeld's party. She was convinced that he'd get drunk and try to grope her again. It was the wrap party — the movie was in the can — she couldn't threaten him with unemployment anymore.

"I told her she didn't have to go. But Sunnerfeld was my friend, my director, so I was going, regardless. That was enough for Jessika. She threw on her

mink and stalked out to the Jag. No way was she going to let me out all alone on New Year's Eve, at a party full of eager starlets.

"As it turned out, it wouldn't've mattered if she'd stayed home. It didn't matter that she was there. Because once I saw Bridget, I forgot that Jessika even existed.

"Ah, Bridget." Franck sighed, paused. *"What can I say about the first time I saw Bridget? She was tiny and golden and bright-eyed. I recognized the dress she was wearing as one of Jessika's from the previous year. It was beautiful — Jessika didn't own any clothes that weren't beautiful — it was shimmery and spangly, but it was too big on her. Roger introduced us, and then he, too, faded into the periphery.*

"You may laugh, Carol, but the very first thing I noticed about Bridget was the way she looked at me. She was smiling and attentive — her eyes communicated a kind of fond amusement — but she didn't have that hungry look, that who-are-you-pretty-boy-and-what-can-you-do-for-me? look."

Ruthanne, still standing by the computer, paused the recording again. "Are you laughing at him, Carol?" she asked. I frowned, and gestured for her to hit play again.

"It was refreshing, the way Bridget looked at me. I could tell that she didn't want anything from me — it made me feel like I could immediately trust her. She chirped happily about how nice she'd found everything to be in LA. She told me how grateful she was for the great job Mr. Yerdlay had given her, about how generous was her pay. She told me about her little girl, and how much she loved her, how important little angelic Maribeth was to her, how glad she was that the child was in her life. As I would later learn, Bridget was a wonderful mother and her little girl loved her very much."

I heard papers rustling again, and I wondered how Maribeth was taking Franck's description of her mother. I wondered if it made her sad — I imagined a tear in her eye.

Again Franck sighed. *"We danced, we chatted. She asked me about where I'd grown up — when I mentioned the farm, she giggled and admitted how much she loved cows. How beautiful she found their soft, trusting brown eyes. She said the only thing that she missed about Kansas was the cows.*

"She never asked me about the business. Not once. In all the time we were married, either. If I'd bring it up, she'd discuss it with me, but other than that, she never asked me about it. It was just not something that interested her.

"And the rest, as they say, is history. No one ever looked at me the way Bridget did. That happy, twinkling, amused expression – I'll take it with me to the grave."

Which yawns right there off-stage for you, eh, Franck ol' pal? I thought nastily. *You can't have too many years left, and I bet a day doesn't go by that you don't think about that. How's that for an old chestnut? Nobody thinks you're quite so pretty anymore, do they? Except maybe the Grim Reaper, standing just over there in the wings.*

"When the party was over," Franck was saying, *"I walked out to the car with Bridget and Mr. Yerdlay. That's how she'd referred to him the entire evening – Mr. Yerdlay. He was nothing but a generous employer to her.*

"I waved good-bye as they drove away. Then I went back inside and scared up Sunnerfeld's chauffeur and had him take me to Jessika's house. There was screaming. She threw things at me. Any woman-scorned cliché you can think of. She knew it was over between us, just that quickly. In the end, I told her I was sorry, and went home.

"By the time the Oscar ceremony rolled around in April, Bridget and I were already engaged. Even though we hadn't even been nominated, the studio wanted us there, anyway, me and Jessika and Sunnerfeld. Manhattan was still in the theatres, and the studio insisted that Jessika and I attend the festivities together, even though I had already announced my engagement to Bridget.

"It was okay with Bridget, though. She didn't have anything to wear, and like I say, the thought of all the bright lights and flash bulbs and famous people held no interest for her at all.

"Jessika had calmed down by then. She was nice – she only propositioned me once, in the limo on the way to the show, and she did it in such a way that she could laugh it off as a joke when I turned her down.

"And Jessika continued to be nice. She never once said anything disparaging to the press. She came to the wedding, accompanied by Roger, who was also nice. She even took drunken Bobby and his drunken comments diplomatically.

"We all seemed to settle down as friends after that. Jessika made a pass at me when I got back from our honeymoon, but she was drunk, and she apologized for it the next day. Roger continued to invest my money, turning out huge profits for me. Maribeth and Dolores hit it off immediately, and soon became inseparable little friends."

"Tell us about Dolores," Maribeth's voice said.

My ears pricked up. That wasn't a question on my list. Ruthanne and I hadn't been able to figure out a way to ask about that indelicate situation, so we'd just decided not to mention it at all. I'd considered it rather chickenshit of us, but still, how does one ask about such a thing?

I'd figured at the time that it was going to be Maribeth answering the questions, anyway. I'd figured at the time that the book was going to wind up not being about Franck, after all, nor any of the crimes alleged against him, because at the time, I'd still believed Franck was dead. So I'd just let all the inquiries about Dolores slide. But Franck wasn't dead, and now Maribeth had broached the thorny subject all on her own.

There was a long pause. So long, in fact, that Ruthanne and I both looked at the TV, to see how much time was left in the audio file. But there was still plenty of time left. Either Franck was going to answer the question or there was going to be quite a bit of dead air.

At last he spoke. *"Dolores was a willowy girl, tall for her age,"* he said slowly. *"She favored her mother quite a bit: the same blonde hair, the same gray eyes. Even as a teenager, when I saw her last, she had the potential to grow up to be the same kind of ravishing beauty as her mother."* He paused. *"But who knows? Not everyone lives up to the potential of youth, and youth has long passed for Dolores. God only knows what she looks like now."*

There was another long pause. It was broken by more paper rustling. Then Maribeth said, *"But what was she* like, *Franck? How did she feel about you? What was between you that would lead her mother to lodge those awful accusations?"*

In the ensuing silence, Ruthanne said, "Did you put all that in there?"

I shook my head. "We couldn't think of a good way to ask about it, remember? I didn't put anything about it in there. I didn't bring it up at all."

"Hot *damn!*" Ruthanne said again. "This little interview seems to have taken on a life of its own. It looks like we're going to get all the answers without even asking the questions!"

For another couple of seconds, the only sound out of the television was the mike hiss. At last Franck said, *"Don't you think you're getting a little ahead of things, Mari? It's too early to be discussing Dolores. We're still quite aways away from Jessika's awful accusations. I haven't even gotten to tell Carol how Bridget was taken from me, yet. How you were taken from me."*

Again Franck paused. I thought I'd discerned a shade of anger in his otherwise perfectly modulated actor's voice, but I couldn't quite be sure if that was what it was. Maybe it was sadness, as the tale was about to turn sad; maybe it was resignation at the sadness he was about to impart. Regardless, the delightful, subtle, unmistakably mocking tone was gone from Franck's exceptional voice, replaced by this new one. I would have to say that it was anger. Almost definitely.

"In fact," Franck said, *"I think I'd like to take a little breather before we get into the saddest part of the story, how I lost my wife and my little girl. Be back with you in a little while, Carol."*

There was the sound of a chair scraping across the floor, the rustling of paper, then the mike hiss stopped.

.

THIRTEEN

It was getting late, and we were getting drunk. But our curiosity would brook no pause. I could see it from the look on Ruthie's face: what was sleep, what was sobriety, when the legendary Franck O'Day was telling us his life story?

"We're almost out of whisky," Ruthanne commented as she handed me yet another drink. She pulled a chair over next to where the laptop was hooked up to the television, so she didn't have to keep jumping up to stop the recording when she wanted to make a comment.

"We'll just have to switch to something else," I replied. I looked at the TV and noticed that the next file was dated a day later than the previous ones. Gesturing with my glass, I said, "Hit it."

"There were never any signs, never any hints, that one day Roger would lose his mind," Franck began, without preamble. *"We seemed like one big happy family to me. Bridget and I; Jessika and her brother; Dolores and Maribeth."* Franck paused and I wondered if he was waiting for Maribeth to interject again. When she remained silent — there was not even any rustling — he continued.

"We celebrated holidays and birthdays together. Life *did a spread on Bridget and me, and there was Jessika and Roger in the background, there were the girls. All smiling, all happy. I'm sure you've seen the pictures on Mari's website."*

Maribeth's voice sounded a little muffled, like she was in another part of the room, instead of sitting right beside Franck and the mike, when she said, *"The* Life *pictures aren't up there, Franck."*

"Why not?" he asked, that little edge of irritation creeping back into his voice.

"I just haven't gotten to them yet."

Franck paused, and I wondered if he was thinking the same thing that I was: it wasn't like these were pictures that were taken yesterday. It wasn't like Maribeth was swamped with new pictures to put up. It wasn't like there were *any* new pictures at all. Here were some showing everybody happy — why hadn't she gotten around to posting those?

Franck sighed. *"One big happy family. Through three years of Christmases and birthdays and anniversaries. Just three years. And then Roger went insane. He blubbered on and on in his suicide note about how he couldn't live without Bridget, how we'd been best buddies and I'd betrayed him, how he was going to kill me. It was all craziness — something he'd just made up inside his sick mind. He said —"*

"I'm sure Carolyn's read it, Franck."

Another pause. Then incredulously: *"You didn't get around to posting the* Life *photos, but you posted Roger's suicide note?"*

The file ended abruptly. So abruptly that Ruthanne looked at the TV, to make sure that there hadn't been some kind of electronic malfunction. There hadn't been. Franck had just stopped talking and shut the mike off.

Ruthanne said, "I always did think that it was a little ghoulish of her, posting the suicide note left by the man that shot her mother in the back. What? No autopsy photos?"

I shrugged. "People like that kind of gory detail, Ruthie. It lends authenticity to the tragedy. Pathos."

"Apparently Franck didn't even know that she'd put it up there. He sounded a little pissed, didn't he?" Ruthanne shook her head. "It doesn't belong on a fan site. I remember thinking that the first time I read it. On one of those Hollywood death sites, maybe. But not on a fan site. Fan sites are supposed to be about the star, and his movies, and how much we all love him — not about the bad things that happened to him in his personal life. I always did think that Maribeth put up a little bit TMI about her mother's death. There's nothing up there about how much her mother meant to her, or anything like that. Just the gruesome details of how she was murdered."

I thought Maribeth put up entirely TMI about herself, as well, and devoted entirely too much space to skewering Jessika. But I had to admit that the site was very in-depth about Franck's personal life — he hadn't told us anything about Jessika and his immediate family that hadn't already been covered on *TwoGreenKeeys.com*.

Those parts about the gay directors — now *that* had been news. I reflected that Maribeth hadn't known anything about Franck's adventures in Tradeland — it had all happened long before she and her mother had ever entered the picture. And that's why it wasn't on the site. *TwoGreenKeys.com* might've been devoted to Franck — but it was definitely a devotion exclusively from Maribeth's perspective.

I looked at the television. The next audio file was recorded a day later than the previous one. I thought that perhaps Franck had been appalled at the posting of his wife's killer's suicide note. He'd sounded pissed, as Ruthie had observed. Perhaps there'd been words between step-father and step-daughter. Or maybe he just didn't feel like talking anymore that day. He was eighty years old, after all.

Ruthanne clicked on the next file, and Franck's sterling voice filled the room once more.

> *"Since Mari assures me that you've no doubt read Roger's suicide note, I think there are a few things that need clarification, Carol. Roger and I were never friends. He was an employee that just happened to be Jessika's brother. So he was there at my parties, like the gardener was not – but, like the gardener, he was still no more than an employee to me.*
>
> *As far as I know, he'd never declared any love to Bridget – she never mentioned anything along those lines to me, and Jessika never mentioned anything along those lines, either. Jessika couldn't keep a secret if her life depended on it. At least not where other people were concerned. She could easily and completely keep secrets about herself . . . but that's another part of the story.*
>
> *"That part about planning to kill me - why hadn't Roger gone through with that? Why had he shot Bridget, who he claimed to love so much, instead of me? It was just another agonizing question, another one for which we could never know the answer.*
>
> *"Bobby had trouble getting a flight over here, but he arrived as soon as he could. He showed up on the morning of the funeral. He refused to come to Jessika's house – they hated each other's guts. He met me at the funeral home. He was about half in the bag when he got there, but he insisted on being a pallbearer, anyway. It was great to see Bobby again, the only person left in the world whom I could trust. We cried together.*
>
> *"After the service, he insisted that I go back to the hotel with him. Jessika started to throw a fit, right there in the cemetery – but then she took stock of herself: she was standing in a graveyard, holding the white-gloved hands of two devastated little girls. One's mother was dead, the other's uncle was dead. She realized that she had to think of someone besides herself for a change. So she just shut up and took Dolores and Maribeth and got in the limo and went home.*
>
> *"Bobby started drinking again as soon as we got into his limo. He was my best friend, and he was distraught over my loss. 'Oh, Franck, my darling!' he kept saying. He always called me his darling, good times or bad. 'I'm so sorry!' And he cried. He cried for Bridget, and he cried for Maribeth – but he hadn't known Bridget and Maribeth. He'd only met them a few times in the three years we were together. Mostly, Bobby cried for me.*
>
> *"When we got back to his hotel room, he immediately knocked back another Scotch. Then he looked at me, his eyes red from crying, bloodshot from the transatlantic drinking binge he'd no doubt been on. My friend was a mess. But his eyes seemed sober, no matter how much drinking he'd done. Bobby's sober eyes in his*

drunken face communicated all his pain, and I took his hand and sat next to him on the sofa. It seemed like he needed comforting more than I did.

"He said, 'I'm only going to say this once, Franck, my darling. But I have to say it — it'll kill me if I don't. I'm only going to say this once, and we'll have it out, then I'll never mention it again.'

"I searched his puffy, bleary face, his not-drunk eyes. I remained silent and waited for him to say whatever it was he had to say. I couldn't imagine what it was.

"'Jessika did this.'

"'Oh, Bobby, that's just insane,' I said, somehow relieved. 'Jessika was on the set with me when it happened.' I don't know what I imagined that he'd been going to say, but it wasn't this.

"I knew that he hated Jessika, and in his grief, he'd chosen her to blame for Bridget's death. But the idea was just that, a product of his grieving mind. Jessika couldn't kill anybody.

"'I'm not saying that she was there, that she pulled the trigger,' Bobby went on. 'Although that possibility has also crossed my mind, that she was there, that she shot them both.' He shook his head. 'I doubt that she actually did it, I guess. But still, I know that she was behind it. Somehow. She always had Roger in her hip pocket. And you — I've never seen a woman — hell, I've never seen a person, *man or woman — as obsessed with someone as she is with you.*

"'She's Jessika Yerdlay! Film star, legend in her own mind! Did you think that she was going to stand idly by while some adorable Kansas farm girl just waltzed in here and took her man away from her?'

"I felt like I was talking to a child. A distraught, broken child. 'I was never Jessika's man, Bobby.'

"But Robert Ecksmith was not a child. He was a brilliant director, a student of the shameful secrets and perverse foibles of his fellow man. He stopped me right there. 'You're nobody's man, Franck, my darling. You were someone's husband once, for a short time . . .' a tear rolled down his face. 'But you're nobody's man but your own.

"'But in Jessika's mind, you're her *man. You always will be. As far as she's concerned, she's marked you. The inconvenient reality of your love and marriage to someone else didn't change that for her. And I'm telling you, she's behind this. Somehow — she said something to Roger, convinced him to do it. Roger was always weak. I'd never said more than six words to the man, but still, his weakness was palpable to me.*

"'But Jessika's never been weak about anything in her life, now has she? Except for you. And she hates herself for feeling the way she does about you, and she hates you for making her feel that way. She hates you for not loving her back, Franck. But mostly, she hated Bridget for taking you away from her. I know she did. And I know that she's behind this somehow.'

83

"*Poor Bobby. He wanted someone to blame, and the sick, deluded person who was responsible was dead. Bobby couldn't accept that. He couldn't hate a dead man — he wanted someone who was still alive to hate, someone he knew and hated already, and could continue to hate. That was the only way he was going to be able to cope.*

"*But while I would never trust Jessika — not the way that I trusted Bobby and Bridget — I knew her. I was pretty sure she wasn't a murderess. And there was also the unavoidable fact that I could never know what had transpired between her and her brother. Not ever — there was no way to ever know. And I wasn't going to destroy myself with suspicions about things I could never, ever know the truth about. Destroying myself with suspicion wouldn't bring Bridget back.*

"*So, yeah, Carol. There's a possibility that Jessika and Roger discussed their loves. There's a possibility that she knew how much he apparently loved Bridget. Roger knew how much his sister loved me — hell, the whole town knew it.*

"*But I wouldn't believe that Jessika put him up to killing her. I refused to believe that. Not so much because it wasn't possible — anything is possible when a person is obsessed. But I refused to believe it because there was no way I could ever know for sure.*

"*I looked at Bobby and he looked at me. When I didn't reply, he said, 'I had to say it. It had to be said. I'll never mention it again.'*

"*I nodded, and hugged him. 'I'm so glad you're here, my friend,' I told him.*

"*And Bobby was true to his word. He never brought up the subject of Jessika's possible involvement in Bridget's murder again, not even after everything else that happened.*

"*He left for England the following day. He was in the middle of a shoot, and this business doesn't allow for extended mourning. There's no profit in it. Bobby could mourn between takes — that's how the producers felt.*

"*Before he left, he suggested that I pack up Maribeth and bring her over to England. The film he was working on was scheduled to be completed soon, he told me, and after that . . . he had a few ideas for a couple of new vehicles, each starring Francis Joseph O'Day.*

"*I smiled and Bobby smiled, and I clapped him on the back and told him I would sincerely consider it. He grabbed my head and kissed me on the mouth, as he was wont to do on the rare occasions when he knew he could get away with it. He said, 'You do that,' then turned and walked across the runway and climbed aboard the waiting jet.*

"*I returned to Jessika's house. I remember that she was pacing angrily back and forth in the foyer when I arrived, smoking a cigarette. Waiting for me.*

"*'That's bad for your skin,' I said in greeting. 'Makes you old before your time.'*

"She looked furiously at me for a split second, then her gaze softened and she said, 'Your daughter has been asking when you'd be back. And Dolores, too.'

"My daughter. I found her, playing half-heartedly, sadly, with Dolores. I gathered her up in my arms and hugged her.

"Jessika and Dolores watched us, their identical gray eyes somber and somehow expectant. What did they expect? I didn't know, but I knew I had to get away from them. I had to take Maribeth somewhere else, get her to some new surroundings, get her away from all the memories of her mother's death, if only for a little while. So we went to the Chateau Marmont. *It wasn't the best place, but it was more secluded than the* Beverly Hills Hotel. *Quieter.*

"I had the house packed up, put it on the market. I pondered Bobby's offer. It would be good to get Maribeth away from all the bad memories. It would be good to get away from Hollywood for a while, away from the never-ending, absolutely worthless, insincere condolences, from Jessika and Dolores's solemn, expectant faces.

"I'd just made up my mind to go ahead and do it, had just filled out our passport applications, gotten our pictures taken — when Peter McSwale, Attorney at Law, showed up in town, demanding his daughter back."

Ruthanne stopped the recording. "What do you think, Carol? Do you think Jessika put her brother up to killing Franck's wife? So she could get him back?"

I looked back at Ruthanne. I was feeling all those mint juleps, so maybe I was a little bit more honest than I would've been sober. I said, "I haven't the foggiest, Ruthie. You know a lot more about these kinds of obsessions than me. Franck O'Day. *Danny.* Did you want to kill that little cheerleader Danny took up with after he dumped you?"

"I most certainly did," she said. She was feeling just as drunk, just as honest, as I was; she wasn't offended.

"Well, there's your answer then." I sipped my waning whiskey. "Anything's possible. But apparently, Franck didn't think she could do it."

Ruthanne shrugged. "Maybe Franck didn't understand obsession as well as he thought he did." She clicked play again.

"I listened to McSwale's arguments. He was unreadable to me — I couldn't figure out his angle. Did he really want Maribeth back? Did he really think he was doing right by her? Or was he waiting for me to offer to pay him off? Jessika suggested just that — 'Give him enough money, and he'll disappear,' she said.

"But I hesitated. If he wanted money, he'd ask for it. When he didn't ask, I was glad I hadn't offered. Instead, he filed the injunction, or whatever you call it, that kept me from taking Maribeth out of the country.

"There really isn't a lot more to tell about how McSwale took Maribeth away from me. Legal matters have always bored me, absolutely. That's what we pay lawyers for, to understand and handle all those really important things that bore us utterly.

"I met with the studio's lawyers. I called Bobby — he consulted with his lawyers. The consensus was unanimous — the blood daddy's rights were going to trump a couple of unmarried actors, living in sin in decadent Hollywood. Every time. All the money in the world, all the most powerful show business connections, weren't going to alter that fact.

"So the judge gave custody of Bridget's adorable, blue-eyed, red-headed little girl to her not-at-all adorable, blue-eyed, red-headed father, and he took her back to Kansas."

Franck paused. When he spoke again, that mocking tone was back in his voice. But there was also another edge to it, a touch of spitefulness, I thought. *"Why don't you tell our friend Carol about Kansas, Mari?"*

Papers rustled, but Maribeth didn't respond.

"Ah, come on, Mari," Franck wheedled. *"The fresh air, the wide-open spaces? Bridget's beloved cows? I'm sure Carol would love to hear about it. Have you ever been to Kansas, Carol? I never have. I hear it's nice. Clean. Tell us about it, Mari."*

A moment's silence, then Maribeth's voice, sounding like it was coming from far away. *"Carolyn doesn't want to hear about Kansas, Franck. She wants to hear your story."* Then the slight meanness in her voice matched Franck's own. *"So why don't you tell her about Dolores?"*

Franck laughed. *"There's still more of the Franck and Jessika Show to relate before I can get to the Franck and Dolores Show, Mari. I have to talk about all that first, now don't I? We'll get to sad ol' Lori in her proper season."*

Papers rustled, a chair scraped, a door slammed. Franck laughed. *"I think I can tell you the rest of the story without a moderator, anyway, Carol."*

Franck O'Day, so recently back from the dead (at least in my mind) cleared his throat and continued. *"So, my little girl, so briefly mine, was mine no longer. I'd sold my house, and wasn't much in the mood to look for another one. I stayed there with Jessika, puttering around, feeling sorry for myself. It was convenient. We fell back into the old routine.*

"It was like in the old days, before Bridget. She told me she loved me, I told her that I knew she did. But Jessika had me exclusively to herself now, and I detected a certain smugness, maybe a touch of superiority in her attitude that hadn't been there before. But I didn't care. I was depressed.

"Then, in the first week of January of '67, Donald Sunnerfeld called me. Personally. No assistant. The man himself. He told me that he'd been speaking

across the pond to Bobby Ecksmith, and Bobby had convinced him to pull Two Green Keys *back off the shelf. Sunnerfeld said that since there was so little footage, he could always cast a new lead – but he wondered if I might want to take another shot at it.*

"*It was like the sun bursting through rain clouds, Carol. My mood lightened immediately. I realized that Sunnerfeld's offer was exactly what I needed. I realized that what I needed was to get back to work.*

"*Jessika was ambivalent toward the idea. She'd never been in love with the script, and she hated Sunnerfeld. But she went along for me. We went to a couple production meetings, shot a couple reels.*

"*Then, on the first of February, she told me that she was pregnant. She cried – her mascara ran down her face in flat, black streaks. I'd never seen her cry before – the shock of Roger's insane acts had rendered her unable to cry over that, she'd told me. She couldn't cry then, she'd said, because she'd been left too numb by the whole tragic waste to shed a single tear.*

"*But Jessika cried now. Great, wet, black-streaking tears of joy. She was so happy that she was going to be able to give me a child of my own, she said. We had to get married, she said.*

"*Depression descended upon me once again. Now I had gone and got myself trapped. 'Make whatever arrangements are necessary,' I told her, and fled back to the studio.*

"*She threw a huge party on Valentine's Day to announce our engagement– pink streamers and hearts and giant glass bowls everywhere, filled with those little chalky hearts with words printed on them. It was a boring party, I remember that – the press was there, so nobody was making out in the bushes or putting lampshades on their heads, if you know what I mean. The only high point was when Sunnerfeld showed up drunk, uninvited. He walked in and yelled to me, right when all the flashbulbs were going off. He didn't care about the press. What were they going to say about him? He was Donald Sunnerfeld, after all. It was funny as hell.*

"*Once again, Bobby had trouble getting back to California as quickly as he would've liked. But he showed up in time to turn my birthday party into a smash, at the end of April. His latest film was in the can and he was there to talk me into my next one – Sunnerfeld be damned, he said. 'Forget the* Green Keys *thing,' he said. 'It's cursed. Do your next picture with me.'*

"*I told him we'd talk about it, and in the meantime, he could stay as long as he liked. It would be like old times.*

A door closed softly on the recording, then Franck said, "*Mari has decided to rejoin us, Carol. I hope you're as thrilled as I am.*

"*Anyway, I told Bobby that I was so glad that he was back in Hollywood. 'It's where you belong,' I told him. My depression lifted, took wing, and*

87

was gone. Even the tedious situation I found myself in with Jessika took a backseat – it was great to have my trusted friend back by my side.

"When I told Jessika that Bobby would be staying with us, she flew into what could only be termed a towering rage. Again she screamed. Again she threw things at me. I remember Lori – that's what I called Dolores – I remember her cowering in a corner, sobbing, unable to escape the room and Jessika's rage. Lori always was rather a coward around her mother. A crybaby."

Franck paused. Papers rustled.

"But not even Jessika's intense anger could affect my good mood. Since we were not married yet, I said, it would cause no scandal at all, if Bobby and I got us a little place together for the indefinite length of his visit, if she didn't want him there. There was always the Marmont, *I told her.*

"Shooting had been suspended on Two Green Keys *again – maybe it was cursed. Some relative of Sunnerfeld's had taken ill back East somewhere – so I told her that Catalina was also an option. Bobby had not been to Catalina in years.*

"Jessika relented. She didn't want me hobnobbing with the rich and famous, and the not-so-famous but definitely rich on Catalina Island with famed English director Robert Ecksmith, so recently returned to the States. Oh, the parties they would've thrown to welcome him back! And with us living there? Who knows what we might have got up to? Jessika knew better than to let me loose for all of that.

"The whole miscarriage drama happened at the end of June. In retrospect, something would've had to have happened pretty soon – Jessica was supposedly six months pregnant, and she hadn't put on more than ten or twelve pounds. When I look back on it, I guess I'd have to say that I'd never believed it anyway – mostly because I hadn't wanted *to believe it. I hadn't wanted to believe that I'd let myself do something so stupid. Francis Joseph O'Day, legendary Hollywood smart cookie – how* had *I let myself get trapped like this?*

"So when Bobby and that sharp-dressed little Italian guy he hired showed me the proof – I'd never been more relieved in my life. I wasn't even mad, just overwhelmingly relieved. It was the light at the end of what had been shaping up to be a dark tunnel, indeed.

"I scared up the passport I'd ordered when I was going to take Maribeth to England, kissed Lori on the forehead – she cried and cried to see me go – and went to the airport with Bobby.

"As the plane took off over the ocean, Bobby looked out the window and said, 'Goodbye, Jessika, you twisted, conniving bitch! He's all mine now! We still might never win an Oscar, but at least he's rid of you!'

"Life in England was great. Bobby owned a big estate, and we played tennis and went on fox hunts, and just goofed-off overall, all under the pretense of working on the script for his newest picture.

"Bobby had long been fascinated with the Far East – the culture, the languages, the religions. But Japan had always been his favorite. One wing of his house was dedicated to Japanese art and furnishings. He had a delightful old Japanese housekeeper, who mothered the both of us, and only spoke to Bobby in Japanese.

"Shogun wouldn't be published for years – but in 1967, Bobby was developing a script for a similar kind of story. I never really got all the details – the script was mostly in his mind – but it was basically the saga of a blue-eyed European and the swath he cuts across feudal Japan. Or something like that. I was to star of course, along with an as yet unchosen Japanese actress to be my love interest, and a cast of unknown Japanese others, whom Bobby knew would work for under scale.

"The only tedious part of my English sojourn was Jessika's constant letters and telegrams. She begged, she pleaded, she cajoled. She threatened to get on the next plane. Bobby would read her letters aloud to me, in his best Scarlett O'Hara voice, even though Jessika sounded nothing like a southern belle. I think Bobby just liked imitating a southern belle. He was hilarious.

"Bobby took her threats to come to England as seriously as if she'd threatened to board the next plane to come and murder me, however. After one particularly bitter missive, wherein she made vague allusions to airlines and flight schedules, Bobby said to me, 'Let's go to Japan. She'll never find us there.'

"I sent Jessika a telegram, basically telling her that I was going where she couldn't find me and I wasn't coming back. And then we went.

"Japan was wonderful. We traveled to all the islands, saw all the sights. When we visited the big cities, Bobby had no trouble indulging in the things that he indulged in. He'd leave the hotel alone some nights, and when he didn't return, I knew he was out doing those things that a man such as himself did. He never brought any of his friends back to the hotel – he'd just show up the next afternoon or the afternoon after that, and pick up whatever conversation we'd been having, as if the intervening interlude had not occurred. He didn't tell me where he'd been, and I didn't ask him. He was happy – I think that the absence of the poisoned flattery that he'd always had to put up with in the States was a welcome change.

"But when we traveled in the countryside he went almost completely native, dressing traditionally, visiting Buddhist shrines. I thought he stuck out like a sore thumb – he was a skinny, blonde Englishman with stereotypically bad teeth. There was nothing even remotely Japanese about him.

"But Bobby had a knack for languages, and within a few months was conversing fluently with the locals. At least he seemed fluent to me – my knack is for memorizing long passages in English, usually called scripts – and I only ever picked up a few phrases in Japanese.

"The people we met were kind and respectful to the Englishman in their native dress – they invited him into their homes, spoke to him at length, told him *their histories and their mythologies. I mostly sat around and nodded a lot. But it was beautiful there, and I never missed home once.*

"But one cannot escape from one's past, especially when one's past was helmed by an obsessed harpy who woke up one day and realized that she'd been abandoned via telegram, and then decided that she wasn't going to take it lying down.

"I wouldn't hear the details until that unctuous yes-man Izona showed up to chide me like an outraged nanny. He described the dramatic press conference on the steps of City Hall; the tearful accusations; the gobsmacked reporters. Bobby laughed until tears ran down his face.

"The studio would pay for my representation, if it came to that, Izona said. When that beneficence didn't make me immediately start packing, he next rattled his saber vaguely on the studio's behalf, mentioning the little matter of the unfinished, barely even started Two Green Keys, by now long forgotten by everyone except producers, their accountants, and their lawyers.

"I told Izona conversationally that I would return to the States when I was damn good and ready, and in the meantime, the studio and all its minions (including himself) could just collectively kiss my ass.

"Izona was not offended. He was being paid not to be offended. Dealing with actors and their outrageous whims was his job. He said, 'The longer you stay away, the worse it looks on you, Mr. O'Day. Not only as far as this unfortunate . . . family matter, goes. Your prolonged absence reflects badly on your reliability. Your employability, shall we say?'

"I opened my mouth to ask Izona if he knew who he was talking to, if he knew who this skinny guy in the kimono sitting across from us was. But Bobby held up his hand. He recognized a 'you'll never work in this town again' threat when he heard it, and he took it seriously.

"I was just a dumb actor; I didn't know anything about, nor could I have possibly cared less about, the powerful studio political machine that had breezed in like the fog and congealed in front of us in the person of Karl Izona. But Bobby knew, and I deferred to his advice.

"'Your money's not going to last forever, Franck,' he began.

"'On that point, you are quite mistaken, my friend.' I grinned at him and knocked back a little glass of nihonshu. 'Whatever else Roger was, he was a brilliant accountant. I am diversified. I'm making more money standing here talking to you than I would be on any set.'

"Pride goeth before a fall, my darling, and that's what all those smug bastards thought in 1929, did they not? That their money was as safe as were it in their mother's arms? Your money's a million miles away. You couldn't gather it all to you here, if you tried.

"I recommend that you issue a stern statement for the press. Tell Izona to tell the waiting world that Franck O'Day will be immediately emerging from

90

seclusion to face these outrageous charges. I'll even go back with you. But let Izona go back first, let him herald your approach, tell them that 'in fierce tempest is he coming, in thunder and in earthquake, like a Jove.' Then we'll show up and straighten it all out.

"'I also suggest that you move some of all that money *around, into some more stable, more accessible places. For a rainy day. And you also need to change your will, do you not?'*

"As always, Bobby was one hundred percent right. So I dictated that terse statement to Izona, the one where I called Jessika a liar and looked forward to my day in court.

"Izona went home to handle things, as he was being paid so handsomely to do.

"Bobby and I tied up loose ends. I made some phone calls, and did just what he's told me to do. I moved some money to Switzerland. Just in case. For a rainy day. We bade farewell to our kind Japanese hosts.

"When we arrived at the local airport, there was a lone American photographer sitting at the bar. He recognized me, if not Bobby, and bought us a drink. He told us he'd lost his reporter at the neighborhood whorehouse, and asked if he could hitch a ride with us. We told him that he was more than welcome, but at the last minute, he thought better of leaving his partner behind and changed his mind. He took our picture, wished us good luck, and went back to the bar to wait for his reporter.

"Luck, as it turned out, was something we'd have in spades. Only some of it was good, however."

Franck paused, cleared his throat again. Then he said, *"So what do you think, Carol? Do you still think you'd like to write a book about me? Have these tapes been enough of a tease to keep your interest piqued?"*

Ruthanne giggled and stamped her feet on the floor. "Are you still piqued, Carol? Are you *teased?*" She knocked back the rest of her drink in one swallow. "I know that I sure as hell am."

"I was unable to read much energy from the keys you sent in," Franck O'Day said to me through the television. *"But I figure that anyone who wants to cover my life story must be an intelligent and perceptive young woman, if nothing else."* He laughed. *"I think the saga of the plane crash should be something that I tell you in person, however.*

"I also think that the details of my . . . for lack of a better word, relationship, *with Lori are also something best saved for a face to face interview. I guarantee that you'll be surprised when you hear the full skinny on all that. It was not what Jessika accused it of being, not by a long stretch. But you might not believe me if I just recite it to you by this electronic means. I'd like to look you in the eye*

91

when I tell you about that part, Carol. So, if you're still interested, please feel free to give me a call. My number is –" and he recited a number with an LA area code.

"I can come to you, if you don't mind picking me up from the train station. Or you are more than welcome to visit me. And bring your friend, the one that you said showed you Mari's website in the first place. I believe Mari told me you said her name was Ruthanne."

Ruthanne screamed so loud that I jumped. "Oh, my God! Oh, my God! Oh, my God!" she squealed. "He just said my name! *Franck O'Day just said my name!"*

From our TV, Franck's voice concluded, *"I have every confidence that I'll be seeing you soon, Carol. And your friend, too. In the meantime, please accept my thanks for all the interest that you've shown so far."* The mike hissed for another second or so, then fell silent.

Ruthanne slid the button back on the file, clicked play, and wrote the number down. Then she let the rest of it continue, so she could hear the legendary Franck O'Day say her name again, oh, my God. Breathlessly, she asked, "You're going to call him? First thing in the morning, right?"

"First thing in the morning, I'm gonna be sleeping off this whisky," I said. I shook my glass, wanting to hear the ice cubes rattle. To my surprise, they had long ago melted. The only thing left was a few wilted mint leaves.

"And then you're going to call him, right? You want me to call him for you?" Ruthanne immediately reconsidered. "Oh, no. I could never do that. What would I say?"

"I'll call him," I said, and Ruthanne clapped her hands together and jumped up and down like a school girl. A decidedly drunken school girl, but a school girl nonetheless.

Of course I was going to call him. I still thought he was an arrogant, full of himself son-of-bitch. He had *every confidence* that he'd be seeing me soon. *Every confidence,* I reflected, was his middle name.

I couldn't say that I liked Franck O'Day very much, after listening to him tell his story, no matter how much I liked his incredible voice, no matter how sexy he'd been when he was young. You'd think the years would've tempered that ego a little bit, humbled it somewhat. But that wasn't the case.

But I was intrigued, despite myself. I found that I wanted to hear what he had to say about Dolores, and I wanted to look him in the eye when he said it, just like he'd suggested. And I also wanted to hear about the plane crash, and how he'd lived until he'd immigrated back to the States in 2006. And I wanted to hear what became of Ecksmith. Besides, if I tried to back out now, Ruthanne would never forgive me.

FOURTEEN

I woke up the next morning to discover the dire circumstance of no coffee. I groaned, but that just made the hangover worse. I gathered up my purse and dragged myself to the door, where I was confronted by a note from Ruthanne: *Went to get coffee. Call Franck!* She was an angel.

I flopped on the couch and looked at the clock. It was ten-thirty. Were eighty-year-old men awake at ten-thirty on a Saturday morning? There was only one way to find out. I thought it would be a good idea get the call out of the way before Ruthie returned, so she wasn't standing there looking at me with all her nutty fan-girl-ness hanging out while I was trying to be professional.

I dialed the number that Ruthanne had insisted on putting into my phone before she staggered off to bed the night before. It just said *OMG* followed by three exclamation points. I'd have to change that.

After a couple of rings, Franck O'Day's unmistakable voice said, "Hello?"

For a split-second, I was struck dumb. One part of my mind echoed Ruthanne: *Oh, my God, it really is him.* Then another part of my mind declared, *So what?* I said, "Mr. O'Day? My name is Carolyn Adyon. I listened to your CD – it was so nice of you to answer my questions that way. I was wondering if you were still interested in an interview."

"Of course, Carol. It was kind of fun to answer your questions that way. No one likes to talk about Franck O'Day more than me." He laughed.

You ain't just a whistlin' Dixie on that score, pal, my grandpa's voice said in my head.

"I want to apologize for the poor quality of the audio," Franck continued. "I don't have access to the same kind of recording equipment that I once did." He paused, then said, "When would be convenient for you? My schedule is currently open." He laughed again.

Not today, I thought. My head, still innocent of life-giving caffeine, pounded. On the other hand, Ruthanne would make every living second in the interim a living, breathing hell of breathless, oh, my God, anticipation, so I didn't want to put it off for too long. I had nothing else prepared to ask him, but he'd said he wanted to tell *me* the rest of the story. "Is tomorrow too soon?" I asked.

"Tomorrow would be perfect. Shall we say brunch? About eleven o'clock?"

"That sounds great."

"Let me give you the address."

I hopped up off the couch, searching for a pen. Some professional I was. Professionally hung over, that's what I was. I found the pen and paper that Ruthie had used to write his number down the night before, still lying conveniently by the laptop. "Okay," I said.

He gave me a street address, said it was in Beverly Hills. "There's an intercom at the gate," he added. "Just press the button."

"Thank you, Mr. O'Day."

"Please, Carol," he said. "It would do my vanity so much better if you'd call me Franck. Mr. O'Day was my father, like they say, and recalling how long he's been dead makes me feel old, indeed."

"Thank you, Franck," I said dutifully.

"I'm so looking forward to meeting you. And your friend, too."

"We're looking forward to meeting you, too," I said. *Especially my friend*, I thought. *I doubt she's ever looked forward to anything so much in her life. Except maybe nailing Danny Tripplewhite.*

"Goodbye till then, then," he said.

"Goodbye . . . Franck."

I pushed the button and set my phone down, then unhooked the laptop from the television, and sat back down on the couch with it. I considered – should I think up some more questions to ask the legendary Franck O'Day on the occasion of this, his very first interview since coming back from the grave?

Yes, I thought, *I certainly should.* But the hangover was still running the show, and I didn't feel up to it – the only thing of which my brain was capable was remembering how wonderful coffee was, as if I hadn't had any for years.

I forced myself to think. I called up *Wikipedia,* and typed in Robert Ecksmith's name. The black and white studio portrait was in profile, showing a plain blonde man smoking a cigar, looking all sophisticated and director-ish. He looked nothing like the smiling long-hair in the picture from 1968, unknowingly about to meet his fate.

The article was short. Famed English director Robert Ecksmith was not remotely so famous anymore. He was born in London, educated at Westminster. There was no mention of his sexual orientation, only that he'd never been married, never had any children. At the tender age of forty-two, I noted, he was listed as missing and presumed dead along with American actor Franck O'Day, after the plane they were riding in disappeared in Japan in January of 1968.

His cinematic style was *often marked by a subtle, yet controversial eroticism,* according to *Wikipedia.* He'd made twenty-five films, starting with *Miami Moonglow* in 1953. Several of his productions had been nominated for Academy Awards and/or BAFTA's. I'd heard of not a single one of them, excepting of course, that bomb of a Franck O'Day vehicle, *George and Benedict.* I was curious to see what *Wikipedia* had to say about the film, but the title wasn't even linked.

The sum of Robert Ecksmith's career – so many movies, so much fame, so much wealth, such a high life, such an ignominious death – all so completely and utterly forgotten. I reflected that popular culture and its creators were as fleeting as a summer rain. Even the most powerful movers and shakers of yesteryear were as dust now, in the collective memory. If you had to ask, "Do you know who I am?" chances are, no one would. Except for maybe a handful of hardcore devotees, such as Ruthanne. I thought that, "Do you know who I *was?*" might be a better question, even though the answer would still be, "No."

Franck's name was linked, where the plane crash was mentioned. I clicked on it. There was the same picture, the still from *High Times in Manhattan.* Francis Joseph O'Day was an American actor, born April 29, 1933. (The wrong date, according to *TwoGreenKeys.com.*) Presumed dead, January 1968 (age 34). I clicked on the picture, and once again, Franck's face, with his smug, knowing smile and his ever-so-slightly crooked teeth, filled the screen. He seemed more attractive this time, somehow. Perhaps it was because I'd seen him act, heard him tell his stories in that incredible voice, heard him say my name.

I again thought it was a shame that he'd made only two movies. Maybe someone besides Ruthanne and his step-daughter and a handful of others would still remember him, if he'd made just a few more movies. Maybe he'd be up there in the pantheon with all the other dead greats, like . . . like . . . I couldn't think of any other movie stars from his era – my brain was only partially functioning due to its recent soaking in whiskey – but I was sure that Ruthanne could name them. Just because I'd forgotten them or had never known of them, didn't mean that they weren't famous to multitudes of fans. Their names would never be forgotten, at least not by these people.

I pondered what it must be like for those actors – unlike Franck (in the mind of the world), who'd long outlived their heyday. Seldom did one see a photo of a famous movie star grown old – unless it was a grainy snap in a tabloid, those modern-day purveyors of *schadenfreude,* above a caption like *Sad last days of So-and-so.*

Look how the mighty have fallen, was the message. *Look how poorly So-and-so has aged. It's not only you, standing there in line at the grocery store, who's been ravaged by Father Time. Buy me, and feel better about yourself. Read all about it – while you might never have had anything yourself, never been either rich or famous, never lived the high life – at least you haven't lost it all like So-and-so has.*

I put all these sad reflections on old age and obscurity down to the hangover, and again dreamed of the glory that was a hot, sweet, steaming mug of coffee. As if on cue, Ruthanne came through the door to answer my prayers.

The only evidence of her own night of drinking was a slightly disheveled appearance: her normally flawless presentation had fallen off a few notches; one could tell that she had not re-braided her hair after sleep; she was wearing sweats and a t-shirt. But her happy smile was in place. My headache forbade a smile like that. It would've made my face ache.

"Well?" she said, slightly bloodshot eyes still all a sparkle. "Did you call?"

I gave her the thumbs-up, and her squeal pierced my brain. It was no less annoying for being expected. "We're going to see him, in Beverly Hills. Tomorrow. We're supposed to be there by eleven."

"Tomorrow? So soon? What should I wear?"

I hauled myself off the couch and took the grocery sack from her. "Coffee first. What to wear later."

Ruthanne smiled and hugged me. "Thank you so much for taking me with you!"

"I couldn't do it without you, Ruthie," I told her, and staggered out to the kitchen to concoct the soul-saving brew.

FIFTEEN

I truly couldn't have done it without Ruthanne. Oh, I could've gotten to LA on my own, but I would've forgotten something, or gotten lost. Ruthie made everything as smooth and effortless as a tour guide. We'd decided that we'd take my car, because it got better gas mileage than hers, and she went out and gassed it up the night before, had the oil and water and tire pressure checked, so we'd be as safe and prepared as possible. She even ran it through the car wash, just so it would look its best. She printed out directions. It was only about an hour or hour and a half drive, depending on the traffic, but Ruthanne saw it as an adventure. The adventure of a lifetime.

I dressed conservatively, trying to look like I thought a writer would: I wore a nice blouse and jacket with my jeans. Even the legendary Franck O'Day couldn't get me to wear a dress on a day that I didn't have to go in to the office. Ruthie wore a simple, adorable green sundress that played up the color of her eyes, and a pair of cute little pistachio colored wedges. I noticed an ankle bracelet flash in the sun as we walked down the steps, and I wondered vaguely if it said *Franck* on it.

As the gate to our parking lot rattled open, releasing us upon an unsuspecting world, Ruthanne plugged her iPod into the jack on the car's radio tuner. "I made us a playlist for our historic trip."

I groaned inwardly as the opening violin strains of *At Last* filled the car. More oldies. Ancient oldies. But Ruthanne had a wonderful singing voice, and I smiled when she sang along with Etta: *At last/The stars above are blue/My heart was wrapped up in clover/The night that I looked at you.*

And after that there was *Hello, Time Bomb*, by the Matthew Good Band. It was obscure, but I remembered it from when I was a kid. They mentioned Ritalin, and I always remembered the song, because they'd put my cousin on Ritalin. But that wasn't the part of the song that Ruthanne was feeling. *Dirty enough/I've got me a love/And it's so bad/It's sooo bad*, Ruthie sang. *Life's for the living/So check me tomorrow/We'll see if I'm kiddin',"* she growled along with Matt, serious as a heart attack.

Ruthie was most assuredly not kidding, I thought. This was not so much an historical road trip medley, I thought, as much as a songs-that-reminded-Ruthie-of-Franck-O'Day-and-her-obsession-with-him mélange. Next up was Nine Inch Nails' *Closer*. I rolled my eyes at that one. It was a little out of her musical oeuvre, I thought, but the sentiment was right up her alley on this particular day.

Then there was Tom Jones, of all dinosaurs, singing *You Can Leave Your Hat On: You give me reason to live/You give me reason to live/You give me reason to live/You give me reason to live . . .*

And so on. Songs of love and devotion, across every possible decade. Ruthie had disco: Peter Brown sang, *And then I knew I had no choice/But to heed the command of the Devil's voice/Do you wanna get funky with me?* Followed by an aging Sinatra singing *LA is My Lady.*

Down the 60 Freeway to the 10, to the 101, to Sunset Boulevard, I listened to Ruthanne's oldies, interspersed with not so oldies. The oldies reminded me of the dream I'd had, where Franck and I had talked and danced. I imagined that if I told him about it, the idea that my sleeping subconscious had summoned him up for a whirl around the dance floor wouldn't surprise him at all. I imagined that he'd have *every confidence* that I'd enjoyed myself. I wondered if he really knew how to dance like that.

At 10:40, we pulled up to an elaborate wrought-iron gate. It was the only visible break in a long, high wall, behind which grew tall shrubbery. The house was not visible from the street. *That's the thing that separates rich people from the rest of us,* my mother's voice said in my head. *The privacy.*

I pushed the red button on the intercom, and when a woman's voice said, "Yes?" I said, "Hi. I'm Carolyn Adyon. I'm here to see Mr. O'Day?"

There was a pause. Then the woman's voice, sounding a little discomfited, said, "Carolyn? I didn't know you were coming so soon."

My heart sank. Had Franck taken ill or something? Were we going to be turned away after such a long drive? Was I going to have to listen to Ruthanne's interminable Jurassic playlist again so soon? "I spoke to Mr. O'Day on the phone yesterday. He invited us to –"

"Of course." The gate began to slide open. "Come on up. You can park right in front of the house."

The drive showed only trees for a moment, then curved to the left. The house seemed to materialize suddenly out of the greenery – it was breathtaking. It was brick, two stories tall. There were four arched, floor-to-ceiling windows, two on each side of an ornate wood and glass front door. Above the door was a balcony, supported by four Doric columns. An arched glass door, echoing the shape of the windows on the first floor, led out onto the balcony, which was topped by a gleaming white pediment. A terra cotta tile roof off-set the color of the bricks in the forenoon sunshine. I parked in front of the long, steep stone staircase that led up to this mansion.

"This is Jessika Yerdlay's house," Ruthanne whispered in amazement. "I've seen pictures of it – from *Life Magazine*." She looked up at the front door solemnly. "I'm sure of it. This is Jessika's house. Why would Franck be living in Jessika's house?"

I shrugged and said, "Jessika's dead."

We got out of the car; I walked around to Ruthanne's side, and we just stood there, gazing up the stone steps at the magnificent house. I took a deep breath, and was just about to start up the stairs, when the front door opened.

Franck O'Day walked out and paused at the top of the stairs. He smiled, held his arms out in greeting, and said, "Welcome, ladies!"

I studied him as he descended the stairs. He was about six foot tall, and wore a flawlessly tailored, slate gray, double breasted suit. He wore it effortlessly, like he dressed this way every day – one got the impression of a very wealthy, very confident executive. His hair was a shiny, dark, battleship gray. He was spry – he sauntered quickly down the steps, as if he wasn't doing it on eighty-year-old knees and ankles at all.

But it was Franck O'Day's face that was the most amazing thing about him. He reached out and took our hands – my right and Ruthie's left – and just stood there, smiling. He raised his black, slightly manicured eyebrows at us – what eighty-year-old man still had black eyebrows? – and a few lines appeared on his forehead. Most of those were covered by wavy bangs of dark gray hair. He had a web of crows' feet beside each eye, and smile lines on either side of his mouth. But he had the tight, strong jawline of a man half his age.

Franck O'Day looked like an incredibly well-preserved sixty. Incredibly. Well. Preserved. Or even a prematurely gray fifty. In no way did this man look even remotely his age. He'd obviously had work done and it had to have cost a king's ransom, I thought, because you surely couldn't *tell* that he'd had work done. But he'd gone under the knife at some point – no one looked this good at eighty. There was no other way.

His eyes were a clear and depthless dark blue. He tilted his head a little, studying us for a second. He gave us a cheerful little smile. Still holding our hands, he looked from me to Ruthanne.

I looked over at her, also, wanting to see her reaction to meeting her idol. She smiled as if pleasantly drugged. I didn't think she was breathing. Her green eyes were dilated, the pupils huge and black like marbles. Her skin was flushed a becoming pink.

"You must be Ruthanne," Franck said to her. He released my hand, then enclosed Ruthie's in both of his. My friend nodded, clearly unable to speak. You can't speak if you're not breathing. I thought with alarm that she might just faint dead away if she didn't inhale soon.

I said, "She's your biggest fan."

Now the cobalt blue eyes looked at me. "And you must be Carol." I cannot tell a lie – I, too, experienced a tiny jolt of pleasure when Franck O'Day's incredible voice said my name. He released Ruthie's hand – it hung there in the air, as if it had a mind of its own – before dropping to her side. He gave me a firm, single-handed handshake, then said, "I'm Franck O'Day. Welcome to my home."

"This is Jessika's house," Ruthanne said in a dreamy whisper. Then her mind seemed to clear and she added, "Isn't it?"

"As a matter of fact it is," Franck replied, a little surprised. "Or it was. I purchased it from Jessika's daughter, not long after her death." He smiled at me. "Through a third party, of course. Shall we go in?"

He turned, and the three of us walked up the stairs, side by side. He placed his left hand lightly on my shoulder for a second, but clasped Ruthie's hand in his for the entire walk up. I knew she must've surely believed that she'd died and gone to heaven.

Ruthanne must've believed that quiet was expected in heaven, because she still didn't raise her voice above a whisper when she asked, "Why would you want Jessika's house?"

Franck paused at the top of the stairs and smiled at my star-struck friend. I would've bet the farm that she stopped breathing again when he looked at her. "The best revenge is living well, Ruthie," he said, and chuckled. "Besides, this is one of the finest houses in Beverly Hills, and I acquired it for a song. It has a screening room in the basement. I can't wait to show it to you."

The massive front door opened, and an old woman stepped out. "Mari," Franck said, "this is Carol," he gestured at me, "and this is Ruthanne." He squeezed Ruthanne's hand. "Ladies? This is my daughter, Mari."

The appellation of daughter upon the little old lady that stood before me seemed somehow sadly cruel. Maribeth McSwale O'Day was twenty-two years her step-father's junior, but she looked much older than him. She was tall, but impossibly thin and positively frail looking, as if the merest Santa Ana wind might blow her away. Her face was lined and sallow, like an ancient parchment that had been folded and unfolded, over and over again, for centuries. She had white hair, cropped short and mannishly – it was not at all a flattering style on her. In contrast to Franck's snazzy, impeccably cut suit, Maribeth wore a shapeless print housedress. Her watery gray eyes considered us nervously.

After a pause she said, "Welcome to our home." She gestured at her attire. "I'm sorry, I wasn't aware you were coming today." She and I looked at Franck; Ruthanne had never stopped looking at Franck.

"I apologize, Mari," he said. "I talked to Carol yesterday morning, while you were napping. It completely slipped my mind to tell you that I'd invited them for a visit."

Mari narrowed her eyes at him for a split second, then smiled at me. "Shall we go in? Brunch is just about ready."

A bifurcated grand staircase dominated the view from a foyer with a parquet floor of alternating mahogany and cream colored tiles. In my mind, Jessika Yerdlay's ghost paced back and forth before us, angrily puffing a cigarette, impatiently waiting for her beloved's return. Well, he was back now, was he not? I blinked and the image disappeared.

Franck led the way between the twin prongs of the staircase, out to a terrace where a table that sat four overlooked an enormous swimming pool. This was where Jessika had feigned her miscarriage, I thought. The blue water, the same color as the cloudless California sky, was as still as glass. Franck pulled out a chair for each one of us in turn.

Complete with mimosas, brunch was served by a silent, middle-aged Asian man. It was all like a cliché from some old movie about Hollywood decadence – the silver and the china and the crystal were all exquisite, impossibly expensive. Everything we could see was so superb as to defy compliment. *Gee, nice place ya got here, Franck,* just wouldn't cut it.

Mari offered small talk. She asked if there was anything else I did for a living besides write, and Ruthanne told her that we were legal secretaries. Franck used this information to segue from a slightly off-color joke about Hollywood lawyers into several anecdotes about all the actors and directors he'd known and worked with. Ruthanne, her bubbly charm returning, laughed and made eager comments – the names of everyone Franck mentioned were more or less familiar to her. As I'd never heard of most of these luminaries of yesteryear, I just smiled and nodded where it was appropriate, and observed Maribeth as she watched Franck, silently and coolly, over the rim of her mimosa.

When brunch was finished, he asked if we'd like to see the screening room. Again taking Ruthanne's hand in his, he led us downstairs to a small theater. I estimated that it might seat as many as twenty people. The curtain, the walls, the seats, were all done in a midnight-blue crushed velvet. A dark, impossibly polished hardwood floor was beneath our feet.

102

Still holding Franck's hand, Ruthanne – again whispering – said, "Can we watch it? Can we watch *Manhattan?*"

Franck grinned. He looked politely surprised, but somehow not surprised at all. "You want to watch it now?" Ruthanne nodded. The interview was forgotten. I was forgotten. Franck glanced over at Maribeth and me, standing a few paces behind him in the aisle.

"I've seen it," Maribeth said flatly. She glared at Franck – the look was unmistakable this time. "I'm sure you have, too, Carolyn," she said without looking at me.

Franck picked up a large remote control that had been sitting on the arm of one of the midnight-blue seats. He pointed it at the curtain, which rolled back to reveal the biggest big screen television I'd ever seen. It said *Panasonic* at the bottom. I looked at the wall at the back of the screening room and noted that there were no longer any little windows where the old-timey projectionist once sat. Franck might be eighty – *although he certainly doesn't look it*, my mind said automatically – but he was technologically up to date.

"Come on, Carolyn," Maribeth said, still not looking at me. "I'll show you the rest of the house." She turned and stalked out. Ruthanne and Franck were busy seating themselves in the first row. Franck aimed the remote at the ceiling, and the lights dimmed.

Taking this as my cue for an exit, I walked toward the door. I paused to look back at them, as the opening credits of *High Times in Manhattan* rolled up on the almost-as-big-as-a-real-theater screen. In silhouette, Franck gestured at the credits, then leaned in close and said something into Ruthanne's ear. She giggled. I smiled, knowing how deliriously happy she had to be. Then I followed Maribeth out of the little theater.

SIXTEEN

Maribeth McSwale O'Day gave me the grand tour of the grand house. It was impressive – and if I'd been a fan of old Hollywood architecture any more than I was a fan of movie stars, I might even have been awestruck. As it was, I viewed the house about the same way as I did movie stars: I'd never get to meet any of them, and this was a beautiful, ostentatious, impossibly expensive mansion, of a kind I could never hope to inhabit, either. Next topic.

The brunch things had been cleared away, except for a big pitcher of mimosas and two fluted champagne glasses. Maribeth and I sat, and she poured us both a drink. She studied me cautiously, then said, "What would you like to ask me, Carolyn? Surely you don't really want to hear about Kansas?"

Surely I do not, I thought. Ever since discovering that Franck was indeed alive, I had kinda forgotten about Maribeth, as well as anything I'd previously wanted to ask her. He was the main attraction, after all. But as I sat across from this non-descript little old lady, the thought struck me that another perspective might be invaluable. Franck was only going to offer the *Me-me-me, but enough about me, what do you think of me?* angle. Here was someone who could give me a different take. Sure, she was his biggest fan and all that, but the annoyed looks she'd been shooting at him made me think that maybe all was not happy child and doting daddy so much anymore, as it had once been.

I considered. What did Maribeth, with her increasingly irritated glances at her once-famous step-father know, that Franck wouldn't tell me? I asked her the most obvious question first. "Where did Franck get his surgery?"

Maribeth blinked rapidly in surprise. "Surgery?"

"Was it in Japan? Wherever it was, they did a fabulous job. He doesn't look a day over fifty. If he dyed his hair, he could pass for a well-preserved forty-five, or maybe even forty. It's amazing what they can do these days."

Maribeth looked at me in confusion, then the realization of what I was talking about dawned on her. She uttered a dry laugh. "Oh. You're talking about *plastic* surgery. Face lifts and nose jobs and stuff like that."

I nodded. "Whoever he is, the doctor that worked on Franck is a genius."

Maribeth smiled widely, revealing perfectly straight, perfectly white teeth. They reminded me of my grandmother's, and thereby, I knew that they were dentures. "Franck hasn't had any plastic surgery, Carolyn."

I smiled back at her. "It's okay, Miss O'Day, I won't put it in the book," I told her. I wouldn't have to. One look at Franck, and everyone would already know. No one looked like that at eighty without a little surgical assistance. It was impossible.

"Seriously, Carolyn. Franck hasn't undergone any kind of plastic surgery. Nor, as far as I know, has he ever been sick a day in his life." She sipped her mimosa. "We just use that as an excuse, if he doesn't want to do something right away. It's just something I put up on the website, to drum up a little anticipation for when he makes his first personal appearance."

I'll come back to all that personal appearance business in a minute, I thought. She wasn't going to get me off of the topic of Franck's preternatural state of preservation that easily.

When my look of skepticism didn't fade, she continued, "It's the energy, Carolyn. The *Reiki*. He learned how to harness it during all those years he spent in Japan."

"The energy?" I repeated. I'd completely forgotten all about that crazy shit.

Again Maribeth smiled. "Did you ever see *The Matrix?*"

I nodded. What, did she think I lived under a rock? Who hasn't seen *The Matrix?*

"It's one of my favorites. Certainly, vastly more entertaining than . . ." She gestured toward the house. I had to agree. While he was no blue-eyed, silky-voiced Franck O'Day, Keanu and the rest of the stars in *The Matrix* surely combined for a different, more original kind of movie than *High Times in Manhattan*.

"Anyway," Maribeth continued, "remember the part where Morpheus is first telling Neo about the Matrix? He says, *The human body generates more bio-electricity than a one hundred twenty volt battery and over 25,000 BTU's of body heat. Combined with a form of fusion, the machines had found all the energy they would ever need.*"

Oh, this was even crazier than I could've imagined. Was Maribeth trying to tell me that Franck was a machine? Some kind of cyborg robot, maybe?

When I continued to stare dumbly at her, she explained further. "Morpheus was right, Carol. People produce enormous amounts of energy. That's all we are, really: meat and chemicals. And electricity. But there's more to the energy we produce than just what's needed to keep our bodies alive, our hearts beating, our organs functioning. Our thoughts, our feelings, our emotions – *our words* – they all produce

105

energy, too. Letters, keys – even a happy e-mail packs a little positive energy with it.

"While he was in Japan, Franck learned the secrets of harnessing the positive energies given off by others. He uses it to keep himself young." Maribeth paused, then laughed. "I can see by the look on your face that you don't believe me, Carolyn. It *is* a little hard to believe, I'll give you that. I probably wouldn't have believed it myself, if I hadn't seen it with my own eyes." She sipped her mimosa.

"You've seen the pictures on the website? The ones where Franck is dancing so joyfully on Jessika's grave? Tell me that he doesn't look younger now than in those pictures. And those were taken . . . oh, going on two years ago."

The whole idea was insane. The pictures were grainy and of very poor quality, shot from a distance. That was enough right there to make any little old man look older.

"Not long after those shots were taken," Maribeth continued, *"The Egyptian* held a Robert Ecksmith retrospective. It would not've been complete, now would it, without a screening of *George and Benedict?* Now, judging from what a big fan your friend is," Maribeth again gestured at the house, "I'm sure that you've had the unfortunate honor and dubious pleasure of sitting through Franck's screen debut. As it's inarguably Bobby's worst film, the good people at *The Egyptian* saved it for last. It showed at three in the morning, or so Franck told me. He went to see it, you see.

"Bobby did some great work, almost all of which is still respected and discussed – if not, *The Egyptian* wouldn't have undertaken a retrospective of his films. But *George and Benedict* is neither respected nor discussed too much anymore, unless it's to deride Bobby's misstep, to ask, *What was he thinking?* But once the derision is delivered, everyone, *universally,* recognizes Franck's stellar contribution to an otherwise utterly forgettable film. As you undoubtedly know, his performance – and the scenic New England countryside – are the only redeeming qualities to it. The small crowd that sat through *George and Benedict* in its dismal three am time slot were not there to experience its director's genius, therefore. They were there to see Franck.

"Without a shadow of a doubt, the thirty or so people who were there to see it – young women like your friend, old women like me – a cadre of drunken homosexuals – they were all dyed-in-the wool Franck O'Day fans. No one else would have bothered with such a terrible film at such a terrible time, even for the purpose of making fun of it. Franck sat in the back of the theater and basked in all the adoration that was aimed at his image on the screen.

106

"He looked ten years younger when I saw him the next day. And *Manhattan* is screened all the time at one or another of the little theaters downtown. It was even shown with the *Oscar Contenders of The 1960s Film Festival,* even though it wasn't even nominated. I didn't see him for the whole two months that one ran. I think he was probably at the *Marmont,* reliving the glory days, when he wasn't in the crowd, incognito, absorbing the adulation.

"When he came back, he looked like he does now, except for a little puffiness, which I put down to attending all those late show times. The film wasn't really nominated, after all, so it still played late. He was again a well-preserved forty or forty-five, like you said. And it was all a result of the energy he gathered from all the fans watching *Manhattan.* Not from anything as pedestrian as plastic surgery."

Or, maybe, I thought, *and much more likely, he got cut while he was away for those two months, and* it completely slipped his mind to tell you *that he'd gone under the knife.* It looked to me like Franck must be a fast healer – how long it must take to recover from that amount of work, I had not a clue – but that residual puffiness sounded like a dead giveaway. An extremely well-done facelift, two months recovery in a secret, and no-doubt monumentally expensive spa (or wherever it was one went after one had work done) and voila! Franck O'Day was young again.

I didn't fault him for it. His pretty face had been his life, *all his life,* and I imagined it must've been tragic to look in the mirror and find himself not quite so pretty anymore. Who was I to judge? Who knows how much getting old might debilitate me? Hell, thirty loomed just over the horizon, and I'd already had a few what-have-you-done-with-your-life discussions with myself. Who knows what steps I might be inclined to take when I started to look like Maribeth?

She glanced furtively at the house, then leaned in closer to me. "There's something I'd like to give you, Carolyn," she said in a low, conspiratorial tone. "You'll excuse me, just a moment."

She arose and quick-walked into the house, then reappeared almost immediately. She glanced behind her again, then approached and regained her seat. She had two small, thick, red-bound books in her hand. "These are some of Jessika's daughter's journals," she said. "Apparently, she started keeping them when she was just a child, about eight or nine. There's an earlier one, filled with a little girl's tedious scribblings. I don't think it would be of any use to you. But these . . . these cover the period from the first time her mother brought Franck home, till just after her mother's suicide attempt. I found them at the back of the closet in the room that used to be hers, after we moved in here last year. Franck doesn't know they exist."

107

Ah, the diary, the *deus ex machina* of any good yarn. I looked down at the red books: they didn't have the stereotypical, easily forced locks on them, but *DIARY* was engraved across the front of each, in flowery gold script. Dolores's lost diaries, from whence I could surely glean the *real* story. No doubt it would be a bombshell.

I thought about *TwoGreenKeys.com*, with its faithfully reproduced telegrams between Franck and Jessika, correspondences that Franck's step-daughter could never have actually seen. She was already in Kansas, still a child, when all those telegrams were sent and received. I remembered thinking that Maribeth had made up their contents, just to lend reality to her website. I remembered thinking how crazy *all that* was, and once again, my estimation of Maribeth McSwale O'Day returned to the realm of obsessed mental illness. These weren't Dolores's journals. These were what Maribeth thought her journals *should say.*

She slid them across the white-linen clad table to me. "Here. Put them in your purse, then take them out and put them in your car. I don't want Franck to see them. But since he's going to tell you his side of things, I thought you might also want to read what Lori had to say. If nothing else, it'll make for a more rounded perspective in your book."

"Thank you, Miss O'Day," I said genuinely. *Yes, indeedy, I'm willing to explore whatever stripe of crazy you're willing to hand over to me,* I thought. I slipped the forged diaries into my bag. "I'll get them back to you as soon as I can."

"That's okay, Carolyn," she said and patted my hand companionably. "You keep them as long as you need to. I already know what they say."

Of that, I have no doubt whatsoever, I thought.

Maribeth freshened our mimosas from the pitcher, then held up her glass. The sun glinted off the crystal. "A toast," she declared. "To your book. To the truth!"

We clinked glasses, then I was startled to hear Franck's voice. "Never drink to the truth, Carol." He was leaning cavalierly against the doorframe to the entrance of the house, one arm carelessly around Ruthanne's waist. He released her, then took her hand again and the two of them came over to where we sat.

The Asian servant materialized out of thin air, set down two more fluted champagne glasses, then once again dissolved. Franck poured out a drink for himself and one for Ruthanne, then held his aloft. "One should always toast beauty," he gestured at Ruthanne, and she blushed to the roots of her hair. "But never truth. The truth should never be allowed to get in the way of a good script, a good story. To a good story!"

We clinked glasses – the sound of the crystal was clear and resonant, a perfect counterpoint to the amusement in Franck's amazing voice. He drained off his drink in a swallow, set the glass down. He pulled out a chair for Ruthanne, then plopped down in the one remaining. *Not at all like an eighty-year-old man would,* my mind observed. He regained Ruthanne's hand.

I looked at my friend. The blush had faded, but still the roses lived on her cheeks. She twirled the stem of the champagne glass lightly between the thumb and first two fingers of her left hand, watching intently as it rolled back and forth. A faint smile, which I thought wouldn't leave for weeks, played on her lips. I noticed that her lipstick was fresh; then I noticed that her normally flawless hair was just a trifle mussed – a few flyaways had escaped from the normally immaculate braid she wore. *OMG,* I thought, *it can't be –*

As if reading my thoughts, Ruthanne left off studying the stemware and looked up at me. Her green eyes glowed like the emeralds in some mythical pagan statue. Then one corner of her mouth crooked up in the slyest grin I'd ever seen. The story was as plain on her face as black written upon white.

I was surprised and delighted and appalled all at the same time. In the bowels of dead and forgotten starlet Jessika Yerdlay's sprawling manse, in the midnight-blue, crushed velvet screening room, under the ever-discreet cover of darkness, *Ruthanne had been making out with Franck O'Day!*

I smiled back at her faintly, and the sly grin bloomed into a full-blown leer for just a split-second, then faded back to a modest smile. There could be absolutely, unequivocally, no doubt. Lipstick smudges on his collar (of which there were none, of course) could not have confirmed it more for me.

Franck said, "Has Mari been telling you about the joys of life in Kansas, Carol?"

I looked at him, and discovered I was speechless. *Why, you slick, geriatric roué! You smooth, charming old bastard!*

Maribeth said evenly, "Actually, Carolyn was asking about your plastic surgeon, Franck."

The manicured eyebrows shot up and he smiled. "No plastic surgeon, Carol. Just good genes. And good living." He released Ruthanne's hand, and made the meditative *Om* gesture with both hands, fingers in circles, arms held out above the table. "And being one with the energy of the universe."

109

Franck O'Day winked at Ruthanne, who blushed again – I wouldn't've thought she had it in her. Then he stood and filled all our glasses with the rest of the mimosas. He raised his glass, but before he could offer another toast, Ruthanne said, "To absent friends."

Franck laughed, said, "Indeed," and we all clinked glasses again. Then he said, "I was just about to give Ruth a tour of the house. Since you've already seen it, Carol, we'll take our leave."

Franck offered his hand to Ruthanne, but before she could take it, Maribeth said, "Carolyn was just saying how much she'd like to take a little drive, Franck. Perhaps venture down to *Hollywood Forever*, and pay her respects to Jessika."

I'd been saying no such thing. But Maribeth shot me a glance that I understood with a clarity as clear and sparkling as Franck's fluted crystal. *Time to save your friend's honor, at least temporarily*, the look said. *The hound is loose and the hare is not at all unwilling. Provide her with a little breathing room, a little time to reconsider, before she allows herself to succumb to an eighty-year-old man. She might just thank you for it.*

I doubted if Ruthanne would thank me for it, because I doubted if she would change her mind. I knew that she had devoutly, *vividly* dreamed of just such a consummation. And he didn't look eighty at all. He looked like Perry Calibri after a particular rough couple of years. He was twenty-seven in *Manhattan* and he surely didn't look twenty-seven now. But he just as surely didn't look eighty, either.

But there was always a possibility that I could talk Ruthie out of it, if I was given the opportunity to talk to her. The whole idea was just the tiniest bit – well, more than just the tiniest bit – appalling, after all. Even if he was only the fifty he looked, he was still way too old for her. Even if he was only fifty, which he was not, he would still be almost twice her age. And even if Ruthanne couldn't be dissuaded in the end, it couldn't do her reputation anything but a solid, if she was forced to wait a little while. Even Franck might appreciate that.

So I just looked at them expectantly. Ruthie said, "That sounds like a great idea." She looked at Franck for confirmation. He smiled, and she looked back at me. "I don't know if we can all fit it your car, though."

I noticed Franck glare at Maribeth, just for a second, and noticed her glare back at him, as he removed his cellphone from his breast pocket. I wondered if my friend's number was already entered there, or if the Hollywood legend had intended this as a one-time dalliance. He said a few words into his phone, then put it back in his pocket.

"A limo will be here in five minutes." He smiled at me. "I never drive in LA. I never drive at all, actually. Too much stress."

110

Plus the fact that your eighty-year-old eyes, blue and youthful-seeming as they might be, probably can't see the letters on the wall at the DMV anymore, I thought nastily.

"Drink up, ladies!" Franck said. "We wouldn't want to keep Jessika waiting." He finished his mimosa, and waited until Ruthanne finished hers. Then he again offered her his hand, and she took it and arose. They walked arm and arm back into the house. Maribeth shook her head, sighed, and we followed.

SEVENTEEN

When we visited Jessika's grave at *Hollywood Forever*, Franck stayed in the limo. "I've seen it," he told us with that little smug grin.

Then the afternoon turned into a tour of all the Hollywood landmarks and swinging hot spots of yesteryear. Franck pointed out *The Frolic Room,* and I could almost see Kevin Spacey standing on the sidewalk in front of it, from the iconic scene in *L.A. Confidential.* We drove past the Roosevelt Hotel, where Marilyn Monroe's apparition has been reported. Then Franck had the driver take us out Franklin Avenue to the John Sowden House.

Ruthanne knew all about it. "It's built in something called the Mayan Revival style," she said, as we gawked out of the window of the limo like Midwestern tourists. "Frank Lloyd Wright's son designed it for Sowden. He was some kind of artist."

She paused. Still not a maven of Hollywood architecture, Frank Lloyd Wright once removed or not, I said, "And? So?"

"This ex-LAPD cop wrote a bunch of books. Said it was his dad that killed the Black Dahlia," Ruthanne said, and grinned at me. "This is where dear old dad lived."

Oh, swell, I thought. Ruthanne had once dragged me along on one of those Hollywood death site tours. We rode all over Los Angeles and its environs in a hearse, while the driver pointed out the places where the rich and famous had dropped dead, been murdered, or done themselves in. I found the whole escapade to be soul-crushingly depressing.

Suddenly, I remembered that tour, and imagined that this ride was going to turn into something similar. After the Black Dahlia murderer's house, I thought, perhaps Franck would be taking us by the apartment building where twenty-year-old Diane Linkletter had jumped out of her sixth floor window in 1969, supposedly high on LSD.

Her apartment wasn't far from where Sal Mineo would be fatally stabbed in an alley in 1976. Famous for being publicly gay at a time when such things were practically unheard of, I wondered if ol' Sal had ever made a pass at ol' Franck, back in the day. I asked him, "Did you ever know Sal Mineo, Franck?"

Surprised at my completely out of the blue question, Franck grinned at me. "No. I never had the pleasure. But Bobby knew him."

Of course, I thought, as the limo cruised on.

Perhaps Franck would next take us by Nick Adams' pad, I thought. Adams' house had also been in Beverly Hills somewhere, I remembered – maybe it was right down the street from Franck's own. Adams, now long forgotten, had died from an accidental or on-purpose overdose in 1968, the same year the world had also lost and then forgot about Franck. The two of them had a lot in common.

Thinking of the powerful, unforgiving sedatives that were prescribed to an unknowing public in the oldie-days, I imagined that next Franck might take us by Carole Landis' house – she'd committed suicide by an overdose of Seconal, when a married co-star refused to divorce his wife for her. Or we could cruise on over to Franck's favorite, the infamous *Chateau Marmont,* where John Belushi had overdosed on those two Tinseltown staples, heroin and cocaine, in 1982. Or Franck could just instruct the driver to take us up to the Hollywood sign, so we could see the *H* up close, where aspiring actress Peg Entwistle had jumped to her death in 1932, the year before Franck was born.

I frowned, amazed that I couldn't come up with a single famous dead actor's name yesterday, when I'd been in the grip of a hangover. Today, riding around in a limo with Franck O'Day (himself back from the dead, at least in my mind), suddenly I could remember the names and sad endings of damn near every one of the ones that we'd heard about on that macabre tour.

Of course, Franck didn't take us by any of those places. It was just my imagination making depressing suggestions to me. Perhaps the idea that this geriatric playboy was making a concerted pass at my best friend, and she was positively *digging it,* was bringing on all my musings about dead actors and their unfortunate ends.

By the time we arrived back at the house, the afternoon was shot. No interviewing had taken place.

The limo dropped us off in front of Jessika Yerdlay's palatial estate. Jessika, another starlet who'd tried unsuccessfully to off herself over her lost co-star. She'd obviously still loved Franck, even after all those terrible accusations she'd made against him. Or else, why had she tried to kill herself when he went missing?

But Jessika had been unsuccessful in her attempt to join her one-time lover where she believed he was – in the afterlife. Afterward, she'd locked herself up here, in this very house, for another forty-some years, with only a housekeeper and her long suffering daughter for company. How depressing. No wonder Dolores had unloaded the place immediately after her mother's death.

113

I thought of Dolores's long lost diaries, tucked safely into my purse, and my mood brightened considerably. Regardless of whether Maribeth had written them, which I suspected – or if they were the genuine article, which I sincerely doubted – they should still prove an interesting read. I hadn't heard Franck's take on what had or had not happened between them yet, so maybe it would work out for the best if I read Dolores's take first.

The four of us paused at the foot of the stairs. As the limo pulled away, Franck said, "I'm sorry, Carol. The afternoon seems to have gotten away from us. I'd invite you to dinner, but I know you're probably not looking forward to the long drive home. I imagine you'd like to start back as soon as possible. What with work tomorrow, at all." He smiled, then sighed. "I wish I had some work to go to tomorrow."

"Perhaps you'll be making that comeback sooner than originally planned," Maribeth said evenly. "Maybe Carolyn's book will be just the precursor to make it happen."

"All the more reason for her to get home early and safe." He patted me on the shoulder. "But I have an idea – why don't you two come back next Friday night? Stay the weekend? That'll give me time to recall the old days in more detail. I'll be able to take that walk down Memory Lane by myself first, weep over my sad memories in seclusion for a few days, before recounting them to you." He smiled widely – no weeping would be taking place. Franck was not the weepy type. "If you don't want to drive, you can take the train, and I'll send a car around to the station for you."

"That's very generous of you, Franck."

"Nothing's too good for my biographer." He winked.

"Actually, I have plans for Friday night. An old friend of mine will be in town, and –"

"Bring him along," Maribeth suggested. "There's plenty of room."

"He's not that good a friend," I said, a little embarrassed at having to explain. For lack of a better word, he'd been my high school sweetheart, at least for senior year. His name was Doug. He was coming back to town on Friday to visit his family for the first time in years. And while I was not averse to spending some quality time with him on Friday, quality time that might just spill over into the wee hours of Saturday morning, I wasn't going to drag him to LA and have him experience all this weirdness. Besides, he might be inclined to snicker at my writer-ly aspirations.

After whatever romantic hijinks we got up to on Friday night, my plan was to send Doug on his way to visit his family on Saturday

114

morning. And then he could just toddle back to Portland or wherever he was living these days. No muss, no fuss. He was cute enough, and parts of me surely missed him, but like I'd said, he wasn't that good a friend. Just someone that I used to know. Fun, safe, familiar. Temporary.

I said to Franck, "We could come back on Saturday. How does that sound?" I didn't even have to look at Ruthanne for confirmation. I was pretty sure that she'd stay right here with Franck now if he but suggested it. Friend? What friend? Job? What job?

"That sounds great," Franck said.

"It was so nice meeting you, Carolyn. And you, too, Ruthanne," Maribeth said abruptly. "I have to go in and see about dinner. I'll see you next week." She fluttered a little wave at us, then climbed the stairs and disappeared into the house.

"I'm sorry that the time got away, Carol," Franck said again. "But when you come back next weekend, I'll finish the rest of my sordid tale, and you can start pulling everything together for your book."

"I'm looking forward to it." I shook his hand and walked around the front of my car and then climbed into it. I hoped his and Ruthanne's goodbye wouldn't be a lengthy one. It *was* a long drive home, and I was starting to get hungry.

Franck and Ruthanne stood by the back corner of the car, and although I knew it was rude and voyeuristic, I found that I was powerless not to watch their farewell, especially since they were framed perfectly in the passenger-side mirror. I was fascinated, despite myself.

Yesteryear's leading man had just met my friend today. She was a stranger to him. But Ruthanne *knew* Franck O'Day. Not only the story of his life – she also had picked up little details, like that his preferred drink was a mint julep. She had a copy of probably every available photograph of him, and she'd watched his two movies over and over again. She knew his voice, and his smile; his little mannerisms. They were as familiar to her as were mine, or her mom's, or anyone else she knew IRL.

Ruthanne had dreamt about Franck O'Day, both asleep and awake. She'd longed for him to hold her hand, and God-only-knew-what-else they'd been doing in the little theater, with that impossible longing, that special kind of yearning, that singular kind of ache that's known only to fan-girls, and fan-boys, too, for that matter. With that unique brand of desire, reserved for attractive, famous people that they've never met. *Even though you're a celebrity and don't know that I'm alive,* that longing says, *if only a merciful God would allow me to meet you, to talk to you – just* once *– then you would see, you would know, as I do, that we're perfect for each other. We are soul mates.*

Ruthanne couldn't be anything more than just an attractive, adoring young woman to Franck. Something that he'd been looking at since he was thirteen years old, as he'd told us more than once. But I knew that he was Ruthie's most impossible fantasy, now come inexplicably to walking, talking, making-a-play-for-her life. Meeting him – boy, the anticipation of that had thrilled her. But all this – *this* was unbelievable. It must be damn near supernatural to her.

They stood face to face, with their arms linked loosely around each other's waist, like teenagers. Then Franck reached up and tenderly brushed a stray hair out of her eyes. It was a gesture right out of *High Times in Manhattan*, or, to be fair, any other romance. He took her face in his hands and kissed her on the forehead, then on the mouth. I looked away.

When I looked back again, he was whispering something in her ear. Then he turned and looked right at me in the car's mirror and smiled – that smug, knowing little grin. He stepped forward and opened the car door for Ruthanne. She slid in and he shut the door.

He leaned over so I could see him through the window and said, "You ladies drive carefully now. I'll see you on Saturday." He stood up and tapped the roof of car. I started it up and we took off. Ruthanne waved.

EIGHTEEN

We drove in silence for a moment. Then I said conversationally, "Oh. My. God. Ruthanne."

She squealed shrilly, unable to hold it in another second. "I know, right?" she said, unable to come up with anything more poetic than that.

I smiled. "What *are* you going to do next weekend?"

She clutched my shoulder, squeezed it. "Anything he asks me to do," she whispered in awe.

We'll see if I'm kiddin', I thought.

I wouldn't insult my friend's judgment by bringing up the fact that Franck O'Day was eighty years old. She was a bright, intelligent young woman, and I wasn't her mother. She was free and twenty-six, and more than capable of making her own decisions. She hadn't insulted me by trying to talk me out of my planned one-night-stand with Doug. She liked Franck galaxies more than I would ever like Doug – who was I to say her nay?

But maybe that was just the problem. Maybe that was what was making me uncomfortable about this whole thing, even more than the Grand Canyon-sized age difference between them. Just how attached did Ruthanne think she was going to get to legendary matinee-idol Franck O'Day? How attached did she think he was going to get to her? But still, it was really none of my business.

My curiosity was alive – it writhed and slithered in my head. What must it be like for Ruthanne to have met Franck O'Day in the flesh? And not just as a shriveled up old geezer, which is what he should've been, but as a vibrant, confident, still attractive, middle-aged man? I remembered her poetic description of his photograph. I had to know how actually meeting him had affected her.

"Well?" I said. "So?"

Ruthanne gazed out the window at the gathering darkness, as if transfixed by the red tail lights ahead of us. She spoke in a low, throaty whisper – I turned down the radio in order to hear her clearly. "Oh, my God, Carol. When he took my hand in front of the house – I have never been so excited in my life."

"I can imagine."

"Can you?" She looked at me suddenly, and the pupils of her eyes were again as big and as black as marbles. "Can you, really? It was all so much beyond what I'd ever imagined, myself. From the moment he came down the stairs – oh, my God, all I could think was – *It's him, it's really him!*

"What was I gonna say? What was I gonna do? And then he took me by the hand – if I would've known ahead of time that he was gonna do that, I think I would've come right there, as soon as he touched me. But it was a total surprise.

"And he kept holding my hand. After a while, to my amazement, I kinda got used to it. Can you imagine? I got used to holding hands with Franck O'Day! Then he showed us the theater, and the anticipation, the excitement started to build again. I wouldn't have believed that I could become any more excited, but I did. All I could think of was watching *Manhattan* while I was holding his hand.

"I'll never forget it, not till the day I die, Carol. The house lights dimmed, went out. He was sitting on my right. He leaned closer to me and said that they'd had to shoot the title sequence twice because of some camera malfunction. I could feel his breath, warm and soft and tickly in my ear.

"I turned to look at him. He moved in even closer, as if he would kiss me – oh, my, God, Franck O'Day was going to kiss me! I leaned toward him – the most impossible thing in my life was about to happen, and I wanted it *so bad*, Carol! Never have I ever wanted anything as badly as I wanted Franck O'Day to kiss me.

"But when our lips were almost touching, he stopped. He hesitated, for just the merest second. Just long enough for the idea to flash like lightning through my mind, that maybe he wasn't going to kiss me after all. The anticipation, the sudden unsureness of that split second – it nearly undid me, Carol. I looked at him. He smiled. And then he kissed me." Ruthanne exhaled.

"And then what happened?" I asked, before I even knew the words had formed in my mind.

I'd really never been much for listening to Ruthanne relate the details of her conquests. As we approached thirty, there was very little breathless anticipation like this involved in the telling anymore. It usually went, "He did this, and then right away, he asked me if I would do that, can you imagine?" And in conclusion: "It was okay. Maybe I'll see him again." It was not that Ruthanne was jaded, so much as it had just become one of those things – enjoyable, sometimes *highly* enjoyable – but still, there weren't too many surprises anymore.

And I was almost incapable of giving any descriptions of my own. When I told her that Doug and I would be having a little rendezvous, Ruthanne wanted me to remind her about all the things we'd done in high school. I reminisced about the cool summer nights, the texture and smell of the black vinyl backseat of his car. But when it came to the description of all the delightful things we'd done, I mostly said, "And then he, well, you know . . ." and fell silent.

I could think about it – though maybe not as clearly and to such pleasant ends as Ruthanne could. And I could most assuredly do it, and with perhaps less compunction than Ruthanne. If I'd gone ahead and picked up that Marty guy, based solely on the way he looked, as Ruthanne had done? I most assuredly would've gone right on ahead and found out about the rest of him. I wouldn't have tempted myself, teased myself like that, and then not gone through with it, the way Ruthie had. I was a sucker for temptation, every time.

But for some inexplicable reason, I just wasn't very good at *talking* about it. And I didn't usually care to hear Ruthanne's somewhat clinical, morning-after play-by-plays. They depressed me for some reason. I guess that I wanted to hear a two thumbs-up, rousing review. Just once.

So I was fascinated with Ruthanne's description this time. I knew how she felt about Franck O'Day. I'd watched her watch *High Times in Manhattan*, witnessed what it did to her: the parted lips, the glassy eyes. What must it have been like to actually be there with this guy? I could not begin to imagine what it must've been like to kiss someone that you wanted that much. Call me frigid, but I've never wanted *anyone* that much.

Again Ruthie sighed. "Not much else happened. We kissed. Oh, my, God, Carol, he kisses like an angel. Like the Devil himself." She grinned at that conflicting image, but I knew exactly what she meant.

"He smelled so good . . . he tasted *so good.* He put his hand on my thigh once. Only once, and just for a second, but that was all it took." Again she grinned at me. "I would've done anything he asked, Carol, anything, right there in that little theatre, with an unlocked door and you and his daughter liable to walk in at any second.

"But nothing else happened. We kissed through most of the movie, and he touched my leg that one time. But that was all. I wanted him to do more, Carol – oh, my God! I've never wanted anything so much in my life. But that was it. I guess you could say he was a gentleman. I have never been so turned on in my life. It was the most incredible thing I've ever experienced."

Incredible, indeed, I thought. As the act commences, how seldom do we get to want a man more than he wants us, how seldom do we get to experience that aching longing and desire – even for just a moment – before consummation? How much better would it all be, if that happened once in a while?

Atta boy, Franck, I thought with not a little admiration. *Always leave 'em wanting more.* "What do ya think would've happened if you'd taken the house tour?" I asked.

"Anything he wanted," Ruthie whispered again.

The entirely vulgar term *cock-block* popped into my mind, and I felt compelled to explain. "You know, it wasn't really my idea to go for a drive. Maribeth came up with that all on her own."

Ruthanne blinked at me, like she was having trouble remembering who Maribeth was. Then she shrugged. "It's all good. Saturday'll be here before you know it."

And you have all week to think about it, I reflected. *A sweaty, sticky fever of anticipation, that's what you'll have, all week.* I smiled. Saturday came after Friday, and that was when my old boyfriend Doug would be dropping by for a little walk down a sweaty, sticky Memory Lane of our own. I began to feel a little anticipation myself.

NINETEEN

Franck called Ruthanne every evening at about 6:15. I knew it was him from the way she would lower her lashes for a second, softly say, "Hello?" and then flash a brilliant smile at me. And then she would take the call into her room.

As expected, Ruthie walked around all week with a little thoughtful smile pasted on her face. I discovered that I was smiling a little bit my own self. It wasn't the same Anthony and Cleopatra, Napoleon and Josephine kind of anticipation that Ruthanne encompassed, surely, but it was nice, nonetheless. It had been a little while since I'd had a date like this to look forward to. Doug was cute, and I was fond of him. That was good enough for me.

In honor of my imminent accessibility, no doubt, Doug treated me to surf and turf. I was flattered by the extravagant gesture. He'd always been cheap in high school, so I enjoyed this unexpected magnanimity to its fullest, consuming more than my share of the not-inexpensive champagne he bought to toast our reunion.

After dinner, without further ado, I took him home. We staggered up the steps to my apartment. Giggling, I put the key in the door and stepped into the dark living room. Then I stopped dead in my tracks. I heard Franck's voice coming from Ruthanne's bedroom, and I thought that he was actually here, in our apartment – that she couldn't wait for one more day.

But then Jessika Yerdlay's voice answered, not Ruthie's, and I realized that what was taking place in my roommate's bedroom was nothing more than a private screening of *High Times in Manhattan*. How *could* she watch the same ancient movie, over and over?

I forgot all about Franck and Jessika and even Ruthanne, then, and concentrated on giving my full attention to Doug.

TWENTY

Earlier in the week, Ruthanne had insisted that I go through all my dresses and pick out something nice to wear once the sun went down on Saturday night. Franck was throwing us a dinner party, she said, and she wanted me to look my best.

"A dinner party? Who else is going to be there?" I asked. "You mean like a *formal* dinner party?"

Ruthanne shook her head. "No, nothing like that. It's just going to be the three of us, but I still want us to look nice."

"Maribeth's not gonna be there?"

Ruthie blinked at me. "Oh, yeah, Maribeth. She'll be there, too, I guess." My friend had forgotten about Maribeth, no doubt because, besides hellos and goodbyes, they hadn't said three words to each other. She'd only talked to Franck, looked at Franck.

I wound up borrowing a dress from Ruthanne, because none of mine passed her inspection. It was wine-colored, a little bit more low-cut than I usually sport, but beautiful, nonetheless. I looked great in it, if I said so myself. Ruthanne picked out an emerald-green number, also daringly low-cut, that played up the color of her eyes.

It was a good thing, I reflected, that the walls were high and the shrubbery thick around Jessika's estate, lest the neighbors think that someone there had hired a couple of professionals for the evening. In other words, I thought the dresses Ruthie chose were a little too much for just dinner, even if it was at an opulent manse it Beverly Hills. They were more like dresses for dancing, bar-hopping – definitely after-dark attire. But she would not be dissuaded, so I dutifully put the red gown onto its padded hanger, covered it with its dry cleaner bag, and took it out to the car.

The ride to LA for our second visit with the legendary Franck O'Day was a little different than the first one. We still took my car, because it got better gas mileage, but there was no Jurassic playlist, no breathless anticipation of the unknown. Ruthie just smiled to herself, hummed along with the radio, and pointed out the sights along the way. She knew what she was walking into this time, and was just quietly thrilled about it. She was still filled to near-bursting with anticipation – but it was not of the unknowable, *I wonder what's going to happen?* sort. Ruthie knew what was going to happen. She was going to *make it* happen. One of her wildest fantasies was about to come true. She was serenely in control of herself.

When he strolled down the stone staircase to greet us, I was astonished to see that Franck had dyed his hair in the week since we'd seen him last. He wore a cream-colored linen suit that played up the inky blackness of it. The stunning illusion that this man was not a day over forty was now complete.

I was amazed at how natural the color looked on him. When the sun shone through his hair, there was none of that tell-tale reddish-brownness, which is a dead-giveaway to dyed hair. If your hair is really black and not just chemically blackened, it's black all the way through. But sometimes some of the more stubborn grays only partially absorbed the dye, and you got that brownish cast. The texture also looked natural, luxurious. I knew that Ruthie would be running her fingers through it later.

But then, this coloring was not derived from some mass-produced, boxed amalgam that he'd purchased at a drugstore on Sunset, and then had Maribeth slap on his head, I thought. He'd no doubt visited the finest salon on Rodeo Drive. Ah, the things money could buy. Extraordinary plastic surgery. A flawless dye job. The illusion of youth.

We arrived in time for lunch, and Franck again seated us at the table overlooking the pool. The silent Asian man – Franck called him Kimura – served us the best salmon I'd ever tasted, again on impossibly expensive bone china. I noticed that it was a different service than the one from which we'd had brunch the week before. Ah, the things money could buy!

After he cleared the dishes away, Kimura presented Franck with a bottle of champagne for his perusal. Franck nodded. Kimura left, then swiftly returned with four glasses and the opened bottle in a bucket of ice.

"To absent friends," Franck toasted.

Oh, you're good, Franck, ol' boy, I thought. He had remembered Ruthie's favorite toast.

We toasted to our friends, absent though they were, then Franck said, "You wanted to hear about Lori." He removed a little digital audio recorder, also expensive, from the breast pocket of his plantation-owner's suit and set it on the table in front of him. "I took the liberty, Carol. I hope you don't mind."

The girl-reporter/best-selling author picture that I'd painted in my mind had somehow totally skipped the mechanics of an interview. I hadn't even brought a steno pad. I nodded gratefully at Franck.

He smiled and pushed the button on the recorder. "I can't remember precisely the first time I met Lori, but it was at some party

123

that her mother threw, no doubt. She was tall for her age, slender. She was only four years or so older than Maribeth, but she seemed older, because she wasn't giddy and child-like. She didn't giggle and fidget and run around like a kid, like Maribeth did. Lori was always quiet and watchful, always there on the periphery.

"She liked to be around adults – she always wanted to stay up and attend her mother's parties. She'd just blend into the background, watching. Sometimes, I'd forget she was even there. Jessika would discuss the most outrageous studio business in front of her, deride people in front of her, because I think Jessika forgot she was there sometimes, too. Lori had learned to be quiet because she knew that her mother wouldn't tolerate being upstaged." Franck laughed.

He looked at his step-daughter. She narrowed her eyes in her own kind of anticipation, I thought, anticipation of whatever it was that Franck was going to say next. He asked, "What do you remember about Lori, Mari?"

Maribeth cleared her throat. "She was always very kind to me. I think she loved me very much."

"Although she didn't show it very much, eh?" Franck said with a grin. "I remember her chucking you into the pool a couple times."

"I was probably just annoying her then." Maribeth looked at me, as if to explain. "I was just a child."

"Lori was very fond of me," Franck continued. "But she was aloof, always watchful. She was always aware of her mother's presence and made sure, like I say, to never attempt to be the center of attention. She knew that this was an offense that her mother would just not brook. No one was allowed to be the center of attention except Jessika.

"But I could tell that Lori liked me, that she was glad I was around. She wasn't jealous of the time I spent with her mother, like some kids might've been. She didn't feel like I was taking her mother's attention away from her. Her mother never paid her that much attention, anyway – she was a very self-sufficient child.

"Lori was always reserved, not demonstrative. She'd never climb up into my lap and kiss me and hug me and call me *Daddy* like Maribeth did. But she watched me. When I was depressed after Bridget died, and after Maribeth went back to her father, Lori would tell me how sad I looked. She was very sensitive – I could tell that she felt my pain very much."

Franck sighed. "As far as our *relationship* was concerned – as she grew older, Lori seemed to grow farther away from her mother. Their own relationship had never been overly affectionate, and as she got older, Lori sought the affection she was missing from me. She never passed up an opportunity to sit by me, talk to me, hug me. And she watched me.

"When I left with Bobby – I felt bad about leaving Lori here in this big house all by herself. But Cecilia, the housekeeper, was here, and I knew Jessika would be returning in a few days. Lori was always close with Cecilia. She was more of a nanny than a housekeeper.

"When I left with Bobby, I remember that Lori hugged me, squeezed me very tightly, like she never wanted to let go. But we were in a hurry. We had to catch a plane – I remember I had to take Lori's arms from around my neck, because we had to go.

"The tears were streaming down her face. She was very sad that I was leaving. I was the only father-figure she'd ever had, except maybe for Roger, and Roger had betrayed us all. Roger was a murderer, a suicide. I was the only adult man that Lori had ever been around in her life." Franck paused.

After a second, when it became apparent that Franck would say no more, Maribeth spoke up, a trifle stridently, I noticed. "That's all you're going to say? That she was *fond* of you?"

Maribeth looked at me, and I suddenly remembered Lori's diaries. They were still in my purse. I'd forgotten all about them in all that looking forward to my big date. I shook my head, almost imperceptibly, to communicate to Maribeth that I hadn't read them yet. She understood my gesture, and looked at Franck again.

"Lori was much more than merely fond of you, Franck," she told him. *"Lori loved you.* I was just a little girl, but even I could see it."

Franck resumed, as if Maribeth had not even spoken. "There was never anything more than a remote, respectful affection between us. Like I say, she was not a bubbly child, like Maribeth. She was not always asking to be kissed and hugged and rocked in her rocking chair, like Maribeth was, even when she was too big for it. I was always afraid that rocking chair was going to collapse with both of us sitting in it.

"I don't know why Jessika said the things she did about Lori and me, Carol." He looked at me, and his blue eyes seemed perplexed, a trifle hurt, even after all these years.

But I didn't allow myself to be taken in by his wounded expression – at least not entirely. Franck O'Day was an actor, after all, and a very good one. I remembered the tale of woe he'd told in *Manhattan*, with those blue eyes alone, when Perry believed he was going to lose Dora forever. It had been a performance of Oscar caliber. Maybe this was, too.

"I think Bobby had it right. Jessika was Hollywood, through and through. And using people to further your own ambition is a staple here, as utilized to people's advantage as is Method acting. Some people'll sell out their own mothers to get what they want, so why not their own daughters? Bobby said that Jessika had concocted the whole repugnant story, for no other reason than to get me to come back to the States. He was convinced that Jessika would've dropped the entire issue, if we ever would've made it back here. Once we came back, he was convinced, she'd let it all go, and try to patch things up with me.

"'You'll never see the inside of a courtroom,' he said. 'She'll clasp you around the knees and beg for your forgiveness. She'll try to explain it all as a testament to how completely she's missed you, how utterly she's needed you, how desperately she loves you.'

Franck shrugged, smiled. "Before the term *drama queen* even existed, Bobby was one. But that didn't make him any less correct in his estimation of Jessika's motives." He sipped his champagne. "I think Jessika would've done anything to get me to come back to California. And that included making up those horrible accusations and using her own flesh and blood as a ploy to force me to come back."

Now Franck acknowledged Maribeth's presence. "Based on what you think you know of the events – even though you were a little kid in Kansas at the time – do you have anything you'd like to add?"

Maribeth glanced at me quickly, then looked at the table in front of her. She shook her head.

"I didn't think so." Franck looked at me again. "What about you, Carol? Do you have any other questions about sad Lori and my non-existent relationship with her?"

"I can't think of anything at this time," I said neutrally.

"Well, if you do, please don't hesitate to ask." He pushed the button on the recorder.

Nobody spoke for a second, then Franck smiled at Ruthanne, sitting forgotten at his side; he took her hand and kissed it. "I hope you ladies remembered to bring your suits. I'm in the mood for a swim!" He released Ruthanne's hand and stood up. "I'll re-join you momentarily." Then he turned and went into the house. After waiting a proper amount of time, Ruthanne followed him.

When she was sure they were out of earshot, Maribeth said, "Go ahead, Carolyn. Jessika's pool is impeccable. You just be sure to read Lori's diaries before you write your book."

"I apologize, Miss O'Day," I said, feeling like an ass. "I had a very busy week." *A very busy week, what with looking forward to getting at Doug,* I thought.

"It's okay, Carolyn," she offered her white, false-toothed smile and patted my hand. "I'm sure you're curious now." She nodded at the house. "Go on, go put your suit on. We'll talk again, maybe after dinner. I'm a little too old for public bathing, I'm afraid." She winked at me, then arose and walked into the house. After a moment, I followed.

TWENTY-ONE

Ruthanne met me on the stairs, already attired in a silver, one-piece suit. She returned to my room with me, sat on the bed and waited for me to change.

"So, what do you think?" I asked her from the bathroom, as I put on my own light-blue one-piece. "Do you think he's telling the truth about Dolores?" *I'll soon be finding out*, I thought. *Or at least I'll be hearing another take on the whole thing. The hardest part will be figuring out if it's fiction or not, and from whose perspective.* When Ruthie didn't answer, I looked out of the bathroom door at her. She met my eyes.

"How can I help but believe him?" She answered my question with a question.

Now dressed for the water, I came out of the bathroom and looked at her. "I understand that these things happen all the time, Ruthie. Especially back in the day. He said she was tall and mature for her age. Maybe he —"

"No," Ruthanne cut me off, offended. "If he says that there was nothing between them, then I believe him. Why would he lie? The statute of limitations ran out decades ago. Why would he lie about it now?"

"Maybe he wants to protect his reputation? Maybe he wants to underline what an unrepentant bitch Jessika was? She's not here to defend herself, is she? Nor is Lori here to tell us what really happened." *At least not in the flesh*, I thought, again remembering the diaries. I wondered how hard it might be to actually track down the daughter of the late Jessika Yerdlay. I didn't even know if she was still in LA. I didn't even know if she was still alive.

"No." Ruthanne shook her head firmly. "I could never believe that the man I . . . I could never believe that Franck's a liar."

I raised an eyebrow at that. She'd almost said, *the man I love.* I wondered, not for the first time, how Ruthanne's yearning, unrequitable, impossible obsession with a dead movie star was translating into real life. Was she just channeling all the feelings she'd had for the Franck she knew from the internet, from his movies, from *TwoGreenKeys.com* — a persona that really amounted to nothing more than a one-dimensional *Wikipedia* synopsis — was she just transferring those feelings, wholesale, onto the sexy, attentive, freak of nature that was the impeccably preserved man himself?

Or was she paying attention to the words he used? Was she listening to the things he said, trying to ascertain what kind of man he truly was? Was she trying to glean what kind of heart and mind lived behind those cobalt-blue eyes and charming smile, like I was attempting to do? I thought not. Ruthanne would love Franck O'Day with all her soul, even if he turned out to be an ax murderer.

But still, she was an adult. Who was I to pass judgment on her decisions? If she thought she was in love with Franck O'Day – with the man *he really was,* and not just Perry Calibri, the character he'd played in *High Times in Manhattan* – who was I to say one damn word to the contrary?

What a tiresome and pointless existence it would be, if we believed that dreams can never really come true. There had to have been at least one happily ever after, or we'd never have heard of the concept.

Ruthanne looked up at me and smiled brightly. "Let's go swimming!" She grabbed my hand, and we ran out of the room and down the sweeping staircase. Ruthie giggled, as if she was the kind of carefree schoolgirl, wanting for nothing, that might've once inhabited this palatial house. I wondered if Dolores had been that carefree schoolgirl. Franck had not described her as such, and I wondered what inner demons had kept her watchful and quiet. Perhaps her diaries (if they were genuine) would help me to find out.

Franck was waiting for us when we returned to the pool. He was wearing Ray-Bans and a beige, straw porkpie hat, complete with dark brown hatband and bow – *gotta keep the merciless sun off of all that expensively, flawlessly doctored skin,* I thought. It was a hat right out of 1965 – or something he might've snatched off the head of a hipster strolling down Vine Street this morning. He wore a matching beige short-sleeved shirt, unbuttoned, and Persian green board shorts. Board shorts. He might be eighty, I thought, but modern fashion had not passed him by.

I waited with no little curiosity to see if the rest of him was as well preserved as his face. He smiled at us, and after a minute, doffed sunglasses, hat, and shirt and threw them onto a lounge chair. His chest was smooth, and he was a little pale – the sun was the enemy, after all, ask any dermatologist – and one couldn't say he was cut. But his body also looked forty: he was muscular enough, trim, broad-shouldered, sturdily well-built. And when he jumped up onto the diving board and executed a flawless, Olympic-caliber jackknife into the pool, I couldn't help but notice that he had a really nice ass.

The afternoon passed in idyllic Southern California indolence. Franck and Ruthanne splashed and played in the water like teenagers, then floated around on matching rafts, holding hands. I reclined on a lounge chair, soaked up the rays, and read a trashy novel. All the summer-afternoon-by-the-pool clichés. Kimura materialized with a pitcher of mint juleps.

I reflected that Ruthanne and I could be engaging in the same activities at home – our apartment building had a pool. We had the same sunshine, although it was a little hotter at home, being, as we were, quite a few more miles from the coast. But our water was just as wet. You could even drink a mint julep at our pool, as long as you disguised it as something else, and didn't drink it out of a glass container.

It was what was missing from Jessika's large pool as compared to our little community one back home that made the difference – here there were no teenagers playing loud music and cannonballing off the diving board; no squealing children and crying babies, no people of other cultures speaking in foreign languages to each other. No suspicions that they might be talking about you. Here all was quiet and serene and private. Here was all the pluperfect ambience that money could buy.

I considered Ruthanne. She and Franck were sitting in the water, on the steps, smiling and talking, drinking their juleps. I think that all the opulence had totally passed her by. She was too dazzled by Franck himself – there wasn't any part of her left to be dazzled by Franck's house, Franck's pool, Franck's *money*. Ruthanne wouldn't have cared if Franck was a pauper, because he was *him*. The grandeur of her surroundings had gone unnoticed, the moment she became lost in his blue eyes.

But I couldn't help but notice it. When the Joneses get a new barbeque, you feel a little twinge of jealousy, because you can't get a new barbeque till next payday. And when they get a new car, you feel that little twinge again, because you can't get a new car until next season. That's why they call it *keeping up with the Joneses* – without too much hardship, you *can* keep up.

But here was opulence and luxury that I could never attain in a thousand legal secretary's lifetimes. Franck's was old Hollywood money. He'd made his fortune more than fifty years ago, and the bulk of it had no doubt been sitting somewhere in Switzerland, collecting stupendous interest ever since. I imagined that Franck was wealthy beyond my ability to imagine it.

Not that the lavishness of Jessika's house didn't impress me. It was just too far beyond my reach. It would be like aspiring to someday live in Buckingham Palace. It just wasn't ever going to happen, so I didn't ever wonder about what it would be like to live here, to laze around the pool at my leisure, to have Kimura step and fetch and cater to my every whim.

They say that the average person believes they receive more value for their money when they spend it on visiting exotic locations. Experiencing that expensive cruise or two-day, one-night stay at that posh hotel – the memory of these adventures is much better to them than simply purchasing expensive things. It was not so with me. To me, the trip was over once it was over. Even while I was there, I couldn't pretend that this was my lifestyle. I didn't have the imagination to enjoy the rented luxuries as if I could afford to sustain them for any length of time.

I much more enjoyed our big TV and its attached home theater components, for which Ruthanne and I had shelled out a small fortune. These were my expensive things – concrete, utilitarian. So much better than the fleeting memory of a white sand beach that I would only ever be able to afford to visit for a day or two. I might live in a crappy two-bedroom walk-up, and drive a twelve-year-old car, but I could watch television like a recently drafted NFL running back.

"Let me tell you about a little trick Esther Williams taught me," Franck said to Ruthanne. I looked at them over the top of the bodice-ripper I was reading. "First, you have to be floating on your back."

Ruthanne obeyed, legs together, pink-nailed toes peeping above the water. She held her arms out from her shoulders, gracefully moving them back and forth to stay afloat.

"Good." Franck held her by the heels for a minute, smiling at her. Then he gently drew her alongside him through the water, so he could whisper something in her ear.

Ruthanne said, "Oh!" kicked herself upright and splashed him, then ducked him under the water. Franck came back up smiling, shook the hair out of his eyes and hugged her. He winked at me over her shoulder, and I smiled back.

Not privy to what he'd whispered, I didn't get it. Whatever.

As the sun began to sink into the west, Kimura appeared on the terrace. Franck noticed him and nodded. Kimura faded back into the house. "Time to dress for dinner, ladies," Franck said. He offered his hand to Ruthanne and she dutifully followed him up the steps out of the water. He said to me, "I hope you like Italian, Carol."

"It's my favorite," I replied, mostly just for something to say. I was sure that whatever the nationality, Kimura's dinner would be excellent.

Ruthanne and I showered and coiffed and put on our faces, giggling like teenagers getting ready for the prom. Her happiness was infectious. I even forgot my aloof, none-of-this-could-ever-be-mine realism for a little while.

At last we were ready for our close-up, and glided down the staircase, again hand-in-hand. Franck was waiting for us at the bottom, looking like Rhett Butler, with his impossibly natural-looking black hair and angelic blue eyes. He wore another perfectly tailored suit, black this time. The man certainly knew how to dress. He told us we looked beautiful and took us both by the arm and led us into the formal dining room.

It was not ostentatiously large, only about as big as half of our entire apartment. There was an enormous, sparkling, immaculately clean chandelier. The dining table was small, however, almost modest. The room could've accommodated one three times its size, and I imagined that it once had, back in the days of Jessika's swank Hollywood soirees. Perhaps it had been depressing for Franck to sit alone at such a vast table, just he and Maribeth. Perhaps it depressed him to remember that the luminaries of yesteryear that had once dined here were all long in the ground, that he was one of the few left. Maybe that was the reason he'd gotten rid of the big table in favor of this smaller, cozier one.

Maribeth was already seated. She had dressed for the occasion, too – she wore a lacy white dress, white like her hair, white like her skin, white like her dentures. It was lovely, but I thought that all that whiteness made her look ghostly, wraith-like. As if she was just a spiritual visitor, returned from one of Jessika's long forgotten parties, and not really alive and here with us at all.

The Italian dinner was delicious, as I knew it would be, but I kept thinking about the scene from *Sunset Boulevard*, where Norma Desmond and her silent-movie cronies sit around and play bridge, pretending as if the world had not passed them by. Our little dinner party reminded me of them. Here we were, all alone, just four people in this huge, multi-million dollar, old Hollywood mansion – a place that had no doubt once hosted hundreds of people at a time. I wondered, if, when it was just Franck and Maribeth dining – even more alone – if he ever realized that the world had also forgotten him, had also passed him by.

After the dinner things were cleared away, Franck left the room, and music swelled from hidden speakers. Again I was struck with how technologically up-to-date the place was. Ignoring Maribeth completely, Franck asked me if I wanted to dance. Remembering my dream, in which we'd meshed together so perfectly, I might even have blushed when I declined.

"I don't know how to dance," I told him in embarrassment.

"A pity," he said, and offered his hand to Ruthanne.

Ruthanne didn't know how to dance either, but it didn't matter. She wouldn't have hesitated if Franck had asked her to go sky diving, right then, in her green party dress. She'd do *anything he wanted.*

Franck instructed her softly, and after a few minutes, they were gliding slowly around, using the empty space that had once been occupied by the bigger dining table, as if the dining room was a familiar ballroom on New Year's Eve.

Even though there was no live band, and the music was a little more modern, and even though Franck was not wearing tails – he did look *absolutely divine*, however, I had to admit – again, I was reminded of Norma Desmond and Joe Gillis dancing in *Sunset Boulevard.*

Consulting his watch, Joe says, *"It's quarter past ten. What time they supposed to get here?"*

"Who?" Norma asks, eyes closed, her head nestled on Joe's shoulder.

"The other guests."

"There are no other guests," Norma replies. *"We don't want to share this night with other people."*

I knew that Ruthanne didn't want to share her night with Franck with other people either. Maribeth and I were once again forgotten.

After they whirled around the make-shift dance floor for a few numbers, the music faded. Franck dipped Ruthie dramatically. He put his forehead to hers, smiled, whispered something, then gracefully set her on her feet again.

Still holding her hand, he turned and smiled at Maribeth and me, seated at the little table. "Are you ladies down for a movie? I promise it will be something a little more up-to-date than non-Oscar-winners from the dim reaches of time."

I looked at Ruthanne. She looked back at me, unblinking, then one corner of her mouth crooked up in a tiny smile. The message was unmistakable.

"Ah, thanks a lot, Franck," I said. "But I think I got a little too much sun today." The other side of Ruthie's smile lifted. "I think I'd like to turn in early, if that's not too rude of me."

Franck's smile matched Ruthanne's. "Of course not, Carol. We'll talk again in the morning. Have a pleasant night."

Maribeth's plans for the rest of the evening were not consulted.

Franck and Ruthanne turned and left the room, hand in hand. She looked over her shoulder and winked gratefully at me, and then they were gone.

I said to Maribeth, "Now I'll have a chance to take a look at Lori's diaries."

She smiled evenly at me. "I think you'll find them enlightening." She stood. "It's so nice having you here, Carolyn. I'll say goodnight now. Brunch is at eleven – but then you already know that. I'll see you then."

"Thanks for all your hospitality, Miss O'Day," I replied.

"Oh, Carolyn, please call me Mari," she finally said.

"Thanks for everything, Mari. Goodnight."

TWENTY-TWO

I walked up the grand staircase to my room. I'd been given one of the two in the back of the house, the ones that overlooked the pool. I took off Ruthanne's beautiful wine-colored dress and carefully hung it in the closet. I threw her shoes in the general direction of my open suitcase, which was sitting on a chair.

I rummaged through it until I found the oversized t-shirt that I'd packed for pajamas, wondering vaguely if Ruthie's step-by-step script of what exactly was going to transpire tonight had included a scene involving lingerie.

I had no such aspirations. I flopped down on the soft bed. By the somewhat dim light of the lamp on the bedside table, I opened the first little red book, supposedly the diary of Jessika's daughter. *Dolores Adamson* was written in the corner of the cover. It came as a shock that it didn't say *Dolores Yerdlay*. But of course, her last name wouldn't have been Yerdlay. Jessika had had a husband at one time, and Dolores, a father. Yerdlay was Jessika's maiden name, her stage name.

The first entry was dated December 17, 1960. Ruthanne had informed me that Dolores's birthday was April 15, 1951. So she was not quite ten years old when she'd begun this journal. I sighed. My friend was living out her wildest fantasies, and I was reading a little kid's diary from twenty-something years before I was a twinkle in my father's eye. The things I did for my art.

December 17, 1960

   Mama and Uncle Roger just returned from a Christmas party. She came up to my room and hugged me. Her mink tickled my nose. She's so happy! She'll be starting work on her next film in the New Year. It's a romance. The only thing she doesn't like about it is the director but then Mama never likes her directors.

December 25, 1960

   Merry Christmas! Uncle Roger got me a pair of beautiful pearly earrings. They are clip-ons, because Mama says that I'm too little to have my ears pierced yet. But then Mama said that I was growing up, and in honor of that – that's what she said – in honor of that – she gave me a big box. Inside was a beautiful, cream-colored dress! And a pair of shoes to go with it, with heels, almost like the ones Mama wears! I ran upstairs and put it on right away. They told me that I look lovely!

December 31, 1960

    Mama had a New Year's Eve party for all the people that are going to be in her movie. She told me to put on my new grown-up dress, and she even let me stay up and meet some of them. First I met Mama's director. He shook my hand and said my dress was exquisit. I curtseyed, like Cecilia told me to do when a gentleman gives you a compliment. Mama laughed, and then Mama's director started talking to Uncle Roger.

    Then Mama ~~intra~~ introduced me to Mr. O'day, her co-star. He has the bluest eyes I've ever seen. He smiled at me and pretended to kiss my hand. He called me Miss Lori. He told me that I looked just like Mama. I don't look just like Mama, who is a beautiful, famous movie star, but it was still nice of him to say so.

    After Mr. O'day was there, Mama told me that it was time to go to bed, and Cecilia took me upstairs. I pretended to be asleep until I knew she was gone. Then I snuck over to the window so I could watch all the ladies in their ~~beu~~ beautiful gowns and the gentlemen in their pretty tuxidos come to Mama's party.

    I watched three or four cars pull up. People got out. One lady was wearing a very pretty red dress. Then I saw Mr. O'day walk down the steps. He said something to the valley, and the valley ran away. Then Mama came down the stairs after him. Why was she outside? Was Mama leaving her own party? I slid the window open a little so I could here what they were saying.

    I'm sorry, Jessika, Mr. O'day said. I have to make the rounds. If I don't show up at Bobby's before midnight, he'll cry.

    Who? Mama said in her beautiful voice. Mama's voice is like music!

    Mr. O'day smiled and kissed her on the cheek. Thanks for inviting me, he said.

    The valley brought Mr. O'days car up and he drove away. Mama stood on the bottom step for a minute, then turned around. She wasn't smiling when she turned around. She looked up and I jumped back into bed! Maybe she wasn't smiling because I was supposed to be sleeping.

    The plot was thickening already. Franck said he couldn't recall at which of Jessika's many functions that he'd first met Dolores, but she'd recorded the exact date for posterity.

    I reflected that Jessika was already interested, as early as New Year's, and Franck was already playing hard to get. What a bastard he is, I thought again. Why had he even bothered showing up at her party, if he was only going to stay for five minutes?

    I was impressed with the seeming authenticity of the document, already, however – the spidery child's hand, the endearing misspellings, the almost complete lack of punctuation. Perhaps this first volume really *was* little Dolores's diary. It was sure as boring as hell, just like Maribeth had indicated that it would be. Nothing but a child's tedious scribblings. Maybe this one had indeed been written by not-quite-ten-year-old Dolores. If this volume was genuine, then I sincerely doubted that there were going to be any bombshells in it. I believed that there would be bombshells – why else had Maribeth handed the journals off to me so secretively, if there was nothing revealing in them? But I was still pretty sure that when the mortars did begin to fall, it would be in the second volume. And I was still not completely convinced that Dolores had written that one.

I skimmed over pink decorations for Valentine's Day and an entry about Mrs. Larson, Dolores's new private tutor, whom she found to be *yucky*. There was a description of an Easter egg hunt, complete with Easter bunny. Billy and Susie and Andy were present, no doubt all offspring of Jessika's Hollywood peers. They were all either dead now or in their early sixties.

It was gonna take a minute to slog through all of Dolores's colorful ramblings and childish observations. She was quite long-winded for a little girl. I supposed that this unfortunate tendency might spring from being the pampered child of privilege, from not having to ever worry about a single thing.

I read with interest that Mr. O'Day had attended Easter dinner.

He wasn't wearing a tuxedo this time. We had ham for dinner. After dinner, he asked me if I would show him my Easter basket, and told me that my Easter dress was very pretty. He's got the bluest eyes.

I took him into the living room and was showing him my colored eggs. Mama and Uncle Roger were still in the dining room and they started raising their voices at the dinner table, which Cecilia says is very rude.

Suddenly, Cecilia was standing in the doorway to the living room, telling me to come to her. She looked embareassed.

Even though she couldn't spell it, Dolores was already familiar with the notion of embarrassment. I tried to recall if I had understood the concept at her age, but couldn't. I recalled vividly, however, the first time I had felt the emotion myself. I was a few years older than ten.

Mr. O'day saw Cecelia standing there too, and he took my hand and we went out to the foyer with her. Then he told me goodbye and Cecelia told me to go up to my room. She always told me to go to my room when Mama was having raised voices. I ran upstairs and watched Mr. O'day walk down the steps and get into his car and drive away.

Mama didn't follow him this time, because she was still downstairs at the dinner table with Uncle Roger. Now that company was gone, they were not just

137

having raised voices. They were yelling. I stayed in my room, because I don't like to be there when Mama is yelling. Cecilia knows it, too.

Later, Mama came upstairs. She said I've got some good news and some bad news. What do you want to hear first? It was a little game she taught me. She said I should always ask for the bad news first because then the good news sounds even better.

So I did. Mama said that the bad news was that Uncle Roger left. He wanted to live in his own house, Mama said. He would still be back to visit us, Mama said.

Now came the best part. I got to ask what the good news was! Mama sat next to me on the bed and hugged me. The good news is that we're going to be seeing a lot more of Mr. O'day. Mama smiled and kissed me. If I played my cards right, she said, Mr. O'day might even be my new daddy. I told Mama I didn't know how to play cards and she laughed and hugged me again.

Later that night, I heard a car door slam. It was getting warm already, and my window was open, or I wouldn't of heard it. I peeked out the window to see who was coming to our house in the dark.

It was Mr. O'day. I watched Mama run down the steps and give him a big hug. She said Roger left in a huff. He said he wasn't going to stand around and watch me have a sorted affair in front of Dolores.

Mr. O'day said that he would never have guessed that Uncle Roger had a bone in his back. Then he said to Mama Is that what this is? A sorted affair?

Mama laughed. Her laughing was like music, too. Then she kissed Mr. O'day.

April 12, 1961

I asked Cecilia what a sorted affair was. She asked me where I heard that, and I told her what Mama and Mr. O'day said. She told me to stop listening in when other people didn't know I could hear them. She said I should especially not listen in when Mama didn't know I was there. Cecilia said it was very rude and ill-mannered.

The next entry was from Dolores's tenth birthday party, whereat Mr. O'Day presented her with a king-sized stuffed unicorn, *the same color blue as his eyes.* A budding poet, was little Dolores. A thoughtful mother's boyfriend, was Franck. It wasn't a real pony, which is what her little spoiled brat ass had requested, but since she reasoned that she couldn't keep a real pony in her room, anyway, she guessed she liked Mr. O'Day's present well enough.

I skimmed the rest of the year's entries. Mr. O'Day was around a lot, while he and her mother were filming *Manhattan*. Mr. O'Day taught her how to swim in Jessika's pool. Mr. O'Day took her horseback riding. She and Mama and Mr. O'Day went to the beach, went sailing. Mr. O'Day had the bluest eyes, just like the ocean. Dolores and Ruthanne were in agreement on that point, I thought.

Mr. O'Day was there for Thanksgiving dinner – he carved the turkey. Uncle Roger was there for that and he wasn't mad anymore.

That was no doubt because he was already in a fever of unspoken love for his secretary by then, I thought. Still, he was obviously too gutless to do anything about it, else he would've asked Bridget to Thanksgiving dinner at his sister's palatial estate. Or perhaps, he had just not wanted to expose the object of his secret desire to the charms of Franck O'Day.

Christmas arrived. Mr. O'Day gave Dolores a jewelry box, and Mama gave her another big girl dress and another pair of shoes. Whoopee.

Then came New Year's Eve. The night that Franck had dumped Jessika, the same night he'd first laid eyes on Bridget. I was eager to hear what little Dolores, not yet eleven years old, had to say about that.

December 31, 1961

Mama and Mr. O'day went to a New Year's Eve party. I hope that I get to go to a New Year's Eve party soon. Mama said maybe in another few years. Mama was wearing my favorite black dress and her diamond necklace. She was beautiful. Mr. O'day looked very pretty in his tuxedo.

I'll bet he did, I thought. Another point on which Dolores and Ruthanne could agree. What had Ruthie said in her description of Franck's picture? *Is there any icon more enduring, more alluring, that a man in a tuxedo?*

Mama woke me when she came home from the party, because she squeeled the car to a stop in front of the house and slammed the door. Then she slammed the front door too and stomped up the stairs. I could tell she was mad from all the noise she was making. I didn't even peek out of my door. Mama scares me when she's mad.

I went back to sleep. I didn't wake up until I heard Mama yelling downstairs. I heard something crash, then Mama yelling some more. I heard the front door slam again, so I peeked out the window. Mr. O'day walked down the steps. He was still wearing his tuxedo. He got to the bottom and turned around and looked up at the house. I didn't duck quick enough and he saw me in the window. He smiled and waved at me. I waved back. Then he got in his car and drove away.

That's when I heard Mama crying. I'm not afraid of Mama when she's sad, only when she's mad. When she's sad and crying, she always hugs me to her and squeezes me very tight and tells me she loves me.

I snuck out of my room and peeked over the stairs. Mama was sitting about three steps up on the left-hand staircase. She was crying very hard. I walked down and hugged her. She looked up at me, and her eyes were red from crying, and her makeup was running down her face in black lines.

I said What's the bad news, Mama?

She laughed, even though she was still crying. She said The bad news is that Mr. O'day won't be staying with us anymore. And this bad news makes Mama very, very sad. She hugged me to her and started to cry again. She got black streaks on my pajamas.

I asked Why won't Mr. O'day be staying with us anymore, Mama? But she just cried. She didn't tell me why. I was very sad for Mama, so I said the other part, the part she always told me to ask after the bad news.

What's the good news, Mama? Mama said, There isn't any good news, Dolores. Not right now.

Then Mama put me back in bed, and kissed me goodnight. I was very sorry for how sad Mama was and I was sad because I would miss Mr. O'day. He's got the bluest eyes.

OMG, *the humanity,* I thought. It was all so appallingly sad, and Franck was a bastard, but I thought if I had to read *He's got the bluest eyes* one more time, I might scream.

But the Fates took pity on me. Or perhaps Maribeth had gauged correctly just exactly how many childish journal entries I could bear. Because after two blank pages, the next entry was dated April 15, 1965, Dolores Adamson's fourteenth birthday. I would soon discover that she'd morphed from a tiresome, wordy little girl into a tiresome, know-it-all, tragically ironic, wordy teenager. But at least she'd learned a little punctuation, and now her spelling was flawless.

April 15, 1965

I just found this diary in the bottom drawer of my nightstand. I was looking for something else. That's called serendipity, when you find something good or useful when you're looking for something else. Or is it kismet? I can't remember. One or the other. Something we talked about in English last week.

I don't know if finding this journal is either good or useful. When I read it over, I sound like such a stupid little kid. Talking about how beautiful Mom is, and how happy I was with my big-girl dresses.

What I should've been talking about is how good-looking Franck O'Day is.

140

Oh, snap, I thought. *Hot damn, here we go.*

"He's got the bluest eyes" — how many times did I write that? He's got the bluest eyes and the blackest hair and the sweetest smile. I don't know what Mom did to drive him off. It was probably something to do with her terminal bitchiness. But it was a mistake. It was a mistake that I bet she regrets everyday of her life. How could she let him get away?

I read over the last thing I wrote, from that New Year's Eve, the night he left and never came back, at least not to stay with us anymore. It seems like a million years has gone by since then.

Even through my childish innocence, it's clear that it had to have been Mom's fault that he left. I remember Cecilia sweeping up the foyer the next day. What had they argued about? She threw things at him. She screamed. I'd leave, too. Lucky him. He got to leave. I've got to stay with her.

I didn't even see "Mr. O'day" for a while after that New Year's Eve. Then just like that, he was married to someone else. Mom and Uncle Roger and I, we all went to the wedding. I remember that the bride was beautiful. I don't remember too much else, but in retrospect, I'd be willing to bet that the groom was scrumptious.

I also remember being scared to death at one point, at the reception. Mom was standing there, holding my hand, and that English director guy stood up and made some kind of a toast. I don't remember what he said. But whatever it was, it sure pissed Mom off. Her face didn't change, but she was holding my hand, and she squeezed it until I thought she would break my fingers. She didn't let go until that English guy sat back down, and I said, "Ow!"

But we're all one big happy family now. We hang out. Franck and Bridget and Maribeth come over here sometimes. Mom and Uncle Roger and I go over there sometimes. I look after Maribeth sometimes. She's an adorable little kid, but she can be a little brat, too.

I'm not a little kid anymore. I can see how my mom looks at Franck, when she thinks no one knows she's looking. And I remember how it was, before he married Bridget. I remember how he practically lived here with us, how I would always catch him and Mom kissing.

Speaking of kissing, I guess I should record for posterity that I had my first kiss yesterday. Kevin Flaherty told me he had something he wanted to show me on the side of the music building. Like a dummy, I followed him. As soon as we got around the corner, Kevin declared, "I love you, Dolores!" and pinned me to the wall with his mouth. I was surprised at first, a little scared, but after a second, it was all right. After a few more seconds, I discovered I like kissing Kevin Flaherty just fine. Finally he stopped kissing me, and told me happy birthday. I said thanks. We kissed some more. Yes, I like Kevin Flaherty just fine. He's got the bluest eyes.

But he ain't no Franck O'Day.

Somehow, I'd failed to notice how attractive Franck is, until just last week. Maybe it's because I'd always been a kid before. When the accident happened last week, I was acting like a kid. But I'm not a kid anymore. I was chasing Maribeth around the pool, and I slipped, and busted my knee open. It positively squirted blood. A big drop fell on Mom on the lounge chair.

Everybody froze. Mom, Uncle Roger, Bridget. Even Maribeth stopped yapping for a second. I'm screaming. I'm bleeding to death, right there by the pool, and nobody's moving.

Except Franck.

In a heartbeat, he scooped me off the ground and carried me out to the car. He kissed me on the forehead, told me I'd be all right. He called back to the rest of them – they were just making it out to the top of the steps – he called out to them to follow in another car, this was an emergency! He was taking me to the hospital immediately.

When we arrived, Franck carried me out of the car and into the emergency room. He was so strong, and he smelled so good. I thought, this man could've been my dad, should've been my dad, if my mother wasn't such an utter bitch. If my mother hadn't driven him away.

Anyway, Franck burst through the door to the emergency room, still carrying me, demanding to see a doctor at once. Couldn't they see that they had ~~an emergency~~ a crisis on their hands here? Hospital personnel scattered before him.

They showed us to an examining room, and Franck set me gently down on the table. He held my hand, and told me I was going to be all right. Then – still holding my hand – he looked down at my knee. Blood was caked, it still oozed. I was still crying.

"It doesn't look so bad," Franck said. Then he looked up and smiled at me. "I guess you're too old for me to kiss it better, huh?" He kissed me on the forehead again, instead, and squeezed my hand.

It was at that moment, ladies and gentlemen, that I realized that I was in love with Franck O'Day. I'd never seen just how incredibly beautiful he really is until that very second. How entirely perfect he is, and how utterly stupid my mother is for letting him get away.

But on the other hand, I'm grateful for her stupidity. If she hadn't driven him away, then he might've wound up being my dad. And now I don't feel very daughterly to him. So it's just as well that he doesn't live here anymore. I might not be able to help myself.

Today is my fourteenth birthday, and all I want is for Franck to kiss me. Just like Kevin Flaherty did!

Later

> *It was really nice of Franck to come to my birthday party, even if he didn't kiss me. But he did give me a copy of "The Rolling Stones, Now!" which just came out in February. I love him! He's so cool!*
>
> *Kevin came to my birthday party, too, and he stayed long after Franck and Bridget took Maribeth and went home. He stayed later than everybody. Kevin kissed me, even if Franck did not find the opportunity to do so, and I liked it just as much as the first time.*
>
> *But I wasn't thinking about Kevin when I was kissing him, however. He asked me to be his girlfriend, and I guess I will. Franck's not free right now. Bridget is the luckiest woman in the world!*
>
> *Maybe it won't last. Maybe Bridget'll drive him away, just like my stupid mother did. But in the meantime, I guess I can be Kevin's girlfriend. He'll never know who I'm thinking about when I'm kissing him.*

OMG, the little tramp! I thought. But not really. I recalled that first time I'd come to understand embarrassment, and it made me speculate that it was at just this age, at fourteen, that a girl's burgeoning sexuality first makes itself apparent to her. It had to be at just about fourteen when a girl starts noticing boys – and then she starts to formulate plans about what she wants to do about all that. Sometimes in writing. Even though she has not the remotest clue as to what she's talking about.

Witness Dolores's claims of not being sure if she could control herself if then thirty-two-year-old Franck still lived with her. I'm sure she believed it with all her heart. I'm sure she felt it in all the places where she'd just begun to feel things. But at fourteen, it was all still romance, still all in her head. It wasn't like she was going to climb up into his lap and seductively call him *Daddy,* like she might've done at sixteen, or eighteen.

I was absolutely sure of all this, because when I was just the same age as Dolores, I'd done the exact same thing. I'd poured out my heart to my diary about Mr. King, my English teacher. He was so poetic, and he was so beautiful – his eyes were so warm and sparkly and brown, I wrote.

I wondered if his mustache would tickle when I kissed him. I knew he would be surprised when I just marched up to his desk and planted one on him, but I was also sure that he'd like it, and would immediately kiss me back. I wondered how long it would take him to divorce his wife so that we could run away together.

I wondered and knew and was sure of all these things in black and white, in writing, in a diary not unlike Dolores'. I kept it under my pillow. One day, I returned home from school, eager to write down more about how much I wanted to kiss Mr. King, about how much I knew Mr. King was going to like kissing me right back.

There was a Post-It Note over the last such entry. It read: *You shouldn't be writing things like this about your teacher, Carolyn. Mr. King could get in a lot of trouble if someone read this and thought that it was actually happening. Besides, how would you feel if he read it? How would you feel if his wife read it?*

Cue the embarrassment.

My mom hadn't signed the note, but I knew it was from her. I suddenly felt like the little girl I still was – sure, I'd written all those things, and I'd felt them, and I thought about them all the time. But the idea of actually putting any of them into action had not even crossed my mind. The manner in which I might even begin to go about putting them into action had not crossed my mind, because I was only fourteen years old, and I didn't know anything about the reality of such things yet. I didn't even have the experience Dolores had – no Kevin Flaherty had yet kissed me. I didn't know anything about anything, yet. But I'd taken the first step, as Dolores had, as we all did – I was thinking about it.

And the idea of Mr. King ever reading what I'd written was just too horrible to even be contemplated. For him to ever know how I felt – or his wife? I couldn't even entertain the idea for more than a few minutes without breaking out into the oft-mentioned cold sweat.

Immediately after my mother's terse advice, I switched from writing journals to writing fiction. And my prose was just as purple and over-blown as Dolores's excited, exaggerated tale of her mad dash to the emergency room, chivalrously carried as she was by her shining hero. And I wrote about how much people sometimes wanted to kiss other people, and about how sometimes people did kiss other people. But I didn't name names, and I was so petrified that someone might see through to who I was actually talking about, that I always made my princes and princesses in some far off land. And I always made them the same age.

So I knew that Dolores's robust claims of love and lust for Franck were just the innocent ramblings of a young girl feeling her oats for the very first time. And that wasn't even accurate – she wasn't feeling them quite yet. She was just discovering that they were there, and was writing about what she thought she might like to do now that she'd discovered them.

But she had no idea what *not being able to stop herself* meant. Not the foggiest. Not yet.

There were a few more entries for May and June. Dolores decided that she didn't want to kiss Kevin Flaherty anymore, after someone told

144

her that they'd seen ol' Kevin out beside the music building, kissing someone else. She decided courageously to save her kisses for Franck.

Then came the entry dated Friday, July 16th, 1965, the day after the murder-suicide.

Words cannot express the sadness I feel for those left behind in the wake of this tragedy. I cannot grieve so much for Bridget — she's gone on to a better place. And I certainly can't grieve for Uncle Roger — he had to have been possessed by some devil to do what he did, and I'm confident that he's now where he belongs, right alongside that devil.

Mom has lost her only living relative besides me. When I saw Maribeth's curly red head, I just wanted to hug her and hold her to me forever. Franck looks lost, haunted. I would like to just cradle him in my arms and cry with him.

July 20, 1965

Bridget's funeral was today. It was so sad. Mom started to squeeze my hand really hard again, when Franck said he was going back to the hotel with that English guy. But then she just stopped, and we left and came back to the house.

Maribeth's 10. She's old enough, but just barely, I think, to understand that her mother isn't ever coming home. She seems to be in shock about the whole thing. She'll cry for a minute, then she'll seem to be thinking it all over, trying to understand. Then she'll cry for a while again.

Franck was gone for a few hours. Then he returned and gathered Maribeth up and left. He didn't even really say goodbye to me. He just sort of nodded and left. He's so sad. He's even beautiful when he's sad.

Mom just sat out on the terrace for the rest of the day, and stared at the pool. I tried to talk to her a couple times, but she just kind of waved me off. I guess she's sad, too. We all are.

Again I skimmed. Dolores had learned where to put her commas and her quotation marks a little bit better; but her diary was still pretty boring. Franck was beautiful, she loved him so much, he had the bluest eyes, blah, blah, blah.

She found a new boy to kiss, one Dean Sands. Surprise, surprise, young Master Dean looked — to Dolores at least — just like a teenaged Franck O'Day, black-haired and of course, blue-eyed.

I reflected that while there was only one Franck — *there can be only one!* I thought, and giggled. While there was only one Franck, he'd sure had more than his share of look-alikes over the decades. There was this Dean kid. And of course, Marty. *Will the real Slim Shady please stand up?*

But then the idea struck me that perhaps the resemblance was all in the eye of the beholder, and I wondered how many black-haired, blue-eyed young friends Bobby Ecksmith had entertained back in the day. Because all dark-haired, blue-eyed men don't look like Franck. But they look more like Franck then blondes and gingers. Sometimes, I thought, all it takes is a little imagination.

Dolores dutifully made note of each of Maribeth and Franck's visits through the rest of 1965, mooning over him each time. I noticed that the confident tone of lust, completely ignorant of real life that it was, slowly gave way to a more impossibly romantic, yearning tone.

Her greatest triumph was when she was able to trap him under the mistletoe at Christmastime. She had schemed and planned and dreamed about that one for weeks, the purple prose practically bleeding off the page.

But Franck, unknowingly, was just as much of a spoilsport to the daughter as he had frequently been to the mother. Unlike the passionate smooch she'd so thoroughly anticipated, Franck had just kissed her quickly on the forehead, as was his fatherly wont.

Dolores was undaunted. Jessika allowed her to stay up and attend her very first grown-up New Year's Eve party that year. Dolores detailed how she began stalking Franck about ten o'clock, angling for that kiss at midnight.

> *I'd managed to be standing right there next to him when the counting began. Ten-nine-eight . . . the countdown would get to one, and everyone would scream, "Happy New Year!" and he'd look around for someone to kiss, and I'd step up, and he would kiss me. That was the plan.*
>
> *He'd kiss me, and I'd kiss him back and I'd whisper, "I love you, Franck!"*
>
> *And he'd say, "And I love you, Lori." And then he'd pick me up, like that time when I busted my knee, and he'd carry me upstairs.*

And then what? I thought with amusement. I was sure that the *and then what* was just as fuzzy to Dolores at fourteen, as it'd been to me at the same age. But, I recalled, that didn't make the yearning, the desire, any less real. I'd loved Mr. King completely, to the height and depth and breadth of my little girl's soul.

Ignorance didn't make the anticipation any less deliciously unbearable. Not knowing exactly what it was you wanted so badly didn't make you want it any less. Not being completely sure what was going to happen next, still made you long for it to happen as quickly as possible.

Seven-six-five . . . Franck turned and smiled at me. It was going to happen, he was going to kiss me . . . four-three-two . . .

And then my mother appeared out of nowhere and jumped roughly into his arms. He seemed a little jostled by her, like he'd just as soon have dropped her as caught her, seeing as she'd just jumped out of nowhere and surprised him.

But then she was kissing him, one arm wrapped around his neck, the other red-taloned hand holding onto the side of his face. Mom made a loud "Mmmm" sound and kissed him like she was kissing him for the first time.

So I didn't get to kiss Franck at midnight because my mother barged right on in. My only satisfaction of the entire evening was when I noticed that Franck really didn't kiss Mom back at all. He just more or less stood there and allowed himself to be kissed.

She'd jumped on him from out of nowhere at the last possible second, and he'd only caught her out of reflex. I'm sure he would've caught me, too, if I would've thought to just leap into his arms. How undignified she can be sometimes! What else could he do, but stand there and let her kiss him?

January 12, 1966

We were driving down Sunset today, and I saw the Chateau Marmont up on the hill, emerging out of the greenery like a fairy castle in the clouds. My prince is there, in that castle, I thought. My beautiful, blue-eyed prince.

Dolores was somewhat of a one-trick pony, I thought again, something of a harper upon just the one string. I wasn't sure if I was going to be able to use any of these syrupy adolescent musings in the book. Yes, Jessika's daughter had certainly had a major league crush on Franck when she was only fourteen. But by the evidence of her own diary, her love was entirely unspoken. If Franck had looked at her twice, or anything else, I knew that it would've been gleefully recorded herein.

Valentine's Day, 1966

We had a very nice dinner — the house looked beautiful. Valentine's Day is Mom's favorite, and she always has it decorated in all the pinks and reds in the world. She and I wore almost matching pink gowns, and Maribeth wore an adorable red dress with pink and white hearts on it. Still, I thought it was a little young on her. She is almost eleven.

I like Maribeth very much. She used to be something of a yappy little brat. But she's turned into a calm, thoughtful child, ever since her Mom died.

Franck wore a dark suit and a blue tie. It wasn't a tux, but I guess he can't wear a tux to every single occasion, now can he? He was still devastating.

147

Mom saved the very best for last. "I've got some good news and some bad news, Dolores," she said. "What do you want to hear first?"

"The bad news," I said, as I'd been taught to say.

"The bad news is that you're going to have to share your bedroom with Maribeth for a few days, while I have the back corner bedroom painted.

"The good news is – Franck and Maribeth will be staying with us for a while! Starting today!" Mom smiled, giggled – she couldn't hide her happiness. The bright, glorious smile the world knows from her movies had nothing on this.

Mom's joy could not even begin to equal mine, however. Franck was going to be back, living in the same house with me! All my prayers had been answered!

I looked at him. He didn't look all that happy. I couldn't blame him – I wouldn't want to come back and live with Mom, if I ever got to escape from her.

"Just for a little while," he said. "We might be going to England."

There were a few more entries, covering the moving in of Maribeth and Franck. I learned what the sleeping arrangements had been, all those forgotten decades ago.

The room that I now occupied had been Jessika's. She had been connected via a bathroom to Franck's room, which was where he lived now, once more. Maribeth was in the room across the hall from me, which she had also taken back when they moved in here again. Maribeth's room was also connected by a bathroom to what had been Lori's bedroom. This room had been assigned to Ruthanne, and I guessed that she would be seeing very little of it, unless the Fates were extremely unkind. This room was separated from Franck's by the balcony on the front of the house.

There were more descriptions of Franck's beauty, more recitals of Dolores's undying love for him. I stifled a yawn.

Then there was an entry for her fifteenth birthday. The party had been great, Mom had let her taste champagne for the first time. Franck had admired her dress. They had shared a brief, glorious dance, a happy birthday hug.

Shit. I'd read through all the wearisome outpourings, the laying bare of the romantic soul of a teenage girl with a crush on her mother's boyfriend. The critical fourteenth year, the period when the transgressions were alleged to have occurred had passed. She'd turned fifteen now, and not a damn thing of any kind of shocking note had occurred. Somehow I hadn't expected anything, but I still felt a little cheated at the amount of time I'd wasted reading her tiresome diary. Time, as they say about bad movies, that I could never get back.

So far, Franck's estimation of their relationship rang true. Although I couldn't believe that he wasn't aware that Lori was more than just *fond* of him. After all, he'd been seeing that look in the eyes of men and women alike, since he was thirteen years old. But maybe he had his hands too full with Jessika to notice. Maybe Dolores just hid it exceptionally well.

I plunged on. I'd come too far to quit now. Mercifully, at fifteen, Dolores didn't have as much time for her diary as she'd had in previous years. She still made a lot of entries, but they were, with a few exceptions, generally much briefer than her previous short-story length accounts. 1966 progressed. Dolores kissed another boy. School let out in June. The four of them spent the 4th of July in San Diego. School took back up in September.

The central thread throughout the whole year was Franck's melancholy. Dolores sighed over it, felt deeply for him. He seemed so sad, and she longed to comfort him. She noted that he seldom left the house, sat around the pool, drank a lot, took frequent naps. Throughout it all, Dolores loved him still. She never took his sadness personally – she often said that living with Jessika would make anybody sad.

Then, at the height of summer, love-sick, fifteen-year-old Dolores acted.

August 27, 1966

Mom took Maribeth shopping. I didn't want to go, because Franck was upstairs sleeping, and I thought he might wake up, and then I'd have him all to myself.

After they left, I went upstairs to check on him. The door to his room was open, so I tiptoed inside. He always leaves the door to his room open when he naps. Napping wasn't the same as sleeping, he always said. He just laid down with his clothes on sometimes, he said. Just call him if I needed him, he said.

He was sleeping on his back when I snuck in, one arm thrown out to the side. He was still dressed, wearing jeans and an undershirt.

I thought that I needed him right then. Nobody was home but us – Mom had taken Cecilia along to help with the shopping.

So I climbed into the bed with Franck, snuggled right up next to him. I wanted to see what it was like. My mom got to snuggle up next to him – why couldn't I? It would just be for a minute. No one was home. No one would know, not even Franck. He was sound asleep.

I curled up next to him for just a second, with my back against his side, and my head beneath his outstretched arm. I held my breath, and just stayed there next to him for a second, listening to him breathe.

Then the scariest, most wonderful thing happened. Franck rolled over in his sleep. He threw his arm over my waist. I could feel his breath, warm and even. I could feel his heartbeat against my back.

I thought I must've died, because I was surely in heaven.

It seemed like I lay there for an eternity, curled up next to Franck, with his arm around me. I wanted to stay there all afternoon. I wanted to stay there forever. I wanted to drift off to sleep in Franck's arms and never wake up.

Then I heard the door slam downstairs. I could've panicked. I could've froze. But I'm too smart for that. I just carefully slid out from under Franck's wonderfully encircling arm and slowly slid out of the bed. I paused to look at him — he was so beautiful. He looked like a sleeping angel.

I tiptoed out of Franck's room and hot-footed it down the hall to my own. I jumped on my bed and picked up the nearest thing. It was a copy of Vogue.

I opened it and pretended to be reading it. I discovered that it was upside down, so I quickly turned it around, just as Maribeth came running up the stairs and into my room. She was all excited to show me all the stuff that they'd just bought.

But I told her that I wasn't feeling very well, and was going to take a nap. "Go wake up your daddy," I told her. "And shut the door on your way out."

Waking up Daddy was still fun for Maribeth, and she ran out of the room without argument, closing the door behind her.

I curled up on my bed and closed my eyes, wanting to just lie there and relive the incredibleness of what had just happened. After a minute, I took my shirt off and buried my nose in it, because it smelled like Franck, from where his chest had been pressed up against my back. It was the most delicious smell in the world.

Well, I'll be a son-of-a-bitch, I thought. Dolores was turning out to be a lot gutsier in the pursuit of her desire than I would've predicted from the previous entries in her diary. She'd seemed to be the typical yearn-from-afar kind of teen, the same as I'd been.

Now I thought I could see how it'd been possible for her to keep the longing out of her eyes — maybe Franck was telling the truth, and he hadn't seen it there. Maybe Dolores was adept at keeping it hidden because she was a little schemer.

It was turning out that Dolores was quite the go-getter, after all. Finally, things were starting to get interesting.

September 26, 1966

They're taking Maribeth away from us. She's leaving in the morning, and she'll never be coming back. They're taking her to Iowa or Kansas or somewhere.

I am devastated.

I knew that Maribeth's real dad was in town. He's been here for a while, I think, or maybe he left and came back a few times. I know Maribeth's even been to see him a few times. I even knew that Franck had been to court once or twice.

But no one told me that her real dad was trying to take her away from us. No one had the courtesy to treat me like an adult and inform me of this Damoclean sword hanging over our heads. Maybe then, I could've prepared myself a little bit. I could've tried to figure out how I would cope with losing my little sister. I would've been nicer to her, hugged her more often.

I hate Mom for keeping me in the dark. How <u>could she</u> not tell me that this was going to happen?

Franck is devastated. It's like a replay of how it was after Bridget died. Since they came back from court this afternoon, he's just been rocking Maribeth in the rocking chair in her room. Maribeth's sitting in his lap, dry-eyed and silent. Maybe she doesn't understand. She's really too big to be sitting in his lap and the rocking chair is squeaking extra loudly from the weight of both of them. But he used to rock her when she was little, and I guess it's some kind of a comfort to her.

Mom seems to realize for once that she should just leave them alone. There's nothing that she can do now, and it's best if she just lets them be alone for the few hours they have left together.

She's out sitting by the pool. I tried to talk to her, but she brushed me off again, just like she did after Bridget's funeral.

If Dolores saw Franck's mood as melancholy before, he was downright depressed after Peter McSwale took Maribeth back to Kansas. He continued to mope around the house, drink, and sleep.

Jessika went to a costume party on Halloween without him. Dolores noted that she was costumed as a she-Devil, complete with horns and tail and pitchfork. Dolores commented that the outfit was perfect for her mother. *It's a true and accurate outward expression of the inner her,* Dolores wrote, her poesy on full display.

It seemed to me that Dolores was feeling the natural friction that occurs between mother and daughter during the adolescent years a little more keenly than most girls her age. I reasoned that this was undoubtedly because most teenage girls don't want to do their mother's boyfriends quite as desperately as Dolores did. That little unnatural catalyst only added to the mix of tension common at such a time in a young girl's life. Or maybe Dolores just truly hated her mother. It happens.

Thanksgiving dinner was sad and depressing, Dolores reported. Franck missed Maribeth terribly. He had three mint juleps with dinner, she noted, then went up to his room and passed out before eight o'clock.

Dolores wrote at length about the nobility of Franck's sadness at the loss of Maribeth, and how she empathized so much with his pain. She mentioned peeping in his door and watching him nap, even sneaking in and sitting in a chair in the corner of the room to watch him on one occasion. He was so beautiful, so angelic, yet still so troubled, even in sleep. Dolores longed to comfort him.

December 16, 1966

Mom took Cecilia with her to go Christmas shopping. I told her that I was tired, and that I would go next time. Franck was upstairs napping again so I tiptoed into his room. I love to watch him sleep.

He was lying on his side, facing away from the edge of the bed, so I couldn't really see his face. He was again wearing a pair of jeans and an undershirt.

I feel so sorry for him. I know Christmas is going to be tough this year, because Maribeth is gone.

I wanted to be near Franck again, so I could hold him, so I could comfort him while he slept. It would be easy, just like the last time. No one would ever know.

So I just wriggled in there next to him, under his arm, facing him this time. I laid my head on his chest, just under his chin. I held my breath and listened to his heartbeat, listened to him breathe, smelled him. It was heavenly.

But it was also a little awkward, too. I found that it's a little difficult to snuggle up face to face with someone when they're sleeping. I didn't know where to put my arms.

I must've wiggled around too much, because all of sudden Franck put his hand on the side of my face. He said, "Jess, I don't really want to —"

I looked up and he looked down and saw that it was me, and not Mom. He was stock still for a second, just looking at me. Then he said, "Lori. What are you doing?"

Apparently Franck wasn't one to panic either, I thought. I imagined that most men his age would've leapt up immediately if they awakened to find their girlfriend's fifteen-year-old daughter all cozied up in bed with them. They might have leapt up and immediately climbed the wall, just to get away from her.

But not Franck. He didn't freak out, didn't immediately try to get as far away from this definition of jailbait as possible. He didn't move. He just calmly asked her what she was doing. The thought crossed my mind that perhaps this was not Franck's first rodeo – perhaps he'd awakened to find underage girls in his bed before.

Funny how he hadn't mentioned *this* episode.

I said, "I just wanted to give you a hug. You've been so sad, lately."

He slowly took his arm from around me. He slowly sat up, then slowly stood up. His shirt was lying on the chair. He picked it up his threw it on. Then he turned around and looked at me. He said, "Get out of my bed, Lori." But he didn't even seem mad.

I did what he said. He sat back down on the corner of the bed, and ran his hand through his hair. He sighed. Then he looked up at me. "Tell me again what you were doing?"

"I just wanted to hug you, Franck," I said, and took a step toward him. He held up both hands as if to ward me off, and I took a step back.

He looked up at me for a second, like he was trying to decide what to say. He looked a little embarrassed. Finally, he said, "You can't be climbing in bed with me when I'm asleep just because you want to give me a hug, Lori." He paused, like he still didn't quite know what to say. "You're too old for that. And . . . and you're way too young for that. Hasn't your mother talked to you about —?"

"I'm not a child, Franck," I told him, and again stepped forward. He again held up his hands, and made a little pushing gesture. I stepped back again.

"If you want to give me a hug, Lori, you have to do it while I'm awake," he said. "While I'm standing up. You can't just be crawling into bed with me." He ran his hand through his hair again, covered his face for a second. Then he looked up at me again. He said, "You're fifteen years old, for Christ's sake. It's just wrong. Promise me you'll never do anything like this again."

"Is it wrong because you love my mother?"

Franck looked at me and blinked. He said, "What?"

Now that it was out in the open, now that he'd caught me, I found new courage. I was prepared to declare my love to him and to the whole world. I'm not afraid of them, and I'm certainly not afraid of him. I love him. If I told him, if he knew how much I loved him, I knew he'd protect me from Mom. Because I _am_ afraid of her. But I knew I had to tell him, first. I had to speak up. He couldn't read my mind.

"I said, is it wrong for me to crawl into bed with you because you're in love with my mother?"

"I'm not in love with —" he began, then stopped. He ran his hand over his face, then started over. "It's wrong because you're fifteen, Lori. I'm old enough to be your father —"

"But you're not my father," I said. I leaned forward a little, and was going to take a step toward him, but he held his hand up again before I could.

He shook his head. "It doesn't matter. You're only fifteen. It's not allowed."

Something dawned on me then, something wonderful. I decided that it wasn't necessary to declare my love. Instead, I said, "I'm sorry, Franck. You just seem so sad. I promise that I'll never do it again. Will you forgive me?"

153

Now he smiled at me, just a little bit, like he might be trying not to smile, but wasn't succeeding. He said, "I forgive you. Now get the hell out of here."

I skipped toward the door to his room, standing open as it always was. I turned back and said, "Promise me you won't tell Mom?"

He rolled his eyes and smiled all the way this time. "Cross my heart and hope to die, I won't tell Mom."

"Thanks," I said.

Franck stood up and walked to the door. "I don't want you to think you're not allowed to hug me anymore, Lori," he said. "Just do it when I'm awake, okay?" And then he hugged me, to prove it was still allowed.

I hugged him back. He smelled so good. "Okay," I said, and skipped back to my room.

I'm so happy. I've never been so happy in my life. Why am I so happy, after Franck ran me out of his room and told me to never crawl in bed with him again?

I'm happy because he said he didn't love Mom. He didn't actually say it, but he started to say it. He said that it was wrong for me to be in bed with him because I'm only fifteen. Not because he was in love with Mom.

Well, I won't be fifteen forever.

My mom is a bitch, and Franck knows it. I see how annoyed he gets with her sometimes. I know that she'll drive him away again, eventually. It's inevitable. They're wrong for each other. And when she drives him away again, I'll be waiting for him. He'll come to me, then, because he'll finally be tired of her. I can tell he's getting tired of her already.

And I won't be only fifteen then.

This had to be the bombshell that Maribeth had wanted me to uncover. Still, I thought it was a dud. Unexplosive.

I tried to give Franck, and the tale as he'd related it to us, the benefit of the doubt. Most men are basically civilized, and would not even consider a fifteen-year-old girl, even one that crawled into bed with them, and I tried to look at him as one of those. Maybe this incident was what he was referring to when he'd said that, as she got older, Dolores had *started to seek affection from him.* Maybe this episode, to him, was just one more of those opportunities to hug him, one of those opportunities that he said Dolores made sure not to pass up.

Perhaps it was all explosive and revealing, but only to Maribeth. Maybe Franck hadn't told us about it because it hadn't seemed that big a deal to him.

I thought that he'd handled this delicate situation expertly. A trained psychologist couldn't have trod the tricky minefield of young Dolores's ego and psyche and teenage self-esteem any better. He didn't tell her that he didn't want her. He didn't tell her that she was a bad girl. He didn't even say that what she'd done was wrong in and of itself – it was only wrong because it was not allowed, because she was only fifteen years old.

As far as I could see, the version of their relationship that Franck had related was true, if a little vague on a few of the chapters. He remained innocent of any wrongdoing, in my eyes. Not a jury in the world would've convicted him.

Dolores's diary briefly mentioned Thanksgiving and Christmas. Franck was still sad. Apparently he didn't treat her any differently than he had before their little encounter, or I was sure she would've mentioned it, for better or for worse. So perhaps it had meant nothing to him.

Franck and Jessika went out on New Year's Eve. Dolores attended a soiree thrown by one of her school chums. She kissed a new boy at midnight. She was growing up.

The January 4th, 1967 entry found Dolores rejoicing for the change in Franck's mood. Shooting was slated to begin again on some movie he and Jessika had been working on before Bridget's murder. Even Dolores didn't mention it by name. I thought *Two Green Keys* had been doomed, cursed indeed, destined to be forgotten, from the very start.

February 3, 1967

I can't think of any other way to say it, so I'm just going to say it. Mom just told me that I was going to have a little brother or sister. She said it just like that, like I'm six years old, instead of almost sixteen. Like I'm ignorant as to where babies come from. As if I don't know what she and Franck do.

And the bad news is, she and Franck are going to be getting married.

I had to be very careful when Mom told me that. A big bright bolt of anger shot through me – she's trapping him. He doesn't want a baby. He's not over losing Maribeth yet.

He's just getting back to making movies again. He's happy again. He doesn't want this. He doesn't want her.

But I couldn't let Mom know I was anything other than ecstatic for her. Any other reaction might make her suspicious. So I gave her a big hug and said congratulations.

I could easily fake being happy for her. Why shouldn't I be happy? If Franck marries her, he'll be around a while longer. And they can always get a divorce. It happens every day.

Still, I had to know what Franck thought about it. I knew I'd be able to tell his feelings by just one look. For an actor, he's got a very open face. He doesn't hide his feelings well. I can always read him.

How we do delude ourselves, I thought. Dolores thought she could read Franck's face. Franck, consummate actor that he was, had *a very open face.*

Right. I thought Lori could only read what it was she wanted to see there, and nothing more.

I waited for him to come home from the studio. I sat halfway down the steps, so that when he got out of the car we would be eye to eye. When he finally showed up, the sun was starting to go down. He got out of the car, looked at me solemnly, maybe a little curiously, over its roof. The sunset's golden rays were like a fiery nimbus around his black hair.

I returned his solemn look, then said, "Congratulations . . . Daddy."

He gave me that little smile that I love so much – this time it was tempered with a little bit of embarrassment. As I knew it would, his expression told me everything. He didn't love Mom any more than he ever had – he loved her maybe a little less for trapping him like this.

He shrugged. "What are ya gonna do?" his expression said. He didn't like being trapped, but he wasn't resentful. At least not yet, or at least not much. The wedding, the baby – they were still all a long way off. Who knew what might happen in the meantime?

I stood up, and he put his arm lightly around my shoulder, gave me a little hug. We walked up the steps together. He paused before the front door and took a deep breath.

"I believe this is what they call going to hell in a hand basket," I said.

Franck hung his head for a minute, looked at the ground, exhaled. Then he cocked his head to one side and smiled at me. He said, "When did you get so smart?"

I shrugged and we walked in the house.

"I got smart that day when I fell and busted my knee open," I wanted to tell him. "That was the day that I fell in love with you," I wanted to say. But I was still only fifteen (almost sixteen), and I knew that it wasn't allowed. Not yet. So I didn't say anything.

Valentine's Day, 1967

Mom threw an enormous party. All her friends were here, as well as all the studio people and the press, too. It was all in honor of her big announcement. She and Franck were engaged! Oh, raptures of joy!

156

No date for the actual nuptials was announced, however. And that was because Franck's still trying to figure some way out of marrying Mom, I think.

March 25, 1967

I overheard Franck on the phone. He was out on the terrace, and I was just inside the house where he couldn't see me. I wasn't intending to eavesdrop. Cecilia has been telling me how rude that is, all my life. I was just watching Franck. I like to watch him. I like to stand back and look at him for a few minutes. I was going to go out and talk to him. But I just wanted to look at him for a few minutes first.

I know he was talking to that English director guy, because he said, "Oh, for Christ's sake, Bobby, will you shut up for one minute and let me talk?" Franck held the phone away from his ear - there was a noise coming from the other end that sounded like little dogs barking. "Are you done?" he said. "Look. You remember how Loretta Young played it in the thirties? Maybe we'll be coming to England for a visit after all." The little dogs barked on the other end.

"Actually, Jess said something about Germany. Then she can come back with a little adopted German Madchen oder Junge. There are lots of dark-haired, blue-eyed Germans, are there not? Besides, maybe it won't look like me. Maybe it'll look like her."

Bobby spoke from across the ocean. I couldn't hear what he said.

"I know nobody's gonna buy, it Bobby. Who cares? This way, we won't have to get married till next year sometime."

Or maybe not at all, I thought.

Franck sipped his drink, then changed the subject. "How's your latest coming along?"

I went back into the house. Movie-talk always bores me. But it made me happy to hear that Franck was still in no hurry to marry Mom. No hurry at all.

Dolores's sweet sixteenth birthday party was a big hit. Jessika let her drink a half a glass of champagne, and at Franck's suggestion, she was allowed to drive the Jag from one end of the driveway to the other. A magician performed. Franck didn't wear a tux, but still looked scrumptious. Yawn.

April 30, 1967

Mom threw a surprise birthday party for Franck. He'd been at the studio all day, and seemed a little annoyed when everybody jumped out and yelled, "Surprise!" when he walked in the front door. I heard him say, under his breath, "Jesus Christ, Jess, you know how much I hate surprises." But he smiled and shook peoples' hands and thanked them for coming. He didn't let anybody see how annoyed he was.

Then, out of the blue, that English director guy showed up. Bobby. Franck's friend. Now here was a surprise Franck liked. I've never seen him so happy.

Bobby kissed my hand and told me that I looked "ravishing." I like the way he talks.

Mom frowned when he complimented me. I think that she's jealous of how happy it made Franck that he was there. I like him very much. He's Franck's best friend, and any friend of Franck's is a friend of mine. He even snuck me a glass of champagne.

Then, disaster struck.

It was getting late, and I was just about to go to bed. All the guests had already left, except for Bobby. I think he might've still been out by the pool. Mom and I were in the living room. She was sitting on the couch, and I was sitting in a chair close to the door. Then Franck came in by himself.

"Did you put the world's most boorish British fag in a cab?" Mom asked. "I hope they drive him off a cliff." Always a lady, that's my mom.

Franck grinned. "I put him in Maribeth's . . . in the spare bedroom. I told him he could stay with us for as long as he likes."

Mom stood up, put her hands on her hips. Her face turned red and she screamed, "Are you out of your mind? That son-of-a-bitch isn't staying in my house!"

"Then we'll just go to the Marmont, Jess," Franck said without hesitation, and turned to leave.

Mom picked up a vase from the coffee table and hurled it at him. Of course, she missed. She wouldn't dare to really hit Franck with a vase. It struck the wall inches from my head, and a piece of glass flew off and cut my cheek. It's not a deep cut, but I started to cry. I couldn't help it. The sound and the sudden pain surprised me, plus I realized that Franck was going to leave us again, to go with his friend, just because Mom was being a jealous bitch.

"You're not going anywhere," Mom said. Her face was a furious mask. Not what the paying moviegoers ever get to see. But I get to see it all the time. Anytime she's mad.

Franck turned and looked back at her. "You just watch me," he said, not even raising his voice. He turned toward the telephone, then noticed me crying. He saw the blood on my face. He glared at Mom, then took me into the bathroom.

He wet a washcloth and gently wiped my face. I couldn't stop crying, because he was going to leave me. "There's no glass in it." He kissed me on the forehead. "It's nothing. You're all right." He looked at me searchingly for a second. He's got the bluest eyes. "You are all right, aren't you?" I nodded, and tried to stop crying.

Mom appeared in the bathroom doorway. "I'm sorry, Franck." She touched his shoulder, but he flinched away from her hand. "Of course Bobby can stay. He's your friend, after all. And it is your birthday."

Franck ignored her and said to me, "Are you sure you're okay, Lori?" I nodded again, and stopped crying. I was okay now. He wasn't leaving.

"Go on up to bed, then," he told me.

I wanted to hug him, to tell him how glad I was that he wasn't leaving. But I didn't dare do it in front of Mom. I squeezed past her. She didn't even look at me. I ran upstairs.

I was so relieved that Franck wasn't leaving, that it took me a few minutes to realize that Mom hadn't told <u>me</u> she was sorry for busting that vase next to my head, or for cutting my face.

July 2, 1967

I was staying at Cindy's house for a few days, but I'm home now. She's back from boarding school, and it was great to see her. It was also great to get away from Mom. She's put on about twenty pounds, and that's making her bitchy, and the fact that Bobby's still here is making her bitchier.

She called Cindy's mom this morning with the bad news. Cindy's mom said, "Oh, Jessika! I'm so sorry to hear that! Are you all right?"

I heard Mom's voice say my name, and Cindy's mom handed me the phone. Mom told me that she was at the Beverly. That English fag had pushed her into the pool, or something, and it had caused her to lose the baby. She didn't sound sad at all, just furious.

I thought it was all supposed to be a big secret that she was even pregnant, yet here she was telling Cindy's mom that she'd lost the baby that nobody was supposed to know that she was even going to have. I guess it doesn't matter now.

I told her that I was sorry about the baby. She brushed off my condolences and told me that she was going to go over to Catalina for the 4th, because she couldn't stand to be in the same house with Bobby. She told me to borrow some clothes from Cindy and have their chauffeur bring me to the Beverly right away, so I wouldn't miss the boat.

I thought fast. I told her that I was having a particularly bad woman-time this month. "Please don't make me go to Catalina right now!" I begged her. "I just don't feel up to it."

"I don't want you along, then," she said, "if you're just going to be whiny and weepy all week. Just stay there at Cindy's. I'll see you in a couple of days." The phone went dead.

I said, "Sorry about the baby, Mom," to the buzzing dial tone. Then, "Love you, too." I waited another second, then handed the phone back to Cindy's mom.

"I'm so sorry, Dolores," Cindy's mom said.

"Thanks," I said, pretending to be sad. She's a really nice lady, and I hated lying to her, but I had to get home to see Franck. "Mom asked if you could get Jonathan to take me home?"

"Oh, yes, dear, of course. Right away."

Cindy hugged me and her mom called the chauffeur. Within twenty minutes, I was on my way home to see Franck.

The good news, the very best news, I thought, was that now there was absolutely no reason that he'd have to marry Mom.

When I arrived, I found him sitting by the pool with Bobby. He stood up and gave me a hug. "I'm so sorry about the baby, Franck," I said, holding on to him.

He sighed. "These things happen," he said.

Bobby didn't seem upset at all.

July 8, 1967

A very nice dressed man came to see Franck and Bobby today. The three of them went into the office and closed the door. I tried to eavesdrop (even though Cecilia says it's rude). But she was in the kitchen making dinner, and she didn't see me standing outside the office. I couldn't hear anything, anyway. The door's too thick.

The man in the nice suit stayed to dinner with Franck and Bobby and me. In the middle of dinner, Franck excused himself for a minute. I saw him out of the corner of my eye, talking to Cecilia by the door to the dining room. Then he came back.

After dinner was over, they all shook hands and the nice-dressed man left. Bobby went upstairs to his room. Franck sat on the stairs and asked me to sit down with him.

"I'm going away for a little while, Lori," he told me. "With Bobby. I didn't want to just leave without saying goodbye."

I looked into the foyer and saw a suitcase sitting by the door. Cecilia must've packed it for him during dinner. I was relieved that it was only one suitcase. I knew that he couldn't be going away for too long, if he was only taking one suitcase. Mom always took fifty suitcases, even if she was just going to be gone for a few days. He couldn't be going away too long if he was only taking one suitcase.

He's probably going to the Marmont to stay with Bobby, until Bobby goes home to England. I'd heard him say that he'd be going back soon. What with all that's happened, Bobby probably doesn't want to be here when Mom gets home from Catalina.

Still, I'm going to miss Franck, every second, even if it's just for a few days. But I didn't want him to see me cry, so I tried hard not to.

Franck enfolded me in his arms and kissed me on the top of the head. He smelled so good.

160

Bobby came down the stairs. He had two suitcases. He made a short phone call, then the three of us went outside and waited. When the limo pulled up, Bobby kissed my hand and said in his delightful British accent, "It was very nice seeing you again, Miss Lori."

I said it was very nice seeing him again, too. Then he carried his suitcases down to the limo.

Franck said, "I'm gonna miss you, Lori." Then he kissed me on the cheek and turned to go.

I threw myself into his arms and hugged him as tightly as I could. I started to cry. I couldn't help it. "I love you, Franck!" I said.

He held me for a long moment, then carefully took my arms from around his neck, because I wasn't letting go. He put his hand on my cheek, and wiped away a tear with his thumb. He said, "I love you, too, Lori." Then he picked up his suitcase and said, "You be good."

Then he walked down the steps and put his suitcase in the truck of the limo. He turned and waved at me. He smiled. He's got the sweetest smile. I waved back. I was still crying. Then he got in the limo and they drove away.

July 10, 1967

I want to die.

Mom got home today. She looked all tanned and glowing from being on Catalina. Not like she'd had a miscarriage at all. As soon as she walked in the door, she asked where Franck was. Cecilia told her that Franck wasn't here.

There was a telegram waiting for her in the foyer. It'd been there since this morning. When Cecilia was making lunch, I picked it up and held it up to the light, but I couldn't see anything through the envelope.

When Mom went to open the telegram, I noticed that Cecilia backed quickly out of the room.

I watched Mom take the letter opener and slice through the envelope. She put the envelope and the letter opener down on the little table in the foyer and read the telegram. I watched her face turn white. The scarlet of her lipstick looked like the red ring of a bull's-eye when she screamed, "No!"

She picked up the letter opener and hurled it at the mirror. The sound of the shattering glass echoed through the house. Then she swept a vase full of roses and all the glass figurines off the little table in the foyer and screamed "No!" again. She wadded up the telegram and threw it on the floor, and then, with black tear-streaks already running down her face, she ran up the stairs to Franck's room. I could hear her sobbing.

I looked up the stairs after her, thinking that I should probably go up there and try to comfort her. Instead, I went over and recovered the wadded up telegram. I smoothed it out on the now empty foyer table.

161

It was from Franck. It read: "Two Green Keys shelved indefinitely. Ecksmith on flight back to England by the time you receive this. I'm with him. Return indeterminate."

I folded it up and put it in my pocket. I slowly climbed the stairs and went to my room. I had no desire to comfort Mom any more. I'd always known that she'd drive him away again, eventually. I just never imagined that she'd drive him so far away. All the way to England.

Franck's gone, and it's all her fault. There is no good news. I want to die.

The summer entries were punctuated by the lows of Jessika's histrionics when Franck didn't reply to her letters and telegrams in the manner in which she demanded. Dolores came to dread the arrival of the Western Union man. The downstairs seemed to drain of breakable things.

But there were also highs – Franck sent Dolores three postcards. One showed Big Ben, the other a fox hunt, and the third, a picture of Shakespeare's birthplace in Stratford-Upon-Avon. This one was her most treasured, because he'd signed that one *Miss you, Love, Franck.*

Then came Franck's final insult to Jessika, the last straw.

August 28th, 1967

Franck has finally tired of Mom's constant letters and telegrams. The woman has absolutely no pride, no dignity whatsoever. She can't accept that he doesn't love her. Why won't she just leave him alone? He's obviously enjoying his vacation in England with Bobby.

I wish I could take a vacation. I would love to go where Franck is, of course, but anywhere else in the world would also be fine, as long as it was away from Mom.

This time, she threw a little end table against the wall, gouging a big piece of plaster out of the wall and splintering the end table. She also busted the foyer mirror again, this time throwing my favorite crystal paperweight through it. She destroys everything that I love.

Only my mother could continue to alienate someone, even across the Atlantic Ocean. She pushed him all the way over there, and apparently that wasn't far enough away for her, because she's continued to push him even farther, all summer, with her constant letters and telegrams. I can only imagine how nagging and whining they are.

Franck doesn't want to hear it anymore. He doesn't want her anymore, hasn't for a long time. After she threw my paperweight through the mirror and flew upstairs, I again dug his telegram out of the debris.

It reads: "Leaving with Ecksmith for Japan tomorrow to scout locations. Forwarding address unknown. Will not be returning to US in the foreseeable future. Don't wait for me. Look for someone else. Best of luck, Franck."

Even though it's to my mother, I feel as though he's speaking directly to me in this telegram. He knows that I'm waiting for him. He's trying to be magnanimous. He doesn't want me to waste my time waiting for him, when he doesn't know how long he's going to be gone.

It's very heroic of him, offering to set me free. But I don't mind waiting. No matter how long it takes. I know he'll be back. It's Mom that he wants to forget about him, not me, and he wants to stay away until she does. But I'm never going to forget about him. I will wait for him for as long as it takes.

Dolores didn't write another entry in the first volume. I shuffled through the rest of the pages, but they were all blank. I imagined that she might've been too sad over Franck's absence to write anymore. Apparently, there were no postcards featuring a snowy Mt. Fuji. So I opened the second diary, and found that things had gone from bad to worse for Dolores. Things had gone positively *nuts*.

September 9, 1967

I want to die. I don't think I have far to go. I feel half dead already. But I have to write this down, so someone will find it, so someone'll know, in case Mom comes back in here and kills me.

When I got home from school, at first, I couldn't find her. She wasn't in the living room, she wasn't in the dining room. She wasn't out by the pool. I even looked in the screening room, but she wasn't there. I knew she was home, because the Jag was parked out front.

I went upstairs, calling for her. She wasn't in her room. Then I went into my room. She was sitting on my bed. My diary was in her hand. She tossed in onto the bed and stood up. She walked up to me, until she was right in my face. Her gray eyes blazed with hatred.

In a low, growling whisper, she said, "Did you honestly think that you could take him away from me? Do you really think he would ever choose you over me?" Then she screamed, "Tramp!" and backhanded me. I flew across the room and landed on the floor and busted my knee open. I rolled over on my side.

"What kind of a whore have I been harboring under my roof? What kind of a whore just crawls in bed with a sleeping man, uninvited? Did you think he would fuck you?" And then she kicked me. I doubled over. It hurt so bad, but for some reason, I didn't cry. "Do you know what you've done? Do you know that he could go to jail, if anybody ever finds out about this? You stupid, filthy whore!"

She leaned over and grabbed the front of my blouse, and pulled me up until she was right in my face again. She whispered, talking very fast, and spit flew into my eye. "Do you know why he left? He left because of you! He left because you're a dirty, stinking whore! He went all the way to the other side of the world to get away from you! How disgusted he must've been! Did you think that Franck O'Day was going to fuck a conniving whore like you, just because you crawled into his bed and begged him to?" She shoved me back down and the back of my head hit the floor.

"You're going to pay for what you've done. I'm gonna tell the whole world what a stinking tramp you are. And when Franck comes back, I'm gonna send you away. I'll see to it that you never set eyes on him again!" She kicked me again. Then she picked up my diary and stomped out of my room, slamming the door so hard that it made a crack in the frame.

I laid on the floor for a second, then got up and went into the bathroom. Still I didn't cry. I looked in the mirror. I've got a fat lip from where she backhanded me, and a cut on the back of my head where she slammed me into the floor. There's a couple scrapes on my side where she kicked me. My ribs hurt, and my side is already starting to bruise up.

My knee is still bleeding. There's no Franck to carry me tenderly to the hospital this time. Now I'm going to have two scars. A little thin one on one knee from when Franck took me to the hospital to have it tended to, and a big, ugly one on the other knee, from where my mother just left me here to bleed to death.

But as I write this, I'm still not crying. Franck didn't leave because of me. He left because he finally saw the golden opportunity to get away from her, because she's a <u>crazy, psycho</u> BITCH!!

Franck told me that he loved me. I never once heard him tell Mom that he loved her.

He won't come back to her, now that he's finally escaped. But he'll come back some day. He's a movie star, after all. Where else is he going to make movies?

I can wait for him. I'm already not fifteen anymore. I'm already sixteen and in another six months or so, I'll be seventeen. He'll come back, someday, but it won't be to her. I can wait for Franck. I can wait for him forever.

I said, God damn, I thought. *God damn!* Here was the real bombshell. Now things were heating up. Now we were getting into some Joan Crawford territory.

I tried to imagine my mother beating my ass like that, after she'd found my diary with its sweaty scribblings about kissing Mr. King. I couldn't picture it. Her methods of discipline used sarcasm and a raised eyebrow, instead of a raised hand. When she'd discovered my slightly blue adolescent ramblings, she'd simply left me an instructional sticky note. That was sufficient to curb my confessionals. She never mentioned the incident again. Not even after I grew up.

On the other hand, I'd never climbed in bed with Mr. King, and my mother wasn't obsessed with him, like Jessika was with Franck.

Franck hadn't told us about Dolores's misstep in her quest for his . . . *affection*, because we might have thought ill of her motivations because of it. And that's precisely what her mother had thought.

September 10, 1967

Mom came into my room this morning and told me that I was not to come out until Tuesday. She told me that I was to pack a suitcase, because on Tuesday, she was sending me to boarding school. In Sacramento. If she thinks I'm the least bit unhappy about that, she's got another think coming.

September 23, 1967

I've been here at the Academy for about a week and a half now. I love it! All the girls are so nice, and the teachers, too. And the classes are fun and easy, for the most part.

I'm only sad at night, because that's when I finally have time to miss Franck. One of the girls here has an autographed picture of him. She said she got the address of his fan club from a magazine and sent away for it. I didn't even know he had a fan club. I could be president of his fan club. The picture is all wrinkly and tattered around the edges, because she keeps it under her pillow.

No one here seems to know who I am, who my mother is. My last name isn't Yerdlay, after all. None of the other girls know that I used to live in the same house with Franck O'Day.

No one knows that I once snuggled up next to him in bed. No one knows that he once told me that he loved me.

September 25, 1967

Everybody knows who I am now.

Susan Anderson went home over the weekend. She saw my picture in the paper. She came up to me after First Bell today and showed it to me. There was my mother, that bitch, holding up my picture on the steps of City Hall.

Dolores had taped a copy of the clipping into her diary. It wasn't very long, but it said all that needed to be said.

Jessika Yerdlay Levels Abuse Allegations Against
Co-Star Franck O'Day

Actress Jessika Yerdlay called a press conference today to
accuse former co-star Franck O'Day of abusing her
daughter, Dolores Adamson. Yerdlay and O'Day are best
known for their starring roles in the critically acclaimed,
"High Times in Manhattan."

O'Day and his step-daughter, Maribeth McSwale, lived with
Yerdlay and Dolores until the death of his wife in 1965.
Maribeth returned to live with her biological father in
September of last year, by court order. In February of this
year, Miss Yerdlay announced her engagement to O'Day.

"I come here today to tell the world that I'm no longer
engaged to Franck O'Day," Yerdlay said yesterday, tears
streaming down her face. "It has come to my attention that
he and my daughter Dolores have been engaging in unlawful
activities of a sexual nature, starting when she was only
fourteen years old. I found out about these shocking events
not long after he fled to Japan. I am here today to demand
that the District Attorney extradite him immediately, so he
can stand trial for what he did to my little girl!"

The District Attorney's Office would not comment on
Yerdlay's claims, citing an on-going investigation.

*Susan grinned at me. "Is it true, Lori?" she asked. "Did you and
Franck O'Day . . .?" They all gathered around and looked at me, expectant little
grins on their faces. I suddenly saw an angle to all of this. All of my mother's lies
might seem terrible to all the teachers here and everyone else in the whole world. If
what she'd said had actually happened, the world wouldn't understand our love. It's
not allowed.*

*But my friends understand. They love Franck almost as much as I do. If I
really had engaged in "unlawful activities of a sexual nature" with him, then they
thought that was just as cool as it could be. I smiled broadly at them. "I'm not
allowed to say anything," I said, and nodded at the paper. "There's an on-going
investigation." I winked.*

They begged me to tell them if it was true, to give them details, but I just shook my head and insisted that I couldn't talk about it. "He's got the bluest eyes," is all I'll tell them, and they already know that.

Thanksgiving, 1967
I'm here pretty much all alone. Everybody's gone home to be with their happy little families. I love having the place almost all to myself. The library seems huge and echoey with no one else in it. Mom hasn't written or called, but apparently, she's still paying for me to be here, because here I remain. And that's fine with me. If I never see that bitch again in this life, I'm just fine with that, too.
There hasn't been anything else in the paper about me and Franck, and I think everyone has forgotten about the whole thing. Another thing that is also fine with me.
I miss him terribly, but I know I have to wait. I'll be 17 in April, then I'll be 18 next April. Susan says that when you're 18, you're officially an adult. You can do anything you want. "You can do anyone you want!" she said and giggled. So, I've made a plan. If Franck doesn't come back after I turn 18, I'm just going to go and find him.

The rest of the year's entries are happy and chipper. Dolores thrived out from under her mother's roof. While before she'd only mentioned one of two girlfriends, now she wrote about six or seven by name.

January 4, 1968
My life finally has meaning again. My entire universe has lit up, as if from a thousand suns!
Susan came back a few days early from Winter Break. She said it was just so she could tell me the good news. She was so excited, she couldn't even tell me. She just showed me the newspaper. Here it is:

Franck O'Day Returning to US to Face Abuse Charges

In September of last year, actress Jessika Yerdlay accused her former co-star Franck O'Day of engaging in activities of a sexual nature with her then fourteen-year-old daughter, Dolores Adamson. By the time she discovered the relationship, Yerdlay claims, O'Day had already fled to Europe.

Now O'Day is returning to the US to face Yerdlay's allegations. Through his publicist, he issued the following statement: "Miss Yerdlay's accusations have wounded me deeply. While I loved Dolores like she was my own daughter during my brief stay at her mother's home, no improprieties ever occurred. Anyone who disputes this is a liar. I look forward to my day in court to answer Miss Yerdlay's sad charges. I have no doubt of my certain exoneration."

O'Day's publicist said that he expects the actor to be back in California by the end of the week. As of press time, Jessika Yerdlay could not be reached for comment.

FRANCK IS COMING HOME!
For once in my life, there is absolutely no bad news!

Five days later, Dolores plunged from the height of joy to the very pit of despair. Her world imploded.

January 9, 1968
The headline reads, "Franck O'Day Presumed Dead: Hollywood Mourns" The article says that the plane he was flying in with Bobby has disappeared. I can't allow myself to believe it. It must be some kind of publicity stunt. I will not believe it!

If Franck is dead, I'd be able to feel it. A yawning, empty, irredeemable hole would open in my soul if he's really dead. And that hasn't happened, so I know he's still alive, somewhere. He's going to remain alive to me until someone shows me a body.

Mom didn't even call. Could that be guilt? I hope she believes he's dead. I hope she hates herself as much as I hate her. Because if he really was dead, it would be her fault. It would be her fault for driving him away in the first place. Then it would be her fault for trying to force him to return by publicly shaming him with those lies she told the papers. So if he really was dead, it would be doubly, triply her fault. I hope she hates herself every waking second.

I know he's not dead. I just KNOW it!

What a trouper she was, I thought. The things a person can talk themselves into. But on the other hand, what other choice did she have? If she allowed herself to accept that Franck was dead, like her mother believed, like the rest of the world believed – what else did she have in life? The grief would have killed her. Far better to be a little delusional, then to face such a debilitating loss.

I wondered how long Dolores held onto that delusion. I wondered how many years, how many decades, she'd believed that Franck was still alive before she found out that he still, indeed, stalked the Earth? Maribeth had said that he'd been back in the States since 2006, that she'd know he was alive for thirty years before that.

When had Franck let Dolores know? Was it only after her mother's death that he'd revealed himself to her? Then, another thought struck me. Maybe Dolores, wherever she was, didn't know that Franck was alive. He'd said that he and Maribeth had purchased the house through a third party.

Maybe, after a lifetime in exile in the wilds of Japan, after waiting for nearly fifty years for his enemy to die, maybe Franck had decided that he didn't want anything to do with her daughter, either. Maybe Franck thought that Dolores *had* told stories to her mother, after all – maybe he thought that it had been the daughter's fault that the mother had flipped out and made those accusations. Maybe that's why he hadn't told us about it.

If he hadn't been on his way back to the States in 1968, surely against his will, then he wouldn't have been on that particular plane when it went down. He wouldn't have spent years, undiscovered, unrescued, in Japan. Maybe he would've returned sooner and jumpstarted his career. Surely he wouldn't have waited almost forty years to return. Surely he would've made more movies.

Perhaps Franck blamed all his misfortunes on Dolores, after all. Maybe that's why he'd taken pains to buy her house through a third party. Maybe he hadn't ever let her know that he was alive. Perhaps Dolores was pining away somewhere, waiting for him still.

Valentine's Day, 1968

My mother can destroy people's lives long-distance. Just like those missiles that the Russians have aimed at us. Steve asked me to go to the Valentine's Day mixer with him last week. I've been looking forward to it ever since. Susan showed me where there was a little space behind the bleachers, just perfect for two people to go and make out in private.

But oh, no. Dolores is never allowed to have any fun at all. If I was a more suspicious person, or if I thought that she cared about me in the slightest, I might think Mom had spies, watching me. Because I had not even finished half a dance with Steve, had not gotten to even think about kissing him, when Mrs. Winthrop tapped me on the shoulder.

I had to go pack, she said. A car would be here for me in forty minutes, she said. It would take me to the airport. My mother needed me to come home, immediately, she said.

What did my mother need me for? Did it mean that Franck had come back? I could think that, because, like I say, I know he's not dead.

So, has he come back, the only thing I'd ever want to go home for? No.

A) Franck will never come home to her, and B) if he did, maybe just to pick up the suits he left behind, or something, Mom would never summon me home for it.

She was going to see to it that I never set eyes on him again, that's what she told me before she sent me here. She's seen to it that the entire world will never set eyes on him again. Or at least it seems that way. The whole world believes he's dead.

But I know better. They haven't found any bodies yet. They haven't even found any wreckage yet. Franck's not dead.

I'm writing this on the plane. I love to fly. That's another reason why I know Franck's not dead. If he was, my soul would know. And then, I think it would tell me to be afraid to fly.

I know why Mom wants me back. It's her first Valentine's Day without Franck. Last year, she was announcing their engagement. This year, he's dead, or at least she thinks so.

If he was really dead, it would be her fault. But she'll never accept responsibility for it. She wouldn't even take responsibility for driving him away. She put all the blame for that on me.

And that's what she wants me back now for. I can picture the house now. Dark and empty, compared to last year. No parties, no friends, no reporters. No pink and red streamers. No Franck. No me. Nobody to blame. That's what Mom wants. She wants to blame me. She wants to yell at me and call me a whore and maybe smack me around again. But I'm prepared this time. If she raises a hand to me, I'll hit her back. I'm not a child anymore.

Later —

Things didn't go at all like I'd expected when I got home. Sure, the house was dark and quiet as the tomb. I was right about that. No pink and red happy celebration of love this *year.*

Mom was standing at the top of the stairs when the cab dropped me off. I looked up at her. She's lost weight. Her face is drawn and pinched around the eyes, as if she's battling some kind of constant, physical pain. Good. She'll get by, I thought. They can do wonders with make-up and camera filters these days. She'll be all right.

I walked up the steps until we were face to face. She moved her arms away from her sides, and against my will, I flinched. Some cowardly part of me thought she was going to hit me again. The rest of me was prepared for it, and was ashamed of the other part's fear. The rest of me said to myself, "If she tries to hit me, I'll throw her down these steps."

But Mom didn't try to hit me. She was raising her arms to hug me, and when I flinched, a look of guilt flashed across her face. She hugged me tightly, and she started to cry, sobbing, "I'm so sorry, Dolores!"

I just stood there, thinking that I was going to have to get the jacket I was wearing dry-cleaned because she was getting mascara all over it. I didn't hug her back. I have no pity for her. What is she sorry for? Beating me half to death? Sending me to boarding school? Calling me a whore?

Was she saying that she was sorry that she had driven Franck off? Was she sorry for dragging our names through the mud? Was she sorry that she'd killed him as surely as if she'd been piloting that plane?

There were just too many things to be sorry for, and Mom didn't specify. So I just stood there like a statue while she cried and hugged me. I forgave her nothing.

Finally, she got a handle on herself and backed away from me. She looked at me, her blackened, tear streaked face hopeful.

"I'd like my diary back," I said, and walked into the house.

March 15, 1968

I've been at home for a month. I keep asking when I'm going back to school, and Mom just snuffles at me and says, "Soon." Mom seems like she snuffles all the time now, like she's always about to start crying or like she's just stopped crying. I have no pity for her.

I'm going to be 17 in thirty days, and then, 365 days from that, I'll be 18. On my 18th birthday, I'm getting on the first available plane to Japan to look for Franck. And Mom won't be able to stop me, because I'll be an adult. Nobody'll be able to stop me. I know he's still alive, and I'm going to find him.

March 16, 1968

I know why Mom's been all weepy lately. She tried to kill herself last night. Unfortunately, she didn't try hard enough. I guess that sounds mean.

But to the very end, or what she thought was going to be the end, she was only thinking of herself. Her note just said, "May God have mercy on my soul." No explanations, no taking responsibilities, no apologies to those she's hurt. Just a prayer for herself.

Mom kept Uncle Roger's suicide note in her bottom drawer for all these years. I read it once when she wasn't home. It was in a little manila envelope with EVIDENCE stamped in red on the side. She could've learned something from that, like saying sorry to whoever you were leaving behind.

171

She did it right there in the foyer. I heard Cecilia scream, a long bloodcurdling wail, like something from "In Cold Blood" or "Wait Until Dark." I ran downstairs. Mom was laying on the floor, bleeding from her neck and wrist, the huge butcher knife clutched in one hand and her self-serving suicide note in the other. It was all very cinematic.

I told Cecilia to get some towels and bandages. I wrapped her wrist up. We just learned about bandaging cuts in First Aid at school a little while ago. I didn't know what to do about her neck, though. It wouldn't stop bleeding. But it wasn't gushing blood, so I wasn't too worried. She had just cut herself a real good one, deep and jagged and wide, and it kept oozing and oozing.

I called the studio. The number was on a little card above the phone in the kitchen. Mom had told me, from the time that I was old enough to dial the phone: if anything ever happened to her, I was to call the studio. Not the cops, not the life squad, not the fire department. I was to call the studio first, and they would handle it.

Within twenty minutes, a Mr. Izona showed up with a doctor. They went upstairs to take care of Mom, and then came back downstairs and talked to me. Why do they always talk to me like I'm a child? I'm 13 months away from being an adult!

"Your mom has been sad," the doctor said. "That's why she tried to harm herself. It's fortunate that you were here to save her." I didn't say anything. There wasn't anything fortunate about it.

"When do I get to go back to school?" I asked Mr. Izona, after the doctor left. Mom was upstairs in her room. I'd overheard the doctor say the word "sedated" to Mr. Izona.

"Wouldn't you like to stay here with your mom, until she gets better?" he said. It looks like I'm never going to get away from Mom. I'm never going to escape from this place. At least Franck got to escape. I miss him so much. He's got the bluest eyes.

And the rest, as they say, is history. This was the last entry in Dolores's diary. I'd been mistaken in assuming that Maribeth had forged her words. I now believed the diaries to be the genuine article. Maribeth had not invented the wording of the telegrams she'd quoted on *TwoGreenKeys.com*. She'd lifted their contents verbatim from Dolores's diaries.

I re-evaluated Maribeth – perhaps she wasn't as crazy as I'd previously imagined. She was just a lonely old woman with nothing else in the world but Franck, the daddy she remembered from probably the best days of her life, the daddy that had loved her mother. She loved Franck – that love shone through the hateful words on her site. She had an overwhelming anger at the wrongs that she felt the world had

172

done to him, a guiding desire to tell his story, to gather his remaining fans to him, to make him famous again. She loved him, as much as Dolores had loved him, or Jessika, or Robert Ecksmith, or even Ruthanne. And she'd loved him longer than any of them. It would all make for great copy. I even thought I might have a title for my book: *He's Got the Bluest Eyes.*

TWENTY-THREE

I tucked Lori's diaries into the bottom of my suitcase, covered them up with some clothes. Maribeth didn't want Franck to know of their existence, and for some reason, I didn't want Ruthanne to see them, either. Not yet. She could read all about it when she was proofreading my book.

I stretched out on the bed, and was just picturing my name at the top of that bestseller's list: *He's Got the Bluest Eyes,* by Carolyn Adyon. Then I heard a scraping sound out by the pool. I arose and looked out the window.

The pool itself was lit from below the waterline, but the rest of the area was in darkness. I could see a figure moving around in the shadows. Then a flame flared to life, revealing Kimura, lighting a tiki torch. He stuck in into the concrete – there must've been a hole there for it. He picked up another one from a pile at his feet and moved on to the next hole. He pushed a lounge chair out of the way – that was the scraping sound I'd heard – lit the torch and stuck it into its hole. He lit five altogether, forming a horseshoe around the pool. Then he disappeared back into the house.

Franck and Ruthanne appeared, hand in hand, as always. Franck was wearing a pair of black board shorts, and Ruthie had donned her tiny black bikini. *Ah, how cute,* I thought. *They match.*

They walked down the steps into the water. When Ruthanne didn't hesitate or shiver of exclaim over the water's temperature, I remembered that Franck had mentioned that the pool was heated. I had only taken a quick dip that afternoon, and hadn't really took note of the warmth of the water. Another improvement since Jessika's day, I imagined, although they might've had heated pools back when the house was built. What did I know about that kind of stuff? It was another luxury that money could buy.

They swam around each other for a little while, then like leaves in a whirlpool, they came back together, embraced loosely. Franck glanced up at the house, then back at Ruthanne. He could've seen me at the window, if he'd known that I was there looking out. I was pretty sure that he hadn't seen me, but I backed into the shadows a little bit, just in case. I didn't want him to think I was watching him – hadn't enough people, like Dolores, like his adoring public, watched him in his life?

The night was absolutely silent, so when he spoke softly to Ruthanne, I could still hear him. "Let me *really* show you Esther's trick, Ruthie."

Ruthie blushed, but she didn't hesitate, stretching out in the water and closing her eyes. Franck cupped her heels in his hands, then paused for just a split-second, and looked up at me. He looked me right in the eye – he'd known I was there all along. In the light from the torches, bouncing off the water, his blue eyes glowed like sapphires.

Franck kissed Ruthanne's toes and she giggled. He smiled at me – that smug, killer smile – and slowly drew Ruthanne's ankles apart. He kissed her on the inside of her calf, the bend of her knee, then inched forward. Ruthanne folded one knee over his shoulder; the other leg floated slightly off to one side. Franck kissed her thigh, and there was a swirl of water as he brought his hands up from beneath her and hooked his thumbs into the bikini strings at her hips. His eyes never left mine.

Realizing what was about to happen, I stepped away from the window, back into the welcoming, concealing darkness of the room. I was surprised to discover that I was panting just the tiniest bit. *That's what I get for being a voyeur,* I thought. *A little more of a show than I'd been expecting.* Apparently Franck *liked* being watched.

I stretched out on the soft bed again and tried to convince myself that I couldn't hear any splashing, couldn't hear Franck's low laughter, couldn't hear Ruthanne moan. I felt self-conscious, guilty – all the things you feel when you realize that, quite against your will and better judgment, you might perhaps be developing a little *warm* for your best friend's boyfriend.

Mercifully, after a few minutes, I drifted off to sleep. I dreamed of green pines and startlingly white snow, seen from above. It looked a lot like Oregon. As the ground started to rush up at me at an alarming rate, I knew that my mind was manufacturing Franck's plane crash for me, the only part of the story that I hadn't heard yet. The terrain looked like Oregon, because I've never been to Japan, after all. Before I actually collided with the ground, I woke up with a start, just like dreamers of nightmares do in the movies.

I consulted my phone on the bedside table. It was 2 am. I stood up and stretched. I went to the window and looked out at the pool. Franck and Ruthanne had retired from their alfresco frolic: the water, still lit from below, was once again as smooth and as still as glass. The torches were out.

If I'd had to venture three guesses, and if the first two didn't count, I would wager every dime to my name that they'd moved the oldest game in the world to Franck's room, just on the other side of the lavishly appointed bathroom from me. But the sturdy old house, built for money in the 1920s, had thick walls and plush carpets. It kept its secrets. I could not hear a sound from that direction.

Maybe they were in Ruthie's room, but somehow I doubted it. I could picture Maribeth, dressed in an old woman's flannel pajamas, with her ear and a glass to the wall of the bathroom that separated her room from Ruthanne's, if they were in there. Maybe she was *in* the bathroom, with her ear and glass directly against the wall of Ruthie's room.

After all, Maribeth was nothing if not obsessed with Franck too, albeit in a different way. But obsession is obsession – I imagined that if Maribeth thought there was a chance that she could hear them, she'd try to hear them. I imagined that Franck could picture it too, and had therefore no doubt chosen his room for his and Ruthie's first night together.

I thought about Franck, and his room. It had stood empty for almost fifty years, until his recent, triumphant return. He'd fled with Robert Ecksmith in 1967, like a thief in the night, taking only one suitcase, abandoning his undoubtedly impressive matinee idol's wardrobe. Franck was obviously a clothes horse – the volume and quality of the garments that he'd left behind must've been extraordinary, indeed.

I wondered if Jessika had kept his room as it'd been the day he left, like a shrine. I wondered if Dolores ever snuck into the closet and pressed her face to his shirts, just to try to get the scent of him again. I wondered if she'd ever crawled into his bed when her mother wasn't home, just to dream of him, to remember the sound of his heartbeat, the feel of his sleeping breath. I wondered if Jessika had ever done the same.

Two passionate women, both so desperately in love with Franck O'Day. Now my passionate friend, no stranger to the concept of obsession with him herself, was in that same bed with him. It was all going to make a great book.

TWENTY-FOUR

I was late for brunch. There was nothing as prosaic and working-class as an alarm clock on the bedside table in the room once occupied by legendary starlet Jessika Yerdlay. As for my phone – well, who sets an alarm for Sunday morning?

It was 11:10 when I opened my eyes, not sure where I was. I blinked and it all came back to me: Franck and Ecksmith, Franck and Jessika, Franck and Dolores, *Franck and Ruthanne*. The palatial manse. Old, shriveled Maribeth. My book.

I jumped up, dressed quickly, and hurried downstairs and out to the terrace. The table was set, exquisitely, as it had been the previous Sunday. A large vase of flowers sat regally in its center. Ruthanne was sitting sideways on Franck's lap, her legs draped over the side of his chair, her arms draped languidly around his neck. They were laughing and whispering to each other like newlyweds, their foreheads touching. Maribeth was nowhere to be seen.

"Sorry I'm late," I said.

Franck looked up at me, the delighted little smile that he'd been sharing with Ruthanne still on his face. "You were not missed," he said brightly. I probably could've taken that as an insult, but the look on his face communicated that he'd not missed me because he was more than entertained by Ruthanne, someone whom I'd brought into his life. The little hint of gratitude in his tone was more than enough to keep me from offense.

"Besides, we don't keep to a lot of strict time schedules around here." Franck indicated for Ruthie to hop up, and she did so, then took her own seat beside him. She smiled radiantly at me, and I smiled back at her, happy for her happiness.

"Kimura has kept everything warm for us." Franck gestured toward the house, to the unseen servant within. I took my seat, and after a moment's hesitation, poured myself a cup of coffee from the antique porcelain carafe on the table.

"I'm afraid Mari won't be joining us until a little later this afternoon, Carol. She's feeling a little under the weather today. I told her that she should've taken a swim yesterday." Franck took Ruthanne's hand and kissed it, smiled at her. Then he looked at me and said, "An occasional dip can be very therapeutic. Don't you think so?"

Franck smiled curiously at me. He was trying to gauge whether or not I'd watched his open-air expression of affection for Ruthanne in its entirety, or if I'd just caught the opening scene. He was asking whether I'd enjoyed it, vicariously, as much as Ruthanne had. Before I could stop myself, I glanced away, embarrassed.

Satisfied with my reaction, he smiled smugly for a second and then said, "But I couldn't talk Mari into a swim. Not with you young ladies here. She's vain. She doesn't like to reveal her old, battle-scarred flesh to an unforgiving world."

A problem you don't have, I thought.

Maribeth occupied the room across the hall from mine, another room that faced the pool, and I wondered suddenly if she also might've caught the Franck and Ruthanne Show. I wondered if, being from an earlier generation, she'd been appalled and embarrassed and disgusted, and if those reactions had contributed to her feeling under the weather this morning.

On the other hand, perhaps their aquatic pasodoble had caused her to feel just the tiniest bit turned on. Even though I wouldn't've looked out the window to watch it on purpose, I'd be lying if I said that the small part that I'd inadvertently witnessed hadn't turned me on a little bit. Perhaps such stirrings, no doubt unaccustomed in a woman of Maribeth's age, had brought on a case of the vapors.

"Ah, here's breakfast!" Franck said, as Kimura trundled a cart up to the table. It didn't rattle as he pushed it across the tile; his approach was as silent as a big cat. Franck's idyllic peace could not be disturbed by clattering dishes.

As Kimura delicately spooned it onto my plate, I was amazed to discover that the meal consisted of eggs and lobster. Kimura paused, and I looked up at him.

"Kimura wants to know if you would like to top your eggs off with some sevruga, Carol," Franck said. "I recommend it, if you're adventurous."

Adventurous is my middle name, Franck ol' boy, I thought, and nodded at Kimura. From out of a tiny silver serving dish, he doled out several generous spoonsful of a black, beaded substance. I first thought it was some kind of jelly – not a usual topping for lobster, but who knows what kind of weird food combinations rich people favor? But when I tasted it, it was salty and deliciously, faintly fishy, and I realized that it must be some kind of caviar. Now *this* was scrumptious.

Franck smiled at my reaction. "Dig in, ladies! I don't know about you, but I feel like I could eat a horse!"

And if you really wanted one, I'm sure you'd just have Kimura fry one right up for you, I thought.

178

We dined in silence, as befitted the amazing dish. *Can't talk now, eating,* Homer Simpson said in my mind. All the flavors and textures blended and melted in my mouth – it was ambrosial, heavenly. *Hot damn!* I thought. I might not be impressed with the house and the pool and the screening room and the silver and the china, but a girl could definitely get used to eating like this.

Kimura had cleared the dishes away and was again pouring mimosas for us when Franck asked if I'd brought the little digital audio recorder down with me.

"I left it on the night table," I said and started to get up to go get it.

Franck touched my hand and nodded at Kimura. I sat back down. He set the pitcher on the table and went back in the house, then returned and set the machine down on the table. He exchanged nods with Franck, then once again disappeared.

Franck pushed the button and spoke. "I suppose the most exciting and mysterious part of my story concerns my sojourn in Japan with Bobby, after our plane went down. The crash itself was unremarkable. One moment we were in the air, in the blue, and the next moment there was a whining sound, then greenness, then blackness.

"Contrary to the rather colorful fable that Mari has posted on her website, we weren't saved by a *yamabushi* and taken to the mountain fastness of his monastery to recuperate in bliss. We were actually rescued by a pair of Russian hikers. We were nowhere near the plane – the location of the plane wasn't discovered until 1982.

"But it must've just happened when they discovered us – we were both unconscious, but we hadn't been out long enough to have been affected by the elements. I awoke to a gentle hand, holding the back of my head and trying to feed me vodka." Franck chuckled. "I had come out of the crash virtually unscathed – I've been lucky all my life." He winked at Ruthie. "All I had was a broken wrist, a concussion, and a cut right here." He indicated the back of his head. "I've still got the scar." Ruthanne reached over and ruffled the hair there.

More luck, I thought. *Even a plane crash couldn't mess up that pretty face.*

"Bobby was worse off: he had a cut over his eye and a broken leg. He was unconscious. Some kind of head injury. The heroic Slavs bandaged our heads and set my wrist and Bobby's leg. They built a travois for each of us. Bobby was out, and through signs and gestures, our rescuers indicated that they didn't want me to walk either, due to my head injury. I don't recall the trip back to civilization. My head must've been worse than I thought, and I lost consciousness.

179

"I woke up in a room in someone's house, dressed in Japanese clothing. Bobby was still unconscious, lying in a bed across from me. He was out for two weeks – I wouldn't call it a coma, because he tossed and turned and talked in his sleep. He called out for me a couple of times. But he wasn't awake. He couldn't talk to our kind Japanese benefactors for us.

"I walked around the village. Try as I might, I couldn't bridge the language barrier. I tried to ask what had become of the clothes I'd been wearing, my passport. I made airplane-crashing gestures . . ." Franck wiggled his fingers in the air, then dropped his hand to the table. "Like any American, I spoke English to the locals, loudly and slowly. They smiled shyly and shook their heads.

"I had no idea where I was. There was not an English speaker, not an English *document* to be found. The Russians who'd saved our lives were gone, although it didn't really matter, because I don't speak Russian, either. I had no money, no passport. The people were kind, however, and took care of me. They didn't ask for anything.

"I walked a lot, waiting for Bobby to wake up. There was a great, curving, black beach. I had not a clue as to what body of water it was on. There were stone paths through the forests, punctuated with shrines. All of it was indescribably foreign to me.

"I had strange dreams. In one dream I saw a temple. I thought about approaching it – it was huge, and I thought that perhaps there might be some educated holy man in there that might speak English. But I hesitated. I had an American's superstitious fear and wonder at the alien beliefs of this foreign place. Bobby had tried to explain them to me, but what I thought I knew wasn't enough.

"There was a towering, two story wooden structure – call it a pagoda – that served as a gate to the temple. Two statutes, twenty feet tall, flanked the passage that led inside. Their expression was fierce, not welcoming.

"What if there wasn't anyone inside that could speak English? What if I broke some taboo by just waltzing into their sanctuary? What if there was some kind of punishment for such an offense? One of the statues turned his massive, round stone head and glared at me. I screamed and woke up. An elderly Japanese woman was sponging my forehead. Apparently, I was feverish. She gestured across the room. Bobby was sitting up in bed, smiling at me.

"'It's about time you woke up,' I told him. Relief flooded me. I was so glad that my friend was awake and alive, but I was also glad that he could communicate with these people. 'Where the hell are we?'

180

"'We're in a little town called Kumano, in a place called the Kii Peninsula,' Bobby said. 'The best thing is – no one here knows who we are. No one out there . . .' he spread his arms to indicate the world, '. . . knows *where* we are. I think we should stay here forever.' He grinned at me.

"'We gotta get back, Bobby,' I said. 'Jessika. The studio . . .'

"'You're dead, Franck, my darling. I'm dead. Mama-san, there, says we've been here for two weeks?' I nodded. Bobby whistled. 'If they knew where to look for us, they would've found us by now.'

"The old woman bowed to Bobby. He bowed to her and she left the room. 'No one knows us here, Franck!' he repeated. 'Here's your papers.' He tossed my passport and other ID to me. Unlike me, he'd known the words to use to ask Mama-san for them. 'I say, let's never go back,' Bobby continued. 'It's a paradise here. We're dead – and we're in heaven. Why should we go back?'

"There was a soft knock at the door. Bobby said something in Japanese – *come in*, I would imagine. Mama-san had returned, and she'd brought a young man with her. He entered the room and bowed to Bobby, and then to me. We bowed back.

"'I am Nakano,' he said in a thick accent. 'I come from *Kimpusen-ji.*'

"'You speak English,' I said.

"'A small,' Nakano replied shyly, and bowed a little again. 'I come to take you to *Kimpusen-ji.*'

"Bobby said something to Nakano in Japanese. He smiled in pleased surprise and said something back. They began a regular conversation. I just stood there like an idiot. I never would pick up much of the language.

"Bobby and Nakano finished their little talk. They bowed to each other, and Nakano left. Bobby clapped his hands and rubbed them together, grinned widely. I was annoyed, still in the dark about where exactly we were, what exactly was going on.

"'Don't frown, my darling, it'll give you wrinkles,' Bobby said. He waited another moment, just to piss me off that much more, because it amused him. Then he said, 'Okay. That was Nakano. He's a monk, of the ancient *Shugendō* religion. It's rather a nature sect, a blending of Buddhist and Shinto. A mountain faith.'

"Bobby started to tell me what they believed. I told him that I didn't care what they believed. But I didn't say, *Can he get us out of here?* Because I'd been thinking over Bobby's suggestion. Maybe we should stay here, for a little while, anyway. It was beautiful country, and if the world thought we were dead, why not stay dead for a while? I had

181

nothing to go home to, no desire whatsoever to go home. That's why I'd left the country with Bobby in the first place, to get away from all the things I didn't want at home.

"He spoke the language, even if I didn't. It would be fun. We could step out of the wilderness for a big comeback, anytime we wanted to. So instead of asking if Nakano could get us out of there, I asked, 'What does he want?'

"'He wants to take us to *Kimpusen-ji*.' Bobby didn't wait for me to glower at him, but instead explained immediately. 'It's a temple.'

"'And why does he want to take us there?' I asked.

"Bobby grinned even wider, shrugged. 'I have no idea, my darling. No idea at all,' he said. 'Perhaps it's kismet.'"

"Kismet. *Fate.*" Franck laughed, shrugged. "I never did find out precisely why Nakano had been sent to fetch us. Bobby told me some story once – he said it had to do with some Japanese good luck charm that he'd been wearing when the plane went down. Some symbol that he wore around his neck. When the Russians brought us in – Mama-san had seen it and got in touch with the monks." Franck shrugged again, sipped his mimosa. "I don't know. Something like that." He shrugged a third time. "Bobby made stuff up a lot, Carol. He was a storyteller, an *artiste*. He never let the truth get in the way of a good story. It was intrinsic to his charm." Franck winked at Ruthanne.

"So, we went. It turned out that it was *Kimpusen-ji* of which I'd dreamed, while we were still in Kumano. I was amazed when we walked up to the gate – the guardians, the *Kongō Rikishi* – they didn't turn their enormous fierce round faces to look at me – but I'd been there. I'd seen them before. I told Bobby that I'd dreamed of them.

"He just smiled and said, 'Kismet, my darling. Kismet.'"

Franck paused, sipped his drink. Then he looked at me and sighed. "I won't bore you with a long diatribe on Eastern beliefs, Carol. Even though I was there for almost forty years, I cannot really explain it to you, not so you'll understand, I don't think.

"Bobby and I went to *Kimpusen-ji*, we were taken to the head guy. His name was Maki." Franck sighed again. "How can I compress forty years into an explanation that you'll understand, that won't bore you? The way they think, their understanding of the universal energy – it's so foreign to Western minds . . ." Franck opened his blue eyes wide and grinned at me. "But it works, Carol. I'm living proof.

"Bobby was able to come up with some money. I'm not sure exactly how he did it, but I know his small-English friend Nakano helped. It was not a lot of money, but enough so that we could get a little place in the mountains, a brisk walk from *Kimpusen-ji*.

'We worked for them – Hollywood heartthrob Franck O'Day and famous English director Robert Ecksmith performed manual labor for Japanese monks. Bobby was happier than I'd ever known him to be, and I liked it there. The air was clean, the water fresh – and not a single studio sycophant in sight.

"Bobby studied with Maki, and he and Maki developed a . . . relationship. I don't know if there was anything physical to it in the beginning. We never discussed the physical relationships that Bobby had. But his tone was soft and awed when he talked about Maki. He spoke of the transcendental oneness of their souls, the complete blending of their energies – as Maki taught him all the steps, as they ascended through the levels of enlightenment together."

Franck paused. "It all sounded like bullshit to me. From all the flowery language, I was convinced that they were lovers." He grinned. "But then Bobby showed me what he'd learned. And the years passed. Maki showed him, and he showed me." Franck stopped talking.

I said, "What did he show you?"

"I learned *Shugendō*. Spiritual power, the balance between humanity and nature. And I learned *Reiki,* the mysterious atmosphere, the supernatural influence, the universal life energy."

I must've looked skeptical, because I was. It all *sounded like bullshit to me.*

Franck barked a short laugh. "Ah, it's nothing, Carol. Just a weird Eastern spiritual practice. *Reiki.* It's not even ancient – it's only been around since the '20s. Harnessing the energy of the universe. It keeps me young." Again, Franck stopped. This time he looked at me, willing me to say something, expecting me to defend my unbeliever's expression.

"Well," I said and smiled at him, "it certainly seems to work."

Franck roared laughter, and Ruthie and I joined him. He clicked the button on the tape recorder. And that was the end of my interviews with Franck O'Day.

TWENTY-FIVE

We spent a few pleasant hours on the terrace, chatting about current events. Franck told a few more Hollywood anecdotes from his heyday, but he didn't talk about himself or Jessika or anything that touched on his personal life. Maribeth did not appear.

At four o'clock, to my utter surprise, Ruthanne announced that it was time for us to go upstairs and pack, because it would soon be time to start that long drive home. I was disappointed, hoping to enjoy more of Franck's hospitality, especially Kimura's exceptional cooking.

But Ruthanne was right, as always. It was time to get ready to go. I went to my room, and she to hers, with a quick stop off at Franck's, I imagined, to recover anything she may have dropped in there.

Ten minutes later, we were walking down the grand staircase. Franck was waiting for us at the bottom. I set my suitcase down and stuck out my hand. He shook it. "Thanks so much for having us, Franck. I'll work on pulling all the info together, and send you an outline in a few weeks."

"Send me a signed copy," Franck said.

"You don't want to read it before it's published?" I asked in astonishment.

"I trust you, Carol." When I continued to gape, he said, "Send me a draft then, and I'll review it for chronological accuracy or something, if you'd like. But you don't have to run it by me first. I'm sure you'll get everything right."

"I appreciate your confidence in me," I said sincerely. It may have been more confidence than I had in myself.

"Don't hesitate to call me if you have any more questions."

I said thanks again, and goodbye. I told him to tell Maribeth for me, that I hoped she'd be feeling better soon. I walked out the front door, leaving him alone with Ruthanne, so they could say their goodbyes in private.

Then Ruthie was running down the steps like a pleasant spring breeze. She paused to wave at Franck, then she got in the car and we drove off.

Again, we rode in silence. At last, Ruthie said, "Do you want to hear about it?"

"Do you want to tell me about it?"

"It was . . . wonderful. He was . . . awesome." Ruthanne stopped, at an unusual loss for words. "*He wanted me*, Carol, can you imagine? As much as I wanted him. He made me feel as if he'd never wanted anyone like he wanted me. It was . . . *unbelievable.*" She stopped again.

I realized suddenly that perhaps my inability to describe these kinds of things sprung from my level of enjoyment – the better it was, the harder it was for me to verbalize it. Where this conundrum originated, I had no idea. But Ruthie seemed similarly afflicted. She could relate dry, clinical, sometimes downright bored chronicles of the ones that had not pleased her. And she could relate juicy tales of anticipations and longings unfulfilled, the aching marvels of consummation temporarily postponed. But when it came to the actual telling of the long awaited dream at last satisfied, Ruthie stumbled. Mere mortal words and phrases could not encompass its glory. But it was okay. I didn't really need to hear the details. Her smile told me enough.

Ruthanne's phone buzzed. "Franck says to check your email. He says Maribeth's sent you a surprise. Let me see your phone."

"My phone died," I said. "Have him send it to you."

Moments passed. Ruthanne's phone buzzed. She squeaked, and then she squealed. Then she read aloud, "Saturday, July 6 – *TwoGreenKeys.com* presents – an evening with Franck O'Day, including a screening of 1961 Oscar contender *High Times in Manhattan.* Mr. O'Day will be available before and after the screening to answer questions and sign autographs. Don't miss the rare opportunity to view this acclaimed film, not shown in Las Vegas since –"

"*Las Vegas?*" I hate Las Vegas. I'd spent a few romantic weekends there that wound up being barely romantic at all, because I discovered, each time, that I hate Las Vegas. The heat. The traffic. The idiots. It's so much worse that LA, and I hate LA, too, at least the driving around in it.

Why would they want to do this in Vegas? *Say it ain't so, Joe!*

"That's what it says. VFW Post 864, Las Vegas Boulevard North."

"Wait . . . what? Franck's having his coming out party in Las Vegas? *At a VFW hall?*"

"That's what it says," Ruthanne repeated.

Not to say anything against our Veterans of Foreign Wars – but it seemed odd to me that legendary screen star Franck O'Day would choose to make his first personal appearance in over forty years at some little bitty hall that probably wouldn't hold two hundred people. I would've expected him to host such a gala event at the ballroom of the MGM Grand. It wasn't like he couldn't afford it.

"Franck says Maribeth wants to know if we want to help her promote it."

185

"*Promote it?* What is this, a bake sale? A car wash?"

Ruthanne shrugged, typed on her phone, waited for a reply. "Franck says Maribeth went back to sleep. She just told him that all the arrangements had been made, then said she still wasn't feeling well. He says he'll let me know all the details tomorrow." She paused, then said by rote, "I hope she's feeling better soon." I didn't get a lot of heartfelt sentiment out of that. It's not like they were buddies and Ruthanne was truly concerned. It's not like she and Maribeth had ever had a chance to sit down and visit.

The following evening, Ruthanne put Franck on speakerphone, and he gave us the rundown on his first personal appearance in nearly four decades.

"We're booked at the *Wynn,*" he began.

That made it a little better. If I was being forced to go to Las Vegas, at least we'd be in a nice hotel. Don't get me wrong, I find the gambling Mecca tolerable – in other words, I don't loathe it completely – if I can stay at a nice hotel. If I don't have to venture outside in the withering heat, nor drive through the insane traffic, then it's almost okay.

"I thought it said a VFW Hall?" Ruthanne asked. "Isn't that what the flyer says?"

"Oh, yeah, the screening is at the VFW Hall," Franck said. "But we'll be staying at the *Wynn.*"

"Why not just have the whole thing at the *Wynn?*" I asked. I pictured myself battling inching Vegas traffic back and forth between the famous hotel and the anonymous hall.

"This is kind of a grass roots thing," Franck replied. "I want to start small, in a small venue. There'll only be publicity on the website and through a few flyers – almost a *by invitation only* kind of thing. I want to see what my real fans look like, Carol.

"If I called *The Times,* or notified *TMZ,* I know I'd get a bigger response. Hell, I might get a huge response. It's not every day that a movie star reappears after being dead for forty some odd years."

And especially not looking like you do, I thought.

"But if I alert the media, as they said, most of the turnout would be people who're just marginally interested." Franck paused, sighed. "What I'm trying to say is that if I make a big announcement, there might be a big turnout, but they won't all be fans. Most'll just be curious, or bored, or not have anything better to do. But if I have it at this little hall in Vegas – the people that show up, they'll be true fans. I want to see who I've got left, Carol."

186

If I get sunburned, you're gonna have one fan less, I thought. God, how I hate Las Vegas.

"Ruthie says she'll pass out flyers at some of the memorabilia stores. All very low key. Will you cover the whole thing for the book?"

"Why Las Vegas?" I whined.

"Again, I want to see only my true fans. If we screened *Manhattan* here in LA – hell, they screen it here all the time. And you get a few of my fans and a few of Jessika's fans and a bunch of Sunnerfeld's fans. I'm selfish, Carol."

You ain't just a whistlin' Dixie on that score, pal, I thought.

"People who just want to see Jessika, or admire Sunnerfeld's masterpiece – they can do it in LA. But people who want to see me – *who really want to see me in person* – they'll come to a little hall in Vegas."

"A small inconvenience, going to Las Vegas," Maribeth said in the background. "Well worth it to any real fan."

A pain in the ass to a biographer, I thought.

"We can come down this weekend to hand out flyers," Ruthanne said. She looked askance at me, and I nodded. I might as well go with her, because I knew she was going, regardless.

Franck reinforced this for me when he said, "I thought you were coming down anyway." He laughed. "Thought we might take another swim."

Ruthanne didn't blush, because she didn't know that I knew just what kind of swimming Franck was talking about. "We can always do that after I hand out flyers."

"Most definitely," he said, and Ruthanne blushed then, perhaps reliving the events in her mind. "We'll see you Friday night."

"I can't wait," Franck said and laughed again.

TWENTY-SIX

The four of us screened *Titanic* on Friday night. It looked incredible on Franck's giant television, and the movie theater ambiance took me back to the thrill of seeing it for the first time, on the big screen, when I was a kid. Ah, the romance! Ah, the tragedy! Ah, the tragic romance! Ah, Leo!

Franck and Ruthanne even behaved like adults instead of hormonal teenagers. Perhaps they were saving all that for the pool later. I retired early – I started an outline for the book – then was fast asleep before any repeat of Esther Williams' trick might have begun.

Ruthanne tapped on my door at 9 am the next morning, whispering something about wanting to get an early start before it got too hot. I told her to come in. She was wearing white sandals and a white t-shirt and a dark green pair of shorts. As always, she was just as cute as a summer day.

I wore jeans. I would've felt exposed looking like a summer day in Los Angeles, even if it was a summer day. People walking around on the storied streets there were different than those in our little Inland Empire burg: more colorful, stranger, bolder. Perhaps more dangerous.

We took a cab and had it drop us off in the heart of Tinseltown. There was no way I was going to drive around all day looking for places to park.

Ruthie was blithe. She sidestepped weirdos and panhandlers with panache. She was not a child, after all, even though she was as gleeful as one. She was on a mission to spread the word. Franck O'Day was making his first baby steps back into public life, and he was only interested in real fans being a party to the historic event. We walked all over LA, visiting old movie theaters and memorabilia shops.

The girl in the box office at *The Egyptian* proved to be a big fan, and I stood by quietly as she and Ruthanne deconstructed the subtleties of *Manhattan*, and bemoaned the fact, as I had myself, that even Franck couldn't save *George and Benedict*.

The girl, the same age as Ruthanne and I, promised to hand out the flyers at the next showing of *Manhattan*. It would be running that Thursday at 1 am. As we turned to leave, the girl said suspiciously, "Is he really going to be there? He's supposed to be dead – I don't want to drive all the way to Vegas if this is some kind of a scam."

Ruthanne looked one way, and then the other, the classic precursor to telling a secret. She stepped closer, lowered her voice. "I've seen him."

"Really?" The girl was stunned. She wanted to believe. "Where?"

"Right outside *Paramount*," Ruthanne nodded in the direction of the famed studio. "They asked for volunteers to hand out flyers, on *TwoGreenKeys.com*, so I sent an email and volunteered. I talked to his manager on the phone – the manager told me that they had a meeting at the studio, and if I was waiting outside at 9:30, he'd give me a bunch of flyers to hand out. I told him what I looked like, what I'd be wearing, and sure enough, at 9:40, a limo pulled up next to where I was standing on the sidewalk. The window rolled down and this guy said hi, and gave me this file full of flyers. And then he said that Franck wanted to thank me personally for being such a big fan. The manager guy sat back a little, so I could see inside the limo. And there was Franck O'Day sitting next to him. He told me thanks, and asked me if I was going to be there in Vegas. I said I wouldn't miss it for the world. So I guess you could say, I got a personal invite."

"Are they still looking for volunteers? What's the name of that site?"

Ruthanne pointed out the name of the website on the flyer. "It tells the whole story of his life. It's awesome."

"How did he look?"

Ruthanne smiled at the girl. "He looked great," she said. "Good enough to make me want to drive to Vegas."

The box-office girl looked thoughtfully at the flyer. "I just might see you there."

"Great!" Ruthie enthused. "Thanks for your help with the flyers." The girl nodded. She had taken out her phone, and was going to *TwoGreenKeys.com*.

After we were out of earshot of *The Egyptian's* box office, I said to Ruthanne, "Why didn't you just tell her that you're sleeping with him?"

Ruthie looked at me like I was stupid. "Nobody's gonna believe that, Carol. I don't hardly believe it myself."

Our next stop was *Mae's Memory Lane,* a memorabilia shop on Hollywood Boulevard. The place was a tiny store front with large windows and a glass door. Inside were cardboard boxes, cut down, set in rows on wooden tables that looked like they might have seen the inside of a school cafeteria about 1956. Inside the boxes, in vaguely alphabetical order, were hundreds of 8 x 10s of Hollywood's famous (and not so famous, I imagined) stretching back for decades. Each photo was encased in dusty plastic and had an old-fashioned price tag,

189

the kind you affix with a plastic gun, stuck on the back. A few curled posters adorned the walls, also dusty.

There was a cash register, also circa 1956, atop a scarred wooden counter. A printed sign stuck to its side read *In God We Trust, All Others Pay Cash.* As if to underline this philosophy, a tattered, handwritten notice was posted below: *All transactions, cash only! No refunds! Choose wisely before you purchase!*

Next to this warning I was amazed to see a framed, autographed picture of William Holden. It was in color; he was wearing a brown suit. He had his right hand in his pocket, and was leaning forward a little, other elbow on bent knee, cigarette in hand, smiling. The autograph read: *To Mae, Keep up all the good work! Your friend, Bill.*

Behind the cash register sat a large, sweet-faced old woman, drinking a Pepsi. I could tell she had been lovely once, before time and perhaps too many sodas had made her fat. Twinkling blue eyes surveyed us from behind half-spectacles on a chain. She had round, rouged cheeks; a pink-lipsticked bow mouth smiled from above many chins. Her hair, in gray ringlets, framed her face. I was put in mind of a somewhat overly made-up Mrs. Claus. She wore an animal-print muumuu. When Ruthie entered the store, the woman exclaimed, waddled from around the counter and embraced her. They performed air kisses.

"Carol," Ruthanne said, "this is Aunt Mae. She was an extra in *High Times in Manhattan.* Aunt Mae, this is my friend, Carol."

"So nice to meet you, Carol," Aunt Mae said. Her voice was low and cultured, but with a little rough edge to it. "What brings you to see me, Ruthie?" she asked as she returned to her stool behind the cash register. She perched upon it, like a big bird on a little branch, and lit a cigarette from a pack laying on the counter.

Ruthanne winked at me. "I met Franck O'Day, Aunt Mae."

Aunt Mae took a drag on her cigarette. I noticed that she had small, delicate hands, the fingers crowned with long, red-lacquered nails. She looked over her half-specs at me, a trifle suspiciously, then exhaled a cloud of smoke and narrowed her eyes at Ruthanne. "Don't lie to an old woman, Ruthie."

"I'm not lying, Aunt Mae." Ruthanne lowered her eyes, looked at the floor, as if she might be lying. Then she looked up and said, "Tell Carol about making *Manhattan.*"

Now Aunt Mae narrowed her eyes at me. It was a look I'd seen Ruthie give before, the same look she'd shot at Marty when he had foolishly elected not to read the back of the box that had contained *The Criterion Collection* release of her favorite movie. It was a look gauging my worthiness – did I really want to hear her story, or was I just being polite? Would my attention wander halfway through it? Might I be rude and interrupt, or even just walk out in the middle of it?

I smiled with an eagerness I did not feel. She was Ruthie's friend, after all. And what would it hurt me to listen to one more *High Times in Manhattan* story? Now Aunt Mae smiled back, and it was with that slightly rapacious smile that crosses an old storyteller's face when she realizes that she's found a new victim.

"The director was polite, but not kind. He still ordered us around like we were cattle," Aunt Mae began. She took a drag on her cigarette, exhaled. "We called ourselves the chorus. We were in all the ballroom scenes, dancing gaily in the background. There were ten of us altogether. There are only two of us left, and Candace really doesn't count. She's in a nursing home out in Chino now, with the Alzheimer's. It was a generous shoot – all the dresses fit to a T, and they always fed us well."

"Tell her about Jessika, Aunt Mae," Ruthanne prompted.

Aunt Mae took another quick, short puff on her cigarette, leaving another coat of pink lipstick on the filter. "Ah, yes. *Miss* Yerdlay. She was a bitch and a half. She was about thirty, and we were all in our early twenties. She pretended that it was too much trouble to remember our names. She'd just call us *girl*. As in, 'You – girl in the blue chiffon – you're dancing too close to me in this scene. You need to back up a bit.' That was the only time she spoke to us, or even looked at us – when she was giving us some kind of correction. She didn't really deign to speak to any of the other actors, either, and you could tell that she despised the director. She'd glare and roll her eyes when he spoke. It was very disrespectful. *Miss* Yerdlay was so much better than the rest of us, you see. She always had her nose in the air."

Aunt Mae glanced slyly at Ruthanne, who grinned back. She'd heard this story. I could guess what was coming next. "Except when Franck O'Day was on set." Aunt Mae took another drag on her cigarette and set it down in an ashtray beside the cash register. "Are you a fan, Carol?"

"As of just recently," Ruthanne answered quickly for me.

"I've seen a lot of actors in my time, and I'm sure you'll agree that few of them look as absolutely delectable in a tux as he did. When Franck would arrive before a scene, we'd all stop what we were doing and just look at him. Then we'd all run over and gather around him, all talking at once, like the silly gooses we were. But Franck didn't mind. He'd smile and say something nice to each one of us. He'd tell Candace that she looked lovely today, and she'd blush to the roots of her hair.

191

Candace doesn't remember much these days — she thinks I'm one of the nurses, and always gives her daughter a lunch order, because she thinks she's a waitress. But I'll bet she still remembers Franck.

"He'd ask Janice how her ankle was mending — Janice had tripped over a cable on the first day of shooting and sprained it slightly. He always had something nice to say to all of us. He'd stand there, with one of us on each arm — we used to plan out ahead of time whose turn it was — and just chat and smile with us until it was time to begin.

"When the show wrapped, he took us all out to dinner — just the ten of us. Ten unknown extras from the chorus and famous Franck O'Day. He bought us champagne." Aunt Mae paused to recollect.

"When we'd all gather around him on set," she continued, "Miss Yerdlay would stand off to one side. She was way too high and mighty to include herself in any conversations between Franck and a bunch of extras. But I watched her sometimes, when she didn't know anyone was watching her. She would just look wistfully at Franck — all the hard, I'm-better-than-you-and-we-both-know-it big star attitude would just melt away, and she'd just look like a woman gazing at the man she loved. It almost made me feel sorry for her. But only almost.

"Franck was polite and respectful to her on set — still, we all knew they were sleeping together. He was never anything but kind and friendly to us and everybody else — but he was always professional toward Miss Yerdlay. She hated it — you could see it in her eyes — she wanted him to hold her hand or steal a kiss in front of everybody. She wanted the world to know that not only were they sleeping together — she wanted him to demonstrate that he loved her, as much as she loved him. She wanted — what are those initials, Ruthie?"

"PDA, Aunt Mae. Public display of affection."

Aunt Mae took a final drag on her cigarette, and stubbed it out in the ashtray. *Are you gonna finish that cigarette*, my grandpa's voice said in my head, *or is that cigarette going to finish you?*

"Exactly," she said through the exhaled smoke. "That's what Miss Yerdlay wanted from Franck. *A public display of affection.* But he wouldn't give it to her. He was more affectionate with us girls in the chorus — he would give us a little pat on the back sometimes, or a quick little hug around the shoulder. But Franck was always professional to Miss Yerdlay — civil, courteous. But not affectionate. It was almost as if he wasn't sleeping with her at all — even though we all knew he was."

Aunt Mae smiled, her teeth just as white and incongruous and false in her old face as Maribeth's. "But sex is just sex, is it not, my young friends? Remember *The Shoop Shoop Song*, Ruthie?"

192

Ruthie burst into song: "*If you wanna know/If he loves you so/It's in his kiss/That's where it is!*"

"You can tell how a man truly feels by how affectionate he is," Aunt Mae continued sagely. "Franck was fond of all us girls in the chorus. He could've had any one of us at a wink, but he wasn't that *fond* of us." She chuckled. "But he was a man, just like any other man, and Miss Yerdlay made herself available to him – she was beautiful and famous, just like he was – so why wouldn't he take advantage of it? But he never loved her, not the way she loved him. We could tell from how he looked at her, from his complete lack of affection to her. And like I say, it almost made us feel sorry for her. But only almost. She was a bitch. And a few years later, when he dropped her like a bad habit and left town with Bobby Ecksmith, the ten of us lit up the switchboards laughing at that."

"Did you believe what Jessika said about him in the papers, Aunt Mae?" I asked. "About him and her daughter?"

She made a pushing away gesture. "Franck O'Day could have had any woman he wanted. For a wink. What would he want with some little girl? No, I didn't believe a word of it. No one who'd ever met him believed a word of it."

Then Aunt Mae paused and her face sobered. "And then we heard that his plane had gone down. That's how Carole Lombard went, in the war. I remember my mother telling me about it. All of us girls that'd been in the chorus for *Manhattan*, we gathered together at Candace's house when we heard the news. We were all on different movies – just unknown faces in the crowd, that's all any of us ever were – but we found time to get together. We drank, we cried. Candace cried the most – we all had a crush on him, but hers was the biggest." Aunt Mae narrowed her eyes and considered Ruthanne again. "Now Franck O'Day's biggest fan over here tells me that she's met him."

Ruthanne removed one of the flyers from its folder and handed it to her. Aunt Mae's skepticism remained unabated. "Oh, yeah? And Sinatra's playing at the Hollywood Bowl. Only it ain't him. It's just somebody that sounds like him. It's a – what do you call it?"

"A tribute," I supplied.

"That's right. And that's what this is, too. You've been snookered, Ruthie. Franck O'Day is dead. May he rest in peace." Aunt Mae frowned, and her age showed fully on her face. She lit another cigarette and looked at Ruthanne. She didn't smile.

"Must I recite the facts to you, Aunt Mae?" Ruthie winked at me. "No bodies were ever found. They're not even sure the wreckage they found is from the right plane. But most importantly, I'd never lie to an

193

old chorus girl." She smiled kindly at her friend. "He's living in Jessika's house in Beverly Hills. With Maribeth McSwale. I've met him."

I noticed that while she didn't give her old friend the fiction about the manager and the limo in front of *Paramount,* she also didn't tell her the extent of how well she knew Franck. Aunt Mae wouldn't believe that. *Nobody would believe that.*

"I even got his autograph." I watched in amazement as Ruthanne pulled down the collar of her white t-shirt to reveal Franck's signature in Sharpie, just above the swell of her right breast.

I think Ruthie had expected to shock her friend. But Aunt Mae wasn't easily shocked. She'd been in the chorus, after all. She put her cigarette in the ashtray and her eyes narrowed again. "You young girls today. Didn't you have any paper? Haven't I always told you to get it on paper, Ruthie?"

Ruthanne released the collar of her shirt, and reached into the folder. She brought out an autographed copy of Franck's still from *Manhattan.* She held it up so I could see it. The autograph read: *To my Dearest Mae – Is there still a place for me with the chorus? Your co-star in an almost Oscar-winner, Franck.*

But still the old woman was not convinced. "You could've got this off the internet, Ruthie. Anybody could've signed it."

Ruthanne turned the 8 x 10 over. *Mae's Memory Lane,* the address on Hollywood Boulevard, and the phone number were stamped in the corner. "This is my photo, Mae. I bought it from you, remember? The first day I came in here. I told him about you and he remembered you, right away. I asked him to sign it for you."

Aunt Mae's pink bow mouth formed a perfect O of astonishment. "He's really not dead?"

Ruthanne shook her head. A tear ran down Aunt Mae's wrinkled cheek and she embraced Ruthie across the counter. "He remembered me?" Ruthie nodded. It was the sweetest thing I'd ever seen.

Aunt Mae released Ruthanne and reached around the cash register. She retrieved the framed photo of much-more-famous but also definitely-dead William Holden. She removed his picture, opened a drawer beneath the cash register and tossed it carelessly in there. She slid Franck's picture into the frame. She studied it, ran her finger lightly across the autograph, then replaced the picture in its place of honor beside the cash register.

Then she picked up her cigarette, stuck it in her mouth, and picked up the flyer. "Vegas, you say? I'll have to have the Caddy checked out. It's a long drive. Whatever will I wear?"

194

TWENTY-SEVEN

We hit a few more memorabilia stores, but didn't find any more fans. Franck was standing at the top of the stairs when the cab dropped us back off at Jessika's house. He descended, smiled at us, then took our arms and we walked back up the stairs. He didn't ask us how it went.

After an excellent dinner of filet mignon, Franck asked me what movie I'd like to watch. Who knew movie stars liked to watch movies so much? But then, if I had the set-up he had, I'd never leave the house. I'd watch movies all day.

"How about *Sunset Boulevard?*" I suggested, thinking about how Aunt Mae had summarily replaced ol' Bill Holden's photo with Franck's own.

He smiled at me. "How topical of you, Carol! Who's ready for their close-up more than me?"

Maribeth frowned. "That one always depresses me. I'll pass. Good-night, ladies. Franck."

Franck nodded and Maribeth left us. After the movie, I, too, retired, telling them that I was going to work on the book outline again. The truth was, I felt like a third wheel. They were just so cute together. *Affectionate.*

Franck was cute, all by himself. I don't know how I hadn't noticed it before. I guess I'd just been fighting it, always noting what an arrogant bastard he was, without observing that he had a good reason for it. I felt that little pang of guilt again at my appreciation for someone else's man.

On Sunday, we had brunch, and lazed around the pool all afternoon in studied indolence. As the sun began to set, Franck once again bid us farewell. It was getting to be a habit.

TWENTY-EIGHT

On the following Friday night, Ruthanne and I went to the local gay bar. It was our favorite. The music was loud, the drinks were strong and cheap, and the men were sexy and adorable, even if they were not in the least bit interested in us, past laughter and conversation. And the occasional dance.

We didn't go to LA, because the Inland Empire was due for a rare visitation, all unbeknownst to it. Legendary screen actor Franck O'Day was riding out on the train from his brick palace in Beverly Hills on Saturday to visit his biggest fan. They planned to stay at the local Hilton. After all, the walls in our apartment were not nearly as thick and protecting of secrets as those in Jessika's mansion. It was difficult to imagine yourself even remotely alone, when your roommate was sleeping mere feet away. I was grateful for their discretion. I knew that I'd hear, I knew that I'd *listen,* if they were just across the hall.

But on Friday night, Ruthanne and I went out. We drank, we danced. We saw all our gay friends. The two of us had gone to school with the bar's DJ, David. We'd always suspected that he'd come out someday, because he'd been just fabulous in high school. Ruthanne had even gone out with him a few times – he was dark-haired and blue-eyed after all. Now he was living the gay dream – he was tattooed and ripped and beautiful, and had more men, just as attractive as he was, than Ruthanne and I could ever hope for.

At one point, Ruthie went over and stood in front of the DJ booth. I watched her wave to David, and hold up her phone. Then she typed, and David looked at his phone. He nodded and Ruthie climbed up the three steps and joined him in the booth.

When the song ended, David said into the mike, "You all know my friend, Ruthie." Scattered cheers and applause. "She'd like a moment of your time."

Ruthanne kissed David on the cheek and took the mike from him. "Thank you, David," she said. "I only have one question, and then we can all get back to dancing." A whoop from the assemblage. "I only have one question," she repeated. "Are there any Franck O'Day fans out there?"

Oh, no, she didn't, I thought. I hid behind my drink in embarrassment for her. No one of our age group, except for one box-office girl in LA, had ever heard of her used-to-be-famous boyfriend. The silence stretched out for maybe five seconds, then there was a whoop, then another one. "Gentlemen!" Ruthanne said, a smile in her voice. "Please meet me on the patio. I have a surprise for you."

She handed the mike back to David, then kissed him on the cheek again and left the booth. She walked out to the patio, where it was quieter, where wild horses couldn't have kept me from following her. This I had to see. By the time I made it outside, five men, not one of them more than thirty, were gathered around my roommate. I couldn't hear what she was saying – I was having a little trouble maneuvering through the crowd to where they stood. I watched her hand them each a flyer, watched her pull down the corner of her t-shirt again, and show them the faint outline of Franck's Sharpie signature, not entirely washed away yet. There was a flash as someone took a picture of it. One of the men, a muscular blonde wearing nothing but jeans and a leather vest, actually bounced up and down in glee, and elbowed his companion, gesturing at the flyer. I noticed that he had pierced nipples.

"Tell John and Andy, too," Ruthie was saying as I finally made it through the crowd. She smiled at me. "Evan already knew about this," she said. Evan was a tall, brown-haired hipster type. He smiled at me. "He belongs to the fan club."

Evan reached into his pocket and brought out his keys. He dangled them in front of my face, so I could see the two green ones at the bottom. "We'll definitely see you there, Ruthie." Evan gave her a hug, and the five of them melted back into the crowd.

"Mission accomplished," Ruthie said. "Let's dance!"

TWENTY-NINE

The following evening, Franck and Ruthanne and I dined at *Paul's*, the most expensive restaurant in town. It was nice, but I had already been spoiled. The meal couldn't hold a candle to Kimura's cuisine. But it was nice.

"I've been thinking about taking Franck over to the gay bar," Ruthanne said as the three of us enjoyed a digestif. That's what we called the place. *The gay bar.* It was really more a dance club than a bar, actually. And it had a name, of course, but we never called it by its name. Franck raised a manicured eyebrow over his green Chartreuse, and gave her a little half smile. "You have at least five fans there that I know of," Ruthie said and grinned. "Maybe more."

"What can I say?" Franck grinned back. "Some of our gay friends have exquisite taste." He paused. "If you really want to go, Ruthie – I'm sure I'll be flattered by the attention. I always have been." He winked at me. "A gay bar – it's really a perfect place – I don't have to worry about any of them leaving with you, and you don't have to worry about me leaving with any of them."

I considered that for a minute – there seemed to be some kind of subtle insult in there, but I couldn't quite ferret it out. I thought perhaps Franck did not appreciate Ruthanne's transparent attempt to show him off. It did seem a little small of her – just like Franck said, Ruthie would have no competition there, could bask in the gay men's jealousy that their idol had chosen her, without worrying that he might choose one of them *over* her. On the other hand, where else in town did he have a concentration of fans, albeit a small one?

"I'm just kidding, Franck," Ruthie said and squeezed his hand. "I want to keep you all to myself up until the last second. Next weekend, there'll be all your real fans, and then, after that . . . you'll belong to the world again."

I stifled a giggle, almost choked on my Schnapps. Sometimes Ruthie was just a little too dramatic. A little too *cinematic*, as Dolores had termed it in her diaries.

"Every part of me belongs entirely to you," Franck replied and kissed her hand.

Oh, you are *good, Franck, ol' boy,* I thought. *Very,* very *good.*

"I'm not selfish," Ruthie said. "But I'm not ready to give you up to your fans just yet."

I thought of Norma Desmond. *"We don't want to share this night with other people."* I finished my drink, made my excuses. They didn't try to dissuade me from leaving.

THIRTY

The following Friday afternoon found us standing with the common rabble at the United terminal at LAX. I was surprised at my petulance, surprised at how I suddenly missed the borrowed glories: at one point, I whispered to Ruthie, "Couldn't Franck have chartered a plane?"

"Franck doesn't care for chartered planes," Ruthie whispered back.

"My last experience with a chartered plane didn't end well," Franck said. Even over the din in the terminal, he'd heard me. "I figure that the commercial ones might be maintained a little bit better." He smiled a little sheepishly at me. "I've only flown twice since 1967. And the disembarkation on the first trip was a trifle abrupt." He tilted his head and considered me. "You don't like to fly either, do you, Carol?"

Ruthie and Maribeth were no longer paying attention to us. They were now chatting animatedly. Apparently the two of them had finally bonded, and it was over just this subject – both of them just *loved* to fly. Oh, the exhilaration of the take-off, the glory of the clouds, the living map of the earth below! The thrill of the descent, the afterglow of the landing!

I met Franck's eyes. Here was something that the *two of us* could also bond over. It was kind of like that tired old joke – *I'm not afraid of flying, I'm afraid of crashing.* But even that wasn't entirely accurate. I'm afraid of dying as much as the next person, I guess, and I've always supposed a plane crash wouldn't even be the worst way to go. It would be merciful and quick, I imagined. Just a long screaming drop and then nothingness.

But it was the anticipation, the inevitability of a plane crash – these things happen every day, don't they? It was the complete surrender of my fate to unseen hands. That's what got to me about flying. If I was up there, and if the plane started to go down, there was not a *goddamned thing* I could do about it. I couldn't steer out of it – I couldn't avoid it in any way. Chances are, I wouldn't even know it was happening. This concept of my own helplessness damn near undid me.

Flying, to me, made me feel like I'd voluntarily allowed myself to be strapped into a rollercoaster and then blindfolded. Then the paranoia emerged. What was that sound? Was that some kind of bolt falling out of the car? What if the rail was bent? What if one of the billion different things that could go wrong, things that I didn't even comprehend – what if one of them went wrong? What if several of them went wrong? I couldn't see any of them to prevent them. I was as vulnerable as a horse in a trailer, a cow in a cattle car. I had absolutely no control.

The only thing standing between me and certain death was an aging frat boy with good eye-sight, who was probably cheating on his wife and who might have a drinking problem. I would hesitate to let such a person drive me to the market, but I was going to allow him to *fly me to Las Vegas?*

I nodded slowly at Franck. "I hate to fly."

He grinned. "Me, too, for obvious reasons. You want a drink?"

I looked at him in surprise. "A drink?"

He removed a cheap plastic flask from his pocket and hit it, then handed it to me. "We have to finish it. They won't let us take it on the plane. I checked." I hit the flask. The whisky was hot and calming in my belly, like a gentle paternal hand laid upon the brow of my fear. I felt better already. I was handing the flask back to Franck when I noticed Ruthanne staring at us, open-mouthed. "Drink, Ruthie?" I held it out to her.

Ruthanne glanced around like Franck and I had been making jokes about guns and bombs. "You can't drink that in here!" she whispered fiercely.

"You just watch me, Ruthie," Franck said. He took the flask from me and hit it again. "I just can't take it on the plane. You want a drink or not?"

By the time we got up to the checkpoint, Franck and I were like old drinking buddies, simpatico in our belief that drunkenness was a perfectly acceptable defense against a fear of flying. Ruthie only had one shot, and kept looking at us like we were teenagers trying to sneak a bottle into a concert.

Maribeth pretended she didn't know us. When she started through the metal detector, Franck clandestinely dropped the plastic flask into a nearby trash receptacle. He winked at me, and I felt a fondness for him for the first time, past my guilty appreciation of his looks – a feeling of *aw, maybe he's not so bad after all.* Where before, I'd felt him to be full of himself, arrogant, and rather an all-around son-of-a-bitch, the whiskey had warmed me up enough to think that perhaps Franck might be an okay guy after all.

I lied to myself, told myself that I was still immune to his charm, no matter how attractive he was. But I could see a little more clearly how others could succumb so completely to it. *He's got the bluest eyes,* I thought, and almost giggled in the face of the TSA lady who was wanding me. That wouldn't be good. They wouldn't let me on the plane if it was obvious that I was wrecked.

Ruthie, the gleeful flyer, got the window seat, and Franck sat next to her. I was across the aisle from him, and Maribeth, the other happy traveler, formed a bookend to our fear in the window seat next to me.

The plane started to vibrate up the runway, and Franck and I reached across the aisle and held hands, like the scaredy-cats we were. We didn't have time to become completely petrified, however, because the flight from LAX to LAS only lasted, runway to runway, shuddering takeoff to heart-stopping landing, for an hour and a half. But we held hands across the aisle for the entire flight. The stewardess glared at us when we had to let go to let her pass. It was not a man/woman kind of hand holding – just the human comfort of the touch of someone who was just as scared as I was.

The limo driver was waiting for us in the baggage claim area with a sign that said *Frank O'day* on it. Apparently, nobody at the limousine service was a fan. Franck took him aside, said a few words. I watched money change hands. Then Franck slapped the limo driver on back and he walked quickly out of the terminal.

The four of us stood on opposite sides of the carousel. Maribeth and Ruthanne again chatted happily on their side. They had just experienced an uneventful LA to Vegas hop, whereas Franck and I had just withstood an ordeal. Franck stood next to me, facing away from the bumping luggage. We looked at each other – we were not drunk enough, and the jitters were just starting to subside.

"Fuck this," he said, conversationally. I flinched at the profanity, borne as it was on his silky, mellifluous voice. "They can fly back if they want, but not us. I'll hire a car, we'll take the bus, if we have to. But fuck this." He grinned at me a little, and we embraced, as if we felt lucky to be alive. We did.

In the limo, Franck found a pint of Maker's Mark, still in its little black liquor store bag. "What an excellent limo service you picked, Mari," he said, and uncapped the bottle. Mari smiled at him, a little maternally, I thought. She was unmoved by his fear, however – he was just a silly child to her, as far as his fear of flying was concerned. "I've never been a heavy drinker. It's bad for your skin." Franck winked at me. "But, fuck it. I hate to fly." He took a long swig, shuddered. "Carol?"

I reached for the proffered flask. "Welcome to Las Vegas," I said.

The sun was sinking in the west when we arrived at the *Wynn*. Its brightness had subsided, but its heat remained. Curious tourists paused as we got out of the limo, eager to see if we were anybody famous.

They were disappointed. Just a couple girls and their mom, and some good-looking, well-dressed other guy, they thought, and proceeded on their way. Just a little group that had rented a limo at the airport, all part of living the Vegas dream, along with the expensive hotel and its room service. They'd be taking cabs for the rest of their stay, or maybe just walking to see the sites, and Mom would be checking those room services bills, worrying about the credit card balance. Just like they were. If only they knew. Franck had the limo service on speed-dial, and his suit cost more than my car.

I staggered a little as we entered the lobby; Ruthanne supported yesterday's matinee idol. Our rooms were not all the way at the top, but they were at least three-quarters of the way, three doors on the same floor. Ruthanne and Franck had given up all pretense – what happened in Vegas, stayed in Vegas, after all. They were staying together in the same room.

It wasn't as if what was going to happen in Vegas (before the hour was out, I'd wager) hadn't been happening in Southern California for the past month or so, already.

"I'm going to look at the pool," Maribeth said, to everybody's surprise. She walked down the hall and entered her room.

"I'm going to take a little nap," I said. "Call me later." I nodded at them. "Franck. Ruthie."

"Drinkie," Ruthie said and nodded back. It was what we called each other when we were drunk.

I turned and walked down the hall, only leaning on the wall for support once. I slid the card in the slot, and then was enveloped in the glorious coolness of an expensive Las Vegas hotel room. There was nothing like it, I had to admit. Artic, icy, delicious cold. I closed the curtains on the dying sun, without even offering it a salute, and slid between the crisp white sheets. Also cold. That was Vegas – agonizingly hot or mercifully cold. It all depended on what side of civilization you were on. Outside with the peasants or inside, where it cost money to remain. The bed was wonderful, but I still hated Vegas.

I slept the sleep of drunken, ice-cold comfort. Damn the Strip, I just slept. Been there, done that – ya seen Vegas once, ya seen it. My phone rang at 10 am, its six or seven plaintive summonings finally dying away unheeded. It rang again immediately. This time, I answered it.

"How's your head?" Ruthanne asked.

I sat up. My head pounded. "I may live," I said.

"Order yourself some room service, if you want," Ruthie advised. "Charge it to your room. If you want to see the venue, meet us in the lobby at 11:30."

"I wouldn't miss it for the world," I said, looking at the room service menu. "I'll see you then." *Charge it to my room, indeed,* I thought, a little shocked at the prices.

THIRTY-ONE

By 11:30, I was showered and coffeed and fed, and felt like a new woman. The gripping fear of the plane flight was like a story that I'd read, something that someone else had felt. Fear of a plane crash was silly and childish, after all. Plane crashes are rare, statistical improbabilities. You had more chance of being in a car wreck.

But you have a higher probability of walking away from a car wreck, the fear, which was indeed my very own, whispered. *The probabilities of walking away from a plane crash are slim and none.* I knew I would be right there beside Franck if he hired a car, would be right there beside him if he took the bus. *Fuck this,* I thought, and smiled.

I bounced down to the lobby. Franck and Ruthanne were standing outside, waiting for our ride. I waved, but hung back, not wanting to step out into the relentless July heat any sooner than absolutely necessary. I wondered where Maribeth was. A cab pulled up. No limo this time. I thought that perhaps Franck didn't want to call attention to himself just yet, pulling up to the humble VFW hall in a limo, just for the walk-through. But I knew he would so arrive tonight. Tonight was all about drawing attention to himself.

Franck opened the door for Ruthanne, then gestured for me to come on out of the hotel. I braced myself – the blazing heat was just as awful as I knew it would be as the doors opened – and I quickly slid in beside Ruthanne. "Maribeth's not coming?" I asked.

"She's out by the pool," Franck says. "She loves the heat." When I looked askance at him, Franck laughed. "Oh, back at the house? That was just a little self-consciousness on her part. She didn't want you attractive young women looking down on her. The old gray mare, she ain't what she used to be." He winked at Ruthanne. "But here, she doesn't care. There are plenty of oldsters and fatties exposed for the world to look upon with disgust. Nobody's looking at her. She doesn't know any of these people. And she loves the sun. She might even talk some young man into rubbing a little sun screen on her."

Franck told the driver where we were going, and after about twenty minutes of interminable start-stop, start-stop traffic, blocks before it passed under the 515, Las Vegas Boulevard South turned into Las Vegas Boulevard North. A few moments after that, we had arrived.

The cab pulled into the strip mall driveway beside the hall, then came to a stop before a thick flagpole, topped with the stars and stripes and a black MIA flag. Beside the flagpole was a square block of concrete, maybe three feet on a side, painted snow white. There was a plaque on the front. Atop the block was some kind of weapon – the barrel was perhaps twelve feet long. It had been painted and repainted, to stop the rust no doubt, although I couldn't imagine how anything could rust in the humidity-less desert. Currently, it was painted gray. On the other side of the building was an empty field, punctuated by a few scrubby weeds.

We got out of the cab. Franck handed the driver a fifty and told him to wait.

The flat façade of the building was painted a pale blue, so pale as to be almost white. Only the contrast from the white block with the gun atop it informed your eye that the building wasn't white at all, but light blue. *Veterans of Foreign Wars* was emblazoned – no other word would do, except *emblazoned* – across the top of the façade in dark blue. The legend was hand-painted in fat capital letters, two feet tall. They ran up at a little bit of an angle, then leveled out, took a little jog downward again, then leveled once more. Large windows framed double glass doors. The doors stood open to the merciless Nevada heat. That could not possibly be good.

I looked at Ruthanne, then we both looked at Franck. The place was ancient, tiny. It was as far below Franck, his past glories and future aspirations, as was the hot, cracked concrete of its parking lot beneath his pricey Italian shoes.

"It's charming," Franck said, not looking at us. "Just what we need."

Speechless, Ruthanne and I followed him into the hall. A plump, middle-aged woman rose from behind a counter. She extended her hand. "You must be Mr. O'Day," she said. "Welcome to Post 864. I'm Betty." Franck smiled, shook her hand, and Betty was charmed, but I could tell that she had no idea who he was, and so she wasn't that charmed. She said politely, "I understand ya'll are going to show a movie?" She had an endearing Southern accent that I imagined would grow annoying very quickly. I was glad my hangover had been cured.

"Yes," Ruthanne spoke up. "It's a fan club meeting. Our first. We're going to screen a movie from 1961." Ruthie didn't go on to describe *High Times in Manhattan*. The almost Oscar contender from fifty-odd years ago was obviously not this woman's oeuvre.

"Let me show you the hall," Betty said. She led us down a dark, narrow, wood paneled hallway, lined with commendations and proclamations, and faded photographs of long-dead veterans. "We've got it all set up for you."

The hall was a large, rectangular room with a low ceiling, painted white. In one corner was a dais, reached by two semi-circular steps, carpeted in the most astonishingly ugly yellow and brown swirly pattern I could imagine, this side of Hell. Satan sat on such a dais in his disco days. Another American flag on a pole, flanked by nine others that I couldn't identify – other VFW chapters perhaps – lined the back of the dais.

To the left of the dais was a large screen, and hanging from the ceiling near the center of the room was a fairly modern projector. A flat podium was directly below it. There was another machine – a DVD player, maybe? on the podium, and wires snaked up to the projector. Two impressive speakers stood beside the screen against the back wall. Perhaps a hundred or so folding chairs were lined up in neat rows on either side of the podium, leaving a wide aisle behind it. *VFW 864* was stenciled on the back of every single chair.

I have to mention the floor, because it clashed with, yet somehow complimented, the hideousness of the carpet on the dais. A pattern of one bright pink tile, surrounded by eight light gray tiles, stalked across the hall, back into the mists of whatever garish era had produced it. The floor was immaculately clean, shiny, polished – but it was just as ugly as homemade sin.

Betty showed us the microphone set-up on the dais, in case we wanted to address the fan club before the movie. She showed us how to work the projector – she pushed a few buttons, and *The Little Mermaid* swam into view on the screen. I was appalled at how indistinct and bleached out it appeared under the fluorescents, but when Betty strode across the ugly floor and flipped the switch, the room was plunged into wonderful darkness. The only thing we could see was Ariel, distinctly now, and a square of dim light coming through the narrow door, and the red exit sign that blinked fitfully over it. Not a ray of harsh Las Vegas light intruded anywhere.

A table for refreshments was set up behind the rows of chairs, and the doors to the men's and ladies' were on the wall in the back of the room. Several more commendations and proclamations and pictures of long dead veterans populated the wall in between the doors.

The place was large, the audio and video were decent, the bathrooms convenient. It was old, but spotless, and despite the front doors being open, nice and cool inside.

Franck smiled at Betty. "It's perfect," he said. "Just perfect."

Betty smiled back. She was pleased that he was satisfied with the hall, but in no way was she star struck. "There's a phone in the front," she said, "and emergency numbers. Just turn out the lights and lock up when you're through. Drop the key through the slot in the door." She handed Franck a single key, attached by a length of wire to half of a wooden ruler, and we walked down the long dim hall to the front counter again. "I told your daughter . . ." Betty looked at us. We shook out heads. Betty shrugged. "I told your daughter that there was to be no alcohol, because we don't have a liquor license or anything like that." She looked at Franck, waiting for him to object, but again he just smiled.

"No alcohol. Check."

"And you'll have to have everyone out of here by 1 am." Franck nodded. "And if ya'll make a mess, we'll keep your cleaning deposit." Betty smiled. She didn't think that this sharp-dressed man and his friends would be likely to make a mess. "What's the movie about?"

"Romantic hijinks at an upscale New York hotel on New Year's Eve, 1940," Ruthanne recited by rote.

"Oh. And who did you say was in it?"

We all stood silently, embarrassed at Betty's ignorance. Finally, Ruthanne just pointed at Franck.

"Oh, so you're *in the movie!* It's your fan club? Isn't that nice!" A more sophisticated person might have been embarrassed at this glaring faux pas, but not our Betty. She said, "I'll be here till five, if you need anything before your event, and my number's by the phone." She shook our hands. "Well, ya'll have fun now. I hope your first fan club meeting is a success."

We rode in the cab in silence for several minutes, before Franck said, "It's perfect, Ruthie. We're out here in the middle of nowhere – no bright lights, no press, no disinterested passers-by."

"Only real fans?" Ruthie asked.

"Exactly. Only real fans. I want to see who I've got left."

When she still looked unconvinced, I said, "It'll be great, Ruthie. Just you wait. It's small, intimate. Perfect for an up close and personal with all the real fans."

Ruthanne looked solemnly at Franck. "If you're happy with it, then I'm happy with it." Because she certainly wasn't happy with it otherwise.

He took her hand and kissed it. "It's perfect. Trust me."

THIRTY-TWO

When we got back to the hotel, Franck suggested lunch. I begged off, saying I was still full from my earlier room-served breakfast. I told them that I wanted to go upstairs for a while, write a little. *And get out of the sun,* I thought. I told them that I would call and catch up with them later. A little bit of that feeling of being a third wheel lingered. They were just so cute together.

I went up to the welcoming cold of my room, and flicked on the lights. I left the curtains drawn on the sun. I sat at the little table provided and considered the blank screen of my laptop. I found inspiration in our recent white-knuckle flight from LA.

> *In January of 1968, Franck and friend Robert Ecksmith chartered an airplane, bound for a commercial airport, no doubt in Tokyo, where they would catch a larger plane back to the States. Franck and Ecksmith were confident as the climbed aboard. As the small plane banked into the sky, they knew that Franck would soon be exonerated of all the specious charges that Jessika had related to the press.*

I frowned. I'd said *plane* three times in one paragraph. It was weak. What kind of plane was it? I thought of calling Franck and asking him for clarification as to the make and model of the aircraft in which he'd crashed, but then I considered that Franck, being as much of a fan of aircraft as I was, probably didn't know himself.

So I minimized my immortal words, weak though they were, and called up Franck's *Wikipedia* entry. I scrolled down to the *References* section at the bottom, hoping to find a link to some other article, one about the plane crash specifically, one that would mention what kind of plane it had been. Maybe there was a link to some article from 1982, when the wreckage had been found.

I scrolled all the way down to the end. No articles specific to the plane crash. I was just thinking that I would Google *Franck O'Day plane wreckage,* when my fingers stopped dead above the keyboard. In the *External Links* section of the *Wikipedia* entry for my close personal friend and legendary matinee idol, the following words had caught my eye:

Bridget McSwale O'Day at Find a Grave
Peter McSwale at Find a Grave
Maribeth McSwale at Find a Grave

My fingers trembled. There had to be some mistake. Some kind of double entry, a typo, *something*.

It's alleged that *Wikipedia* is riddled with misspellings, factual errors, and just plain lies. College professors and 8th grade English teachers alike forbid its use for research papers, for just these reasons. But I'd learned a little trick during my time in legal secretary school. We'd been assigned to do a paper on landmark legal cases. Ruthanne had picked *Brown v Board of Education* and I'd picked *Roe v Wade*. I went to *Wikipedia*, first – the teacher's prohibitions be damned – because *Wikipedia* is the best thing to hit the internet since cats. There it was, all the information I could possibly need, all un-citable, due to the proscriptions of academe.

But at the bottom of the page, in itty-bitty font, in the *References* and *Further Reading* and *External Links* sections were all the sources that the diligent author of the page had used in his or her own research. These references were real, legit. These were, like Caesar's wife, above reproach.

I wrote my paper, cited a few of the sources from the bottom of the forbidden *Wikipedia* entry for *Roe v Wade*. I got an A+.

I clicked on *Bridget McSwale O'Day at Find a Grave*. The page was lilac-colored. Bridget's claim to fame was simply, *wife of Franck O'Day (1933-1965)*. There was a black and white photo of a lovely, smiling blonde woman. It was the first likeness I'd viewed of Franck's beloved, murdered wife: I'd skipped the photo section of *TwoGreenKeys.com*. There was a shot of her tombstone, which was located at Forest Lawn Memorial Park in Glendale, California.

Under family links, Franck was mentioned – his name wasn't linked, because there was no grave for Franck O'Day, now was there? Franck O'Day was somewhere in sunny Las Vegas, having lunch with my best friend. The only grave he'd ever reserved for himself was now occupied by the earthy remains of Jessika Yerdlay.

Below Franck's listing as Bridget's husband, there was Maribeth's name again – *daughter (1955 – 1970)*. I clicked on the link. The page was also lilac-colored – this was the theme for *Find a Grave*. There was no entry saying that Maribeth was a little red-headed girl who had loved her mommy and step-daddy very much. There was no photo. Under family links, it listed her mother, her father, and of-course, her famous step-father.

She was interred at Penwell-Gabel Cemetery in Topeka, Kansas. There was a photo of her tombstone. *Beloved Daughter*, it said. *Maribeth. May 1, 1955 – June 12, 1970.*

I clicked on the link for her father. Only Peter's occupation was listed: *Attorney-at-Law*. There was a grainy photo of a young man in cap and gown; no doubt it was taken at his graduation from law school. There was a shot of his tombstone – *Peter McSwale. January 8, 1929 – June 12, 1970.* He and Maribeth had died on the same day.

Perhaps it was kismet. *Fate.* But at the same time that I noticed that Peter and his daughter had died on the same day, I noticed an advertisement from *Ancestry.com* at the top of Peter's *Find a Grave* page: *search obituaries for free*. Then the ad was gone, replaced by one from Southern California Edison, informing me that I could check my account online, anytime.

I knew it wouldn't be completely free – I'd have to sign up for a 14-day trial. But I knew Ruthie already had an *Ancestry.com* account – she loved history, and genealogy, and what fan's treasure-chest of memorabilia would be complete without a copy of Marilyn's death certificate? So I entered Ruthanne's username and password, and clicked around until I found the *Search Obituaries* page. I entered Maribeth's birthdate and alleged death date.

No results.

I put *Maribeth O'Day* instead of *McSwale*. Still nothing. But I'd seen a picture of her tombstone. *Find a Grave* didn't make stuff up – they didn't find graves that didn't exist. So I typed Peter McSwale's name into the obituary search box, typed in his birthdate and death date. And there it was.

June 13, 1970

Local Attorney and Child Die in Auto Accident

Local attorney Peter McSwale, 41, along with his daughter Maribeth, 15, were killed yesterday when the car in which they were riding was struck by a train in Topeka. Peter is best remembered for his successful campaign against actor Franck O'Day in 1966, to win back custody of his daughter. Maribeth's mother Bridget had married O'Day in 1962, but after her death in 1965, Peter journeyed to Hollywood. After a short legal battle, custody of Maribeth was awarded to Peter and he returned to Kansas with her.

Services will be held for Peter and Maribeth at Cochron and Sons Mortuary on Saturday. Flowers and contributions to the charity of your choice are both welcome.

Maribeth McSwale O'Day was dead. She'd died at the age of fifteen. She's been dead for more than forty years. Who had I been talking to? Who was the old woman sitting out by the pool, soaking up the desert sun, waiting in joy for Franck O'Day's triumphant return to public life this evening? *Just who in the hell was she?*

I left my room, rode down on the elevator. *Who is she?* repeated over and over in my head. I went out to pool. Maribeth — *no*, not *Maribeth*, I thought. *Maribeth is dead.*

The woman masquerading as Maribeth was stretched out on a lounge chair, wearing a modest, old lady's swim suit, complete with high neckline, wide straps, and demure skirt-thing, that covered her to mid-thigh. She wore a huge pair of Jackie O style shades. As Franck had said, she was no longer recalcitrant about exposing *her old, battle-scarred flesh to an unforgiving world.*

I sat down next to her on another lounge chair. The heat was intense, the sun merciless. God, how I hate Las Vegas. "Hi, there, Maribeth!" I said brightly. "Are you enjoying the weather?"

She looked over her sunglasses at me, her gray eyes smiling. What had Franck said? *So the judge gave custody of Bridget's adorable, blue-eyed, red-headed little girl to her not-at-all adorable, blue-eyed, red-headed father, and he took her back to Kansas.*

This woman had gray eyes, not blue.

"I love the heat," she said. "It soaks into my old bones and makes me feel young again. The sun has life-giving energy, did you know that, Carol?"

"Oh, yeah. Vitamin D and all that." *Who are you?*

She removed her sunglasses and wiped her brow with the back of her hand. She smiled at me, a genuine smile, one that reached her eyes. It was something that I hadn't seen before. "I love the sun," she said. "I'd love to live here in Vegas, just for the sun. But Franck would never go for it. The sun's bad for your skin, you see. It gives you wrinkles. Not that I care, anymore."

I studied her seamed face. *Who are you?* I noticed that one of the wrinkles that climbed up her right cheek took a little jog, before continuing upward to blend in with the crow's feet around her eyes.

There was a tiny scar there, almost imperceptible, in the ruin of her face. A tiny scar, not more than a quarter of an inch wide.

The old woman that was not Maribeth put her sun glasses back on. She settled back in the lounge chair, drew her knees up. "You must be sweltering in all those clothes," she remarked.

I looked at her knees. There was a scar on both of them. *My knee is still bleeding. There's no Franck to carry me tenderly to the hospital this time. Now I'm going to have two scars. A little thin one on one knee from when Franck took me to the hospital to have it tended to, and a big, ugly one on the other knee, from where my mother just left me here to bleed to death.*

The years had not erased the scars. Not the one on her face from Jessika's flung vase, not the ones on her knees. The woman sitting before me wasn't Maribeth at all. Maribeth was dead. This woman was Dolores Adamson. There could be no doubt.

She looked over her sunglasses at me again, because I'd not responded to her comment about being hot in my clothes. Her gray eyes looked expectantly at me – I heard Franck's voice in my head – s*he favored her mother quite a bit: the same blonde hair, the same gray eyes.* Father Time had robbed her of the blonde hair, but he couldn't change the color of her eyes.

I stared at Dolores Adamson for another second, then said abruptly. "You're right. It's entirely too hot to be out here unless I'm going swimming. I'm gonna go back in now. I'll talk to you later." I arose and walked toward the entrance to the hotel.

"I'll see you later, Carolyn," she called after me.

Once inside the welcoming, arctic-cold confines of the lobby, I collapsed into a chair by the desk. I had to think, sort all this out. Maribeth was dead. She'd been dead since 1970. The woman pretending to be Franck's long lost step-daughter was, in reality, none other than she who had pined for him her whole life, Dolores Adamson, daughter of his one-time paramour, famous Hollywood starlet, Jessika Yerdlay.

I thought that I could go back out to the pool and confront her, in the stifling heat. What would I say? What would she say? She'd deny it, I thought. We would perhaps have a scene, *have raised voices.*

All those words, all those emotions, all that aching longing for her mother's boyfriend, etched for posterity in Dolores's diaries – they'd all been written by this woman sitting by the pool. It had not been Maribeth's inability to get over childhood wrongs that had produced the vituperation against Jessika at which I'd marveled on *TwoGreenKeys.com.* It had been Lori's hatred of her own mother.

213

All those sentiments had come from this woman, who'd been our hostess at Franck's house. Who'd stood by and watched him bill and coo and make love to Ruthanne.

How could he do that to her? I thought. But then, maybe Dolores had never confessed her undying devotion to him. Maybe she'd carried her torch, all unspoken, for all these years. But how unlikely was that? Dolores's pluckiness and nerve had come through her diaries. She'd aimed to get at Franck the moment that she was of age, the moment that she was *not fifteen anymore*. She'd been prepared to travel halfway around the world to track him down, just because she was the only one in the world that didn't believe he was dead. And apparently, she *had* found him.

Surely, she wouldn't have kept such an all-consuming passion bottled up inside for all these years. Surely, she'd confessed her desire to him at some point.

Then another idea struck me. Maybe Franck didn't know. Maybe he thought she *was* his step-daughter, as much as the rest of us did. Maybe Dolores *had* flown to Japan when she turned eighteen, like she'd sworn she'd do. Maybe she'd found Franck, but had lied and said she was Maribeth. But he would've recognized her. He'd just seen her, not three years before. There was no way that Dolores could've passed herself off as Maribeth. Franck would've recognized her. *Ecksmith* would have recognized her.

All the lies and half-truths and what-ifs swirled in my head. I had to talk to Franck. I hoped he was somewhere in the hotel. I didn't know what I'd say to Ruthanne, how I'd get rid of her for a moment. But I had to talk to Franck alone about this.

Kismet led me to Franck, in the hotel's bar. It was cool and dark in there, and I almost missed him. Then I heard his voice, his laugh. He was talking to his waitress. He was just finishing lunch. Uncharacteristically, he was alone.

"Ah, Carol," he said as I walked up. "Would you care to join me in a little mid-afternoon drink? I find that I'm having a few opening-night jitters, and nothing cures that better than a quick julep."

There was absolutely nothing nervous about him. The legendary Franck O'Day could be nothing but looking forward to meeting and greeting his die-hard fans, after a more than forty year hiatus. I doubted if this man, possessed of the confidence lent him by his pretty face, had ever been nervous about anything in his life. Except flying.

But I found that I could use a drink. I sat down and told the waitress that I'd have whatever he was having, and she left.

"Where's Ruthanne?" I asked evenly.

"She found she wasn't that hungry after all. She's upstairs napping," he said. "I'm afraid all the excitement has taken its toll. She wants to be fresh for the show tonight."

The show, I thought. *I had a show for him.* "I know, Franck," I growled at him.

The manicured eyebrows went up in surprise at my tone. "You know?" he repeated. "What is it that you know, Carol?"

How many other secrets do you have? I thought. I nodded over my shoulder. "That little old lady out by the pool? That's not Maribeth McSwale. Maribeth McSwale has been dead since 1970. She died in a car wreck. Hit by a train. That little old lady soaking up the sun's energy is Dolores Adamson. Jessica's daughter. That's what I know."

Franck smiled. After a heartbeat, he said, "Well, aren't you just the little Lois Lane!" He leaned forward and chucked me under the chin. "Atta girl, cub reporter!"

I was struck dumb by his reaction. No denial, no angry demands to know how I'd found out. He just admitted to it, and sat there smiling at me. "How?" I said. "Why?"

"It all seems so much more heartwarming this way, doesn't it?" He said. "A joyful reunion with my long lost child, ripped so cruelly from me in my grief, all those years ago. Living out the rest of our lives in familial bliss. It's enough to bring a tear to your eye, isn't it?" Franck's smile curdled a little bit. "So much better than the alternative. So much better than the truth. Instead of the grateful step-father and the loyal daughter of my murdered wife living together with our memories, people might assume that I'm just shacking up with Jessika's daughter, in Jessika's house. Living with the girl who I'd been accused of seducing when she was but a tender teen. You know, those things do happen, Carol. And sometimes, they even work out. What was that teacher's name? Didn't she marry that little boy, and didn't they live happily ever after, once he became a consenting adult?

"People might've thought that. That I'd been waiting all these years, just waiting for Lori's mother to die, so we could be reunited and continue our no-longer-forbidden love affair."

The look on my face must've asked if that had indeed been the case.

Franck rolled his eyes. "Have you *seen* Lori, Carol? Taken a good, hard look at her? She's got one foot in the grave." He smiled. "But why should you believe me? You just go right on ahead and ask her. She'll tell you the whole story."

He removed his cellphone from the breast pocket of his immaculately tailored suit. He pushed a button, waited. Then he said,

"Carol would like to have a word with you, in your room. She knows, Lori. She wants to hear everything. It's time for your close-up, dear. Your long-awaited moment in the spotlight. Be sure to make it good." Franck listened, then disconnected. "She'll meet you upstairs in ten minutes. You know where her room is?"

I nodded. "It's right across the hall from mine." *Just like at Jessika's house*, I thought.

"Someday, you'll have to tell me how you figured it out," he said, as the waitress brought our drinks.

I slammed half my drink in one swallow. The Kentucky whiskey was welcome fire in my belly. They made 'em strong here in Vegas, just like Ruthanne made 'em. But this mint julep had nothing on one of hers.

"You don't have to wait till someday. I'll tell you right now. You're famous, Franck, although not as famous as you used to be." I couldn't help that little jab. I was angry. He'd lied to me. He'd lied to Ruthie. "And famous people can't hide anything on the internet." I drained the rest of my drink and left the bar.

Dolores Adamson was waiting at the door when I knocked. She must've been standing right behind it, because she opened it immediately, then turned her back on me and seated herself at her own little table, just like the one in my room. She didn't look at me. I sat down across from her.

She began without preamble. No explanations, no apologies, no denials. "Franck was declared legally dead on January 1st, 1976. I think because he'd disappeared overseas, they'd given it an extra year. It's usually takes only seven years before someone can be declared legally dead. Maybe Mom had something to do with it." Dolores shook her head. "Maybe she wanted an extra year to hope that he'd turn up. I don't know. On New Year's Day, all the holdings Franck had left to Mom were now hers. There was a trust account for me, but I couldn't touch it until I was twenty-five. I was twenty-five on April 15.

"A man with a British accent called the house the day after my birthday. Cecilia called me to the phone. Mom was in her room, where she always was. The man said his name was Marish, and that he was a lawyer, and that he needed to speak to me on matters concerning my trust fund. He said that he could meet with me that very day, if it was convenient for me. I said that I could come immediately. I took a cab to his office.

"Mr. Marish was stereotypically British in appearance, clad in a tweed three-piece suit, with thinning gray hair and crooked teeth. He shook my hand and led me into a posh office, with bookcases lining the walls, and fat, red-leather chairs. He directed me to one of them in front of his desk. He sat behind it, and said, "'I represent the estate of Robert Ecksmith,' he began. 'Is the name familiar to you?'

"'Bobby,' I said. How could I forget Bobby? 'He was Franck's friend.'

"Mr. Marish nodded, then removed a tape recorder from a drawer in his giant desk, and set it on the blotter. He removed a large, crumpled manila envelope from another drawer and held it up. 'This arrived some time ago, with instructions for me to contact you on April 16th. If you were amenable to meeting with me, I was then to play the enclosed cassette for you. With your permission, I'll do so now.'

I nodded. The office was very quiet. I remember all the little plastic and metallic sounds being very clear – the *click* when he lifted the lid on the machine, the *snap* as he fitted the tape into it, the *clunk* as he pushed play.

"'*Hello, Lori. This is Franck.*' There was a pause, then Franck's laugh from the tiny speaker. *'I'll bet you're glad I'm not dead.'*

"Mr. Marish slid a black and white photograph across the desk to me, as proof, I guess. As if the sound of his voice was not proof enough."

I had to agree with Dolores on that point. No one else had a voice like Franck O'Day.

"The photo showed Franck and Bobby, smiling, in Japanese clothes." Now Dolores met my eyes. "Franck was going to be forty-three-years old in two weeks. He was going to celebrate a birthday, I thought, because he wasn't dead. I'd celebrated his birthday, on my own, every April 30th in all the intervening years, because I'd believed all along that he wasn't dead." Dolores smiled faintly, paused. "I actually lost my virginity on Franck's birthday, to a young man that I thought looked just like him. But that's an entirely different story."

Dolores paused again. "In the picture the lawyer gave me, Carol, Franck didn't look as good as he does now. Oh, he looked healthy enough. Like I told you, I don't think he's ever been sick a day in his life. But it was obvious that he'd spent the last eight years out in the sun, and like I say, the sun is not kind to one's skin. He looked as though crows had barn-danced around his eyes – the black sheen of his hair had gone to salt and pepper. Franck O'Day, idol to millions, was not aging well. Not well at all. He was going to be forty-three, but he looked fifty, already, if he looked a day."

Dolores shrugged, sighed. "The upshot of it all was that he was contacting me because he needed money. Something about his assets being frozen, his being legally dead, all that. He wanted me to travel to

Japan immediately and bring him some of the money I'd just inherited. It was his, after all.

"Mr. Marish had already made all the arrangements. The plane was leaving at nine o'clock the next morning. Mr. Marish gave me my ticket, and to my surprise, a passport that I hadn't even applied for. The picture was from an old college ID. Lawyers can do anything. I shook his hand and went home. He kept the cassette tape. Neither he nor the disembodied voice of Franck O'Day had mentioned that I should keep all this incredible news from my mother. It didn't need to be said. She could go to her grave believing he'd died in a plane crash in 1968, for all I'd ever say to her."

And that's just how it went, I thought.

"I packed and unpacked my suitcase – one would be enough for me, just like it had been for Franck, when he'd left all those years ago. I tried to sleep, but couldn't. All I could think of was that all the years of waiting had not been in vain. I'd known all along that he wasn't dead, that one day he would send for me. The good news was that it had finally happened. My dream had come true.

"The pinnacle of rudeness – I left only a note for Cecilia and Mom. Some fiction about how I'd gone to visit friends in Tahoe or Frisco or somewhere. It was none of Mom's business where I went. I was twenty-five years old, and I'd spent the last eight years in that mausoleum with her. She never left the house, and expected me not to, either. She'd quit acting after trying to kill herself – the scars just couldn't be disguised. Or at least that's what she told me. They could've put her in a turtleneck. But I think the heart went out of her when she thought Franck died. So what? I could not possibly have cared less.

"The flights were interminable, unmemorable. Eventually, I landed at some little airstrip in Japan. To this day, I couldn't point it out to you on a map. The lawyer had made all the arrangements. I didn't care where I was, anyway. Franck and Bobby were there on the runway when I stepped off the plane. Bobby was aging a little better than Franck. His hair was still blonde.

"Franck enfolded me in his arms, kissed me on the top of the head. He smelled the same as he always had, and the memories rushed back, and I began to cry. I loved him so much.

"'I've missed you, Lori,' he said.

"Bobby said he had an appointment, said he'd let us catch up on old times. He said it was good to see me again, told Franck he'd meet us at the hotel for dinner, and walked away.

"I don't remember what the hotel looked like from the outside. My room was small, almost cramped. Nothing like this." She gestured

218

at her spacious, ice-cold, modern Las Vegas accommodations. "But there was a table and two chairs, just like this. And Franck sat down across from me, just like you are, and he told me the same story he told you, about the plane crash, and his God-sent, Russian rescuers. He left out the part about the *Reiki* and his studies of it, and all that. I wouldn't have been interested, anyway.

"I just looked at him. Sure, he was older. But he was still Franck. He still had the bluest eyes. I still loved him with my entire soul. At one point, he stood up and began pacing the room. I watched him, then made my decision.

"I might've lived a sheltered life, locked up there in my mother's house, Carolyn, but it had not been entirely so. I didn't have to work, of course, but I did go to college, and had done my share of slumming on the Sunset Strip. In other words, I was no virgin, no shrinking violet. It was 1976 – I was liberated. I reacted to the presence of Franck O'Day alone with me in a room with a bed in it, in no doubt the same way your friend did, the first time she found herself in a similar kind of room."

I recalled the little pool scene. *Hell*, I thought, *they didn't even need a room.*

"I watched him pace back and forth. He was talking about something – Bobby, Japan, I don't know. I wasn't listening to his words. I was just listening to the golden sound of his voice, so familiar, so missed, so *anticipated*. I was just watching him stride back and forth. I was just watching him, listening to him.

"Then I just stood up and embraced him. I'd like to tell you that I fired off some clever little bon mot, something cinematic – *I'm not fifteen, anymore, Franck* – or something like that. But I didn't say anything. I just put my arms around his neck and kissed him. He kissed me back. Then we looked at each other – he seemed surprised, but somehow not surprised at all – then he picked me up, like he did when I *was* just fourteen, and carried me to the bed."

Dolores grinned slyly at me. On her lined face, it was not an attractive expression. "Did your friend tell you that sleeping with Franck O'Day was everything she'd dreamt it would be?" It was a rhetorical question, thank God, because Dolores continued immediately, not waiting for a response. "But your friend hadn't dreamed of it for as long as I had. I'd dreamed of it my whole life. Your friend hadn't seen his face in every black-haired, blue-eyed young man she'd ever taken a fancy to. Your friend hadn't been disappointed when they didn't sound like him, didn't smell like him. Your friend hadn't been disappointed *every single time*, because they were not *him*. But at last,

219

at long, long last, it finally was *him.* So I think I can honestly say, that I surely enjoyed my first time with Franck more than she did."

I dunno, old girl, I thought. *My friend pretty much knows what she likes. Her imagination is pretty monumental. Ruthanne didn't have to suffer through watching him with her mother, either, and from what I've heard, she didn't have to corner him in a motel room. All the instigating had been on his part.*

Dolores sighed. "He stayed with me for the entire night, and it was glorious. In the morning, he looked five years younger. An outdoorsy forty-five, still older than he actually was." She paused and looked pointedly at me. "It was the energy, you see, Carolyn. All my love and adoration, all my longing – it just detonated, the moment we were together, like an atom bomb. All that energy, all my love – the good people there in Japan had taught Franck how to utilize it, to absorb it. They taught him the life-giving power of it. The love and adoration of others. It was like a nutritional sustenance for him. He hadn't summoned me for money. He didn't need money. He needed *me.* It wasn't like he could get the same kind of devotion from some local Japanese girl. He would've had to have married her or something, and he didn't want to get involved with all that.

"I stayed for a week. He and Bobby and I walked around and visited the sights. We went to the temple, and Franck told me how he'd once dreamt that one of the big stone statues had turned its head and looked at him. Even the unliving rock is moved to turn and look at Franck O'Day.

"Then, he put me on a plane and sent me back to my mother. He promised to write, and he did. But his letters were vague – he mentioned no names, no places, no specific events. *Things are great here, the weather's fine, miss you much.* Nothing that could identify that the letters were from him, that he was still alive. He didn't even sign them. He knew what a sneaky bitch my mother was, and he didn't want her going through my room some afternoon and discovering our secret. He never knew about my diaries, about Mom finding them. We never discussed what she'd said to the papers. But he knew she was a sneaky bitch.

"In comparison, my letters to him were poetic, sometimes literally. I wrote sonnets to his beauty. Paeans to the wonderfulness of the week we'd spent together. I compared myself to a delicate flower, him to a stallion, our love to a rising tempest that had carried us both away. I begged and pleaded to be allowed to return to Japan and see him again. And about every five years or so, he granted me permission. A certified letter, deliverable under my personal signature only, would arrive from Mr. Marish or one of his subordinates. Inside would be a round-trip ticket to Japan.

"Franck always looked the same as in the picture Mr. Marish had first shown me – a rode hard and put away wet fifty. But he always looked five years younger when he put me back on the plane.

"This went on for *thirty years*, Carolyn. Every five years or so, Franck would permit me to visit him in Japan, to shower him with my undying adoration. He would allow me to give him the energy of my love.

"As time went on, my health began to fail. Not long after I returned from seeing Franck in 1996, the doctor gave me the bad news – I was diagnosed with a heart murmur at the ripe old age of forty-five. The doctor was concerned – I told him blithely that the good news was that I was in love, that it was simply the rejoicing of my heart that he heard through his stethoscope. I always felt lighter than air, poetic and free when I returned from visiting Franck. Emotionally, anyway. Physically, I usually felt like crap, which is why I'd paid a visit to the doctor in the first place.

"The doctor was not poetic. He recommended against any exertion; he recommended against travel. I told him that I wouldn't be traveling again for another five years.

"When I returned from visiting Franck in 2001, I almost died from congestive heart failure. Collapsed right there at LAX. I spent nearly a month in the hospital. The doctors debated whether I should have a pacemaker implanted – in the end they decided against it. I was only fifty – far too young for such a procedure, surely. They were convinced that a little more exercise, a little better diet, and I should be all right. One doctor told me to quit smoking. I didn't smoke. It seemed that my poor heart, which so loved and longed and pined for Franck – was just not up to his actual physical ministrations.

"I glossed over my health problems in my letters to him. But Franck knew. I had read the look on his face when I'd stepped off the plane in 2001, even before I came back and collapsed. Even in 2001 – he still looked like he was fifty. Sure, maybe a little tired, a little worn – but it was a little tired and little worn *fifty*, not the sixty-eight I knew him to be. I *was* fifty – but I was an *old* fifty. I looked older than him. My face was lined. I'd gone gray at thirty-five, then white.

"I'd dyed my hair blonde when I went to visit him in 2001, but it looked bad on me, unnatural. A little old lady with Marilyn Monroe's hair. I saw the look of disappointment on Franck's face, the minute I got off the plane. I wasn't fifteen anymore. I was *old*. But still, he entertained me like he always had, and if there was a little distance, a little pulling away, a fleeting look of disgust on his face, I tried to tell

221

myself that I was imagining it. He still loved me. He told me that every time I boarded the plane to come home. And I certainly loved him.

"When the time rolled around for me to visit him again in 2006, there was a surprise for me in the certified letter. The party with whom I'd been corresponding – that's what it said, Carolyn – *the party with whom I'd been corresponding* – would be arriving at LAX the following evening. There was an airline and a flight number. What I was going to do about it, was left up to me. The letter contained nothing else.

"I picked him up at the airport, drove him to the *Marmont*, where he already had reservations. I tried to show him how glad I was to see him, in my most favorite manner. Franck gave me some really bad news then – he took me by the shoulders and gently told me no. He was concerned for my health, he said. Such activities were not good for people with heart problems. His concern seemed genuine – the idea that I was a shriveled up old bag and that he was disgusted by the very suggestion hardly showed in his eyes at all. He still looked an outdoorsy fifty or fifty-two.

"Franck only stayed at the *Marmont* for a week. Things had changed, he said, and while he enjoyed the changes – he found the town to be as vibrant and alive as it had ever been – the hotel was a little less private than he remembered it. Under no circumstances did he want my mother to find out that he was here. Under no circumstances must she find out that we'd been in contact. So I got him a nice little apartment, paid for it with his money. He'd spent very little of it while in Japan. I visited him. We took walks on the beach.

"A few months after he came back to California, he wondered aloud if he'd been totally forgotten by the world; he seemed sad, like he'd been when he'd lost Bridget and then Maribeth, all those years ago. I was inspired.

"I'd had a little mail-order fan club going since 1976, when he'd first contacted me. Mom never even knew it existed. The one that had been around when he was famous . . . that one had disappeared. Mine never had much of a response, either.

"I still use the same PO box for the website that I did for the mail-order club. I hired a computer guy and had him write it, had him teach me how to post to it. Thus *TwoGreenKeys.com* was born. The response to the site has been great. There are over five hundred people in the world, besides myself, that still remember Franck O'Day. At least a hundred and twenty of them say they're going to be here tonight."

I thought that Ruthie's tireless stumping might have had something to do with that.

"The energy from these fans – what they send in with their keys, and what comes through in the nice little posts and emails they send – it's been enough to keep Franck going. I still love him – I'll always love him – and the energy from my love helps, too. But since we've had the fan club, since he came back in 2006 – he doesn't need my energy so much anymore. Between what he receives from the website, and what he receives from the fans attending all those midnight showings of *Manhattan* – there have only been a few occasions when he's felt pity on me and allowed me to demonstrate my love for him in a physical manner. My bad heart and all."

Now there's a visual, I thought, trying hard not to change the expression on my face. *The old gray mare, she ain't what she used to be.*

"And since he's met your friend, well . . . I think my time has passed once and for all. I can't say it wasn't a good run, though."

I did not believe for a second that this woman would give up the one love of her life that easily. But if Franck wasn't having any, then he wasn't having any. What could she do about it?

Dolores sighed. "When Mom finally died, and he moved back into the house, Franck started to get the idea of a personal appearance. Even though I still love him – my energy – it just wasn't enough. It wasn't cutting it anymore. The adulation of a room full of people – it would be just the ticket, just the thing he needed. We called it *his comeback,* even though it's only a personal appearance.

"Then you emailed, and he met your friend. Franck didn't dye his hair, Carolyn, although I know you think he did. It just turned black the day after your friend left. He used her energy, you see, her love, her anticipation – to make himself younger, to knock another five years off his looks." Dolores sighed again. "I know you don't believe me," she said.

Not in a million years, I thought. *Even if it wasn't nuts in and of itself, I still wouldn't believe you – after all you've told me so far? After slipping me your own diaries, so I would know of your undying devotion to that son-of-a-bitch – all the while pretending to be poor, dead Maribeth – his innocent, lost little girl? If you told me the sky was blue, I'd have to go out and check, because you're a liar and you're just as crazy as a shithouse rat.*

"It was my idea to become Maribeth on the website," Dolores was saying. "It only took a few phone calls to Kansas to find out what had happened to her. Franck wept when I broke the news to him.

"The fans enjoy the idea that Franck and his long lost child are reunited, that she never forgot about him, despite all their years of separation. The truth is so much more complicated, so much more . . . ignoble."

223

"Aren't you afraid that someone will root it out, after his big comeback? Aren't you afraid that someone will discover that you're not Maribeth?"

"I've already thought about all that, Carolyn. All personal references to me have been removed from the website. It doesn't say that Franck and Maribeth live together anymore, it doesn't say *email Maribeth* anymore. It now says *email the webmaster*. After a few of these personal appearances, the press might consult my site. They'll find no mention of a living Maribeth. The idea that Maribeth once ran the website has already disappeared. Franck's not going to tell anyone, and I'm not going to tell anyone. And I'm sure you wouldn't include this chapter in your book, would you? It would only hurt him, and me. You won't include it, will you, Carolyn?"

Damn right, I'm going to include it, I thought. Franck wants to be famous again? This whole thing was the real bombshell, the angle I'd been looking for all along. Young woman pines for Mom's cute boyfriend, Mom's cute boyfriend delivers, in spades, for thirty-five some odd years, then gives up on woman as too old, and starts getting younger action. Franck'll be famous again, all right.

Then I thought of Ruthanne. I didn't care about hurting Franck or Dolores, but I wouldn't want to hurt Ruthanne. Not for the world. I said to Dolores, "I won't include it, Miss Adamson. I don't want to hurt anybody."

"I appreciate your discretion, and I know Franck will, too. And please, Carolyn," she said. "Call me Lori."

I nodded, and said, "Well. I'll let you get back to the pool." I stood up and left, trying not to move too quickly. But I really wanted to get out of there.

THIRTY-THREE

I immediately got on an elevator and rode downstairs, on the off chance that Franck might still be in the bar. In light of all this new information, I wanted to look him in the eye. All the warmth and good feelings I'd recently felt toward him, the result of the whisky and our mutual fear of flying, had evaporated. Franck O'Day was a bastard, like I'd thought all along, and I wanted him to see that I thought so.

Franck was still in the bar, but he was not alone. He was at a different table, with two women, each a couple of years older than me. At first I thought that they might be hookers – they were all made-up and decked out in short skirts and high heels, and it was still the afternoon. But this was Las Vegas, after all, and after watching them for a little while, I realized that they were just tourists, out to start their good time a little early that day.

Franck saw me and nodded, but didn't invite me over. So I sat down at the bar and watched him and his two new friends. I saw it as a rare opportunity to observe the preternaturally preserved pretty boy at work. He sat between them, intimately close. He touched them frequently, on the shoulder, on the hand. He put his arm around one and whispered something in her ear, then put his arm around the other one while she whispered something in his. They laughed, they whispered further. Then they all finished their drinks and stood up. Franck put his arms around their waists and the three of them walked toward the door of the bar. He looked over his shoulder and winked at me as he passed.

He paused at the door and said, "I'll get this, ladies. You just go on up to your room. 714, wasn't it?" The two women nodded. "I'll be up to see you in a little while." He patted them both lightly on the ass. They walked away, turning around twice to wave at him. Franck waved back. Once he was sure they were gone, he turned around and smiled at me.

He came up to the bar where I sat, and after paying his friends' tab, he gestured at the table at which he'd been sitting when I'd found him earlier. The waitress appeared, and he ordered drinks for us. When she left, he sighed, then at last spoke. "I wonder if you can imagine what it's like, Carol. From the moment that I first arrived in California, when I was nothing more than a boy – I've never once had to proposition a woman. Can you imagine that? Not once. The first girl I kissed . . ." he shook his head. "She kissed me. The first girl I seduced .

. .." again he shook his head. "She seduced me. I was fifteen at the time. She was almost twenty. She was Uncle Jesse and my step-father Howie's baby sister – technically, my aunt by marriage." Franck smiled. "It was her idea. I've never had to seduce anyone, Carol, never had to talk anyone into it, never even had to ask. They always ask me. Sometimes, I accept . . ." his eyes drifted toward the door to the bar, so recently vacated by his eager new friends. "And sometimes I decline. I'm not saying that the entirety of womanhood has always thrown itself at my feet."

That's precisely what you're saying, I thought.

"There are girls too young and women too old, and happily married women, and girls that like girls. I'm not everyone's type." He grinned. "But if I am their type, and they're bold enough, they always wind up asking me, sooner or later. Except for Bridget. And after we were married, I didn't have to ask her, either."

He paused while the waitress set down our drinks. He gave her a fifty, and told her to keep the change. "And then there's you. You look at me like Bridget did, with sort of a wry amusement. Though without her accompanying fondness, I might add. You don't look at me with that hunger. You don't look at me with that certain curiosity, that overwhelming desire to know what it would be like." Franck grinned again. "Although I have every confidence that the thought has crossed your mind. You are only human after all." He winked. "When you walked in here just now, while I was chatting with those hopeful young ladies, the thought crossed *my* mind – that if anybody was going up to anybody's room, then it should be you and me going up to *your* room."

Franck's charisma, concentrated now, instead of merely ambient, channeled directly at me, was difficult to resist. Instead of the usual polite interest, his eyes now held a different kind of interest, explicit, just for me.

I knew what Ruthanne meant when she'd said, *He made me feel as if he'd never wanted anyone like he wanted me. It was . . . unbelievable.* Franck was communicating that he wanted me, with only his stunning blue eyes and that breathtaking, silky voice. It wasn't what he said, it was how he said it. We were friends, after all, and no one, not even Ruthie, would suspect anything shady if they saw us going into my room. But I knew what he meant, because he wanted me to have no doubt.

"You can't know how refreshing it is to me to have to ask, to anticipate, to wonder if you might say no," he said. "Look at me, Carol. I'm all a flutter, like a school boy." I opened my mouth to speak but Franck held up his hand. He wasn't finished. "It could be our little secret, Carol. Much more easily hidden than . . ." He again glanced at the door to the bar. "I imagine that you're better at keeping secrets than those young ladies. They'd want to take pictures, post it all on Facebook. And they're not even fans. They've never heard of me." This did not seem to bother Franck in the least.

"But you and me, we could keep a secret. Just like this whole sordid, tiresome business about Lori. If Ruthie heard about that from you, before I had a chance to sit her down and explain it to her . . . and I will explain it to her, Carol. Just not right now. There's too much going on right now. Better to wait until we get back to LA.

"Why, if Ruthie were to hear the story from anybody but me, it would just break her heart. It would break her heart as surely as if I were to . . ." He again glanced at the door to the bar, then looked back at me.

I suddenly perceived that all the simmering lust in his eyes, there just for me – it wasn't real at all. Franck was just acting. As breathtaking as it was, it was a sham. *Damn, he was good.* Franck wasn't propositioning me. He was threatening me. He was saying that if I told Ruthanne the truth about the Franck and Lori Show, before he had a chance to, then he was going to hurt me.

He was telling me that if I spilled the beans to Ruthie, he'd hurt me in the only way he could. He'd hurt my friend, break her heart, as effortlessly as walking out and riding up on the elevator to Room 714. If I opened my big mouth to anyone about what Lori had told me, then he'd break Ruthanne's heart, and it would be my fault. He'd hurt me by hurting her.

Franck continued to look at me, then, when he was satisfied that his point had been made, he said, "So, Carol. Should we go up to your room?"

"No, Franck," I replied evenly. "I can keep a secret, but I'm not inclined to want to have to keep that one." Even though, had our situation been different, had there not been him and Ruthie, I knew I'd have taken him up on it in a heartbeat. Son-of-bitch or not. I wouldn't have cared. I admitted it to myself. He was right. The thought had crossed my mind. And if the suggestion had been real, and if circumstances had been different . . .

"I'm sorry, Carol. You're going to have to explain the meaning of that word, *no*, to me. I've never heard it before." Franck O'Day laughed. The lust glowed for another moment in his eyes and then winked out. Then he looked past me and smiled. "Ah, Ruthie, my darling!" He stood and pulled out a chair for her. Not a scintilla of worry or guilt crossed his face as he glanced at me again. It was as if

227

our conversation, his threats, had not taken place. It was as if I'd imagined them.

"You missed the excitement," he was telling Ruthie. "Two young ladies from Wichita were just here. They were very friendly. A might too friendly, wouldn't you say, Carol?" He didn't wait for me to answer. "Carol arrived just in time to save me from the embarrassment of declining. She just walked up and looked at them. They thought she was my girlfriend, and they beat a hasty retreat."

Ruthanne said, "Oh, yeah? Will they be at the show tonight? Perhaps I'll have a word with them." She smiled at me – she wasn't really jealous. She believed that Franck was hers – had he not told her, *Every part of me belongs entirely to you?* She was confident that their love was impervious to the adoration of mere fans.

"Oh, no," Franck said. "They didn't even know who I am." He smiled and kissed her on the cheek.

THIRTY-FOUR

Ruthanne brought one of her suitcases and our dress bags and her make-up kit over to my room, so we could get dressed together, like we'd done for every big event since high school. Ruthie, in her ignorant graciousness, even asked Maribeth (who was not really Maribeth) if she'd like to join us in getting ready. Maribeth seemed genuinely flattered, but knowing what I knew, I couldn't imagine that she would be able to pretend giggling prom night antics with Franck's newest young plaything. I was correct. She arrived already dressed, and sat at the little table in my room and quietly surfed the internet on my laptop while we engaged in giggling prom night antics on our own. She wore a sea-foam confection that looked great on her. She nodded and smiled in relief when I said, "Your dress is beautiful, *Maribeth.*"

While Ruthie and I donned our gowns, I thought about Franck and his charm and his threats. *He was old Hollywood, not someone to be trifled with.*

I thought back to the taped interviews he'd sent to me. He'd spoken of what a wonderful mother Bridget had been – I'd thought it had been a tribute, because it was little Maribeth sitting beside him, grown up. *Remember your wonderful mommy?* was what it'd seemed he was saying.

But it hadn't been that at all. When I realized that it had been Lori sitting beside him, I saw that Franck had just been pointing up to her much how much her own mother had not cared for her, by recalling how much Bridget had loved Maribeth. Instead of recalling Jessika's affection for her daughter, if there'd even been any, he'd mentioned how much Lori had feared her mother - *I remember her cowering in a corner, sobbing, unable to escape the room and Jessika's rage. Lori always was rather a coward around her mother. A crybaby.*

I remembered how, when she had insisted that he talk about Dolores before he had been ready, Franck had slammed her looks – *Dolores was a willowy girl, tall for her age. She favored her mother quite a bit: the same blonde hair, the same gray eyes. Even at the young age when I saw her last, she had the potential to grow up to be the same kind of ravishing beauty as her mother. But who knows? Not everyone lives up to the potential of youth, and youth has long passed for Dolores. God only knows what she looks like now.* I remembered the wheedling, the asking her to hold forth about the Kansas that she wasn't really from, that she'd never been to. That was cruel.

Now I could see the little barbs they had traded during that part of the interview. The fake Maribeth had not posted the pictures of her mother and Franck and herself, because the real Lori didn't want him taking pleasure in the memories of his lost little family.

They were obviously not happy together anymore, if they had ever been. I couldn't imagine what the weight and responsibility of Lori's devotion must be like to Franck, for all this time. It must've been almost like a replay of the days he'd endured with her mother — all the tireless declarations of a love that he didn't feel in return.

I imagined that he was at least fond of Lori, whereas I believed that he had essentially despised Jessika. In every account I'd heard of her, she'd come off as despicable — violent, conniving, willing to sacrifice her own flesh and blood to get Franck to come back, even when she must have known deep down that he'd never loved her. But then, I'd never heard her side of the story — she wasn't here to defend herself, after all.

And beyond mere fondness, Franck seemed to really care for Ruthanne. I couldn't say for sure if he loved her or not. That whole diatribe about never having had to ask would seem to speak against it, at least so far. I doubt if Ruthie had actually come out and asked him — she was too star struck for that — but she had not hesitated when he kissed her, nor when he performed Esther Williams' little water ballet. And I was sure she had not played shy once they got behind closed doors.

But still, I could tell that maybe Franck cared for her as much as he could for any former fan. He was affectionate, that tell-tale sign that Aunt Mae had instructed us to look for. So maybe all the threats had just been Franck's way of looking out for Ruthie's feelings. If or when his whole secret relationship with Lori ever came out, it really couldn't hurt him too much. It was a tame thing, compared with the escapades that modern Hollywood got up to. He was protecting Ruthie, not himself.

I decided to take the high road and give Franck the benefit of the doubt. I decided to believe that he was trying to shield Ruthie's feelings until he got a chance to explain to her, and that made me think that he really cared for her. I still thought he was a son-of-a-bitch — even though I could no longer deny that I found him to be one sexy old beast — but I couldn't find it in my heart to seriously dislike him. Anyone that was good to Ruthie and made her happy, couldn't be all bad to me.

We waited in front of the hotel for the limo. Franck wore a black suit that wasn't quite a tuxedo, but was just as spiffy as one. He looked amazing. Ruthie and I had traded the gowns that we'd worn to Franck's dinner party: she wore the wine colored one now, and I the emerald green. We opened a bottle of champagne and had a glass in the limo on the way, because Franck reminded us that there was to be no alcohol at the hall, *because they didn't have a liquor license or anything like that.*

The limo pulled into the strip mall parking lot, parallel to the venue, because it was too long to pull into the non-limo sized parking space beside the hall. The strip mall itself was dark and deserted. The place consisted of a dry cleaners, a nail salon, a tailor, and a tax consultant, all concerns that close when the five o'clock whistle blows. Only a pizza parlor at the farthest end from the hall was still open.

"This is good," I said, as Ruthie frowned at the depressing emptiness of the strip mall. "Plenty of room to park."

Franck gave the limo driver a tip and asked him to return about 12:30. The big car executed a three-point turn in the empty strip mall and trundled back out into traffic.

An arc sodium fixture at the top of the hall's façade cast a round pool of light in front of the double-doors – it looked like something out of film noir, if you used your imagination.

Franck extracted the rude key fob from his pocket, unlocked the doors and propped them open. We walked inside, turned on the lights, and I got the feeling that we were way too over-dressed for this place. But then, the real fans were coming, and they expected to see their idol and his entourage suitably decked out.

I thought that some of them might faint dead away when they beheld Franck, looking not more than ten or fifteen years older than his still from *Manhattan*. His unnatural state of preservation had become second nature to me – I had to remind myself that he was not the trim and attractive forty that he looked, but twice that. It was all part of the Hollywood mystique that the real fans were coming to see.

Maribeth walked around and seated herself behind the counter. Apparently, she would act as concierge. I wondered if she would be MC, too, or if Ruthanne would be awarded that coveted spot. I wondered if they would fight over it, or if Franck had handled all of it ahead of time.

Ruthanne, Franck and I walked down the dark, narrow, wood-paneled hallway. Franck flipped on the fluorescents. Ruthie went over to the podium and removed a DVD case from her bag. She inserted the DVD into the player. When the credits to *High Times in Manhattan* rolled up on the screen, she pushed the stop button, satisfied that the cinematic portion of the night's entertainment was ready to go.

231

A caterer arrived with two helpers, and quickly set up sandwich platters, paper plates and cups on the table in the back of the venue. They brought in two coolers full of sodas and ice and put them under the table. Franck signed an invoice, shook hands with the caterers, and they left. The three of us sat in the folding chairs in the front row and waited.

The first fan to walk down the hallway was Aunt Mae. She was dressed to the teeth in a flowing muumuu, patterned with great blue and black flowers. Accompanying her was a slight, frail old woman wearing a plain tan dress. Rouge dotted her pale cheeks. She glanced nervously around the room, then looked back at Aunt Mae.

Franck leapt up and strode across the ugly floor. "Mae!" he exclaimed. "And Candace!"

Ruthanne and I followed at a respectful distance.

Aunt Mae enfolded Franck in a big bear hug, pounding him joyously on the back.

"It's so good to see you after all these years, my old co-star!" he said, and kissed her lightly on the forehead, careful not to muss her painstakingly applied make-up.

"Oh, go on, Franck," Mae said, smiling from ear to ear. "We were never co-stars. Let me look at you." She lightly grasped his elbows. "You look great!"

"As do you, Mae." He turned and smiled at her frail, lost-looking friend. "And Candace," he said softly, embracing the old bones carefully. "I think I can tell you, after all these years, that I kinda had a little crush on you while we were shooting."

Candace looked up at Franck, her watery eyes shining. "And I, you, Franck, my dear. As soon as Nurse told me about your little get-together, I insisted that we had to be the first to arrive, fashion be damned." She hugged him again.

"Would you like something to drink, Candace?" Franck asked. "I'm afraid we have no champagne, like in the old days, but would a nice cold bottled water suffice?"

Candace nodded. Franck took her gently by the arm and they walked slowly back across the floor.

Aunt Mae said to us, "Candace still doesn't remember me. She still thinks I'm a nurse from the home. But she remembers Franck, just like I knew she would. I told her daughter, *the waitress*, that I'd take good care of her. I told her what a thrill it would be for the old gal, and she gave me permission to bring her, and here we are." She narrowed her eyes at Ruthanne. "But you did lie to an old chorus girl, Ruthie."

Ruthanne blinked in surprise. "What do you mean, Aunt Mae? I told you Franck wasn't dead. There he is!"

Aunt Mae looked across the hall at Franck, again seated in the front row, chatting with Candace. "Not dead at all, and looking like a million bucks, tax free," she said appreciatively.

Aunt Mae did not comment further on Franck's phenomenal youthfulness. Her friend had forgotten all the intervening years, as well as so many other things, and in the magic of the moment, so had Aunt Mae. Candace's inability to remember made it easier for Mae to pretend it was 1961 again, that she was still a beautiful, silly goose in the chorus.

She looked again at Ruthanne. "You didn't lie to me about Franck's being alive, Ruthie. You know exactly how alive he is, don't you? You just said that you'd met him. You have obviously so much more than just *met* him." Aunt Mae winked. "I could always tell by the way that Miss Yerdlay looked at him, that they were sleeping together. We all could tell. You look at him the same way, Ruthie. But unlike Miss Yerdlay, I can tell from the way he looks at *you*, that he loves you back. What a fortunate girl you are!" Again, the immense age difference between Franck and Ruthanne went unmentioned, unremembered.

"Thanks, Aunt Mae," Ruthie said, and blushed a little.

"You'll have to tell me all about it when you get back to Hollywood." Aunt Mae winked again, and crossed the floor to join Franck and Candace.

The girl from the box office of *The Egyptian* arrived next. She had brought three friends. They scanned the hall and when they saw Franck, they released muted squeals and grabbed each other's hands, whispering, *"There he is! It's really him!"*

The box office girl – she said to me, "My name is Penny, by the way" – embraced Ruthanne like they were old pals. She held Ruthie's hands out, not unlike Mae had done to Franck, so she could admire Ruthie's wine colored gown.

I glanced over my shoulder and watched Franck pat Candace on the hand. He arose and approached. "Ladies!" he said, smiling expansively at them. "How nice of you to come. I'm Franck O'Day."

I think that they're aware of that, ol' son, I thought.

Franck took each of their hands in both of his, shook them warmly. Each of them had the same dreamy, slightly drugged look in their eyes – the same expression Ruthanne had borne when she had first clamped peepers on her idol in the flesh. They were each struck speechless.

I mentally shook my head. *Too bad you can't bottle it and sell it, Franck,* I thought. *Your inestimable charm. You could make a fortune. Enough to keep you in plastic surgeons and black hair dye for another eighty years.*

And I would be your very first customer.

Franck didn't allow the girls' dumbstruckness to stretch out into embarrassment. He said, "Allow me to introduce you to some of my friends, ladies. When the show begins, you'll see them up there on the screen with me. They were extras in the little film we're screening tonight."

This seemed to thrill the young women almost as much as meeting Franck. They were his fans, but they were also fans of *Manhattan* itself, and were familiar with Jessika and Sunnerfeld and their careers, as well as Franck's. They eagerly accompanied him across the room.

When the film came on, I wondered if they would be struck by the fact that Father Time had robbed Mae of her looks and slimness and Candace of her mind and memory, while he seemed to have only laid ten or fifteen gentle years upon Franck.

Ruthanne stayed with me by the door. She was more than willing to share Franck with his adoring public. He'd be going home with her in the end.

The next party to enter Franck's shabby ballroom was Evan, the tall hipster from the gay bar, and the blonde with the pierced nipples, and five other young men. They each embraced Ruthanne, admired her gown and her shoes.

"Where *is* he, Ruthie?" Evan whispered.

Ruthanne nodded across the hall, where Franck was chatting with the four young women and the two matrons. He met Ruthie's eye and nodded.

"He looks fantastic!" Evan said in awe.

"Good enough to eat," the blonde rejoined.

You're not the first one to think so, I thought and smiled, thinking of Patrick Morrison, long dead, and Bobby Ecksmith, he whom Franck had allowed to call him *my darling.* Wouldn't these get a kick out of that! I had seven buyers for my book right here. I reminded myself to ask Franck what had ever happened to ol' Bobby. Was he still in Japan? Was he still alive?

One of the young men whispered something to Ruthanne, and she blushed, and they all giggled like school girls.

Franck came over and introduced himself, giving each of them a firm handshake. They were not quite as dumbstruck as the girls from *The Egyptian:* each was able to remember his name and repeat it when Franck shook his hand.

234

I looked back over at the six women seated in the folding chairs. They were leaning together, whispering and giggling, four street-wise young Hollywood hotties and two old chorus girls. All generational differences had been forgotten in their shared appreciation for Franck O'Day.

Others arrived, men and women, young, old, middle-aged. Franck shook hands, smiled, signed autographs, posed for pictures. I was amazed by the turn-out. It was not the one twenty-five that Lori had predicted, but all-in-all, seventy-five fans had braved the horrors that are Las Vegas to meet their idol. It was a good sixty more than I'd expected.

Oh, ye of little faith, I chided myself. I had underestimated the drawing power of the forgotten star. He'd only appeared in two films; he'd been missing and presumed dead for going on fifty years. All this mattered not in the least. I had underestimated his fans.

It had also been a day of underestimating Franck O'Day, himself, on my part. I had underestimated his ability to devise a dark, malicious threat – how devious had all that been? He would hurt me by hurting Ruthie if I hurt him by hurting Ruthie. I had convinced myself that he wouldn't have ever gone through with it – he was extremely fond of Ruthie. He might even have loved her. But he had devised the cruel trick, had executed the first part of it. He had showed me that he could tap into that special brand of Hollywood mendacity, and relish doing it. He showed me that I underestimated him at my peril.

I had also underestimated the full force of his magnetism, whether real or sham, once he concentrated it upon me. *Hot damn, but he was fine!* I had underestimated how quickly I would've abandoned myself to him, had our situation only been different.

The guests ate, chatted. Franck mingled.

Just before the scheduled show time, Franck took me by the elbow and led me off to one side. "Can you do me an enormous favor, Carol? Lori's going to be furious with me." He'd dropped the pretense of calling her Maribeth. Maybe he had told Ruthie already, or maybe he was just calling her Lori cause no one was listening to us.

"She only gave me one thing to do," he continued. "She bought a beautiful, leather-bound guestbook. The only thing I had to do was to remember to bring it with me, and I forgot it. Could you go back to the hotel and get it for me?" He looked at me solemnly, his blue eyes plaintive.

Oh, you're good, Franck, I thought, *very, very good. But we both know that, don't we?*

235

"Lori's been very kind to me all these years, Carol, not even to mention setting this whole thing up. She'll be crushed if people don't get to sign the book she gave me, because I was thoughtless and forgot it. I'll give you my room card. I'll call you a cab. I'm sure you've seen *Manhattan*. You shouldn't be gone for more than a half hour, forty minutes at the most. You'll be back in time for the uplifting finish, and the meet and greet. The fans can sign the book on their way out. I'll be so grateful, Carol, and Lori won't have to be disappointed."

Lori had encompassed enough disappointment in her life, I thought, and not a little of it because of Franck. I nodded.

"Thanks, my friend. I owe you one." Our little threatening conversation this afternoon had never happened. He kissed me quickly on the cheek, then reached into his pocket and handed me a wad of money and his room card. He took out his phone, spoke into it, put it back into his pocket. "They'll be here in ten minutes." He looked at me for what seemed like a long time. Then like an afterthought, he said, "Why don't you take Ruthie with you?"

"She won't go, Franck. She's having too much fun." I looked at Ruthie. She was in her element, the perfect Hollywood hostess, laughing and chatting with the faithful. "Maybe if you ask her, but not if I do."

"I'll ask her."

I watched Franck cross the ugly floor to where Ruthie was chatting with Evan and Penny from *The Egyptian*. I watched Franck ask for a moment alone with her, watched Penny and Evan drift away and begin chatting with Mae and Candace. I watched Franck speak to Ruthie, watched her resolutely shake her head. Well, that was the name of that tune.

Ruthie walked up on the dais, resplendent in her low-cut, wine-colored dress, and picked up the mike. "Good evening ladies and gentlemen!" she said, her voice clear and full of love and enthusiasm. "Franck would like to welcome you to this screening of *High Times in Manhattan*, and would also like to thank you for coming all this way to see him. If you would please take your seats now, we'll start the film."

The people did as they were asked. Franck sat in the first row, with Candace on one side, and an empty chair on the other, reserved for Ruthanne. I noticed that Franck was holding the faded chorus girl's hand. This touched me.

Lori had heard the announcement, and was standing by the light switch. I crossed the room and told her to save me an aisle seat – I would be back in a few minutes. She looked at me questioningly, then nodded. The room went black and I went outside to wait for the cab.

THIRTY-FIVE

I was not looking forward to the drive back to the hotel. It wasn't that it was that far, but Vegas traffic, never anything less than annoying at the best of times, was a particular bitch on a Saturday night. I told the driver that there was a fifty in it for him if he could get me to the *Wynn* and back as quickly as possible. He was not as impressed as I thought he'd be. I'd never thrown a fifty at anybody in my life. But he was impressed enough. "The 15 should be a little quicker," he opined. "Might shave a few minutes off."

I told him that I figured he knew what he was talking about. He got on the 515 and transitioned to the 15. So far, so good. Then, all traffic stopped. Not slowed. Just stopped. Red taillights for as far as the eye could see. There were cops and emergency vehicles and road flares and just one lane where there were supposed to be several more. And there were cars and red taillights.

Taking the 15 probably might've been a quicker route back to the *Wynn*, had it not been for the big rig that had jack-knifed in the middle of it.

By the time I made it back to the hotel, went up to Franck's room and recovered Lori's precious guestbook, returned to the cab and got back on Las Vegas Boulevard, an hour and a half had passed. Where traffic had been a bitch before, it was impossible now, what with the mess on the nearby freeway. By the time we were approaching the underpass to the 515, another twenty-five minutes had passed.

As we stopped under the 515, I could see the smoke. The traffic was at a standstill. We inched up a few more car lengths and I could see the flames licking up into the sky. I threw some money at the cabbie and got out of the car. I hobbled up the sidewalk as fast as I could in my heels.

The building that had housed VFW Post 864 was fully engulfed. One fire truck squirted vainly at the yellow flames through the broken glass at the front, another rained water down on the roof from the vacant lot next door.

Barricades were set up to keep the looky-loos back. I did not run up and scream at the firemen, "My friends are in there!" like in the movies. It would have indeed been too *cinematic,* to use Lori's term. And it wouldn't have done one bit of good. I just stood there with the rest of the there-but-for-the-grace-of-God-go-I curious and watched it burn.

When I couldn't stand it anymore, I walked back down Las Vegas Boulevard. After a block or so, I hailed a cab. I told him to take me to the *Wynn;* I paid him with the rest of the money that Franck had given me. I went back to my ice cold room and cried until I passed out.

At 9 am, my phone rang. Cruel hope flooded me. It would be Ruthie, calling to tell me that she had somehow escaped out the back door, and in all the confusion she hadn't been able to call me until just then. But I remembered the layout of Post 864. There was no back door.

It was a cop. My name and cellphone number had been listed on some invoice for the hall rental as a contact number, after Maribeth's and Ruthanne's and Franck's. No one had answered those numbers – *those phones were all little melted blobs of metal and plastic now,* a hard-bitten, no-nonsense detective's voice said in my mind. So Las Vegas PD was calling me.

The cop asked if he could stop by and ask me a few questions. I met him in the lobby. He shook my hand, and said, "Betty from the VFW says that they were showing some kind of a movie?"

I showed him the flyer. "Franck O'Day, *the actor?*" The cop said in amazement. "My mom's a big fan. She's got a copy of this movie. I always thought he was dead."

He's dead now, the Sam Spade in my mind said.

Perhaps the cop's intuition read my mind, or perhaps he just realized what an awful thing it was that he'd just said. "Can you tell me what happened?"

"Happened? I have no idea what happened!" I yelled at him, and burst into tears. "My best friend burned to death, that's what happened!"

"I'm sorry for your loss," he said. "You weren't at the VFW when the fire –"

"No." I got a hold of myself. "I was there earlier, then I went back to the hotel."

"This is a hard question to ask, Miss Adyon," the cop said, his eyes full of compassion. "Please don't be offended. But, why weren't you there? Why did you go back to the hotel alone?"

I wasn't offended. "Franck asked me to go back. He'd forgotten the guestbook. It was a present from his friend, Lori."

"Lori?" The cop asked.

"Yes. Dolores Adamson."

"Was she there, too? In the –"

I nodded. The cop wrote her name down. I thought there was no reason to keep up the Maribeth charade any longer. I wondered what name she was registered under at the hotel. But the real Maribeth was already dead. *It would only confuse the investigation,* the detective in my mind said. *Now they'll know whose dental records to order.*

"Franck knew Lori's feelings would be hurt because he'd forgotten the guestbook. So, I went back to the hotel to get it for him," I told the cop. "I got caught in the traffic from the wreck on the freeway. When I finally got back . . ." I started to cry again.

"You said your best friend . . .?" I gave him Ruthie's name. He wrote it down. "Did you know anyone else personally?"

I told him just Ruthie. And Franck. And Lori. I told him that there was a girl name Penny that worked at the *Egyptian Theatre* in LA and three of her friends. And a guy named Evan from Riverside, and six of his friends. And Aunt Mae, of *Mae's Memory Lane* on Hollywood Blvd, also in LA. And her friend Candace, who lived at an old folks home in Chino. He wrote everything down, including my full name and my address and the address where I worked.

Because I was still crying, the cop patted me on the shoulder. "Is there someone I can call for you?" he asked, and again I thought it was all like something out of a tragic movie.

I shook my head. "I'll call Ruthie's mom," I told him.

"That'll be very kind of you," the cop said, and handed me his card. "Just have her call this number. And if you think of anything else, any other names . . . or if you need anything."

"No one got out?" I asked him suddenly. "No one at all?" He shook his head sadly. "Do they know what caused it?" I asked, trying to get a grip on myself. But the tears, unstoppable, just continued to roll down my face.

"Nothing official yet. But the Fire Chief told me he's pretty sure it was electrical. Seems to have started right in the middle of the hall. It doesn't take more than a little spark, and those old buildings just . . ." He again seemed to realize that this was not the kind of thing to be saying to someone in the throes of grief. "I'm so sorry for your loss," he said again. "You're free to go home now. I don't have any more questions. But I have your number in case anything comes up."

I started to walk away, and then I said, "What about their stuff? Upstairs?"

"I'll talk to the manager. The hotel will handle everything. Again, Miss Adyon. I'm so sorry for your loss."

I nodded, and went back upstairs. I still had Franck's room card. Housekeeping had already been there. The bed was made and Ruthie's nightgown was folded neatly on the pillow. I picked it up and buried

LM Foster

my face in it, and the smell of her perfume made the tears begin anew. *Oh, Ruthie! I miss you so much!*

I took Ruthie's nightgown back to my room with me. After the tears finally subsided, I packed and checked out of the *Wynn*. I caught a cab, and told him to take me to the strip mall, next to where the fire had been last night. I had to see it for myself.

The cabbie parked next to the pizza place, because most of the parking lot was still taped off. I told him to wait. In one of those cinematic twists that all my dead movie buff friends would've appreciated, there was a *Las Vegas Sun* newspaper box right in front of me when I got out of the cab.

75 Feared Dead in VFW Hall Fire

In the largest loss of life since the November 21, 1980 MGM Grand fire, which claimed the lives of 85 and injured nearly 700 more, another tragic disaster has struck Las Vegas. Fire Department units arrived at VFW Post 864 at approximately 10:12 last night, to find the structure already ablaze. LVFD released a statement early this morning, claiming that arson was not suspected. "The fire was probably the result of old wiring," Fire Chief . . .

That was all I could see. I didn't purchase one.

I walked down the sidewalk until I was standing in front of the hall. The smell of smoke, the thick greasy stench of the aftermath, was not there. Then the wind shifted and it was overwhelming, like someone had shoved an ancient ashtray down my throat. I covered my mouth and nose with my hand, trying to block out the smell.

The fire had spread to the drycleaners, and had also taken out part of the nail salon next to it. Three coroner's vans were parked in the vacant lot next door.

All that left of the VFW Post 864 was the blue façade, now smoke blackened, and some outbuildings at the back of the lot, that I hadn't even known were there. But from the sidewalk, if I walked past the facade just a little bit, I could see through to them now. The hall was gone, the roof had collapsed. The place had *burnt to the ground*, as the old chestnut went. All that was left was the façade – a piece of yellow construction equipment, a small bulldozer of some kind, was parked in front of it – waiting for the order to knock it down.

240

What lay behind the façade – I could see it from the sidewalk – was an unrecognizable pile of blackened debris, through which several people in yellow hazmat gear combed. The tape kept onlookers far enough back that we couldn't identify anything that the fire team discovered. But every now and then there would be some kind of a signal – and the men in the hazmat suits would hold up a tarp, shielding the area from our view. Another group would come over. Then the tarp would be lowered, and two men would carry a black body bag over to the waiting coroner's vans.

THIRTY-SIX

When I couldn't stand it anymore, I had the cab driver take me to the nearest Avis. I sat in the parking lot and called Ruthanne's mother. It was the hardest act I've ever had to undertake in my entire life. She was so cheerful when she answered, the sound of her voice tinged with pleased surprise. "Oh, hi, Carol! How are you?"

Again I felt like I was in a movie. How do you tell someone that their daughter is dead? "There's been an accident, Mrs. Midley. A fire. Ruthie's gone. I'm so sorry." How could I say such clichéd words? Surely there had to be some more poetic way to put it? But there was not.

I gave her all the details that I knew, gave her the contact numbers. I told her that there was nothing I could do here; I told her I was coming home. We cried together for what seemed like hours, but when I hung up, I noticed that the call had only lasted for eight minutes. Destroying a woman's entire life only took as long as riding a frenzied bull in a rodeo.

The effort of driving helped me to get a little more of a grip on myself. I stopped to get gas in Barstow, and called Ruthie's Uncle Ted, our boss. He said that he'd already heard the devastating news from his sister. We cried together, too. He told me to take as much time off as I needed.

I went back home, to our little apartment, silent and dusty as the tomb. I crawled into Ruthie's bed, covered myself up with her blankets, smelled the faint scent of her. It was already fading, and would be gone forever soon. I cried until I fell asleep. When I woke up, it took me a second to remember what was going on, what had happened. The memory felt like a landslide, like a physical weight pushing down on me. I started to cry hysterically again, and could not get a grip on myself until I left Ruthie's room. I shut the door behind me – I couldn't bear to see her things in there.

A week later, there was a memorial for Ruthanne. In an irony that the Sam Spade in my head failed to comment upon, whatever had been left of her had been cremated, and was placed in a little vault at the mausoleum.

Afterwards, her mom and little sister came to the apartment. I made them a cup of coffee, and we talked for a minute. LVFD had confirmed for them that it had indeed been an electrical fire. Ruthanne had been identified through dental records.

"She always loved those old movies," was her mom's only comment on the reason that her daughter had been in Las Vegas. She had never heard of Franck O'Day.

Ruthanne's mom and sister packed up all Ruthie's clothes and movies, all the little odds and ends in her room. I tried to help, but found that I was unable. Seeing the sum of a young woman's life contained in three suitcases and two cardboard boxes undid me.

Two men came and took away her dresser and her bed, her television and her night table and her lamp.

Ruthie's mom left the *Sunset Boulevard* poster that I had given her hanging on the wall. "I think she'd want you to have it," Mrs. Midley said.

I helped put the suitcases and boxes into Ruthie's car. We stood in the parking lot and embraced, cried together for a long time. Her sister drove her car away.

Time passed. Days. I went back to work. I went into Uncle Ted's oak paneled office and cried with him, cried with my fellow secretaries. Then we got respective holds on our respective selves and went back to work. Life goes on.

Weeks passed, then months. It was a little bit of a hardship on me financially, but I couldn't bear to rent out Ruthie's room. I sometimes went in there and sat with my back against the wall and looked up at her *Sunset* Boulevard poster. Gloria Swanson glared back at me. Ruthie's scent was long gone. Nothing remained but the smell of dust. I told myself that if I believed in heaven, perhaps Franck and Ruthanne and Gloria were all up there together, dancing the night away with Bill Holden and Mae and Candace, and all the other dead luminaries of Hollywood's stellar past.

I didn't turn on our big television too much anymore. The idea of entertainment had not re-entered my world.

I shelved the whole idea for Franck's biography. I took all the files off my computer, burned them to disk and threw the disk in a drawer. It had all ended so horribly. And I could never play on tragedy, especially my own.

And then I had the dream.

The hall of VFW Post 864 was dark. There was only a little reflected sheen on the ugly floor from the screen, where *High Times in Manhattan* had reached the climactic scene, where Perry and Dora at last declare their love for each other. Franck stepped in front of the screen. It was like I was standing right there next to him. He held up his hands at shoulder level, palms out, like a preacher before his flock. His face

243

was in shadow. All I could see clearly were the palms of his hands, the white cuffs of his shirt, bright against the blackness of his suit.

Inexplicably, a blue bolt that looked like lightning shot out of his right palm. It zigzagged through the crowd, striking everyone in the eyes and mouths and chests like that scene from *Raiders of the Lost Ark*, where the wrath of God kills all the Nazis. The bolt passed through everyone, gathering speed, turning yellow as it went. At last it struck the back wall, blasting the commendations and proclamations and pictures of long dead veterans to smithereens. Pieces of glass and frames clattered to the floor, followed by charred scraps of photographs, drifting down slowly. The bolt bounced up, hit the ceiling, then shot earthward again. Franck held up his left hand and caught the bolt, like an outfielder snaring a fly ball. I watched as the power of the concentrated energy burnt a quarter-sized whole in the palm of his hand.

I looked at the crowd. Every single one of them was dead. Nothing was left except ashes in the shapes of Franck's fans, like they were all vampires who had been exposed to the sun. The wall and ceiling where the energy bolt had bounced off were ablaze, blue and yellow flames greedily consuming the old building, lighting up the room.

"I'm sorry about Ruthie," Franck's voice said to me. But he wasn't standing beside me anymore. Somehow, he had crossed the room, and in the dim light coming through the doorway, his face was indistinct, just a silhouette – as it'd been when he stood before the movie screen.

"I loved Ruthie," he said. "I didn't want to take her, too, Carol, but when she wouldn't go back to the hotel with you . . ." His silhouette shrugged, noncommittal, then disappeared through the doorway. I heard his footsteps as he walked down the hall – the only way in or out of the building.

I watched, enveloped in the protection of dream, as VFW Post 864 burned around me. The fire moved *so fast* – it sped across the entire ceiling. It spread out from the back wall toward the adjacent walls. The convection of the rising heat stirred the ashes of the dead like a breeze, scouring them away like unseen water, leaving behind only grinning skulls and exposed bones

Franck had held the event here, so he could do this. The little VFW Hall was old, isolated, probably not up to modern fire code. A fire at the *Wynn* would've been discovered, put out. The people would've been saved. After the *MGM* tragedy, there were probably fire sprinklers every other foot at the *Wynn*. Franck had staged his comeback here, so he could kill all these people in private. So he'd never be found out.

The ceiling started to collapse and I raised my dream hand in defense, and snapped awake. I didn't scream.

THIRTY-SEVEN

A year passed, then a year and a half. Doug moved back to town and we started seeing each other. It was nothing serious yet – I was not ready for anything serious yet. But it was nice to have him around, nice to have someone to hold onto when the tears would revisit me occasionally. But their visits were becoming rarer and rarer. Acceptance is supposed to be some stage of grief, and I had reached it, tentatively. Life was getting back to normal again.

The television got turned on more often, but Ruthanne's room still stood empty. Doug had gently suggested once that I might want to start thinking of moving to a smaller apartment. But I wasn't ready for that, either.

Then one Friday evening in June, Doug and I were sitting on the couch, watching television. I really wasn't paying attention to it too much. A woman at work had told me about a fantastic recipe for chicken enchiladas, and I was trying to find it on the internet.

Then I heard Franck O'Day's voice. *"Just blow it, Reggie."*

I looked at the television. The screen went black, then the name *Alvee Smith-Killem* appeared on the black screen. The name meant nothing to me.

Then a bright shot of a steam locomotive – bright enough to make you blink – puffing along its rails through the lonely scrub, heading for a low bridge over a swift moving river.

Another voiceover: *"Not yet, Jody."* I was surprised to recognize Ryan Gosling's voice.

The screen went black again, then, sure enough, Ryan Gosling's name appeared on the screen.

The screen still black, Franck's voice said, *"If you don't blow it, then I will, Reggie."*

Another shot of the train.

"You can't blow it yet, Jody!" Ryan urged.

The screen went black again.

"You just watch me, Reggie," Franck's voice said.

I flinched as if slapped. I'd heard him say those very words, that time in the airport, when the two of us were trying to get drunk, quickly and surreptiously, before we had to board the plane for Vegas.

"You can't drink that in here!" Ruthanne had whispered to him.

"You just watch me, Ruthie," Franck had said. The same words had just come out of my TV, the same voice. *Franck's voice.* Only instead of *Ruthie,* he'd said *Reggie.*

On the television, there was another shot of the train, puffing along. Then the train exploded.

The screen went black. Then it said – *Alvee Smith-Killem. Ryan Gosling. Cheyenne Sundown. This Summer.*

An ad for *DirecTV* came on. I looked at Doug, speechless, stunned. He didn't even notice me looking at him. He just sat there and watched the stupid *DirecTV* ad.

Doug had not just heard a voice from beyond the grave. He knew nothing about Franck and Ruthie, or about my book. He hadn't asked for details about the deadly fire, and I hadn't offered any. All he knew was that my friend and I had been in Vegas together, there had been a fire, and only I had returned. What happens in Vegas stays in Vegas.

"What was that?" I finally said to him.

He looked at me. "What was what?"

"Do you know anything about that movie?"

"Which?"

"The one that they just advertised. *Cheyenne Sundown.* With Ryan Gosling. And . . ." No. Franck was dead.

Doug smiled at me. "You're the Ryan Gosling fan. Google that shit." He turned his attention back to the TV.

There would be too many hits, too much information, if I Googled Ryan. Pictures and movie reviews and fan sites and *IMDb* and *Wikipedia.* Ryan was a huge star, Canadian import though he might be. I needed a narrow field of inquiry, or I'd be there all night.

So I Googled *Cheyenne Sundown.* There were a few entries – the movie was Ryan's latest vehicle; it was a western. It wasn't due out for a few months. I clicked on the official movie site.

It was only a landing page. Apparently, the studio was being just as mysterious on the internet as they had been in their ad. Ryan's face grinned at us from the right side. He was the star after all – we had to see his gorgeous face. On the left of the screen was a picture of someone whom I had to assume was this unknown with the ridiculous name, Alvee Smith-Killem. Alvee was wearing a cowboy hat. He was looking down, and the only parts of his face that were visible were his nose, a wry smile, and his chin.

The chin could be Franck's, maybe the nose. But it couldn't be Franck, because Franck was dead, and besides that rather immutable fact, this guy couldn't be a day over twenty-five. All the plastic surgery in the world couldn't make Franck O'Day look twenty-five again. But the chin, the nose . . . they looked so familiar. And the voice. Somehow, some way – it could be him.

Between Ryan's lovely visage and the obscured face of Alvee Smith-Killem, it said their names again, and the title of the film, and *Coming This Summer*. That was it.

So I Googled *Alvee Smith-Killem*. I was returned the same page for *Cheyenne Sundown*, and an *IMDb* listing for the man himself. *IMDb* said that the young actor with the funny name was born Alvee Joseph Smith, on May 1, 1988, three years and two months after me.

> Alvee decided he wanted to be an actor at a young age. He was born and raised in the little town of Bromley, Kentucky, but spent his teens and twenties kicking around London and its environs, sampling the theater scene. He says the Killem part of his stage name comes from something his first director there told him: "If you ever get to Hollywood, kid, you're gonna kill 'em." The rest of the cast referred to him as Killem after that. The name stuck, so he hyphenated it onto his name for his first movie role, Downpour. "It's so much more memorable than just Smith," he said.

I looked at the photo of Alvee Smith-Killem. Sometimes you'll see a young actor, and you'll think that he looks just like an older actor, from back in the day, when he was young. Sometimes, the resemblance is amazing, uncanny. So much so, that you wonder if this young one could be the old one's son, from some long buried dalliance with one of his first fans, perhaps.

And at first glance, this was what I thought of Alvee Smith-Killem. That he could be Franck O'Day's son.

But then I looked at the picture again. Alvee Smith-Killem considers us smugly from a publicity still from his movie debut, *Downpour*. He has the brow of an angel, crowned with glorious curly hair, worn almost shoulder-length, as black as midnight. Our fingers itch and ache to run gently through those curls. He has enormous eyes, as dark and as blue and as depthless as an angry, stormy ocean. Poets sing about such eyes. He has the cheekbones of a Greek god, a strong, perfect nose; a manly chin.

The eyebrows are a little bit bushier – the slightly delicate arch that I'd always thought of as *manicured* has been allowed to go to seed. It looks good on him, a definite improvement.

Alvee's subtle, knowing smile tells us that he has peered into our soul – he has kenned our desire, something we are powerless to conceal from him. His indescribable, incredible mouth is still dewy, full. I knew that his mouth would toughen up a little bit by the time he was forty, but now we would do anything, *give anything,* for the opportunity to taste that full bottom lip, just once, and Alvee knows it.

He'd gotten his teeth straightened. They were now perfect, like Bradley Cooper's teeth. Stars couldn't have crooked teeth in the era of HD.

I felt like I was losing my mind, because not only did Alvee Smith-Killem resemble Franck a great deal, as if they could be related. Alvee Smith-Killem *was* Franck O'Day.

I knew of no extant photos of Franck at twenty-five – just that one grainy shot of him and the rest of the kiddies from *Sister Sam's Lost Angels*. He'd been twenty-three in that one – and the image he'd been trying to project hadn't been sexy. He'd been going for teenaged and orphaned.

Franck had been about this age in *George and Benedict*, now that I thought about it – he'd been twenty-six or so, had the same curly black hair. But it had been restrained with a little colonial ribbon in that film, and the period clothing had made him look older. Something about stockings and buckle shoes just tends to lay a few extra years on a person. He'd only been twenty-seven or twenty-eight for *Manhattan*, but the evening wear and short haircut in that one had also lent him an aura of sophistication beyond his years.

But if there was a photo of Franck when he was twenty-five, looking just as wild and sexy as he wanted to be, then this would be it.

It was the expression that convinced me, almost more than the familiar face. I'd once stared at that still from *Manhattan* – I had *studied* it, trying to ascertain just what it was about this dead actor's *features* that had so captivated my friend. But I had come to know this *expression* personally. I'd seen him gaze upon Ruthanne with just this look – that little smile, just showing his top teeth – just showing enough teeth for me to see that they weren't crooked anymore. But they were still *his* teeth.

This was a picture of a twenty-five year old Franck O'Day. This was not a son – no, it would have to be a *grandson* – any son of Franck's would have to be in at least his fifties, if not his sixties. It was not some doppelganger. It was him. *Alvee Smith-Killem was Franck O'Day.*

I remembered Lori telling me how the lawyer had slid Franck's picture across his desk to her, as proof that he wasn't dead. She'd never believed that he was dead, and after hearing his voice on tape, she needed no other proof. Now I thought I'd heard his voice coming out of my television, in a trailer for some standard-issue-looking western. The photo on *IMDb* seemed undeniably to be him.

But pictures could be enhanced, changed. Could it really be him? Franck O'Day had come back from the dead before, I thought. There was only one way for me to be absolutely sure. Because it hadn't been Alvee Smith-Killem's face that had snapped my attention toward the television, now had it? His face hadn't even been shown. It had been his voice. Just like Lori, I'd heard Franck's voice, and even after almost two years, I hadn't forgotten the smooth, dark timbre, the melodious masculinity of it. Just like Lori, I'd never forget it.

I could resist the blue eyes – I would not have *given anything for the opportunity to taste that full bottom lip, just once.* Although that was just a damn lie, now wasn't it?

But Franck's voice – I'd never heard another so sexy, so silky. Franck's voice was unmistakable.

I could wait around for another ad for *Cheyenne Sundown* to run on TV, but who knew when that might happen? And he'd just said a few lines in that. I needed more dialogue. I had to watch Alvee Smith-Killem's first feature, *Downpour*. I didn't really even have to watch it at all, just *listen* to it. If its young star somehow really was Franck O'Day, I'd know immediately. Just from his voice.

I clicked on the *IMDb* link for it. *Downpour* was 89 minutes long, a drama/romance. It had been released in the UK, a little more than a year after the fire. It had been written and directed by someone name Maurice Claremount. No bells at the name. It starred Alvee Smith-Killem and a bunch of other nobodies I'd never heard of. The synopsis read simply: *A young man and woman fall in love, but their happiness is marred by tragedy and suspicion.*

The cover photo showed a couple in profile, kissing in the rain. They were wet, their features indistinct. It was a downpour, after all. The man could be Franck, or it could be someone else. It was definitely not Franck as I'd seen him last.

Finding a copy of *Downpour* to peruse proved a lot more difficult than finding its *IMDb* listing, however. It had been a British production, had seen a limited US release, had met with tepid reviews. It wasn't available from *DirecTV,* or *Hulu,* or *Amazon.* It wasn't on *Netflix* to stream, or through the mail. It wasn't in the *Redbox.* I frowned. I had to see it. I had to hear this Alvee Smith Killem's voice again.

Where does one seek a little known, poorly reviewed movie of limited release? There was only one place.

Like a farm boy in the big city for the first time, I took tentative baby steps into those shady neighborhoods of the internet. Like that farm boy, I prayed that I wouldn't catch anything while I was there, doing things that I perhaps ought not to have been doing. There was not a *How to Pirate Movies for Dummies*, but I eventually figured in out.

I found *Downpour*, minding its own business on *Pirate Bay, the galaxy's most resilient bit-torrent site*. Ruthanne had signed us up for U-Verse, so the download didn't take more than a few minutes. After it was finished, I immediately deleted the bit-torrent program I'm used to obtain it. It was like closing the barn door after I might've let all manner of Trojan horses in, but it made me feel better about the risk I'd taken to my innocent computer. Doug, immersed in whatever it was he was watching, had no idea that laws, probably international laws, were being broken right beside him.

I didn't play *Downpour*. If I was right – if Franck O'Day had somehow managed to escape the deadly fire that had claimed my best friend, if he had somehow managed to again circumvent the laws of time and nature and make himself young again, if Alvee Smith-Killem was indeed Franck O'Day – I didn't want to hear the evidence out of the little laptop speakers, nor did I want to hear it through weak ear buds. I wanted to hear it through the surround sound, on the home theater system that Ruthie had so loved. And I didn't want to hear it with Doug sitting there.

So I closed my laptop, stood up, executed one of those theatrical yawns and stretches that Ruthie had been so good at. I even repeated her stock words.

"Boy," I said, "am I tired! I think I must've gotten too much sun." Even though I'd been at work all day, and hadn't gotten any sun at all. How I missed Ruthie!

Doug didn't notice the inconsistency. "Your timing's perfect," he said. "This dumb movie just ended." He arose and also stretched, and gave me a hug.

I didn't ask him what he'd been watching, because I didn't want to hear some drawn-out description of it. I wanted him to go home, to go away. I hugged him back quickly, then moved toward the door. So it didn't seem like I was just throwing him out, I asked, "Are we going to the Farmer's Market tomorrow?"

Doug said some enthusiastic affirmative regarding the Farmer's Market, then gave me a kiss, said good-night, and finally walked out the door.

I set my laptop on the little table next to the television. Ruthie used to put hers right there, when she wanted to watch her pirated movies. She used to hook an HDMI cable right up to the computer – I reached behind the TV, but I didn't find the cable. I looked back there, but could see only darkness. I opened the drawer to the little table, looking for a flashlight. The HDMI cable was in the drawer, wrapped up with a little wire tie. Doug must've have unhooked it from the television at some point, wrapped it up, and put it away. He was neat like that. He didn't watch pirated movies. I didn't watch pirated movies. There was no reason to hook a computer up to the TV anymore, no reason to leave a stray cable hanging off of the back of it.

I found the flashlight, carefully moved the big TV out a little bit so I could slide the cable into its slot. I pushed the TV back, hooked the cable into my laptop. I clicked on the file and sat back down on the couch. I did not turn out the lights for theater ambience.

The filmed opened, not surprisingly, with a shot of a rainy night. But it was a particularly bright and fuzzy rainy night, and I realized immediately that I had downloaded the worst kind of pirated flick. It was a bootleg, filmed right there in the theater by some enterprising individual with a smuggled-in camera. I could tell from the over-exposed look to the picture, the weak sound, and the fact that the silhouette of someone's head drifted quickly across the bottom of the screen as the opening credits rolled.

Some studio I'd never heard of, in association with some other studio I'd never heard of. The title drifted across the screen. Starring Alvee Smith-Killem and some woman I'd never heard of, either. *Directed by Maurice Claremount*. Whoever that was.

Like *David Copperfield*, like *Interview with the Vampire*, *Downpour* was a narrative, and since Alvee Smith-Killem was the star, he spoke first, and continued in voiceover for a while.

The story he was telling was sad, but I didn't listen to his words – only the low, melodic sound of his voice. Even with the bad sound quality, Franck's voice was unmistakable, inimitable. There could be no doubt. After a few minutes, I turned *Downpour* off. The bootleg copy was just too bad to watch any more of it.

THIRTY-EIGHT

First thing in the morning, I called Doug and told him that my monthly had shown up with a vengeance, and I would have to stay in bed for the entire day. It was not a subject that he was eager to discuss, just like I knew it wasn't going to be. He asked for no details. He just asked if there was anything he could do, anything he could bring me. I told him there was not, and told him I'd call him later if I was feeling better. I told him I was sorry that I would miss the Farmer's Market.

I drove to the local Avis, going out of my way to skirt the blocked off streets of the Farmer's Market.

I planned to drive to Beverly Hills in an anonymous rented car. I would drive right up to the gate in front of the late Jessika Yerdlay's palatial estate, push the intercom button, and when Franck answered, I'd say . . . I'd say . . . just what was I going to say? *I know you're in there, I know you're not dead, I know you're somehow twenty-five again?* It was ridiculous. I knew none of those things. But I aimed to find out.

I parked a little bit down the street from the gated drive to collect my thoughts. I suddenly realized that I knew nothing at all. Maybe Franck didn't even live here anymore. Maybe he was staying at the swinging *Chateau Marmont*, as might befit a twenty-five-year-old actor that looked like he did. Maybe he wasn't even in town. Maybe he was still in England, where *Downpour* had been produced and distributed.

Maybe I was insane. Maybe the loss of my best friend and her boyfriend had put me right around the bend. Now only Ruthanne, but Franck, too. Since he was gone, I'd discovered that I missed him almost as much as I missed Ruthanne. I'd discovered that I grieved over Franck's death almost as much as I grieved over Ruthie's. I'd discovered that I'd grown quite fond of Franck. He was dead and I was hearing things, imagining resemblances that couldn't be there.

I sat in my rented car for about twenty minutes, mulling over these ideas. I had just about decided that I should've put a little more thought into the whole thing before going off half-cocked, as they say, when kismet showed me that I had indeed chosen the right day for this little adventure.

A limo pulled up to the gate. The gate opened, the limo drove in. The gate barely had time to clank shut again before limo came back down the drive. I waited until it disappeared up the street, then drove my rented car up to the intercom, and pushed the button.

A man's voice said, "Yes?" It was muffled by static, indistinct. It could've been anyone. I remembered that this piece of technology hadn't been upgraded since that old Hollywood diva, Jessika Yerdlay, had lived here. They could've had a little screen to see who was calling, nowadays, but they didn't. I thought that they might get one installed, after my visit today.

A million things to say went through my mind. I rejected each one of them as too lame, too confrontational, too vague. The man's voice said, "Yes?" again.

At last, I said into the intercom, "I've got a telegram for Franck O'Day."

The same muffled voice. "What?"

"I said, I've got a telegram for Franck O'Day."

I counted to ten before the gate rattled open.

THIRTY-NINE

When I drove up the curving driveway, I beheld Alvee Smith-Killem standing halfway down the steps, looking curiously in my direction. He was wearing a light-blue short-sleeved shirt, unbuttoned, thrown carelessly over a wife-beater. He wore jeans and a pair of black, high-topped Converse. I couldn't gauge the sum of his expression, because he was wearing a pair of Ray-Bans, as perfectly black as the curly hair that reached nearly to his shoulders.

I pulled up in front of the old stone staircase, got out of the car, and looked up over its roof at him.

Alvee Smith-Killem smiled, and Franck's mellifluous voice exclaimed, "Carol!" The man that walked down the steps was not wearing an impeccably tailored, slate gray suit, as befitted an actor in his waning years. No. Alvee was dressed perfectly for someone his age, but he still had Franck's gait.

He took off his sunglasses as he trotted around the car and enveloped me in a bear hug, picked me up off my feet. Then he released me, set his shades on the roof of the car, and held me by the hands. The eyes smiling out of Alvee's twenty-five year old face were Franck's, the teeth, straightened, were his. There could be no doubt.

"How nice of you to come!" Franck's voice said, and Alvee hugged me again.

How nice of you to come? Like I had just dropped in unexpectedly for a little visit. *How nice of you to come? Really?* Not like he had returned from the grave, *again*, younger, more devastating than ever. Not like that at all.

Again, a million things to say flew through my mind. At last I chose the simplest. "What happened, Franck?"

"It was the energy, Carol." He released me and smiled humorlessly at my familiar look of disbelief. Franck retrieved his sunglasses from the roof of my rented car, folded them, put them into his pocket. He took me by the hand and led me up the staircase to where he'd been standing. We sat on the step.

"I've told you before, and I know Lori told you. All those years that I was in Japan – when you love something, you give off a special kind of energy. The things you love, they soak it up – who looks happier and healthier than a beloved child, or a pampered house pet? Even plants respond to love. It's a force of nature. In Japan, I learned to recognize this energy – to harness it, to assimilate it. Through meditation . . ." he made the *Om* gesture, palms up, fingers in circles.

I noticed a white, dime sized scar in the middle of his left palm. Just like in my dream.

"They don't really love me, you know. That's the biggest mistake an actor can make. The biggest trap. They don't love *me*. They love the *character*. I guess there's just something about a heroic, misunderstood Benedict Arnold."

Franck *chuckled*. He was coping with the tragedy quite well, it seemed. "A million years ago, a million women in a million theatres fell in love with Perry Calibri. He was suave, rich, handsome, single. They watched *Manhattan,* thrilled to all that love at first sight between Perry and Dora, who was just a flighty flibbertigibbet. The women in the audience, they knew how it was to be like Dora, nervous and unsure.

"The world was changing in the early sixties, Carol. Not as drastically as it would later, but there were already stirrings. Young men were different from their fathers. They didn't want to wear hats anymore. Young women didn't want to wear white gloves.

"You don't see it in the papers from that time, because the old guard was still in charge, but things were changing. *Manhattan* was a welcome throwback. It wasn't a real representation of New Year's Eve in New York in 1940, but it was a representation of how people imagined it might've been – romantic and carefree. Stable. We were still a year away from entering the war. We were not on the brink of social change and upheaval in 1940 like the real world was in 1961.

"And at the center of the story were Perry and Dora, young, rich, and in love. The women that watched the film – they knew that they were really just like Dora, inside – a little absent, a little confused, putting up a haughty front that they really didn't feel. And just like Dora, they fell in love with Perry. He was perfect – beautiful, carefree, independently wealthy – but he was also a tortured soul, once he saw Dora.

"He loved her so much – and in the end, Perry and Dora were united in their love. If Perry could fall in love with Dora, why, he could fall in love with them, too, all those women in the audience. They could soothe his almost-broken heart, just like Dora did. They loved him as much as Dora did, and he would love them back just as much, if they would just get to meet him – *me* – in person.

"It's a selfish kind of love that fans feel for the characters actors play, Carol. In real life, you have to accept the foibles and eccentricities and sometimes downright meanness of those you love. You take the good with the bad, the wheat with chaff, so to speak. You love your people for who they are. You love who you love despite their weaknesses.

"But the characters in movies are perfect. Fans don't care who or what an actor really is – the character that he plays is their fantasy. In their hearts and minds, if they got to meet you, you'd behave the way they think the character would behave. You'd act just like they'd want him to, *do all those romantic things* that he'd do. They don't want the real man – he might not be amenable to some of those things." Franck grinned evilly. "The fans want the character – they want the delightful fiction that's touched them in that special way.

"The best actors create that fantasy for different kinds of fans – they're a good guy this time, a bad guy the next. A lover, a cowboy, a gangster, a sophisticate. Different characters that appeal to the different imaginations of different people.

"Have you ever heard one of your girlfriends say, *I'm not a big fan of So-and-so, but I liked him in that?* That was the one character, the one that did it *for her*. She doesn't care for the actor so much, but she liked that character. And if she *really* liked that character, she'll find after a while that she likes the actor, too, especially if he plays a similar part in his next film.

"It's harder today than it used to be. People don't have the imagination that they once did. It's harder to lose themselves in the fantasy of a good movie. Maybe the pictures have gotten smaller, eh?" Franck barked a small laugh. "But nowadays, they wonder more about who the actors really are. Sure, Brad and George were great in *Ocean's Whatever*, but what are they *really like?* So, the media provides them with what they want to know, or at least, what they want to hear. It was easier in my time. Fans had no doubt what I was really like. I was Perry Calibri.

"And you can suffer all the emotional angst you want about all that – if you want someone to love you for yourself, don't become an actor. Accept that the adoration is the best part of the job, admit that you need it – but don't ever believe that it's you they adore.

"If you don't realize that it's the character they love and not you, it's devastating when they don't like the characters you play so much anymore. When you're forced to play the dad or the boss or the lawyer, because you're getting old, and some new pretty face is now the lead, the love interest – all the ladies want to do *him* now, and not you, anymore. That's when the depression starts, and then maybe the drugs, or the booze. Or if you were insecure to start out with, maybe they just start to get worse.

257

"It's just a job. A well-paying, exciting job, but a job, nonetheless. If you start to get upset or depressed because all those people's feelings aren't really about the man behind the greasepaint anymore, then you'll lose it.

"It was just a job to me, but the biggest perk *was* all that love and adoration and energy that the masses felt for Perry. I knew it wasn't Franck O'Day they loved. But all that love was still directed at me, of course, because Perry wasn't real. All the fans thought that they loved *me*, because in their minds, I *was* Perry. It was all so much more than good enough for me."

Franck paused, then grinned. "Getting passed up for younger actors was not a problem that I had, of course. But it happens. Because getting old is as inevitable as the seasons, the circle of life and all that. *Oh, yeah, So-and-so doesn't look like much anymore, but you should've seen him when he was young.*

"In the old days, actors made more money, I think, or maybe they were smarter. They retired when they started to get old. No lesser and lesser roles, no older and older characters, no playing Tithonus right up until they cue the grasshopper."

When I looked confused, Franck explained. "Eos was the goddess of the dawn in Greek mythology. She falls in love with Tithonus, a Trojan prince. Eos, being immortal, doesn't age, and she begs Zeus to grant the gift of immortality to her lover also. But in one of those cruel twists that the Greeks were so fond of, Eos fails to request the gift of eternal youth for Tithonus, in addition to eternal life. So he indeed lives forever, but he gets older and older and bent and crushed by all the years, until he eventually turns into a grasshopper.

"Tennyson wrote a poem, in which Tithonus mourns the youth that he's lost: *Alas! for this gray shadow, once a man/ So glorious in his beauty and thy choice/ Who madest him thy chosen, that he seem'd/ To his great heart none other than a God!*

"And so it is with actors. One day you're young and beautiful, the idol of millions, women and men, too, throwing themselves at your feet. You have been made, by their choice, into a god."

Franck paused, grinned at the astonished expression on my face. "Don't look so impressed, Carol," he said. "I'm just a dumb actor. But I did have the benefits of Bobby's classical education. That story about Tithonus? That's just one of hundreds that he told me. Some were more obscure even than that one. We were in Japan together for a long time."

Franck grinned. "You have no idea how intoxicating it is to be made into a god by the masses, Carol. There's the fast life, of course.

The parties, the drinking, the drugs, the women. The cars, the houses." He nodded behind him at Jessika's manse. "The boats, the food, the travel. But businessmen and drug lords know about those aspects. And it's nice, don't get me wrong. But it's not for the material things that you become an actor. That's not why you long to become famous.

"You wanted to be a writer – it wasn't for the money, now was it? You have a little stirring of that desire to be famous, yourself, Carol. To see your name at the top of that bestseller's list, to get fan mail? *Where do you get your ideas?* they'd ask. They'd tell you how wonderful you are, how your work *moved* them. But be warned, Carol – it won't be you they love, but the characters you create.

"It's better for actors. All that love for the character – it's aimed directly at you. To them, *you are the character.*"

Franck rose from the step and held his hands out from his sides a little bit, palms up. "At a premiere – all that love and adoration washes over you from the crowd. It's a palpable thing. When you shake their hands – all that desire shining in their eyes – the glassy looks, the speechlessness – it's not for you, but *they* think it is, because to them, *you are that character that they love so much.* I'd sit in the back of the theater just a few years ago, and I could still feel it – all that adoration directed at Perry on the screen would bounce off and come back to me in waves. It keeps me young.

"The characters we create really are like Tithonus, Carol, how Eos intended him to be. They are immortal, and forever young. It's only the actors that get old."

Franck sighed. "One minute you're young, the lust object of millions, and the next . . ." He slapped his hands on his thighs and sat back down. "And the next, you're playing the can't-even-be-called-supporting-role of the kindly grandpa or villain-with-a-heart-of-gold, and some other blue-eyed thirty-something is the rakish star. And then you just fade away and die. Far better to go out on top, like James Dean. *Live fast, die young and leave a good-looking corpse!*" Franck paused.

I was still speechless. What did all this have to do with the fire? With him being alive and young, and Ruthie and everyone else being dead?

"You know, Dean didn't really say that, or at least he wasn't the first. It was from a movie, called *Knock On Any Door*. John Derek said that line, in that film. He played a street tough who shoots a cop. Bogie was in it, too. It was actually Bogie's film – but it was also a vehicle to show off young Derek. Bogie was already getting old by that time – he played the bleeding-heart attorney. His romantic lead days were long over. No more *Casablancas,* no more *To Have And Have Nots.* He wouldn't even live another ten years.

"The film, forgettable in itself, is a perfect example of what I'm talking about, Carol. Actors get old, start to take the old-guy roles. Not that this is a bad thing in and of itself – some old-guy roles are superb, full of pathos and loss." Franck frowned. "But those are not usually the roles that an actor is remembered for. When an actor dies, they don't show pictures from the twilight of his career – they show pictures from when he was the original Tithonus, the leading man, the star, the love-interest. *Best known for his portrayal of . . .* that young guy.

"And if you go out on top, while you're still young, like Dean, or me, then that's all anyone ever remembers, because that's all there ever was. No need to grow old and get bad parts. No need to lose all that love and adoration of the fans, that wondrous *energy."*

This was all well and good, this treatise on the triumphs and tragedies of fame. But it didn't tell me what had happened. It didn't tell me why Ruthie was dead and Franck was twenty-five and no longer Franck at all but a stunningly attractive up and comer who called himself Alvee Smith-Killem, who was poised to upstage Ryan Gosling. He had offered no explanation at all. "What happened, Franck?" I repeated.

Franck covered his face with his hands. "I lost control of it, Carol. The energy. I was sitting there in the first row, holding Candace's hand. Holding Ruthie's hand." He sobbed. "Ah, Ruthie!" Franck looked up across the curving driveway, at the trees. "I closed my eyes. I felt all the energy, all the love and adoration of all my most loyal fans. Candace – I remember when Candace was a giggly, sadder-but-wiser extra, Carol! And Mae, too.

"My old co-stars, and all the others – they had come all the way out to the middle of Vegas to see me, because – each in their own way, for their own reasons – they loved Perry Calibri. They loved Franck O'Day. And Ruthie. Ruthie's love and energy was the purest of all, because she was starting to believe that she loved me for me, in addition to loving me for being Perry. She thought she was beginning to see the real me, past the 1940's ballroom fiction.

"I just sat there with my eyes closed, feeling the energy channel through me, feeling it wash away all the years. I knew that I'd wake up the next day, feeling alive and refreshed, as if I'd had some incredible spa treatment. Except no spa can do what that adoring energy can do, Carol, if you know how to assimilate it. I knew I would wake up the next day feeling alive and refreshed, but I also knew that I'd look younger. I would *be* younger.

"But then something went wrong. There was just too much! All those people, my biggest, most loyal fans! Suddenly, the projector on the ceiling exploded, and dropped onto the podium, sending sparks and shards of plastic everywhere. The room was plunged into darkness. Flames raced across the ceiling. The podium was on fire. It was the only light in the room. People were screaming and backing up, overturning chairs, getting tangled in them, all to escape the heat.

"People were screaming. I wasn't holding Ruthie's hand anymore. The screen was on fire, and all the flags on that little raised stage in the corner. The place was filling up with smoke. Everybody was trying to get to the door, but the flames – people were screaming, crying. I kept looking for Ruthie, calling her name." Franck buried his face in his hands again and sobbed. I put my arm around his shoulders. He cried, but I remained curiously dry-eyed. His story wasn't quite finished yet.

Franck stopped sobbing, looked out at the trees again. "I don't remember getting out, don't remember running to the pizza place at the end of the plaza. But I remember trying to get in, banging on the window. The door was locked and the pizza guy was sitting at a table, reading. I remember him not even looking up, saying, 'We're closed!' I remember pounding on the window, remember screaming at him, telling him to call someone, telling him that the VFW Hall was on fire. I remember him looking in that direction, scrambling back around the counter, yanking the phone off the hook . . ." Franck drew a long shuddering breath, then let it out again. "There was only one thing for me to do then. I staggered around the corner of the building . . . and I took my phone out of my pocket and called Bobby."

"Bobby? Bobby *Ecksmith?*" But really, was it so impossible to believe? Eighty-two year old Franck O'Day was twenty-five again, standing here in front of me, just as fine as he wanted to be. Why shouldn't Robert Ecksmith still be alive, too? They had been in Japan together, after all. Maybe Bobby was slim and blonde and twenty-five, too, on the boulevard, enjoying the new freedoms.

Franck turned his tear-stained face from staring at the foliage and looked at me. "Of course." He swiped at the tears. "Who else would I call?"

I remembered Lori's diary. *Mom had told me, from the time that I was old enough to dial the phone: if anything ever happened to her, I was to call the studio. Not the cops, not the life squad, not the fire department. I was to call the studio first, and they would handle it.* "What did Bobby say?" I asked.

"Bobby told me to start walking down Las Vegas Boulevard. I'd barely made it under the 515 before a cab picked me up and took me to the airport. A man with an English accent met me there. 'I'm Dr. Urstig, Mr. O'Day,' he said. 'Do you have your passport with you?'

"My passport was in my pocket. That was something else that Bobby had taught me, all those years ago. *Always carry your passport. You never know when you might have to leave the country.*

"I told Dr. Urstig that I didn't want to leave the country, that I didn't want to *fly* anywhere, that there'd been a fire, that they were all dead . . ." Franck buried his face in his hands again. After a pause, he continued. "'You can't help them then, can you?' Urstig replied, not unkindly. We got on a little plane, and Dr. Feelgood gave me some kind of a sedative. The next thing I knew, I was disembarking at Heathrow, still smelling like smoke. I'm sure we changed planes somewhere, but I don't remember it."

"How did you know they were all dead, Franck?"

I remembered the dream I'd had, the horrible dream, where I'd stood in the protective cocoon of the fact that it *was* only a dream, and watched while VFW Post 864 burned down around me. Franck had apologized for *taking Ruthie*, then had strolled out the only exit.

The dream had told me that Franck had sacrificed his biggest fans on the altar of fame – it sounded ridiculously cinematic, even to me. But it could be put no other way. Their energy had made him young again – and since he was young again, he couldn't have a bunch of people pointing out Alvee Smith-Killem's uncanny resemblance to Franck O'Day.

If I'd realized it was him, just from his voice – Mae and Penny and Evan surely would've, too. If a young Jimmy Stewart or Clark Gable all of a sudden reappeared at the local Cineplex – the world would recognize them. They'd starred in enough movies, they still had enough fans. Such a trick would be impossible for any of the true immortals. They would be immediately recognized.

But not Franck, and not now. He'd never been that famous to start out with – no one remembered *George and Benedict* and only a handful – even though some of them were the folks at *The Criterion Collection* – remembered *Manhattan*. He no doubt still had a few die-hard fans left, the ones that couldn't make it to the Nevada desert. That Vegas cop's mother, for example.

But the core of them, the majority of them, had been wiped out in the fire. The ones who would've immediately recognized Alvee Smith-Killem as Franck O'Day, the moment this new movie came out; the ones who would've gathered at *TwoGreenKeys.com* to discuss it. They were all gone.

Not only had these people given their lives to make him young again, now that they were dead, it would be much easier for him to pull this whole Alvee Smith-Killem thing off.

Franck looked at me now, and there was no guilt, no deviousness, not even a shadow of the idea that he knew they were all dead because he'd killed them with some kind of love-energy lightning bolt, that he'd sucked the life out of seventy-five people, just so he could be twenty-five again. He'd isolated them in the middle of that Las Vegas that I hated so much and had stolen their energy from them. He'd killed seventy-five people because he wanted to be young, wanted to be famous again. He'd killed them because he could. That's what I'd seen in my dream.

Sorrow lined his unlined face. I realized with a start that he, or at least Alvee Smith-Killem, was younger than me. I'd turned thirty in March, and he'd turned twenty-seven on May 1st. He wasn't twenty-five anymore already, I corrected myself. But he still looked it. A prime, perfect twenty-five.

"I just knew, Carol." Franck said. "I don't remember how I got out – but if anybody else had gotten out with me, they would've been right there, running to call for help. I knew they were all dead. I could feel it."

He was completely believable. Conflicting ideas flashed through my mind, like slides on a carousel. All the parts of me that wanted so badly to believe that it had been some kind of accident, all the parts that wanted to believe that people couldn't shoot fire out of their hands, couldn't purposefully turn a room full of devoted fans into ash, those parts believed him, believed that it had been an accident.

This whole energy thing – it was all ridiculous, and even if it wasn't, Franck could never just kill a room full of people like that, with no more qualms than stomping grapes for their juice. Franck might be a full of himself son-of-a-bitch, but he wasn't a mass-murdering monster. All the parts of me that wanted to believe him wanted to believe that most of all.

But there was another part of me that said, *It's also impossible and ridiculous to turn the clock back almost sixty years.* Yet somehow, Franck had accomplished exactly that. He didn't just look twenty-seven, he *was* twenty-seven. No plastic surgery on the planet was this good.

This isn't even Franck O'Day, anymore, that one little part of me said, softly, but insistently. *Franck O'Day is eighty-two years old. This is Alvee Smith-Killem, of Bromley, Kentucky and London, England. Fresh-faced, incredibly attractive – not much more than a very sexy boy. Why, he still has milk on his tongue, as grandpa used to say. Just a young actor, with only two films to his name,*

263

one not even out yet. Just a young actor, with Franck O'Day's voice and Franck O'Day's eyes, and Franck O'Day's house, and Franck O'Day's memories.

And all of that was impossible, too, yet here it was. So somehow, I had to admit, the energy thing worked. But it didn't mean that Franck had purposely killed all those people with it, like I'd seen in my dream. It didn't mean that Franck had chosen an isolated venue and then sacrificed a room full of people, including one (or maybe even two) that loved him with all her soul, just to be young again.

Maybe he *had* just lost control of it, like he'd said. It must be a powerful, supernatural thing to work the wonders it did. Maybe it *was* hard to control.

Sitting there and listening to him explain, watching the tears roll down his face — most of me had no trouble accepting that it had all been simply a horrible, tragic accident. An accident, brought on by bad wiring in an old building, or even by Franck's losing his hold on the universal energy. But either way, most of me believed that it had all been an accident.

But one little part of me reserved judgment, kept an open mind to more sinister, more malevolent possibilities. And that other part remained watchful.

"What happened when you got to England, Franck?" I asked.

"Bobby met me at Heathrow. He hugged me. Urstig gave him a little salute, which Bobby returned — then the good doctor faded into the crowd. His job was done. His package had been delivered safely. A little singed, a little drugged, but safely back in Bobby's hands.

"Maki was waiting in the limo. He nodded to me, said something in Japanese to Bobby. 'Papa-san says it's good to see you,' Bobby said, and smiled at me. He said, 'It's *great* to see you, Franck! My darling!' And he kissed me quickly on the cheek. He told me that we'd talk in the morning, and we rode in silence to his estate.

"When I looked in the mirror the next morning, I was young again." Franck looked for that disbelief on my face and was mildly surprised to find it absent. How could I not believe anymore? Was he not young again?

"Bobby told me how sorry he was for my loss, and we cried together for a while, just like when Bridget was killed.

"I knocked around his place for a few weeks. Then he showed me the script for *Downpour.* I didn't want to do it at first, but he talked me into it in the end, saying that working would help me to forget about what had happened.

"'You'll never forget her,' Bobby said, 'but you can try to forget what *happened* to her. Just like Bridget. Think how happy she'd be to see

264

you making films again. If you won't do it for yourself, or for me, do it for her.'"

I felt a little choked up at that the truth of that. Poor Ruthie. She would've been thrilled to see Franck making movies again. *How ecstatic she would have been to see Franck twenty-seven again*, I thought. It was making me a little ecstatic my own self, despite that one little doubting part of me.

"So Bobby and his lawyers created Alvee Smith-Killem. We made *Downpour*."

"Aren't you afraid that someone will find out? That there is no Alvee Smith-Killem?" I asked.

Franck shrugged. "I'm not running for president, Carol. Nobody wastes time vetting actors. It's a twenty-four hour news day. Nobody's got time for that kind of research on people like me. I'm just an actor – my past isn't important. Who cares? Bobby's studio handed out my bio, and the information it contains just gets cut and pasted into each new story. The story's good enough – why would anybody want to start digging into it?

"Besides, Bobby's lawyers are pretty good. There might really *have* been an Alvee Joseph Smith of Bromley, Kentucky. Nobody cares, Carol." He grinned. "At least not yet. I'm still a few projects away from my Barbara Walters' interview. And I'll burn that bridge when I come to it. I have every confidence that ol' Babs'll believe anything I tell her." Franck laughed, paused. "I was telling you about Alvee's debut. *Downpour*. It had a limited release over there, over here. Then it fell off the world."

"I saw it."

Franck looked at me in surprise. "Oh, yeah? And you waited all this time . . . to come see me?"

"I *just* saw it," I amended. "Not when it came out. I saw it last night, as a matter of fact."

"Really?" Franck said. "Where did you see it? It had a limited release, like I said. It'll eventually show up on *Netflix*, but . . . not yet. How did you see it?"

"The same way I saw *George and Benedict*, Franck," I told him. "I downloaded it off the internet. But it wasn't *Downpour* that sicced me on you. I'd never even heard of it."

"You and everybody else," he said and smiled, not upset at all about the lack of commercial success of Alvee's debut.

"It was an ad for *Cheyenne Sundown*. I was sitting on the couch . . ." I almost said, *with my boyfriend*, but thought better of it. Somehow, Doug had totally slipped my mind the moment twenty-seven year old Franck

O'Day had said my name, and I didn't dwell on him now. "I was sitting on the couch, minding my own business on the internet, like Ruthie used to say. The television was on, but I wasn't paying attention to it. Then I heard your voice say, 'Just blow it, Reggie.'"

"So, they decided to run that one? That one's very . . . *bright.*" Franck smiled a little sheepishly, looked at the ground. Then he looked up at me again. "They just show the train in that one."

"It was your voice, Franck. I knew it was you from your voice."

He gazed at me. *He's got the bluest eyes,* I thought, remembering Lori's diaries, her adoration. I looked away quickly, thinking about Ruthanne. I sighed and said, "So I Googled *Alvee Smith-Killem.*"

He continued to smile sheepishly at me. It was entirely adorable. "Don't tell me, let me guess. *Wikipedia?*"

Now I smiled back at him, and it felt like it was the first time I'd smiled, *really smiled,* since before Ruthie died. "You're not famous enough for *Wikipedia,* yet, *Alvee.* I found you on *IMDb,* with that insufferably charming story about your stage name. *You're gonna kill 'em,* indeed."

And then my smile faltered a little bit, because he was looking at me with his enormous blue eyes and his gorgeous twenty-five-year-old's face, and I realized that he *was* gonna kill 'em. He was stunning, irresistible. He was going to leave Ryan Gosling in the dust. He was gonna be a star, just like Bobby Ecksmith had told him all those decades ago. The pictures might've gotten smaller, but Alvee Smith-Killem was going to be their king.

Then the future prince of Hollywood put his hand on my cheek and kissed me. Gently, quickly. It was not a passionate kiss. "Thanks for coming to see me, Carol. I've been lonely. I don't know anyone, anymore."

It was not a passionate kiss, but it was still inappropriate. The insane thought, *He wouldn't've kissed me like that when he was old,* stalked across my brain.

Franck seemed to feel a little ashamed of himself – he cleared his throat, looked at the ground. "So you recognized me from my picture on *IMDb?*" he said, looking out at the trees again.

"Pretty much," I said, "But I wasn't completely sure."

It had been wholly wrong for him to kiss me. Wholly wrong. He had been the love of Ruthie's life. And she was dead, maybe because of him. He shouldn't be kissing me. And I shouldn't be liking it.

"There are a lot of young actors that look like actors of yesteryear," I said. "What is considered beautiful endures, so when this generation begins to age, like you say, the new generation comes forward to take its place, and classic beauty being immutable, some of the new beauties look a whole lot like the beauties of old. So I couldn't be sure." I shrugged. "Franck O'Day had crooked teeth."

He looked at me, a little surprised at this not flattering observation, so rawly put. "The braces were a bitch."

I grinned. "There was only one way to be absolutely sure. So I put on my eye-patch and my whalebone peg-leg and pirated a copy of *Downpour* off the interwebs. I knew it was you as soon as I heard your voice."

"Did you watch the whole thing?"

"No," I admitted. "The quality was terrible. It was a bootleg, and a bad one at that."

He studied me, and I looked back at him, wondering – but not wishing – if he would kiss me again. But he didn't. At last he said, "Would you like to go in the house, Carol?"

Kipling's immortal words paraded through my head. *Pause you who read this, and think for a moment of the long chain of iron or gold, of thorns or flowers, that would never have bound you, but for the formation of the first link on one memorable day.* I paused and I thought, but it was only for a moment.

Who would Ruthie rather see walking up the steps to Jessika's house with Franck? If it couldn't be her, wouldn't she rather it was me?

FORTY

When we got to the top of the stone stairs, Franck said, "There's someone inside I'd like you to meet." He opened the door and we walked through the foyer, then under the bifurcated grand staircase. The house had not changed. *These kinds of houses usually don't,* I thought.

We walked out to the terrace. At the old familiar table was a dignified Asian man, probably in his late forties, clothed in some kind of traditional garb. Beside him sat a thin blonde man wearing a pair of half-specs. He also appeared to be in his mid to late forties. He was wearing a pair of yellow Bermuda shorts and a matching short-sleeved shirt. He was reading a copy of *Variety*. He glanced up at Franck as we approached, but did not smile.

"That only comes out once a week, now," Franck said. "Why don't you check the website?"

"I have a subscription," the man replied. His accent was clipped, veddy British. "I might as well read it. Even if it is old news."

Franck looked at me. "Carolyn Adyon, I'd like you to meet Maurice Claremount." He bowed a little at the Englishman. "Our resident curmudgeon."

The man took off his glasses and rose. He kissed my hand. "I've heard so much about you, Miss Adyon. May I present my esteemed colleague? His name is Maki." He said something unintelligible to the Asian man, who nodded at me. Mr. Claremount sat back down. "You're not here for further research on your book, I hope?" He looked expectantly at me. He still didn't smile.

With dawning astonishment, I realized who I was looking at. I noted a small scar over his right eye – the aftermath of the plane crash. "Franck O'Day is dead, Mr. Ecksmith. I won't be writing anything about him. Or you."

Now the smile bloomed – white, brilliant, straight. Bobby Ecksmith had gotten his teeth fixed, too. "In that case, welcome to our home." He winked at Franck.

"I was wondering if you might like to sit through the rest of *Downpour*, Carol," Franck said. "I have a fairly good print."

I looked at the film's director and smiled. What a once in a lifetime opportunity this was – straight from the horse's mouth, so to speak. I asked him, "Is *Downpour* any good, Mr. Eks – Mr. Claremount?"

He reaffixed his specs, picked up his copy of the now-weekly *Variety* with one hand. With the other, he waved noncommittally. "No . . . it's not very good." He smiled slyly at Franck, then at me. "But he's good in it."

"I couldn't get a higher recommendation than that." Franck offered me his arm, and we went downstairs to the screening room.

FORTY-ONE

I had forgotten totally about Doug's existence by the time my phone beeped as we approached the little theater. I blinked at it for several seconds, unable to place the name.

I opened the text: *Hi! Just wondering if you were feeling any better?* Oh. Yeah. *That* Doug.

I texted back: *Absolutely horrible. I won't disgust you with details. I'll live. Call u tomorrow.* I turned my phone off.

I stayed the night at Franck's house. There was no hanky-panky, however, no Esther Williams tricks in the pool. No more kisses. He didn't even hold my hand while we watched *Downpour*.

Ecksmith had been honest. The film was not very good, just a simple, pedestrian love story. American boy meets English girl, English girl's jealous friend schemes to keep them apart, all is revealed and made well at the last possible second at the train station, in the rain. With a couple of chiffon dresses, a ballroom and a few party hats, it could've almost been an updated version of *High Times in Manhattan*. Ecksmith's direction did not encompass the panache and whimsy of Sunnerfeld's, however. Not this time.

It wasn't a *bad* movie. It was just *all right*. A story that had been told a million times. Unmemorable. But just like Ecksmith had promised, Franck – *Alvee* – was good in in it. There was his voice, of course, clear and familiar and American in the sea of British accents. And the visceral communication of all those feelings of betrayal and woe, just with a glance of his blue eyes. Franck might've been a lot of things, not all of them honorable – but he was a great actor. Try as I might to deny that to myself, I couldn't. He was more than just a pretty face. But on the other hand, that pretty face didn't hurt, either.

Franck and I watched the movie, then had dinner with Ecksmith and the ever silent Maki. I was delighted to see that Kimura was still in the household's employ. The traditional Japanese meal he cooked was excellent. Ecksmith taught me the finer points of the use of *hashi* – chopsticks.

We chatted. Ecksmith asked me if I liked the film. When I hesitated, he said, "Tell me the truth, Miss Adyon. I promise I won't bite you." He winked at Franck. "You're not my type."

"Please call me Carol, Mr. Claremount."

"Please call me Maury, Carol. Just like the television host." He smiled.

"Okay, Maury. Your film was . . . nice. Safe. No surprises." I looked at Franck. "It was an adequate vehicle for a new talent. Like you say, he was great in it."

Franck smiled at me, *just as adorable as he wanted to be,* as my mom always said. I had to remind myself to start thinking of him as *Alvee.* Franck O'Day was dead, along with *George and Benedict,* and Jessika and Dolores and Maribeth and Bridget and Roger and Mae and Candace and Robert Ecksmith. That was old Hollywood. This was new Hollywood. But I would never forget Ruthanne. And I would never forget what old Hollywood had meant to her.

Maury endeavored to look offended, and I was worried for a second – he hadn't really wanted to know my opinion. Who the hell was I to hold forth to legendary director Robert Ecksmith with my humble opinion? Just what I needed to do, offend Alvee's director. *There, I thought of him as Alvee, not Franck.*

But then Maury smiled. "Unfortunately, I must agree, Carol. It was a nice, tame debut vehicle for our lovely, unbruised youth." He smiled at Alvee. "The romance was a little sedate, you might even say. Only alluded to." Now the smile turned into a delighted leer. "Wait till you see *Sundown.* Our youth gets a little bruised in that one. In more ways than one." Maury winked at me. Then, as if the idea had just struck him, he said, "You simply must come to the premiere with us!"

I blinked at him, not quite sure what he meant.

"The premiere! Of *Cheyenne Sundown!* Megastar Ryan Gosling's first western since that forgettable Canadian television thing he did in '98. Unknown – strike that – *newcomer* Alvee Smith-Killem's American film debut! *The premiere!*"

When I still didn't speak, Maury looked at Alvee, said something to him in Japanese. Maki looked embarrassed, coughed into his fist. Alvee looked blank.

Maury smiled at me. "I thought I'd slipped into *The Twilight Zone,* Carol. I thought maybe I was speaking the wrong language to the wrong person." He said something else in Japanese to Alvee. Maki blushed. Alvee shrugged. He didn't understand it any more than I did.

"Okay," Maury said. "Alvee still doesn't understand Japanese, or he would be feigning offense at the suggestion I've just made to him. Just feigning offense, mind you. He secretly lives to consider my sometimes gymnastic propositions."

Alvee shrugged, smiled at me, oblivious. "He does go on sometimes."

Maury said, "Let me try English again. Carol. Would you like to attend the premiere of *Cheyenne Sundown* with Alvee and me? It's at the *Cinerama Dome,* next month."

I looked at Alvee. He wiggled his eyebrows at me. "I'll introduce you to Ryan."

My mouth dropped open. Maury reached across the table and gently pushed my chin up. He grinned at Alvee. "I think that's a yes, my darling."

A movie premiere. They wanted me to *attend* a movie premiere. Not stand out in the crowd, or try to fight through it to get up to the velvet rope. They wanted me to *attend.*

Ruthanne had talked me into going to LA for a movie premiere once. It was *going.* It was not *attending.* It wasn't really even *going* – it wasn't like we were going to actually *see* the movie. It had even been for one of Ryan's films, *Drive.* It premiered at the LA Film Festival in 2011.

"We'll get right up in front," Ruthanne promised. "Maybe you'll even be able to reach out and *touch him.*"

Ryan Gosling affected Ruthanne no more than Franck O'Day – who I hadn't even heard of at the time – affected me when I first saw his picture on *TwoGreenKeys.com.* No, Ryan didn't do a thing for her, but that didn't mean she didn't understand. No one understood obsessions with actors more thoroughly and completely than Ruthanne, and even though mine was not as severe and all-encompassing as hers – I just didn't have that kind of imagination – she knew that I liked me some Ryan Gosling.

On the way to LA, I asked Ruthie how she'd found out about the premiere, and she mentioned some website. I asked how these things worked, and to my chagrin, Ruthie told me that she didn't really know, because she'd never gone out for such an event before. The stars she liked the best were all dead, after all, their movie premieres now just dim echoes of Hollywood's golden past.

It turned out that Ruthie had underestimated the crowd, the awesome drawing power of Ryan, the amount of time ahead (days, apparently) that we would've had to have camped out beside the red carpet if we'd ever wanted to have even the slimmest hope of *getting right up front.*

A contingent of Sirians could have landed an interstellar pod-craft in the middle of Olympic Boulevard and just dropped Ryan off, for as close as we got to seeing him arrive. Or depart. There were just too many people, too many fans.

Now, I got a little choked up, remembering how intensely Ruthanne had apologized to me, how sorry she was about my not getting see Ryan. How she'd railed at herself – of course we couldn't just waltz right up and touch Ryan Gosling! How stupid could she be?

I told her it was all right, but Ruthie was angry at herself. She knew how devastated she would've felt had a similar opportunity passed her by, just because of a lack of planning. I told her that I was not devastated. After a while, she believed me.

And Maury was inviting me to *attend* Ryan's premiere. Not just show up and thrash around outside in the sea of eager faces trying to catch a glimpse of him. I would never, ever do that again. I'd felt like just one more cow in a herd of mooing, mindless heifers. It was just too undignified, and it was not like one could ever get close enough to moo at Ryan directly, anyway.

Now I was being invited to *attend* Ryan's premiere. To get out of a limo. To walk up the red carpet with his director, on the arm of his co-star. To get to meet him, maybe talk to him. Maybe shake his hand. He might smile at me.

"Hot damn!" I whispered to Alvee. He grinned at me. "What will I wear?" I said, still whispering, awestruck at the very idea. "I have nothing to wear!"

Alvee pointed at the director. "You ladies can work all that out. I can't do much, but I can dress myself."

Maury said. "Don't you worry, Carol. I know a few people. We'll scare up something for you that'll be just perfect."

"Trust him, Carol. He knows a little something about dressing women, not to mention dressing as women," Alvee said. "He worked at a geisha school for a little while, while we were in Japan. He was the head geisha.

"Oh, and by the way . . ." Alvee said something to Maury in Japanese. Maki's eyes widened and he coughed into his hand again. Apparently, Alvee understood more of the foreign tongue than he'd been letting on.

Maury grinned, blinked. He arranged his face into one of guileless innocence. He inquired, ingenuously, batting his eyes at Alvee.

Alvee grinned, looked down for a minute, shook his head. "I'm afraid one of us would think he was in love, then, Maury. And I think it would be you."

Maury looked at me. "The story of my life." He paused, then said, "I *was* a dresser at the geisha school, but only for a little while. They have an ancient tradition. They weren't amenable to any updates. It was still fun though. The colors, the silks! Let me make a few calls."

FORTY-TWO

After brunch on Sunday, Maury and Alvee walked me down the stone steps to my rented car. Maury reminded me that I had an early dress fitting on Thursday, kissed my hand, and went back inside.

Alvee gave me a quick, brotherly hug. I noticed for the first time how good he smelled. Ruthanne had mentioned it before, but being a subjective thing, and something I'd never expected to get close enough to experience, I'd not paid too much attention to her appreciation. But she'd been right. He smelled *good*.

Three of my five senses had now been assaulted by the undeniable charisma of Alvee Smith-Killem. There was sight, of course. I might've told myself that he'd looked too old to be *that* attractive when he was sophisticated matinee idol Franck O'Day – he'd looked forty, and even forty was too old for me, really. But all the sly sexiness and mocking charm that he'd embodied when he was old Franck was now all the more breathtaking in young Alvee.

We were peers now, contemporaries. If we were seen together, no one would snigger into their fists, no one would say that I had daddy issues. That woman in Cincinnati would not speculate unfavorably on Alvee's proportions because she thought he could only impress women too young for him. I was no longer too young for him.

I positively blushed at that thought – no one should be speculating on Alvee's proportions, not some woman in Ohio, and certainly not me . . .

There was my sense of hearing – his voice had always been like velvet drawn across the most secret parts of me. That remained the same. And he smelled good, too, I'd just discovered.

I considered the two remaining senses, those of touch and taste. Except for not nearly enough hand-holding and one quick kiss, touch and taste had been left wanting. When I stopped and thought about it – just how *wanting* they had been left, just how willing I would be to touch him, to taste him – I was shocked at myself.

"Are you coming down Wednesday night?" Alvee asked. I blinked at him, lost in the contemplation of my growing aspiration to touch and taste him. When I nodded, he said, "We'll have a luau!"

Imagine that, I thought. *A luau on a Wednesday night.*

"Till then, then," Alvee said. He opened the car door for me, and I climbed in and shut the door. "Drive safely, Carol," he said, and tapped the roof of the car.

On the way home, I thought about my dress. Maury had made some calls, and he assured me that it wouldn't be anything spectacular, that it wouldn't bear a designer name. But it would still be made to my specifications and it would still be more of a dress than I'd have ever dared to dream of in my life. *My fitting was on Thursday.* I'd never had a *fitting* in my life.

I took the rental car back, paid for it, drove home. I thought about ordering a pizza – a giant step down from Kimura's brunch, but hoes gotta eat. I took my phone out of my purse to call for delivery, and discovered that it was still off from the night before. Oops. My loyal boyfriend had only texted me once, early in the morning, again asking me how I was.

The phone buzzed in my hand, made me jump. It was like some kind of accusation, like I'd tripped some kind of where-have-you-been? booby trap. I said hello, and my thoughtful boyfriend Doug told me that he was on his way over with Chinese take-out, and he wouldn't take no for an answer.

I said okay and hung up. I glanced around the apartment, feeling like a fugitive, like a rat in a trap, like a criminal, like someone about to be caught in a lie.

One part of my mind said that I didn't have anything whatsoever to hide. *It was obvious that Doug and I were not that close as boyfriend and girlfriend, he obviously doesn't care too much,* it told me peevishly, *if I'd been able to go out of town for one night and two days, and he hadn't so much as dropped by to see me.*

The more mature part of my mind countered that he hadn't bothered me because I'd told him not to. I'd made up a *lie,* and he'd believed it. He didn't stay away because he didn't care. He'd stayed away because he'd believed my *lie.* And he was dropping by now, bringing me something to eat, because he was worried about me. He was sweet.

I went into the bedroom and changed into a pair of sweats and an old t-shirt, and my ancient house slippers, as befitted someone who had been down with the curse for two days. I didn't have anything to hide. I hadn't done anything wrong. It was none of Doug's business where I'd been. *But there's no sense in messing up a good lie,* I thought. *Might as well look the part.*

The meal was awful. I used to like Chinese takeout. I used to enjoy it very much. But that was before I started hanging out in Beverly Hills and enjoying traditional Japanese cooking prepared by a traditional Japanese chef, meals that cost more than my formerly favorite *Panda Express* took in all day.

275

But it's the thought that counts, after all, and Doug had not a clue as to the high dining that I'd been experiencing. And the chow was not really my problem anyway. My problem was the guilt I felt about lying to Doug. And the other problem was that I was drawing a complete blank on the lie I was going to tell him about where I was going to be Wednesday night through Sunday of the following week.

I read somewhere that a lie comes off best when it's only half a lie. The one that suddenly came to mind – yeah, that's it – was a little more than half a lie, actually. It was an entire lie. "I got a call from Kelley Sanders this morning," I said, choking down my soggy, too salty noodles.

"Who?" Doug asked.

I knew I had him then. "You remember Kelley. From high school?"

"I do not," Doug said, slurping his noodles. I hated slurping. Alvee didn't slurp.

"You don't remember Kelley?" I was making Kelley up. "She wasn't there for more than a couple of months. Maybe only one quarter."

Doug shook his head, said with his mouth full, "Nope. Don't remember her." Alvee didn't talk with his mouth full, either.

"Anyway, Kelley called me this morning. She came back for a visit, and just heard about Ruthanne – they were really good friends, but had lost touch." I paused. I knew Ruthie wouldn't mind me using her memory as part of my deception. She would find it amusing to be included. It wasn't like I was doing anything wrong. It wasn't like I was cheating on Doug, like I was having an affair.

I just didn't care for Doug all that much, and I didn't want to introduce him to my Hollywood friends. I didn't want Alvee to know that he was . . . that we were . . . that I had been seeing him. I wanted Alvee to think I was single, because I wanted to think I was single. Doug was not the man I wanted. Alvee . . . Alvee might not be the man I wanted either, my mind said stubbornly, but Doug definitely wasn't.

"Kelley wants me to come and see her." I paused again. "So I'm going to take a couple of days off and go to LA and hang out with her." I held my breath, waiting for his reaction, prepared for an argument.

But what did Doug have to argue with me about? We weren't married; we weren't even living together. He'd never told me he loved me, or any of that silly high school romance shit. I didn't love him. What we had was just a thing – just a convenient little thing. I didn't owe him an explanation every time I left town.

He didn't even look up, didn't even stop chewing, didn't even wait to swallow. He just said, mouth still full of noodles, "Okay, Carol. You have fun."

And that was it. We finished the soggy meal. We watched a movie. Doug gave me a hug, a little kiss, told me he was glad I was feeling better. Then he went home.

FORTY-THREE

Alvee's Wednesday night luau included hula dancers, Polynesian musicians, and a fire show, not to mention all the awesome food. I didn't know what I'd been expecting, but it hadn't been this. I needed to raise those expectations. When Alvee suggested a luau, he wasn't talking about a canned ham with some pineapple slices stuck to it. *He meant a luau.*

Again there was no hanky-panky, no invitations of any kind. Alvee wore a horribly loud blue Hawaiian shirt that matched his eyes perfectly, and as I looked at him, smiling and chatting with the performers, I realized that some part of me wanted those eyes to look at me again, like they had that time in the bar in Vegas, when he'd still being going by the name of Franck O'Day.

Sure, it hadn't been real – it hadn't even been nice. Franck had just been showing me that he was in control of the situation, that when he said he didn't want me running my mouth off to Ruthanne, he wasn't just a whistlin' Dixie. It had been shocking and threatening and unexpected, and just as sexy as hell.

Time and his charm had worn away the shock and the threat, leaving only the memory of his proposition – the way his eyes had burned into me when he said, *The thought crossed my mind – that if anybody was going up to anybody's room, then it should be you and me going up to your room.*

He'd just been acting, and even if he hadn't been, even if he'd really been propositioning me then, circumstances would've prohibited it. It hadn't been real, then – he'd just been protecting Ruthanne. But circumstances had changed. Ruthanne was gone, and there was a part of me that longed to have Alvee Killem-Smith look at me just like Franck had. A part of me ached to give in to that look, whether it was real or just performance. If I gave in, that would make it real.

I lay in Jessika's bed for a long time after the Wednesday night luau, thinking about Alvee's incredible blue eyes.

The following morning, Maki, Maury, Alvee and I were having breakfast on the terrace, as was our wont. Kimura materialized out of thin air, and once he was sure he had our attention, he bowed. Then six young Japanese girls ran out and stood next to him in a row, three on each side. They bowed. Maki, Maury, and Alvee rose and also bowed. I just looked dumbly at everybody.

Maury said something in Japanese to Kimura and the girls. They bowed, then Kimura took them back into the house. "Your dressmakers are here, Carol," Maury said. I continued to look dumbly, now just at him. "Did you think we were going to Rodeo Drive?" Maury said, smiling. "Did you think we were going to stand around and drink bad wine and do doubtful cocaine off smudged mirrors while some queen draped you with overpriced, domestic satin and exclaimed over your little tiny measurements?"

Now I looked dumbly at him, open-mouthed. Alvee was a little nonplussed himself. After a heartbeat, he said, "Careful, Maury. Your 1960s are showing."

Maury flapped a hand at him. "This is so much better, Carol. We don't have to make polite small talk with the help, because these young ladies don't speak much English. Yet we can talk about whatever we want between ourselves and don't have to worry about them telling our business on the street, because again, they don't speak much English. And they are very talented."

"Well, I think this is my cue," Alvee said. "You ladies have fun. I'm gonna go buy some cigars."

Maury said something to Maki. He nodded. "Take Papa-san with you, will you, my darling? He gets out so seldom."

Alvee smiled and said something to Maki. He smiled back and nodded. Alvee spoke enough Japanese. "You ladies have fun," he repeated, and he and Maki walked back into the house.

"Shall we?" Maury took my hand.

We went into the dining room. The Japanese girls made me feel like Cinderella. They stood me up on a little box in front of the arched window. The sun shone in gaily, and they flitted around me like little bluebirds, chirruping in Japanese to each other. There was neither bad wine nor cocaine, but they did drape me with folds of a dark blue satin, cutting, pinning, twittering, giggling.

Maury stood next to me and observed. One of the girls said something to her friend. When her friend answered, Maury smiled and said something back to both of them. All the girls fell silent and looked solemnly at him – they'd forgotten that he understood them.

I didn't understand anything. "What did she say?" I asked.

"This one commented that the color of the satin – imported, by the way – is stunning." He patted her shoulder and smiled at her. She smiled and shyly lowered her lashes. "And that one agreed, and said it's the same color as Alvee's eyes." He grinned, said something to the girls. All six of them tittered and blushed. "It's a coincidence, I assure you," Maury said to me. "I just told them to bring a nice blue."

279

Maury sighed, and sat down at the dining room table, deciding to observe the proceedings from there. "Ah, my darling Alvee. I can't remember my life before I saw Alvee, do you know that, Carol?"

I'm beginning to feel the same way, I thought, *and I'm not sure what I think about all that.*

"I fell in love with him the very moment I saw him," Maury continued. "A colleague had told me about Alvee, had gotten my *hopes* up with some story about him possessing a certain . . . affability. Alvee was indeed affable, but not in the way I'd been led to believe. He let me go on just far enough to make a fool out of myself – but not a fool out of him. He said that he didn't know what Morrison had told me – *he knew exactly what Morrison had told me.* He wasn't angry or offended or even amused. He wasn't scared. He just wasn't interested.

"He said, 'But I still bet I'd be perfect for the lead in your picture.' He was right.

"The camera loves him, Carol," Maury said, making the director's gesture – thumbs like mirrored L's – he did it quite unconsciously, I was convinced. "Have you ever seen anyone as stunningly beautiful as Alvee?" he asked.

There *was* Ryan Gosling, I thought, but I didn't say it.

"An unkind God chose to curse me and make Alvee heterosexual. And not even remotely curious." Maury smiled at me. He held his thumb and forefinger close together. "Not even the tiniest bit.

"But there's still an element of fate between us, one that goes beyond mere fleeting fleshly pursuits. I wouldn't kick Alvee out of bed for eating watermelon, Carol," Maury leered at me, "but the idea of the impossibility of anything physical between us has fused in my mind with the impossibility of his incredible beauty. He's more perfect to me than he could ever remain if we were to become lovers.

"Don't think I wouldn't sacrifice all this philosophical platonic bullshit in a heartbeat if he were to reconsider . . ." again Maury leered, "but in the meantime, he will always be my muse. Any fragment of plot line that comes to my mind – it stars him. He's an archetype to me – I can make him into anything, any icon – saint or sinner, cop or criminal, butcher, baker, candlestick maker. Whatever character I create, he's always Alvee at the center, gorgeous, eternally fascinating."

You can make him into anything except that one thing that he refuses to be, I thought. *Thus, the agony of art.*

"We've been friends for a very long time. I've watched him go through a lot." Maury considered me. "I know you've heard all the stories. First, there was Jessika. She was a demon. She featured herself desperately in love with our golden boy. But she was mistaken. Jessika could never love anyone but herself. What she wanted was to devour him, to possess him, *to own him*. Alvee's not for sale – although he can be rented for between ninety and a hundred and twenty minutes at a time in large dark rooms where lots of people sit in rows." Maury smiled.

"But he's not ownable. He's like a force of nature. And when Jessika couldn't make him toe the line to her satisfaction, she tried to ruin him. But it all backfired. He and I discovered an incredible secret in Japan, and she shriveled up and died, all alone, in what I hope were painful pangs of self-loathing. One could almost feel sorry for Jessika. But only almost."

She was a bitch, Aunt Mae's voice said in my mind.

"Then there was Bridget. She was sweet, doomed. I think that eventually she would've tired of this town. She had absolutely no interest in the business, and the business *is* this town's business. If you're in it, it's inescapable. It's not something that's done part time. You're up to your eyebrows in it, 24/7. Alvee and I, we wouldn't have it any other way.

"But I think that if she wouldn't have died, he and Bridget would've eventually drifted apart, drifted into bitterness, maybe even divorce. Alvee loves the game – Bridget was too down-to-earth for all that. She'd never have enjoyed all the drama and subterfuge that goes on here, just for its own sake, like Alvee and I do. Alvee needs someone who appreciates this business and his enjoyment of it, as much as he does. How does that line go, from *Pirates of the Caribbean? Take what you can.*"

"Give nothing back," I supplied.

"That's Hollywood," Maury said. We grinned at each other. Then Maury sighed. "But Bridget never got a chance to be disillusioned with Alvee and this town and their love. They never had to lose Paris."

"Alvee's been around for a long time, Carol, and what happened to Bridget happened a long time ago. He remembers Bridget like you would a particularly lovely spring day. But that memory holds no more pain for him anymore than that memory of a particularly nice morning. He's made his peace with it. His mourning for her ended in its natural season.

"There was not one single thing he could've done to alter what happened. Roger was nuts. No one could've predicted that he was going to snap. Alvee never blamed himself – Alvee rarely blames himself. It's not that he blames others – he's just never been the type to brood over things that he can't do a single thing about."

281

Once again, Maury sighed. "And then there was Lori and her tedious yearnings, finally fulfilled after entirely too long. Lori didn't love him either, any more than her mother did. She *wanted* him for too long to ever really love him. She stewed, *fermented* in that desire, and it twisted her inside, Carol, like a deforming disease. Lori believed that her desire for Alvee – her physical *need* for him – she believed that was love.

"You should've seen her when she'd to come to visit him, when she'd to come to Japan. The look on her face – *ravenous*. Frightening." Maury shuddered theatrically. "Like a sailor on shore leave, after way too long at sea. Oh, how Lori *wanted* Alvee, how she *needed* him!" He rolled his eyes. "Between the sheets, anyway. Other than that, Lori didn't need or want much of anything. She was always a tough, self-sufficient little girl. Just like her mother – her only weakness was Alvee.

"But want and need are not the same as love, are they? Love is ethereal, eternal, air and fire. Want and need are like earth and water – too easily stymied and frustrated and turned aside by physical roadblocks. Want and need are like hunger, thirst. They demand to be satisfied, slaked.

"Not tonight dear, I've got a headache. No thanks, Bobby, I don't swing that way – these answers enrage want and need.

"But love understands. Love accepts that he has his own wants and needs. Love is just happy in his company. Love is happy to just look, doesn't always need to *touch. To squeeze.* Love is more than satisfied to have his lifelong friendship."

Maury smiled, paused. "But Lori *wanted* Alvee for too long. She'd longed for him – *and only him* – for so long that the ache turned to selfishness. She thought she loved Alvee, but she really just loved what he'd *finally,* after so many years of impatient waiting, blah, blah, blah . . ." Maury rolled his eyes again. "Lori really just loved what he finally decided to do *for* her, *to her.*

"I cannot imagine how she continued to live and breathe once your friend Ruthie entered the picture, Carol. Alvee had put their sordid little congress to the sword some years before, but I'm sure that Lori lived daily in the eternal hope that he might resurrect it at any moment. But once Ruthie arrived on the scene . . . how Lori must have hated Alvee then. Just like her mother did – she must've hated him and still wanted him in equal measure.

"I wished I'd had the chance to meet Ruthie, Carol. She sounded like a peach. She amused Alvee the way Bridget did, because she just loved him – she didn't want anything else from him than just to be in his company, whatever they were doing."

282

Maury grinned. "But still, I got the impression when Alvee talked about her, that Ruthie was still a little too awed, a little too worshipful for them to have been completely compatible. Alvee has enough worshippers." Maury raised his hand. "Alvee needs someone who keeps him a little off balance, someone who keeps him thinking. Someone like you, Carol."

He smiled at me. "Everyone finds Alvee attractive, to one degree or another. He's stunning. Even militant lesbians from Mars would at least have him as their house boy." Maury winked. "Alvee knows that you don't harbor that abject, unshakeable awe of him, like a fan. You know he can do wrong. It's refreshing. All that glassy-eyed, speechless adoration gets old after a while. He needs someone who doesn't expect him to be on all the time."

"But he is on all the time," I replied.

"Is he? Or is that just what you see? What you expect? Don't get me wrong, Alvee doesn't lose any sleep worrying that you don't find him attractive – he's sure you'll heel over eventually. He won't respect you any less when you eventually do – you don't disrespect the sun for eventually *going down."* Maury grinned. "No one holds out on him forever. No one is immune to Alvee – not even those lesbians from Mars." Maury paused. "I'm not saying that everybody loves him."

That's exactly what you're saying, I thought, remembering a similar conversation with the man himself, on a similar subject, a lifetime ago in Las Vegas.

"Jessika, and Lori, too, wound up hating him. But hate is not immunity, is it? What I'm saying is that Alvee appreciates this time that the two of you are spending together, this time that doesn't involve all those sticky acts of which I have no doubt, after almost sixty years of imagining, that he is sooo good at.

"This time is like the aperitif – it's sweet and light and he's liking it very much. But he's also waiting for the main course, and with anticipation. Make him wait, Carol. For as long as you can possibly stand to. I doubt that it'll be too long. I see how you look at him." Maury grinned. "No one's ever told him no, and you won't either, in the end. I know it. He knows it. I'm not sure you know it yet, but give it time." He winked at me. "But make him wait, Carol. I know that he's liking it very much."

Yeah, Alvee was adorable, but I had a lot more willpower than anybody seemed to give me credit for. Just because he was attractive, didn't mean I was attracted to him. Just because he was irresistible, didn't mean I couldn't resist.

I'd been holding my own pretty well, I thought, all things considered. Sure, the thought had crossed my mind – the thought had begun to cross my mind regularly, if the truth had to be told, ever since he'd sauntered down the steps in his black Converse, young and delightful and just as sexy as he wanted to be. But I was fighting it.

I appreciated all Maury's sharing – I appreciated his advice. So I just smiled and said, "You're the director."

FORTY-FOUR

I made up some other lie for Doug, about where I was going the night of the premiere. I was quite the little out-of-towner to Doug, who had never known me to be anything else, I realized. I'd told him that I had a lot of out-of-town *girlfriends* that I visited, and he just naturally accepted it.

Oh, well, I thought, *what he doesn't know cannot possibly hurt him, now can it?* The truth was . . . *complicated.* I just hoped he didn't see me on *Entertainment Tonight.* Then I'd have some 'splaining to do.

Fuck it, I thought. *I'll burn that bridge when I come to it.*

The dress that Maury's team of lovely Japanese girls created for me was *magnificent.*

Of that stunning blue satin – the same color as Alvee's eyes – it was floor-length, slit up the left leg to above the knee. It was gently ruched at the left hip – the gather went all the way around. It was sleeveless, high-necked, with a black slash of a triangular-shaped collar that reached horizontally from one shoulder to the other.

Maury opened a shoe-box with a flourish, revealing matching dark blue shoes. He lent me diamond earrings. He brought in a hairdresser. He did my make-up personally.

I'd never looked more glamorous in my life. I didn't recognize myself. Alvee smiled, told me rather unimaginatively that I was beautiful.

Damn right, I was beautiful.

But in the limo, I turned down Maury's offer of a Valium to calm my nerves. It wasn't as if anyone was going to be speaking to me, anyway.

Except maybe Ryan Gosling!!!

But no. If I was going to do this thing, I was going to do it undrugged. I was going to do it on my own. I was going to *handle it.* I wasn't going to get all star struck, glassy-eyed and speechless, all the things that Maury said bored Alvee.

Ryan Gosling was just an actor, like Alvee. I wasn't going to forget my name if I got to meet him. I was going to be cool. Cooler than cool. I was going to be ice cold.

I was in the company of Ryan's co-star and Ryan's director, for Christ's sake. If I embarrassed myself, I would embarrass them, and I couldn't do that, not after they'd been kind enough to bring me. I'd never been a *fan* of movie stars, right? So if I acted like an idiot fan now, someone that belonged on *the other side of the rope*, then neither Alvee nor Maury would ever let me live it down.

When we pulled up in front of the *Cinerama Dome*, a person assigned to the task opened the door of the limo and we stepped out. There were scattered cheers. The red carpet was in place, the short distance from the curb to the doors of the concrete geodesic dome was roped off, the sidewalks packed with people.

A few fans called out to Alvee. Apparently not everyone had missed *Downpour*. He signed autographs, leaned over the rope and posed for pictures.

Actor and director spoke a few words to the lady from *Entertainment Tonight*, whose name totally escaped me. I'd never purposely watched *Entertainment Tonight* in my life. But I'd caught of few minutes of it every now and then when Ruthanne would watch it.

The hostess didn't want to talk to me, anyway. I hung back, out of frame, until Maury, his interview completed, stepped back and smiled at me, took my arm.

Alvee was still taking to the hostess when a roar went up from the crowd.

Ryan Gosling had arrived, with splendid Eva Mendes on his arm. The lady from *ET* dropped Alvee like a bad habit and hurried toward the star of *Cheyenne Sundown*.

Alvee shrugged, smiled at me. The three of us went on into the theater.

The best thing about the *Cinerama Dome* was the fact that it had a bar. And the bar was open. I was not surprised at all when Alvee handed me a mint julep. There were no mint leaves in it. It was not a commonly requested cocktail on the West Coast, after all. But there was whisky in it, and that made it good enough for me.

In the lobby, I acquitted myself well when I finally got to meet Ryan and Eva. Alvee introduced me and told them that I was a writer. Ryan asked me if he'd heard of anything I'd written. I didn't stutter, stammer, or look glassy-eyed.

But OMG, I'm was talking to Ryan Gosling!

I was even clever, I thought, when I said, "I don't think *Alvee* has even heard of anything I've written."

Ha, ha. Ha.

We chatted. Ryan and Eva were very pleasant, very nice. Just people, just actors. A few more pictures were taken, and then we all went into the theater together.

Ryan and Eva sat close to the front. Maury said with a leer that he always preferred the back of a theater, so we went up several rows. Alvee sat on my right, Maury on my left.

Alvee did hold my hand this time.

As the lights went down, a thought struck me. I whispered, "You *have* seen this already, right?"

Alvee looked at me solemnly. "Oh, no, Carol. That's why they call it a *premiere.*"

"I've seen it," Maury said. "And I guarantee, you're gonna love it."

FORTY-FIVE

The establishing shot shows Ryan plowing a field. He's behind two big horses, all shirtless and sweaty, six-pack on display. The credits roll. So far, so good.

Then a close-up of Camellia Swanson, gazing out into the distance. Camellia was another newcomer – this was Ryan's film, after all. Couldn't have too many other stars in it to detract from his awesomeness.

Camellia was British, one of Maury's protégés from the *auld sold*, or so I'd been told. She had delicate blonde ringlets and the lightest green eyes I'd ever seen. She was beautiful, in a fragile, antique-doll kind of way. She was sitting three rows ahead of us in the theater. I hadn't gotten to meet her, as she'd arrived fashionably late. She hadn't looked quite so fragile in person, but she was still beautiful.

Camellia rings a dinner bell; she puts a small hand to her brow and smiles when she sees Ryan running up the dirt road toward her. A hired hand leads the horses out of the field.

Ryan runs up on the porch and embraces Camellia, picking her up off her feet. He sets her down gently and starts kissing her, begriming her white dress and her white face with all his sweaty, just-in-from-the-fields, shirtless sexiness.

Then Ryan picks her up and says, "Shall I carry you across the threshold, like a new bride?"

Camellia wraps her white arms around his deliciously grimy, tanned neck and replies, "I'm hardly a new bride." Her accent is fine, cultured. We can tell from one line that she is from a higher caste than her farmer husband.

"You'll always be a bride to me," Ryan says. He kicks the door open.

Cut to a bedroom. Ryan and Camellia are in bed kissing. The scene is hot enough, because Ryan's in it, barely dressed. But there's also a lot of talking and laughter – the intent it to show that they are happily married, comfortable with each other. The passion is there, but also an easy happiness. Fade out.

Fade in to a wide-angle shot. A lone horseman dressed in black, on a black horse, walks slowly up the road to the farm. Ryan's back in the field again, again plowing. The team is heading toward the horseman, and Ryan shields his eyes in the slanting afternoon sun, to see who it is that approaches. Then he smiles. He stops the team and goes running up the road toward the man on the black horse.

We get a reaction shot of the horseman. It's Alvee. He's just as grimy as Ryan, but from the road. He's dressed like a gunslinger, not a farmer. He smiles wryly and kicks the horse into a trot.

As Ryan nears, Alvee stops the black horse and dismounts. The pair embrace joyously, slapping each other on the back. Dust rises from their clothes. *A nice touch of realism, that,* I thought.

"What brings you here, Jody?" Ryan asks, as they start walking up the road, Alvee leading the horse between them.

"Didn't you say your wife was the best cook in all of Texas?" Jody replies. "Didn't you say that, after we pulled that bank job outside of Abilene?" Jody looks up the road at the farmhouse, white and homey-looking in the distance. "I'm here to find out," Jody says.

We get the idea from the look on his face that he has an ulterior motive.

Ryan's hep to it, too. He takes Jody's horse by the bridle and stops it. He looks at Jody across its nose.

"Why are you really here, Jody? I don't knock over banks in cow towns, anymore. I run this farm." Ryan gestures at the house. "I'm married."

"You were married when we hit that bank, weren't you, Reggie?" Jody replies. "And Abilene is hardly a cow town."

"I lied to you, then," Reggie says, looking down at the dirt road, scuffing it with his boot. He looks up and pats the horse on the neck. "If I got killed, I didn't want you bringing the bad news to an unmarried woman."

"If you were dead, then she would've been a widow. Sometimes a widow's better than an unmarried woman," Jody says philosophically. "A widow knows what I'm trying to talk her in to." He squints up at the house. "You're married now, right?"

Offended, Reggie says, "Of course I'm married now!"

Jody smiles at him. "Can she cook?" They laugh and start walking up the road.

Cut to a low aerial shot. We hear Reggie ask again, "Why are you really here, Jody?"

"There's a train, Reggie, old son. A simple, easy train, stuffed to overflowing with gold. It's all right there in the caboose, and it's calling our name."

"I don't rob trains anymore, either," Reggie says.

"Oh, we don't have to talk about robbing it just yet, Reg. We can wait till after I've had your wife's cooking."

Cut to the yard of the little white farmhouse. Camellia's standing on the front porch. Reaction shot of Camellia as she sees Jody for the first time. Her wholesome, happily-married-to-Ryan-Gosling smile fades, and is replaced by one of immediate attraction to Jody. She simply cannot help what she instantly feels.

Reggie isn't looking at her, though, and doesn't notice her un-wifely expression. He's looking at his buddy. "Etta," he says, "I'd like you to meet my old friend, Jody St. Cloud. We met a long time ago, in Missouri. I saved his life once."

Cut to a shot of a boat. Several men throw a sharp-dressed Jody off the boat. He starts to drown. An equally sharp-dressed Reggie dives in and saves him, swims him to shore.

Reggie's voice over: "A bunch of gamblers discovered he was cheating them and threw him off the riverboat. Who'da thought a man like him couldn't swim?"

Reaction shot of Jody. He's ignoring Reggie and his little anecdote, looking at his friend's wife. Attraction to her shows in his eyes, but it's more subtle than Etta's. He's better at hiding it. Maybe it's not there after all, but we're pretty sure it is.

Oh, snap! I thought gleefully. No one loves a good love triangle better than me. Sexy Ryan and blue-eyed Alvee and beautiful, delicate Camellia. This might be good.

Jody touches the brim of his hat, nods. "Miz Etta."

Barely disguised desire glows in Etta's light-green eyes. "Mr. St. Cloud," she says.

Cut to an interior shot, evening. Jody and Reggie are sitting at the table. Etta is serving them. She keeps looking at Jody when he's not looking at her, and Jody keeps looking at Etta when she's not looking at him. The longing in their eyes is plain. Then her hand accidentally brushes his while she's ladling stew or something onto his plate, and their eyes meet. All that longing spills out.

All this time, Reggie is oblivious, talking about the farm. Or is he? When no one answers his last question, he says pointedly to Etta, "I'd like another helping, too."

Rack pan from Reggie to Etta and Jody. They break their forbidden tete-a-tete, and look over at Reggie. Jody is able to hide his sinful thoughts, but Etta is flustered. She almost spills the stew as she ladles some onto Reggie's plate.

Jody says, "I don't know about all of Texas, but you surely are the best cook in all of Wyoming, Miz Etta."

"Why thank you, Mr. St, Cloud," Etta says. She smiles at Jody, but he's ignoring her, smiling at Reggie.

"Good job, Reg," he says. "You always know how to pick the finest things in life. And I don't mean just the safes."

Fade out, then fade in to Jody in a darkened room. He's lying on his back on a bed, shirtless, his hands behind his head, a cigarillo in his mouth. His chest and arms are tanned, slightly sweaty. While not as cut as Ryan, he still looks amazing.

This was the first time I'd seen Alvee shirtless. He'd stayed entirely clothed throughout every scene of *Downpour,* which got to be a little tiresome in some spots, I had to admit. I stole a look at him in the theater, was surprised to find him looking back at me. He smiled, leaned in close to my ear. "Just wait," he whispered. "It gets better."

Jody is looking thoughtfully at the ceiling. We hear the muffled sounds of Etta's laughter, followed by laughter from Reggie. We know what they're doing, because we saw them doing it at the beginning of the film. Jody knows what they're doing, too. He frowns, rises from the bed. He throws on a white shirt, but doesn't button it *(praise Jesus!)* and exits the room.

Cut to Jody standing in the front yard, looking up at the night sky, smoking his cigarillo. Claremount captures the majesty of the Wyoming nightscape in a wide angle shot.

The screen door bangs, and Jody looks over his shoulder. Etta is framed by the light from the interior of the house. She is rosy, disheveled – we know what she's been doing. Jody knows, too, and with a little look of annoyance, he discards his smoke and turns back to surveying the stars.

"Oh, Mr. St. Cloud," Etta stammers. "I didn't see you there." She walks to the front of the porch, stops. She wants to continue down the steps, to go and stand by him, but she dares not.

"A married woman, unattended, strolling her own front porch in the middle of the night," Jody remarks, not turning to look at her.

"Shouldn't a woman be able to stroll her own front porch unattended, Mr. St. Cloud?" Etta replies in her clear British voice. "Married or not? Even in the middle of the night?"

Now Jody turns to look at her. His desire is no longer disguised.

"Your husband didn't tell you much about me, did he?" Jody's need burns in the subtle light coming from the house. His eyes are alive with it.

His desire is almost scary, but Etta is cool. She just got laid, after all. "Why, whatever are you implying, Mr. St. Cloud? I'm not only married, but happily so."

Jody's mouth crooks up in a little half smile. The seriousness of his desire fades to amusement. He says, "So you are, Miz Etta. So you are. For the moment, anyway."

He stares evenly at Etta until she becomes discomfited – she's thinking about *him*, now, instead of her husband. She turns and flees back into the house. Jody smiles in satisfaction at her reaction, and turns back to look at the stars again.

Cut to daylight, the kitchen table. Appropriate modernized cowboy music plays as we go into a montage of Jody and Reggie planning the train robbery. There are shots of diagrams and loading revolvers and spinning chambers. We are shown the plan. They're going to blow the train in half. The front half will keep going over the bridge, the back part will stop on the tracks. The safe's in the last car, in the caboose. They'll just step onboard and open it, take the loot. We're shown that old Reg is a safecracker of some renown.

To our surprise, Etta is in on it. But then, she isn't as pure as we first thought she was, now is she? What with the lusting after her husband's buddy and all? She makes comments, points at diagrams, brings them food.

She keeps stealing longing looks at Jody, but he ignores her. She pouts. He looks at her only once, and she doesn't even know it, because it's when she's walking out of the room. We can tell from just the look in his eyes that his desire is killing him. He wants her, but she's his friend's wife – how can he be having these feelings for her? He might be a train robber, but he's no traitor. Yet . . . he can't help himself. She'd just so beautiful . . .

Alvee conveys all this with just the look in his eyes. I dared not look over at him again.

Rack pan from Jody's face in profile, watching Etta, to Reggie. Reggie sees! He knows! He understands fully his friend's longing for his wife. Rack pan back to Jody, realizing that conversation has stopped again – he looks at Reggie, the pained desire still plain on his face.

But Reggie is looking away. He's decided to ignore it. What can he do about it, anyway?

"I guess I should go into town and buy the dynamite," Reggie says to the scarred wooden table before him. He looks over at his friend. "You wanna go with me, Jody?"

Jody looks evenly, steadily at him. "You know I can't show my face in town, Reg. They still got wanted posters of me up. All the way from Abilene."

Pan from Reggie's resigned face to Etta, coming back into the room with more food. "What about you, Et? You wanna go into town with me?"

Close up on Etta. She flinches to look at Jody, but restrains herself – she looks full at her husband, instead. We can tell it's a great effort for her. But Etta is good, maybe even a little crafty. She smiles at her husband and says in her lyrical British voice, "Why ever would I want to go to town with you *now*, Reggie? When you're buying dynamite?"

Reggie nods, looks at the table again. He could suggest another reason for her to go, but he knows it's pointless.

Pan to Jody. "I'll ride out to the crossroads with you, Reg."

Tracking shot of Jody and Reggie as they plod along the road in a cart, Jody's black horse tied to the back. They realize that it was a dumb idea, because they're not talking, not looking at each other. Reggie stops the cart, still looking straight ahead. Lithe and graceful, Jody hops out. We see Reggie, jaw clenched, still looking straight ahead.

Jody unties his horse and walks back next to the cart.

"I'll see you when you get back," he says.

Now Reggie looks at him. "Unless I see you first," he says. His face is a mixture of anger, pain, betrayal. He knows what's going to happen when his friend goes back to the house, when his friend is alone with his wife. It shows on his face. He's trying to cope with not being able to do anything about it.

Ryan's no slouch at emoting, either, I thought.

Cut to close-up of Jody. His expression says he knows his friend doesn't trust him. He knows his friend has reason not to trust him, but still he can't believe it that his friend thinks he would betray him. He slaps the cart horse on the ass and the cart takes off, jerking Reggie's head back a little bit.

Extremely long angle shot of the farm house and the field and the road beside it. Jody is slowly riding toward the farm house. We hear the screen door bang, and Etta walks slowly out onto the porch. She pauses on the top step. Jody pauses the horse on the road, like maybe he's thinking of going somewhere else, instead. We get a close-up of his face. He looks down, shakes his head, grins a little ruefully. He knows he's not going anywhere else. Then he looks up at the farmhouse.

Cut to Etta. She's breathless with anticipation. Fade out.

Fade in to Jody. He's in the back yard, standing beside the well, shirtless. The camera pans back slowly. Jody arches his back a little and dumps a bucket of water on his head. He shakes the water out of his eyes with a quick jerk – jet black curls twitch and bounce. The camera lingers lovingly over his glistening flesh, traces the rivulets of water running over him. Down, down – across the smooth chest, over the flat belly, the strong haunch it its tight britches – right on down to the scuffed boot.

Ryan might be the star of this horse opera, I thought. *But the director – and the camera – loves Alvee Smith-Killem.*

Etta comes out of the house purposefully, carrying a towel. But she stops – open-mouthed, absolutely *dumbstruck* with his beauty, his lean, wet body. I was pretty damned dumbstruck, my own self.

Jody looks at her, takes in her desire. Then he smiles, looks away.

In one fluid motion, Etta crosses the yard. She doesn't pause, but throws her arms around his neck, crushes him to her. The camera lingers over their bodies, pressed together, the moisture from his chest and arms soaking into the thin material of her white dress.

They kiss passionately – nothing like the playful smooches we saw her share with her husband. Then Jody smiles at her wryly, says, "You don't seem so happily married now . . . *Miz* Etta."

Etta can't speak. She's too overcome with desire. We weren't sure before – maybe they'd already done it and that was why Jody was washing up – but now we know. It hasn't happened yet. She still wants him too much.

Etta kisses Jody again, but he pulls back. "Your husband could come back at any time."

"He won't be back till dark. Besides," Etta declares breathlessly, "I don't care, Jody! Just kiss me again!"

Etta leans forward, tries desperately to kiss him again.

"No, Miz Etta," he says and takes her arms from around his neck. "This is wrong. Reggie's my friend. He saved my life. He loves you."

"I love him, too, Jody!" Etta insists, launching herself into his arms again. "But . . . I love you, too!" She tries to kiss him again.

But Jody takes her arms from around his neck once more, a little more forcefully this time. He says, "Love me? You don't even know me."

He steps back and drops the bucket into the well, then starts to reel it back up again. After a moment of disbelief, Etta stomps back into the house. Close-up of Jody, smiling, as he reels the bucket up and douses himself with water again.

Cut to Etta standing at the kitchen sink, watching through the window as Jody continues his ablutions at the well. Her face is angry, but that desire remains.

The front door slams – another rack pan to Reggie entering through the front, then back to Etta looking out the window.

Reggie walks into the kitchen. Etta turns to embrace him. Reggie goes to hug her, but before he can, he looks at her dress, sees that the front of it is drenched. Etta looks out the window. Reggie follows her gaze, sees Jody out there looking all wet and sexy. Reggie looks back at Etta – she looks down in shame.

Shot from Jody's POV as Reggie runs out of the house, calls him a son-of-a-bitch, and socks him in the jaw.

They fight. I remembered what *Wikipedia* had said about Bobby Ecksmith's direction, that his cinematic style was *often marked by a subtle, yet controversial eroticism* – and there was definitely a little something extra there in the fight between Jody and Reggie. They were fighting over a woman – the standard romantic movie trope – but were they really? Was there something else in this fight, something akin to that love that dare not speak its name? It was very subtle, just the merest whiff – something about how Bobby shot their shifts in dominant and submissive positions, the way the grunting sounded more like some kind of rough lovemaking than a fight.

It was superb. Impulsively, I squeezed Maury hand. He looked over at me and winked. "Just wait," he whispered, "It gets better." It was the same thing Alvee had said.

Reggie is whipping Jody's ass. Finally, Etta runs outside and screams for Reggie to stop. He pauses in mid swing, and turns to look at her.

"Stop, Reggie," she whispers. She gently touches his cheek with one hand, his clenched fist with the other. Reggie lowers his fist. The tears running down her cheeks, Etta kisses him, softly, lovingly. "It's nothing, Reggie."

Rack pan to Jody, bleeding from the mouth, panting. "Yeah, Reggie," Jody says, swiping at his mouth with the back of his hand. He looks at the blood on his hand, grins humorlessly at the damage. "It's nothing."

Reggie looks at him.

"But remember one thing," Jody says. "The train's coming tomorrow. And that is something." Fade to black.

The next scene is the same as from the trailer – a shot of the train, puffing along, heading for the bridge.

Voiceover: "Just blow it, Reggie," Jody says.

The train just keeps puffing along.

Voiceover: "Not yet, Jody."

The train just keeps on going.

Voiceover: "If you don't blow it, then I will, Reg."

The train.

Voiceover: "You can't blow it yet, Jody!" Reggie urges.

Voiceover: "You just watch me, Reggie."

Jump cut to Jody slamming down the plunger on an old-fashioned westerny detonator. Jump cut back to slow-mo of the train exploding. It heads across the bridge for a few spans, then goes over the side, taking out most of the bridge with it, till only one car remains, dangling from the remaining span.

Cut to Jody and Reggie walking down the tracks toward the caboose, which is see-sawing gently from the end of the bridge.

"We waited too long, Reg," Jody says. "Only half of it was supposed to go over. The dynamite was just supposed to blow it in half, not send the whole thing into the river. It was supposed to leave the half with the gold *here!*"

They approach the caboose. Reggie gingerly climbs up the steps. The caboose creaks, lurches forward.

Reggie looks at Jody. He might be going to die, and he wants to know – he doesn't want to know, but he still *wants to know.*

Jody's scared for his friend, knows that the caboose is going to go over at any second, knows that Reggie doesn't care, that he'll go into the car after the safe, regardless of the danger. Jody smiles ruefully. "There's nothing between your wife and me, Reg. Nothing at all."

Reggie smiles. He believes his friend. All is well with them. He turns and enters the caboose.

But he moves too fast, and the caboose falls into the river. Jody rushes forward. It's not the drop that stays him – it's not that far. He can see the caboose filling up with water, can see Reggie struggling to get to the top before it sinks completely, before its rolls over, trapping him.

It's not the drop that stays Jody – it's the water. He can't swim.

Fade to black.

Same extremely long angle shot of the farm house and the field and the road beside it. It's sundown now. Golden bars slant across the road and fields. Jody slowly pilots the cart up the road. We hear the screen door bang, and Etta walks out onto the porch. She pauses on the top step. She puts her little hand to her forehead. She sees that Jody is alone.

Close-up on Etta – different emotions play across her face. Worry – where's Reggie? Then something else . . . she knew it was dangerous, that something could happen to one of them. Jody's alone . . . does this mean that something's happened to her husband? Does this mean that Reggie's dead and Jody has come back . . . for her?

296

Close up on Jody. He frowns, guilt stamped on his face. He couldn't save Reggie because he can't swim. He blames himself. But there's something else there, too, a little bit of a reflection of Etta's thought. Reggie was gone now, but his wife was still there, waiting . . .

Etta goes back into the house while Jody is driving up the road. Now she's standing just inside the door, gazing out through the screen. Jody pulls the cart into the yard in front of the house. He climbs gracefully out of the cart, pauses, looks sadly at her.

Cut to Etta. She realizes what's happened. Reggie's gone. She looks down, starts to cry, to sob.

Jody strides across the yard, opens the screen door. He embraces her, she sobs against his chest. He strokes her hair, murmurs comforting things to her. She looks up at him, her face pitiful and tear-stained. "What happened, Jody?" she cries.

"We blew the train too late. It all went over. Except for the caboose. Where the safe was. It was hanging over the edge. Reggie . . . Reggie climbed up on the car. He was gonna try to get to the safe. The car was too far over. It tilted and . . . it went into the river. I watched it wash away. I couldn't go in after him. Because . . . I can't swim."

Etta sobs into his chest again, and he strokes her hair. We get the sense that Jody is mostly wracked with his feelings of guilt because he couldn't save his friend. But he's holding Etta very tightly.

Then Etta looks up at him, and the look in her green eyes is no longer grief. Jody looks back at her. Jody stops stroking her hair, puts his hands on the sides of her face, and kisses her. Slowly at first, gently. Then harder, *much harder*, as he realizes that he's free from the guilt of being a traitor to his friend. And Etta is free, too. Reggie's gone, and they'll mourn for him tomorrow, but for now . . .

Slow pan into a lamp-lit bedroom. Etta is lying on her back on the bed. The lamplight plays fitfully over her – splashes of light and shadow. The camera pans in to her delicate toes, then to her knees – she's wearing only her shift, which is old and worn, making it gauzy, transparent, in the important places. The camera lingers on her breasts, then on up to her shining face. She smiles slowly.

Slow pan to Jody, silhouetted in the doorway, nude. The important parts are in shadow, but nothing else is left to the imagination. I'm pretty sure I heard myself gasp.

Alvee is shot in shadow and light, planes of flesh and muscle, lines of darkness and desire. He steps into the frame a little more – now the fitful light plays across his face – the lips parted slightly in that smug little smile that I'd seen so many times.

Alvee had never looked at me like that, except for that one strange time in Vegas. And that had just been acting, like this was. I'd watched him bestow that little smug grin on Ruthanne enough times. I'd seen him display it for Jessika in *High Times in Manhattan.* I suddenly wanted to know what it would be like to have him look at me like that, and not be acting.

Alvee Smith-Killem was beautiful – I'd listened to Maury's tributes to his splendor, and I knew how cute he was. But this was what we go to the movies to see. The way Maury had lit him was supernal – he'd made Jody even more beautiful, more flawless than Alvee could ever really be. I could see all the decades of Maury's desire reflected in this one shot – it was Maury's gift, his curse to us, to all of the legions of Alvee's fans yet to be. Maury had desired this for more than fifty years. He could never have it. But he wanted to show it to us, because we couldn't have it, either.

The light plays off Jody's little smug smile, glows in his incredible blue eyes.

He is an immortal, a god. He is Tithonus, lover of the Dawn.

Jody crosses the room, and climbs over the foot of the bed. Things are not shown that can't be shown and still keep a tasteful R-rating. I was proud of the genius of Maury's modesty here – in these kinds of shots, one's imagination is so much better than what is allowed to be shown.

Jody is all light and shadow, delicious concavities and stunning convexities – the arc of his shoulder, the slope of his back, the curve of his entirely, incredibly fine ass, the line of his strong thigh. He crawls slowly, oh, so slooowly up the length of Etta's body. Then he pauses and smiles down at her. Maury gives us another shot of Jody's long, lean, flawless nakedness.

Then a close-up of them gazing at each other. Then Jody slowly lowers his head and buries his face in Etta's neck. She arches her back and gently, slooowly pulls him down onto her. He kisses her hungrily, *devouringly.*

Fade. To. Black.

"Carol," Alvee whispered in my ear. I looked at him. "You're breaking my hand."

I'd been squeezing his hand, without realizing it, apparently a little too tightly. I released it immediately. I shouldn't be holding his hand, anyway.

There is a happy montage of Jody and Etta, all in love. There is a lot of lifting her off of her feet, a lot of spinning her joyfully around, a lot of carrying her to the bed. Lots of smiles and tender looks. We get the impression that this goes on for a while, but not too long. A few days, perhaps.

Same extremely long angle shot of the farm house and the field and the road beside it. A man is riding up the road on a prancing red horse.

Cut to Jody and Etta on the porch. She's sitting on his lap on the top step. They're laughing and talking.

Cut to shorter long angle shot of the man on the red horse. We can't see who he is yet, because his hat shadows his eyes – but we can see he is a dandy, with string tie. A gold watch chain winks from his waistcoat.

Cut back to Jody and Etta. Jody looks out at the road. His smile fades from one of connubial bliss to one of dumb surprise. Etta follows his gaze. She stands up, shields her eyes.

Cut to the man on horseback. He kicks his roan into a gallop.

Cut back to the long angle of the road. We see Jody running down the road. The man slows his horse and jumps off. His hat flies off and we see that it's Reggie. They embrace and pound each on the back. They start back toward the house, arms around each other's shoulders, Jody leading the horse by the end of its reins.

After a moment, we see Etta run down the road and throw herself into her husband's arms. Reggie picks her up and spins her around.

Jody says, "How did you get out, Reg?"

Reggie smiles smugly. "I know how to swim, Jody."

Cut to a shot of the kitchen table. The three of them are sitting at it, Reggie and Jody across from each other, Etta at its head.

Reggie is smoking a cigarillo now, resplendent in his dandy clothes. He says, "The caboose drifted long the bottom of the river for a while. I stayed with it as long as I could, then I had to come up for air. When I dove back down to look for it, it had rolled on down the river." Reggie grins around his smoke. "But the safe fell out. It stuck in the mud on the bottom of the river.

"So I came back up, made a mark on the bank where it was. I walked up the road, and at the first farm I came to, I went in and talked to the farmer. I spelled it out for him, Jody. I said the train had just gone over the side – the people from the railroad would be there pretty soon, and they'd be looking for that safe. I told him they might find it, or they might not. I told him if we waited for them to get done looking for it, then I might not be able to find it again, either.

"He hitched up his team and we drug that safe out of the mud. I opened it right there on the riverbank. I gave the farmer a generous fee for his services, and we pushed the safe back into the river. Then I took a little trip into town. Got some new duds. That fine red horse. I couldn't come home looking like something the cat brought in."

Etta is looking down at the table.

Jody says, "Reg, I thought you were dead. I . . . we . . ."

Reg slaps a hefty sack onto the table. It makes a pleasant clunk-tink sound.

"There's your cut, Jody. I expect you'll be moving on now."

Fade out.

Fade back in to the yard of the house. Jody is once again dressed in his black clothes and hat. His black horse is cropping grass nearby. He and Reggie are talking and laughing. Etta comes out onto the porch. She crosses it, but doesn't come down the steps. She looks at them solemnly, a trifle wistfully.

Jody and Reggie embrace, slap each other on the back. Jody mounts his horse, then looks over at Etta. He smiles gently at her, friendly – all the longing is gone, or maybe just well-hidden. He touches the brim of his hat. "Miz Etta."

Her smile is also gentle. What they shared was glorious, but she's glad her husband's back. "Mr. St. Cloud."

Jody spurs the horse and it trots off down the road.

Reggie watches horse and rider as they dwindle down the road, then turns and smiles at his wife. She smiles back, and runs down the steps and leaps into his arms. He picks her up and spins her around. He sets her down and they kiss. Then they walk hand in hand into the house.

The credits roll on a final shot of Jody, galloping down the road.

FORTY-SIX

The after-party was at the Beverly Hills Hotel.

On the limo ride over, Maury told me, "Don't tell me how you loved it now, Carol. Let it stew overnight. Let it *gestate.* You can tell me tomorrow."

Maury and Alvee again spoke to the lady from *Entertainment Tonight,* waiting in front of the hotel. I again hung back out of frame. Ryan and Eva came up and the five of them, stars, director, hostess, all had a little chat for the masses. Then the light on the camera went out – the *ET* hostess went her way, and we went in to the party.

Alvee and Ryan and Eva worked the room. I silently shadowed Maury, while he received congratulations and little conversations from behind-the-scenes types. I didn't know who any of them were, and they didn't know who I was. They didn't ask. I felt safe there with Maury and the off-screen talent. I was pretty sure that I wasn't going to turn around and find myself talking to Ryan again, or Eva, if I was standing next to Maury. I knew I could relax a little bit, enjoy my champagne. After the bonding experience of the creation of my gown, we were buddies. He was clever and droll and funny, I liked his accent, and I enjoyed his company immensely.

Maury had just introduced me to some functionary from *Paramount.* I immediately forgot his name – the champagne was starting to warm me up a little bit. The man said a few words and walked away. Maury sipped his drink. "Ah, Hollywood! Some things never change."

I followed his gaze. Alvee was across the room, deep in conversation with a paunchy, pale looking fellow. They were dressed similarly – both wearing expensive, expertly tailored dark suits. But there the parallels abruptly stopped. Alvee's companion was as tall as Alvee, but chubby, flabby. He had not much of a chin, and a bad haircut. Alvee, on the other hand, still looked like a god to me, even though he was dressed. I remembered his – *Maury's* – Jody again: the light and shadow, the darkness and desire . . .

When the chubby man turned to take a drink from a passing waiter, Alvee looked over at us and grinned, then turned back and seemed to pay serious, close attention to whatever the man was saying. The man leaned in a little closer, almost whispering in Alvee's ear. Then he moved back again, sipped his drink, and waited for Alvee's response. Alvee paused, grinned. Then he smiled, then giggled. Then he laughed, slapped his knee. He laughed so loudly that some of the people standing nearby turned and looked at him.

Then Alvee stopped laughing abruptly, but looked at his companion like he was having just the hardest time ever keeping himself from busting up again. He shook his head ever so slightly, said something. The chubby man frowned, then turned and walked away. Alvee exchanged a look with Maury, who grinned into his drink. "Some things never change," he repeated.

The chubby man had by this time reached our side of the room. He glanced at Maury, who smiled gloriously at him. The chubby man didn't smile back, but continued out of the room, rather in a huff.

FORTY-SEVEN

We returned to Jessika's — Franck's — *Alvee's* house. I was a little bit drunk, as was Maury. Kimura had left us a midnight snack of cold roast beef and hard French buns, with a little dish of au jus on the side. We devoured it greedily.

Alvee wanted me to tell him what my impression had been of his American film debut, but Maury insisted that I wait until morning to tell them. I had to let it *gestate,* he repeated.

Alvee suggested a swim. Immediately my mind showed me that lamp lit scene of his lean, naked body, followed promptly by his fire-lit blue eyes, looking up at me from the pool, and that smug, killer smile, as he slowly drew Ruthanne's ankles apart, his eyes never leaving mine.

I declined the swim. I told him that I'd had too much to drink. I might drown.

"Unlike Jody, I know how to swim, Carol. If you start to go under, I'll save you."

I might be going under, Alvee, and I might just need saving before too much longer, I thought. *But it won't be from drowning. It might just be from myself, and from your amazing blue eyes.*

Perhaps my vaunted willpower wasn't all it was cracked up to be, after all.

I shook my head, patted my tummy. "I have to *gestate.*"

Maury smiled faintly at me. *Atta girl,* his expression said.

I went up to my room, *Jessika's room,* still feeling the champagne. As a precaution against I knew not what, I locked the door on my side of the bathroom that adjoined Alvee's bedchamber.

Moments after climbing between the crisp sheets, I fell asleep. I dreamed. I dreamed of Alvee, climbing lithe and dangerous over the foot of Etta's bed. Except it wasn't Etta in the bed in my dream. How ridiculous would that be? *It was me.*

"Let me show you a little trick Esther Williams taught me, Carol," he said, just like I somehow knew he was going to, his eyes never leaving mine, that smug little smile in place, just for me.

And then he showed me.

I woke up panting and blinking in the pre-dawn gloom.

Hot damn, but I love the movies! I thought.

After a little while, I managed to go back to sleep again.

FORTY-EIGHT

Brunch was summarily slept through by all parties. It was one of Kimura's rare days off, so Maury, Alvee and I took a cab down to Hollywood Boulevard and ordered lunch at a little Italian place across the street from *The Egyptian*. I learned that Maki was not a big fan of Italian.

I looked at the grand marquee to *The Egyptian,* and thought about dead Penny and her dead friends, and of course, poor Ruthie, and even Aunt Mae, whose shop now stood vacant down the street. Then Maury made some clever remark about a passerby and their ghosts passed from my mind completely.

We ordered. We ate. I was of course a nobody, and no one puts a face to a name with a director, and Alvee's movie didn't open for public consumption until today. We were just tourists having lunch.

I visited the ladies' room, and on my way back, I noticed a folded over newspaper lying on the table in an empty booth. *Cheyenne Su,* the headline read. I picked it up, unfolded it.

Cheyenne Sundown Fades to Night But Not Quick Enough

Quickly, I thought. Not *quickly* enough. What kind of a rag publishes such poor grammar? I looked at the top of the paper. Oh, shit. It was *The New York Times. The New York Times* was panning *Cheyenne Sundown.*

I folded the paper until it was small enough to fit, then went back to the table and surreptitiously stuck it in in my purse. We finished eating, caught a cab back to Alvee's house. The review was burning a hole in my purse, in my head. Had the movie opened on the East Coast already? I didn't think so. Maury would've mentioned it. No, *Cheyenne Sundown* opened today, nationwide. The reviewer must've been at the premiere last night, and phoned it or faxed it or emailed it in. However that stuff worked.

Alvee and Maury went to their respective rooms to change for the pool, and I went out to the terrace to read *The Times'* critique. Maki was there. He rose and bowed to me. I bowed back, and then sat down.

Cheyenne Sundown Fades to Night But Not Quick
Enough

On the heels of the practically G-rated Downpour, English director Maurice Claremount's straight to video tale of not-much seduction and fluffy betrayal, we are now presented with Cheyenne Sundown, a tired oater that should have been put out to pasture before ever being allowed to open in theaters today.

Not only did this guy use poor grammar, his sentence structure was atrocious.

Ryan Gosling's multi-talents

Multi-talents? Seriously? Not for the first time, I wondered how these writers got their jobs, and made good money, when I couldn't sell a movie review to save my life.

Ryan Gosling's multi-talents are wasted in this tale of a high-brow, cheating wife, a botched train robbery, and a bumbling side-kick who can't swim. Camellia Swanson's performance is delicate and vaporous

Vaporous? Really?

Camellia Swanson's performance is delicate and vaporous as the English aristocrat transplanted to dusty Wyoming. But her talents are wasted on the character. She's forced to play the stock, immediately two-timing farmwife. Do we really need another reinforcement of the misogynist fantasy of the devoted bride, seemingly happily married at first, who is nonetheless ready to drop her bloomers the minute a strange man enters the picture? No. We do not.

Neophyte Alvee Smith-Killem's stranger stalks through his scenes, chewing the scenery

Ah, come on! Did anybody really use *chewing the scenery* anymore?

305

Neophyte Alvee Smith-Killem's stranger stalks through his scenes, chewing the scenery and casting overwrought come-hither glances at the unable-to-help herself Camellia, his mouth stuffed with clichéd one-liners about his dangerous ways with the ladies. It's no spoiler to say that when this lady finally takes the initiative and quite literally throws herself at him, however, Mr. Killem takes the coward's way out, spouting platitudes about loyalty and friendship. No one likes a tease, Alvee.

The train robbery falls flat – what, was there only one guy on that train? There is gratuitous, under-lit nudity, for those whom only the idea of the stereotypical horny farmer's wife will not suffice. Marital harmony wins out in the end and we are treated to the inevitable riding off into the sunset.

Don't waste your money on Cheyenne Sundown, my friends. No new ground is covered, and the old ground revisited is riddled with horse apples. Perhaps Ryan Gosling lost a bet to appear in this one. Regardless, he will soon be saying, "If my people ever get me in another dog like this, I'm gonna kill 'em. Kill 'em all."

Damn. I folded the newspaper over and set it down on the table. I looked over at Maki, and he nodded at me, smiled faintly. I wondered what the Japanese expression for *this guy really hated Cheyenne Sundown* might be. I imagined that I might hear it, if Maury got a look at this review.

I looked at the newspaper on the table. Should I get rid of it? It was not like *The New York Times'* circulation encompassed just this one copy. Maury and Alvee were bound to see it sooner or later. Who was I to think I could shield them? Who was I to think that they needed to be shielded?

I was reading the review again when Maury and Franck emerged from beneath the twin staircases. I folded the paper and quickly set it back down on the table, mentally divorcing myself from it. I couldn't shield them from it, but I didn't have to rub their noses in it either.

Maury bowed to his friend, said a few words in Japanese and sat down. Alvee sat down next to me, clad in the same black board shorts that he'd worn when he was . . . that he'd worn back in the day.

This guy could turn back time, and was looking better every minute, at least to me – why should he care about a terribly written review?

Alvee smiled at me. I smiled weakly back at him. He noticed the paper sitting on the table in front of me, beside the familiar vase of flowers.

"Whatcha got there, Carol?" he asked, a lamb to the slaughter.

"Oh, nothing." I frowned, shook my head at the nothingness of it. "Just a review. You famous Hollywood types don't care about reviews, right?"

Maury smiled at me, as if to say, *Of course we don't.*

Alvee grinned at my studied nonchalance. "Oh. You mean the *bad* review. Cary Stuward's review. I can tell from the look on your face." He glanced at the folded newspaper. "Since when do you read newspapers, anyway, Carol? What are you – him?" He nodded at Maury. "And it's not even *The LA Times*. This is Hollywood. Nobody cares what they think in New York."

Maury raised an eyebrow at that but remained silent.

Alvee continued. "Besides, what is this – paper? News? Where'd you even find this? News isn't on paper anymore, Carol. And Cary Stuward is no Roger Ebert. He couldn't write his way out of a paper bag.

"Regardless, there's no great yea or nay critics anymore. There's just too many of them for any one voice to matter." His grin widened. "Besides, there's a reason your buddy Cary gave us such a bad review, and it had nothing to do with his impression of *Cheyenne Sundown.*"

Alvee reached for the paper, but Maury snatched it up, opened it with a flourish. "What exactly did Mr. Stuward say, anyway?" He took his specs out of the pocket of his shirt, put them on, looked at me over them. "I never read the reviews in the *New York Times.*"

"He never forgave them for calling *George and Benedict a dreary attempt at canonizing* a traitor, or for them referring to his script as *atrocious,*" Alvee said.

"They liked you, though," Maury said, not looking up from the entertainment section of *The New York Times*. Then he did look up. He squinted. "Let me see if I can remember. How did it go? *Even the luminous O'Day cannot save this morass of revisionist history. But I see a bright future for O'Day – quick, someone put him in a suit and fix him up with Julie Christie or Elizabeth Taylor or Jessika Yerdlay!*

"And we know how all that turned out, now don't we?" Maury looked at the paper again. "No, I never read *The Times*. I never read reviews at all, unless I should just happen upon one in *Variety.*"

Alvee grinned. *"Variety* savaged *George and Benedict,* too, if I remember." He rested his chin on his hand. "Let's see . . . oh, yeah, they called it *a dismally ill-timed apology for a universally reviled traitor.* And they said I was miscast."

"And they spelled your name wrong," Maury added.

"Yet still you prefer them to *The Times?"*

Maury shrugged.

Oh, no, these famous Hollywood types didn't read reviews. And if they did, why, bad reviews didn't matter to them, didn't affect them at all. That's why they could still remember them, verbatim, more than fifty years later.

Maury read, *"Neophyte Alvee Smith-Killem's stranger stalks through his scenes, chewing the scenery and casting overwrought come-hither glances at the unable-to-help herself Camellia, his mouth stuffed with clichéd one-liners about his dangerous ways with the ladies.*

"Hmmm. There's some imagery for you. *Chewing the scenery. Mouth stuffed full of* clichés. I think Mr. Stuward is trying to tell us something, here."

Maury said something to Maki. He smiled at Alvee, chuckled. Alvee smiled back, shrugged.

Maury said, "Carol seems a little distraught over this . . ." he tossed the paper onto the table, gestured at it. "This unbiased slice of journalistic . . . whatever it is. Perhaps you should read between the lines for her, Alvee, my darling, although Mr. Stuward's prose seems a little transparent to me."

"Did you see the little fat guy I was talking to at the party last night, Carol?" Alvee asked.

I nodded. Maury picked up *The Times* again. *"Nobody likes a tease, Alvee,"* he read. When Alvee looked at him, Maury said, "It says that right here. In the review."

Alvee looked back at me and said, "Remember, once upon a time, in a galaxy far, far away, when a little-known and much-forgotten actor named Franck O'Day told you a true Hollywood story about a director name Patrick Morrison?"

Maury looked up, nonplussed. "You didn't."

"I most certainly did," Alvee said, and grinned. "Lori almost had a cow when I told Carol that Morrison promised me the lead if I'd suck his dick."

I flinched at the profanity coming out of Alvee's flawless mouth, borne on his silky, sexy voice. I was amazed that a little shiver ran down my back.

"Oh, how clever." Maury was reading the review again. "He makes a little pun on your name. He refers to our dear Mr. Gosling's mouth this time, stuffing words into *it*, making him say, *If my people ever get me in another dog like this, I'm gonna kill 'em. Kill 'em all.*

"I do believe you've made your very first new enemy, Alvee. Congratulations! How fun!"

"That was him, Carol, at the party. The guy you saw me talking to was Cary Stuward." He looked at Maury, who was reading again. "Who let a *New York Times* reviewer into my premiere, anyway?"

Maury didn't look up. "It wasn't your premiere, darling, it was Ryan's premiere. You're an un – you're a *neophyte*. It might serve you to remember that."

"Yeah, they always think they can get at the new guy." Alvee smiled. He wasn't upset at all.

"*Neophytes* are hungry," Maury said. "*Neophytes*. What a stupid word. It sounds like a bacteria, something one might get infected with. Perhaps that's it, Alvee? Mr. Stuward longs to be *infected* by *neophytes*.

"New stars think they *need* a good review," Maury continued. "They're not sure where their next dime is coming from." He gestured around him. "Nobody knows that all this has long ago been bought and paid for. Nobody knows that Maurice Claremount and Alvee Smith-Killem are just making movies for the fun of it. Mr. Stuward just naturally assumed that you'd do anything for a little break." He looked at the paper again. "Carol, did you find my *gratuitous* nude scene to be *underlit?*"

I smiled at him. "It was neither gratuitous nor underlit, Maury. It was the highlight of the film."

He smiled back. "I thought so."

We looked at Alvee to finish his story. "So this little fat guy comes up to me, introduces himself, says he's with *The Times*. I don't read *The Times* – or *Variety*, either, for that matter – so I've never heard of this jerk. But I'm a polite kind of guy, so when he says he's from *The Times*, I pretend to be as impressed as he thinks I should be.

"He says, 'I could be a good friend to you, Mr. Killem, if you'd be a good friend to me.'"

Maury rolled his eyes. "How quaint."

"Then he whispers, 'I would be more than willing to write a stellar review of your performance if you'd be willing to suck my dick.'"

Again I shivered.

Alvee grinned broadly at Maury. "You'd think you people would've come up with a more elegant term for it by now."

Maury looked surprised. "Have *you people* come up with a more elegant term for it by now?" Alvee shrugged. "Carol?"

I also shrugged. "None come to mind at the moment."

Alvee continued. "It was like Patrick Morrison had returned from the grave. I laughed at this guy. Then I *really* laughed at him. I said, 'You're not even from *RKO!*'"

Maury barked laughter. "Once upon a time, Patrick used the long shadow of *RKO* to get himself all kind of treats. May he rest in peace." He paused. "But Patrick was all right."

Maury looked at Alvee. Alvee grinned.

"But he certainly was a cocksucker!" they said in unison, and burst out laughing.

Maki looked at Maury and Maury translated. Maki joined in the laughter.

I was sure that I'd just heard the word for *cocksucker* spoken in a foreign language. It was a first for me, and I felt that I had perhaps lived a sheltered life up until that point.

Alvee looked at his watch. "I want to show you something, Carol." But he wasn't looking at me, he was sharing a glance with Maury. "We need to catch a matinee."

Maury held Alvee's gaze for another second, then flapped his hand. "I've seen it." He began tearing the folded section of *The New York Times* into strips.

"I'll be right back," Alvee said.

"Ok, Carol," Maury said when he was gone. "You've gestated. Tell me what you thought of my film."

I took a deep breath, exhaled. I considered this man to be my friend, and you tell your friends the truth. You don't defer, you don't sugarcoat, you don't euphemize.

"As in everything you do, Maury, the cinematography was flawless. Tourism in Wyoming will go through the roof – everyone is going to want to see that sky in person. The repeated use of that wide angle shot of the road – it tied everything together perfectly.

"I thought you could've given a little bit more backstory about Reggie and Etta. What was an Englishwoman doing in Wyoming? And maybe a little more info on Reggie and Jody – how did they become criminals? How did Reggie learn to crack safes? Perhaps you could have shown some other example of Jody getting the woman Reg wanted, from some past time. All these could've been montages, right?

"And Stuward was correct on one point. You should've shown more people on the train – shown 'em all going over, maybe.

"But besides that, it was great." I smiled.

Maury smiled back. "And nobody's going to remember it for any of that, are they?"

I shook my head, delighted. "No. No, they're not. Not at all."

"Such was my intention. Ryan who?"

I turned to watch Alvee walk across the terrace. To his black board shorts, he'd added a loud yellow Hawaiian shirt, his pork pie hat, his Ray-Bans, and a pair of flip-flops.

Maury endeavored to look appalled. "Is this the new incognito?"

Alvee held his arms out. "You don't like it?"

"Whatever's clever, my darling. You'll blend. At least today."

Alvee looked at his watch again. He grabbed my hand and we ran through the house, then out the door, down the stone steps and down to the end of the drive. The cab was already waiting on the other side of the gate.

The red carpet was gone from in front of the *Cinerama Dome,* as were the limos and the velvet rope, and the crowds. There was not even a line waiting to buy tickets for Ryan Gosling's latest, because the next showing had already started.

Alvee went up to the window, asked for two tickets to *Sundown,* slid a fifty to the girl. She hesitated, looked closely at him; Alvee smiled. The girl took in the board shorts, the loud shirt, the sunglasses, the flip flops. She shook her head absently, and slid two tickets to him with his change. "Enjoy the show," she said.

We came in on the extremely long angle shot of the farm house and the field and the road, after Reggie has gone to town to get the dynamite, when Jody is going back alone to the farmhouse and Etta.

In the brightness from the shot, I looked at the audience. There were a few empty seats – it was a matinee. Enterprising young men were probably planning to take their girls out to see Ryan Gosling's new movie this evening. Enterprising young men had no trouble allowing Ryan to warm their girlfriends up for them. It doesn't matter where you get your appetite, as long as you eat at home.

But for the matinee, the house was almost entirely women. I heard Alvee's voice in my mind: *A million years ago, a million women in a million theatres fell in love with Perry Calibri.*

Fade in to Jody. He's in the back yard, standing beside the well, shirtless. The camera pans back slowly. Jody arches his back a little and dumps a bucket of water on his head. He shakes the water out of his eyes with a quick jerk – jet black curls twitch and bounce. The camera lingers lovingly over his glistening flesh, traces the rivulets of water running over him. Down, down – across the smooth chest, over the

311

flat belly, the strong haunch it its tight britches – right on down to the scuffed boot.

Goddamn, but he's fine! escaped from my mind before Alvee tugged on my hand. I'd stopped on the steps to watch the scene.

Alvee found us a couple seats in the back. We watched the movie in silence, as is expected in the theater, until the scene where Alvee is comforting Etta after he tells her Reggie is dead. Then Alvee took my left hand in his right and said again, "I want to show you something, Carol. Close your eyes."

But I couldn't close my eyes because it was *the scene*, and I had to watch it again. As the camera panned over Etta, I looked at Alvee. He had his eyes closed, and was making the *Om* gesture with his left hand. The whiteness of the scar on his palm stood out, even in the gloom of the theater, and I reminded myself to ask him where he got it.

Then I looked back at the screen and became transfixed once again, just like all the other women in the house. There was utter silence from the crowd. No talking, no coughs, no rustling. No movement. Breath was being held.

This was the only thing anybody was ever going to remember from *Cheyenne Sundown*. This scene right here. Nobody was going to remember Ryan or Camellia or the train exploding spectacularly and going over the bridge. Nobody was going to remember the bad reviews, or even the good ones. Nobody was going to remember anything except Alvee Smith-Killem, *neophyte, stalking* into the room in all his *gratuitous* nudity, all his Olympian perfection.

So glorious in his beauty and thy choice/ Who madest him thy chosen, that he seem'd/ To his great heart none other than a God!

Nobody was going to remember anything from this film but this scene. It was exactly like the dream I'd had the night before, except instead of lucky Etta, it had been lucky me. I noticed that Alvee's hand seemed to have grown warm in mine. Then the warmth expanded, becoming agreeably hot. Then my arm started to tingle and the pleasant heat traveled up and dispersed throughout my whole body in the most surprising, most delightful way.

I looked over at Alvee. He opened his eyes and leaned over and kissed me, slowly. The warmth in my body intensified, almost to the point of, oh, my, God! I was *right there,* and Alvee broke the kiss.

The scene faded to black and someone in the theater whooped. Fade in on happy Jody and Etta.

Alvee smiled at me. His eyes seem to glow from within. "I don't need good reviews, Carol. I can get all I need from the audience – love, adoration, *energy*. It doesn't matter what the critics think. Only them."

He glanced at the screen, tugged at my hand. "Come on," he said, "let's beat the crowd. I know how this one ends."

As we walked out, Alvee caught the eye of the ticket girl and smiled. Her mouth dropped open as she recognized him. He winked at her, then put his shades on, all the time holding on to my hand as if he thought I might float away. *I* thought I might float away. I was light and airy and at the whim of the slightest breeze, like the feather from the beginning of *Forrest Gump*.

We walked out to the curb. Alvee took out his phone and called a cab. After a moment, the girl from the box office came running out. She'd brought the poster from *Cheyenne Sundown* with her – one corner of it was missing and I thought she might've just ripped it out of the lobby. She breathlessly asked Alvee to autograph it for her. She was amazed that he was there in the flesh, at his own movie.

Would she start the newest Hollywood legend? That Alvee Smith-Killem attends his own movies, incognito? *How fun!* I thought.

Alvee finally let go of my hand. He smiled and signed the poster for the girl, posed with her while she took their picture. Then she said thanks, told him how much she had enjoyed *Cheyenne Sundown*. She even dared to give him a little hug. He was dressed like a tourist, after all. Then she took her prize and ran back into the *Cinerama Dome*.

I could've had three heads and four arms and she wouldn't have noticed me standing right there next to them.

The cab pulled up and we slid into the back. Alvee took my hand again, smiled at me. I was speechless. I still felt warm all over – it was almost like a sexually sated afterglow. That was only an illusion, I reflected, because I might have been a lot of things, but sexually satisfied was not one of them. Still, I felt light, weightless, joyful. Sexual satisfaction would've only been gravy.

The only word to describe it was the one I'd kept hearing all along – I felt *energized*, renewed. I felt as fresh as a spring day. It was incredible.

FORTY-NINE

We rode in the cab in silence for a while, still holding hands. I suddenly remembered Ruthanne saying, "And he kept holding my hand. After a while, to my amazement, I kinda got used to it. Can you imagine? I got used to holding hands with Franck O'Day!"

I was way used to holding hands with Alvee Smith-Killem, who was just Franck O'Day magically rejuvenated, after all. He was just a hand-holding kind of guy.

I said, "Can you teach me how to do that?"

Alvee blinked at me, shook his head. "That was just a parlor trick, Carol. Done with mirrors, like they say. I just reflected a little bit of the energy from all those delightfully gawping young women to you."

"Is it always so . . . intense?"

He shook his head again, not quite understanding. He hadn't felt the same kind of sensual rush that I had, obviously. He hadn't intended to show me *that*. He just wanted to demonstrate to me that the energy thing worked, that it was real.

That was good. Somehow the idea that he could go around intentionally making women almost climax by just holding their hand and kissing them for a hot second didn't hardly seem fair.

It was bad enough that he could do it unintentionally, that he (and Maury's exquisite lighting job) could just sneak into a girl's dreams, make her want to . . .

"It's not a . . . sexual thing?" I insisted. "Because, what all those women were feeling . . ." *What I was feeling* . . . "You said it comes from their love and adoration . . ."

Alvee tilted his head, as if he wanted to ask me something. Instead, he said, "It's like a fire, Carol." Alvee's eyes widened a little bit, as if he realized that perhaps using a fire in any kind of analogy might not be the best idea.

But he went on. "You need three things to start a fire. Heat, oxygen, and fuel. Once you combine those things, you have the thing called fire. It doesn't matter what kind of fuel it is – it can be wood or gasoline – whatever's combustible. But once it combusts, then it's fire. Its byproducts are more heat, and light, and ash. What it was when it was fuel is consumed.

"The universal energy is like that. The fuel can be love, adoration, desire – even just well wishes sent along with keys." Alvee smiled.

"When this fuel is assimilated, its by-products are well-being and rejuvenation. Does that make any sense?"

I think it might've finally started to. I nodded. "You're saying that all those hormones in that theater don't make you hot . . ."

"They make me young," he said, and squeezed my hand. "Sometimes, two people can attain a sort of equilibrium. Just between the two of them. It takes a great deal of study and meditation." He smiled again. "And it also takes a damn near superhuman melding of love and respect and understanding between two people."

Now Alvee grinned. "A little warm for the guy that was in that western with Ryan Gosling isn't enough. It involves a kind of commitment that I can't really explain, like Maki and Maury share.

"Maury loves me, Carol, and I love him. I've known him for more than fifty years. We're like brothers. Simpatico. But Maury and Maki? They are *Zen.* They are halves to the same whole.

"Sometimes two people can attain that balance, and then it's akin to all the pop iconography borrowed from the East, all the stuff people see and think they understand. Yin and Yang. That's Maki and Maury. The energy flows back and forth between them like magnetic poles.

"The energy that I received in Vegas was much stronger than what Maury and Maki share, much more concentrated, because it came from all those people at once. It was like an inundation, *a baptism.*

"That's why I look so much younger than Maury now – I actually *am* younger than Maury, by eight years. But I look so much younger now because I was fortunate to receive all that energy in one dose. But Maury and Maki, they keep *each other* young."

I thought about how nice all that was, then happened to look down at Alvee's left hand, in my right. I turned it over, opened it, ran my finger over the white circle in its center.

"How'd you get this scar, Alvee?"

He grinned. "It was an initiation. Did you ever see that old TV series, *Kung Fu?* With David Carradine?"

"Oh, my God, Alvee, you're so old!" I replied, and giggled. "I remember my mom saying something about that. From when *she* was a kid."

Alvee laughed. "It starts out – he's a half American kid, applying at a Shaolin temple in China. The hook was the master saying, *When you can snatch the pebble from my hand, it'll be time for you to leave.*" Alvee rolled his eyes. "The show was actually very original for its time. Still, no one questioned why the Shaolins in 17th century China were speaking English.

315

"Anyway, there's this one scene where Carradine has snatched the pebble, and he's getting ready to leave. But there's a large, smoking, red-hot brazier of coals blocking his path. With much appropriately plunking music, we are shown a glowing tiger on one side, a dragon on the other. Carradine throws back his sleeves and presses his bare forearms to the brazier, branding himself with the symbols. He moves the brazier out of his path. A door opens. He walks out, barefoot, into the snow, presses his wounds into its cold. Then he looks up, open-mouthed, at the snowy mountains . . .

"Then he gets in a street fight and kills a member of the royal house. His master is wounded, and gives him all his worldly possessions in a pouch, then dies. This is so Carradine can carry them with him and discover their usefulness and have lots of flashbacks in subsequent episodes.

"He has to leave the country because of his crime, and comes to America and starts working on the railroad, and fighting the good fight."

I looked at Alvee's palm, looked into his eyes. "And you had to do that? You had to burn yourself?"

He looked at me solemnly, then grinned. "No, Carol. I'm just having you on. There's no self-mutilation in *Shugendō.*" He laughed and closed his hand around mine again. "Didn't I tell you once to never drink to the truth? That the truth should never be allowed to get in the way of a good story? That initiation thing, that's just a good story.

"The truth is far more boring. One of the gardeners left a couple of rakes lying out by the garage. I tripped over one of them and landed on the tines of the other one. Lori freaked out. Firing the poor guy wasn't good enough – I thought she was going to get him deported. I calmed her down – it didn't even go all the way through. It's not that big a deal. They stick a little patch and some make-up on it, and it disappears."

He was telling me that this accident had happened *before* Vegas, because *after* Vegas, Lori wasn't around anymore to be terrorizing thoughtless gardeners. Lori was *dead,* as was Ruthie and Penny and Evan and all those other innocent people.

The part of my mind that wanted so much to believe Alvee – it was the bigger part – spoke up. *See,* it said. *If he'd acquired that scar through malice, through mass-murder, then he would've told you that he'd acquired it* after *Vegas. You didn't see him for almost two years after Vegas. If he needed to lie about it, why not just say he'd gotten it in England, playing polo with Bobby, whilst they were concocting their new identities?*

If he'd gotten it in Vegas, as I had seen in my dream, then he wouldn't have told me that he'd gotten it *before* Vegas. If he was lying, then what he'd told me was a risky lie. Maybe I'd been studying his palms from a distance all this time. Maybe I already knew whether or not it had been there before Vegas. Maybe I was testing him.

The truth was, I couldn't tell you if Alvee had a scar on his palm or not at any time before I'd experienced that dream. I'd never noticed one way of another – it might've indeed been there all along, or maybe not. The greater part of my mind explained it away thusly: my subconscious mind *had* noticed the scar on Alvee's palm. Then it'd just brought up the unconsciously remembered memory and plugged the detail into that horrible dream, as concrete proof IRL for something that it had just completely made up on its own.

The mind was a tricky thing.

It was so easy to forget that dream, the one where a blue-bolt of energy vaporized seventy-five people before burning a hole in Alvee's palm. It was so easy to forget that he was pushing eighty-three now, that it was impossible for him to be young and strong and beautiful again, yet here he was – it was so easy to forget *everything*, sitting there in the back of the cab next to him, holding his hand, remembering his incredible kiss in the theater.

It was only a dream, after all. Random synaptic firings during sleep.

The mind was a tricky thing.

But that one little part of me remembered, and remained watchful.

FIFTY

When we got back to the house, Alvee again suggested a swim. I figured that it was safe – it was still daylight, and Maury and Maki were already outside. And I needed a little cooling off after all the hand-holding and energy reflection and near orgasmic kissing that had occurred at the *Cinerama Dome*.

I arrived at the pool before Alvee, and took a seat on one of the lounge chairs beside it, the better to observe Maury and Maki. They were swimming laps together: Maki dog-paddled slowly down the length of the pool, his still mostly black braid trailing out behind him, and Maury stroked along lazily beside him. They laughed and spoke softly to each other. They were *Zen,* as Alvee had said, in synch, perfectly compatible with each other for reasons that I could not begin to comprehend. Watching them together, I could see the affection, even the love that they shared. But there was so much more, as Alvee had tried to explain. They were halves to the same whole.

Sure, Maury would miss Alvee terribly, if he weren't around for some reason. But Alvee would always remain a beautiful, impossible creature to Maury, like a unicorn – that picture made me grin – I was sure that they'd both appreciate the transparent imagery there.

Like in the myth of the magical creature, Maury could look at Alvee, but he could never touch him.

But I could tell that Maury could not live without Maki. It was not a grasping, fervent, passionate, physical thing – at least they didn't show that aspect in public, if it existed. But I could tell that Maury would simply die without his friend, as he'd do if he were deprived of air.

Alvee ran out and leapt upon the diving board, executed another Olympic-caliber somersaulting dive. He flubbed the entry on purpose, splashing the other men.

"And thus does the virility of youth intrude upon the tranquility of meditation," Maury said, as he climbed out of the pool, toweled himself off and sat on another lounge chair next to me. Maki climbed out also, bowed to me and then to Maury, and went back into the house.

"I understand you aspired to be a writer at one time, Carol," Maury said.

"All my life," I told him truthfully.

"A noble ambition," he replied. "But setting nobility aside for a moment, have you ever tried your hand at writing a screenplay?"

Academy-award nominated director Robert Ecksmith was asking me if I'd ever written a screenplay. I thought about the boat anchor of an execrable tome holding down one side of my desk at home. Holding down the other side was a stack of screenplays. Crime stories and romances and science fiction and drama. Period pieces and heist stories and cautionary tales of love gone awry.

"Yes, sir, Mr. Claremount, sir. I've done quite a few screenplays. Nobody's ever read any of them, but I've done quite a few."

Maury grinned at me. "I'd like to see them."

"I don't think so, Maury. They're awful."

"Oh, you're too modest, Carol," he said.

Alvee, swimming laps, splashed us as he went by.

"I have a little trouble with the whole screenplay format, Maury," I said. "Try as I might, things just don't fit. They don't flow."

They have programs on the internet to show you how to format your screenplay, and glossaries, and dictionaries, *stuffed full* of terms. Wide angle shot, smash cut. Interior – Day. Exterior – Night. POV. Spacing and indentation. Screenplays even have a preferred *font*. Fade to black.

Everybody who likes movies wants to *write* a movie. But everyone that likes movies and wants to write a movie is not a screenwriter. It's a special talent – if for no other reason than being able to put all those indentations and camera directions in correctly.

A screenwriter, I was not. I'd given it many attempts, but I'd always felt that all those directions always got in the way of the story I was trying to tell.

"It's not about the format, Carol. It's about the story," famous English director Robert Ecksmith said, as if reading my mind. "Screenwriters are a dime a dozen. It's a technical field, really. Just like you said, it's a format."

"It's a format that I could never do, or at least not well," I whined.

"But you're a storyteller, right? A novelist?"

"I've always fancied myself one," I replied.

"You always see *adapted for the screen by*, am I right? It's never the other way around. No one ever adapts a screenplay into a novel. You can't even buy screenplays."

"You buy novels *for the story*. You go to the movies *to see the story*. Nobody reads screenplays, except people in the business. They're really just instructions. Screenwriting is just making the story into a form that can be shot, Carol.

"Some screenwriters are also excellent storytellers, but I bet you can't name three. Most of them just have a talent for putting someone else's story into a format that can be followed by the director and the actors. It's a technical thing that not everyone can do."

I raised my hand.

"But I want to read your *stories*, Carol. If you're uncomfortable with the *formatting*, we'll hire a screenwriter, or I'll adapt it myself. But I want to see if I can *see* your stories. I am a motion picture director after all –"

"Of no little renown."

Maury flapped his hand. "That's all in the past. My new films are *G-rated*, or *no new ground is covered, and the old ground revisited is riddled with horse apples.*"

"You can't possibly believe that, Maury. No one is going to remember what some hack said. He doesn't even know how to use an adverb correctly."

"That's the writer in you coming out, Carol," Maury said and grinned. "Nobody cares about adverbs."

"It's a good film, Maury."

"Oh, no, Carol. It's a great film. Because of him." He nodded over his shoulder at Alvee.

Because his director knows how to light him, I thought. *Because his director knows how to light him so well that I can't get that scene out of my head, that I dream about it, that after seeing that one scene (twice!), all I can think of is what it would be like to be Etta at that very moment, all I want to do is find out . . .*

"But it's not a great story," Maury continued. "I want you to bring me your stories, Carol, the great ones and the not so great ones. Let me make them into great movies."

I grinned at Maury. "You're having me on, right? You're telling me that you want to make a movie out of something that I wrote?"

"Why not?" Maury said. "Here's some clichés for you: why not? What have you got to lose?" He turned and watched Alvee, smooth and wet and graceful, dive into the pool. "Stranger things have happened. What d'ya say?"

"I'll go home and get them. Right now."

"I think it can wait till after dinner."

I wondered if Maury realized that I would be heartbroken, *crushed,* if this was some kind of famous-Hollywood-director-makes-fun-of-aspiring-writer joke. "Are you serious, Maury? You want to look at my stuff to see if any of it could be filmed? Seriously?"

"What have we got to lose? It's all for the thrill, anyway. If one of them bombs, then we'll just make another one."

"Okay. But just remember that you asked for it."

Alvee swam over to the side of the pool and splashed us again. "Come in the water, Carol. The sun's bad for your skin."

"Your leading man beckons." Maury turned around and looked at Alvee. "And he is irresistible." He turned back and winked at me.

I hopped up and jumped into the pool, my head aswim with all the wondrous things Maury had said. A film – a film from something I wrote! A film, by legendary director Robert Ecksmith, a film, brought to you by Maurice Claremount, the same man, the same *visionary,* who brought you Alvee Smith-Killem's unforgettable, exquisitely well-lit nakedness in *Cheyenne Sundown.* Ryan who?

A film, adapted for the screen by Maurice Claremount – from a story by Carolyn Adyon.

It was a dream come true.

I broke the surface of the water, and there was Alvee. I remembered that other dream, the one where I was Etta.

"Hot, damn, Alvee!" I said and swam closer to him. But not too close. "Maury wants me to help him make a movie!"

Alvee looked over at his director. "Hot, damn, indeed! It's about time we found some fresh ideas!"

FIFTY-ONE

I was nervous during dinner, fidgety. It was good old American steak and potatoes this time, and Kimura had cooked it to perfection, like it was straight off the chuck wagon. But I couldn't savor it, couldn't give it its due, because all I could think of was that drawer full of screenplays, languishing at home, not being perused by my director. *My director!*

I declined the customary after-dinner drink.

"I have to go home, gentlemen," I said.

There was no time for tossing and turning in Jessika's room, unable to sleep for fantasizing about Oscars. There was no time for sex-dreams about Alvee, intoxicating as they may be. There was no time tomorrow for lazing around the pool with my wealthy Hollywood friends, who made movies for the fun of it. There was no time for any of that.

I had to go home. I had to gather up my dusty screenplays. I had to get them to my director. I had to get this show on the road.

"Time is money," Maury said, and smiled. "Commerce and industry. Art." He understood.

Alvee smiled at me, his eyes aglow from the candles that Kimura had set out on the terrace table. No time to think about Alvee's eyes.

He understood, too. "I'll walk you out to the car."

"Can I leave my stuff here?" I said. "My dress . . ." No time to pack. Gotta go.

"Of course," Alvee said, grinning at my impatience. "It's not like you won't be coming back. I'll walk you out to the car."

"Thank you so much for this opportunity, Maury." I leaned over and kissed him on the cheek.

"Don't mention it, Carol," he said. "It's going to be fun."

I stood up and Alvee and Maury and Maki rose, as gentlemen used to do. I bowed to Maki, and Maury also, then skipped under the bifurcated staircase, Alvee in tow.

I thanked him for everything, his hospitality, the premiere, this wonderful opportunity. I wanted to give him a hug, but dared not. If I hugged him, was close enough to smell him, then I might want to kiss him, and then I might start to think of his long, lean nakedness again . . . and I just didn't have time for that right now.

He accepted my thanks graciously. He opened the car door for me, told me to drive safely, tapped the roof of the car. I drove away.

While I waited at the light before the on-ramp to the 101, I thought about my lonely, little, dusty apartment. I frowned. I would drive home, gather up my screenplays, and then there I'd be, in my lonely, little, dusty apartment.

Before the light changed, I called Doug. The premier had taken place on a Thursday, so I had again left town on Wednesday after work. There had been no luau at Alvee's this time. I'd told Doug that I'd taken the time off to attend a several days' long bachelorette party/bridal shower in Rancho Cucamonga.

Now I told Doug that the girl-party had broken up earlier than anticipated. I told him that I'd be home soon, and that if he wasn't busy – *what would he be doing on a Friday night without me, anyway?* I thought. If he wasn't busy, I'd love to see him. I missed him very much, I said.

He said sure, told me he'd missed me, told me he couldn't wait to see me. All the nice little things a boyfriend is supposed to say.

When I walked up the stairs to my apartment, I saw that the lights were on. I smiled. Good old reliable Doug.

I turned the key in the lock. He was waiting just inside the door. I gave him a big hug – unlike Alvee, I wasn't afraid to hug Doug.

I discovered that Doug smelled good. Not as good as Alvee, but good, nonetheless. My senses reveled in his nice masculine smell. I kissed him. Then I really *kissed* him. I forgot about my screenplays for the moment – but only for the moment – and took Doug by the hand and led him to my room.

I exorcised all the demons that had taken up residence in my mind – Alvee's blue eyes, and the delicious sound of profanities issuing from his flawless mouth in his silky voice, his electric kiss in the *Cinerama Dome*, Esther Williams' trick, and the sex scene from *Cheyenne Sundown*.

All the pent-up frustration that these demons had produced in my mind, dancing around in there, pushing buttons and eliciting responses, all the energy that they'd been creating to combat my flagging willpower – I took it all out on Doug, who responded with ardor and pleased surprise. I was enthusiastic, *gymnastic*, giving orders and changing positions.

But when at last Doug collapsed and immediately started to snore – *I bet Alvee doesn't snore*, my mind said – I discovered that all my flying circus acrobatics had been for naught. Sure, I was tired, the edge was off – but a brisk run around the block would've yielded the same result. I found that I couldn't drop off to sleep, exhausted and sated, like Doug.

Lori's words came back to me: *Your friend hadn't been disappointed when they didn't sound like him, didn't smell like him. Your friend hadn't been disappointed* every single time, *because they were not* him.

Doug, who was brown-haired and brown-eyed, didn't look like Alvee, didn't sound like him, didn't smell like him. Not even remotely.

I closed my eyes and watched helplessly while my willpower packed its bags, whistled for a cab, and waved good-bye. I waved back. It was only a matter of time.

Someday, it would be *him*.

FIFTY-TWO

I awoke to the smells of bacon and coffee and the sound of whistling coming from the kitchen. I frowned. Doug was still here. Then I brightened immediately, remembering my director, my leading man, my drawer full of screenplays.

I leapt up and dressed quickly. I rummaged around in the closet until I found a suitable cardboard box. I threw all the little folders into the box, not bothering to look at them. I knew if I started looking at them, I'd start to read them, and biting a fingernail, I'd start to judge which ones were bad and which ones were *really* bad, and then I'd start to take some of them out of the box. Maury said he wanted to read what I wrote, he wanted to make a great film out of one of them.

So I would just send all of them to him, with no second guessing. Second guessing was the enemy. God hates a coward.

Maury was the director. Who was I to decide? I debated throwing the execrable sword and sorcery novel in there, then decided against it. That one was just too awful.

There was a roll of packing tape on the floor in Ruthanne's room. Lonely, dusty, left over from when her mother and sister had gathered up all the odds and ends of her too brief life.

Bring me luck, Ruthie! I thought as I taped up the box. I lugged it out to the living room. It was pleasantly heavy, stuffed full of brilliance, I hoped.

I searched for my keys and found them still in the door. Murderers could've just walked in and killed Doug and me in the middle of our marathon, completely unsatisfying interlude. I was halfway down the steps before I realized that I hadn't even told him where I was going.

I ran back up, stuck my head in the door, called his name. He stepped out of the kitchen, spatula in hand. "I'll be right back," I told him. "I have to run to the post office before it closes." I didn't wait for a reply.

I sat in the car and called the *neophyte*. "Alvee, my darling," I said, echoing my director. I searched for and located a pen in my purse. "I'm going to mail all these Oscar contenders to Maury. Could you tell me the address again?" I could find the place in my sleep, but I didn't know the zip code.

Alvee laughed and told me the address. Then he said, "When will I see you again, Carol?"

Oh, Alvee, I thought, *I see you in my dreams. The very idea of you makes my boyfriend dissolve into fumbling insignificance.* "How about Friday night? That'll give Maury a whole week to plow through this dreck."

"Friday night it is. Till then, then."

How completely adorable he is, I thought.

I started the car and drove to the post office, whistling the appropriately modernized cowboy music from *Cheyenne Sundown.*

FIFTY-THREE

The work week dragged. All the glorious anticipation of my film writing future flagged, then fell, then died. It was all a fantasy. It wasn't real.

Reality was grindingly boring days on the job, eight hours a day, every day, typing briefs and writs, copying testimonies from court documents. It was looking at my meager bank account, noting with a wince what a chunk renting that car had taken out of the bottom line. And then there had been the big bite for putting gas in the rental, as well as the bite for putting gas in my own little beater.

Who did I think I was? I couldn't afford trips to and fro to Beverly Hills every weekend, even if they did feed me and house me and clothe me while I was there. And entertain me. I couldn't forget that. Was I not entertained?

But it was just that. Fanciful, more than I could afford entertainment. Fantasy. Screenwriting and movie making for the legal secretary from a little burg in the Inland Empire?

Right.

Reality was Doug, reliable and just a little boring. Maybe a lot boring.

Reality was that this was my life, and it was never going to change.

And follows so the ever-running year/With profitable labor, to his grave/And, but for ceremony . . .

Ceremony was what Alvee and Maury had, with their million-dollar house and their limos and their movie premieres. With their luaus and their swimming pools and their Japanese chefs, their decades of practically untouched interest on what had to have been stupendous amounts of money to begin with. Ceremony was making movies for fun.

Alvee and Maury, with their supernatural ability to evade the clutches of Mother Nature. They had *ceremony.*

And what did I have? I had a great job and a good boyfriend and a stable future with a successful law firm. What did I know about film writing, about Hollywood, about making movies? What did I know about actors and directors? They were just fantastically wealthy and beautiful people that I was never, ever going to meet.

Except for the two that I already knew, the two that liked me, that I could consider friends. Maury had brought the whole thing up about reading my stuff, hadn't he? Alvee had enthusiastically agreed with him. It wasn't like it had been my idea.

A little ray of the hope that I'd felt so brilliantly when I was last in their company peeped through all those gray clouds of reality. What a tiresome and pointless existence it would be, if we believed that dreams can never really come true. There had to have been at least one happily ever after, or we'd never have heard of the concept.

Happily ever after hadn't happened for Ruthanne, although she'd been on her way to it when tragedy struck. But I couldn't brood on things that I couldn't do a single thing about. Ruthie was gone, and all the brooding and wishing and energy of the universe wouldn't bring her back.

I'd never forget Ruthie. I wouldn't have any of this, neither my stable, boring life, nor the ray of hope that stabbed so insistently through its dreariness, if it hadn't been for Ruthie.

But maybe it was my turn to have a dream come true. Maybe it might really happen. Maybe the three of us could dedicate our film to Ruthie's memory.

Alvee called on Wednesday to tell me that my tedious scribblings had arrived. He didn't put it that way – he said that my screenplays had been delivered, and Maury had them all laid out on the dining room table.

"Does he *like* any of them? Do *you* like any of them?"

"I liked the one where all the people get trapped by a tornado. I thought the love story could use a little beefing up, though."

The Winds of Desire.

"Oh, my God, Alvee, *burn* that one! I wrote that in high school! I didn't even know that one was in there!"

OMG, not *The Winds of Desire!* The love story could use beefing up because I hadn't yet experienced the blissful union of man and woman at the time it was penned. It was a thinly disguised wish fulfillment that I'd written for Ruthanne, about what *could* happen if she and Danny Tripplewhite were trapped underground in a giant storm drain as the result of a tornado.

The cheerleader had been blown away, poor thing, and the water in the culvert was rising. Ruthie had to declare her undying love for Danny, make him see that she was the only girl for him, before they both drowned in rising storm water and purple prose.

"Burn it, Alvee!" I repeated. "Take it out of the stack and *burn it!*"

Alvee laughed. "I also liked the one where Mr. Right turns out to be from another planet. Maury says it's been done, though."

And much better, I'm sure, I thought.

"We both liked the one where the guy's girlfriend leaves him for his buddy, then their daughter turns out to be his. That one's really good."

The Eyes of the Drug Dealer. Coke Dealer is in love with Sassy Redhead. Coke Dealer introduces Sassy Redhead to his buddy, who is Basically a Good Guy. But Sassy Redhead is afflicted like Etta.

Do we really need another reinforcement of the misogynist fantasy of the devoted bride, seemingly happily married at first, who is nonetheless ready to drop her bloomers the minute a strange man enters the picture? No. We do not.

Maybe we did though, if *I* wrote it.

Coke Dealer catches them in the kip, breaks Basically Good-Guy's nose. Coke Dealer leaves town. Sassy Redhead and Basically Good Guy decide that theirs is true love – they get married immediately and a little baby girl is soon born. She is the apple of Basically Good Guy's eye. He loves his new baby almost more than her mom.

The narrator of the story is Basically Good Guy's other buddy, Loyal Friend. Loyal Friend can tell that baby girl is in reality Coke Dealer's daughter – she has his eyes, hence the title. Loyal Friend wonders if Sassy Redhead knows – that's left up to the audience to decide, whether she knows of not.

Some years later, Coke Dealer returns. Loyal Friend sees him at a party – who's on his arm? Sassy Redhead's Daughter, now a rebellious teen.

Loyal Friend confronts Coke Dealer.

"Do you know who she is?" he demands.

"Of course I know who she is. She's Sassy Redhead's daughter."

Coke Dealer intends to corrupt Daughter, has already been corrupting her, to get back at Sassy Redhead for her betrayal.

"Look at her eyes," counsels Loyal Friend.

Coke Dealer tells Loyal Friend that he knows, he doesn't care. He is a seething monster – all he wants is to get back at Sassy Redhead, and Basically Good Guy, too, because Basically Good Guy believes Daughter is his daughter, and loves her very much. Coke Dealer is willing to sacrifice his own flesh and blood on the altar of revenge.

Daughter overhears their conversation. She rushes out into the night and is killed in a car wreck.

Coke Dealer is sorry now. Sassy Redhead and Basically Good Guy mourn.

The audience is still not sure if Sassy Redhead knew who Daughter's daddy was, but we think she might. She has guilt.

The moral of the story – revenge is a dish best served cold, the wages of sin is death.

Fade to black.

"Really?" I said to Alvee. "You guys like *that* one?"

But then they would, I thought. What with all the multi-generational intrigues and goings-on. The motivations were different, but hadn't Alvee and Lori almost lived a similar story? Even the fiction of Maribeth had involved a really big fan that had once been his daughter.

"It's good, Carol. Gritty," Alvee replied. "It would give me a chance to play the bad guy for a change." He chuckled.

"A very bad guy," I said.

The whole story had come to me at my cousin's wedding. She was a sassy redhead – her husband was a basically good guy. His best man was not a coke dealer – he just drove a really nice car.

There had never been a relationship between Best Man and my cousin, so her husband had not stolen her away from him. These people were nothing at all like the characters I made up.

But the idea came to me while they were saying their vows. These three people – what if they *were* this way? What if they did this, and then this happened?

Sometimes inspiration comes from just a simple tableaux like that – three people standing at a wedding. My cousin and her husband and his best man would not have recognized themselves as Sassy Redhead and Basically Good Guy and Coke Dealer. There was no similarity whatsoever between the characters in my story and the actual people that had inspired it. I'd just seen them there, and the *what if's* had started, and the result was *The Eyes of the Drug Dealer.*

I tried to picture Alvee in the role of the heavy. He was too young to be playing the father of a teenage girl, but with movie magic they could make him look older.

Movie magic - make him look older! That struck me as uproariously funny.

In my story, Coke Dealer is a bad man to start out with, what with being a drug dealer and all, but he's essentially an okey-dokey dude. The life of the party. Then he morphs into a *really* bad guy, after his friend's betrayal. The violence of breaking Basically Good Guy's nose unleashes the monster.

Alvee could pull it off, I thought. Instead of longing and lust, he'd have to communicate hatred and revenge with those blue eyes. He could do it.

I'd only hinted at the possibility of an incestuous relationship between Coke Dealer and Daughter – I'd been afraid to actually go there. Coke Dealer was feeding his own daughter drugs in a twisted bid for revenge – that was evil enough, corrupt enough for me. Anything

330

else would've been a little too outré, out of my comfort zone. I was not that edgy.

But Maury was edgy – he of the *controversial eroticism*. He was outré, he reveled in making people uncomfortable. I'm sure that fight scene in *Cheyenne Sundown* had made a lot of people uncomfortable. I thought Maury might actually play up the entirely icky idea of father-daughter incest. Maury might actually *show* it.

Then Alvee would be playing a very bad man, indeed.

I knew he could do it.

It just might work.

FIFTY-FOUR

I didn't even have to come up with a new and different lie to tell Doug, about where I was going this weekend, and why he couldn't come along.

His brother Billy was coming to town for a visit, with his wife and two small tots. They had made reservations, had invited us to stay with them in Anaheim at the Disneyland Hotel. They were planning on making a weekend of it, treating the wee ones to their first visit to the Happiest Place on Earth.

Brother Billy had been two years behind Doug and me in school, and he'd been the most rudely obnoxious person on the planet at the time. I hadn't seen him since our graduation, and had missed him not one single time in all the intervening years. I got Doug to confess that those years and marriage and two kids had not changed Billy's personality. Not in the slightest.

And the only thing that I despised more than Doug's brother was the idea of spending the weekend with him and his little family at the Magic Kingdom. I told Doug as much.

Always the good and thoughtful boyfriend, Doug said he understood. Billy was his brother, after all, and nobody knew better than Doug what a complete ass he was. Doug made a few calls, and it was made up that Billy's wife's sister would go in my place. How the hotel accommodations were going to fall out for that, I didn't know. I could not possibly have cared less.

I was going to be in Beverly Hills with my director and my leading man for the weekend, discussing the finer points of making a movie out of *The Eyes of the Drug Dealer*. Eat your heart out, Mickey Mouse.

And if, for some reason, Doug came back early and discovered my absence, well, that was the glory of a cellphone, now wasn't it? When someone calls, you just make sure you're the first one to ask, "Where are you?" Then you know not to say that you're where they are.

The lie as to where you are usually comes easily, after that. I didn't have a lie already formulated, because the truth be told, I was kinda getting tired of lying to Doug. Not because I was worried about sparing his feelings so much, but because I was getting tired of *him*. He was . . . meh. I was starting to think that it might be getting nigh on to the time to end this little sticky experiment in he'n and she'n, as my grandpa used to say. It already bored me, and the need for all the cloak and dagger was beginning to annoy me.

FIFTY-FIVE

The traffic was an unusually snarly bitch on Friday, and I didn't arrive in Beverly Hills until sunset. As always, Alvee was waiting for me, standing in the middle of the stone staircase, smiling, looking like a million bucks, tax free.

The thought of money again allowed Reality to tear a little gray hole in my sunny mood. *This tank of gas didn't help the liquid assets of Carolyn Adyon, did it?* Reality said. *Not one little bit. Kinda cut into the grocery budget a mite, didn't it? Next week when you're eating ramen, you can enjoy it all the more thinking about how much the drive down here cost you. Maybe you can get Kimura to fix you up a little doggie bag to take home with you on Sunday. When you come back to me.*

But Alvee sent Reality packing, had it get on the same bus as my willpower. Alvee, sauntering down the steps, made me forget all about my boring little Inland Empire life. That was there, and he was here. That was there, and *I was here*, with *him*.

I got out of the car and he gave me a little brotherly hug. That was enough to make all memories of my real life wink out like the glow of a candle wick after the flame has already been extinguished. *This* was my life, right now. Enticing Tithonus and his intoxicating smell.

He took my hand and we climbed the familiar stairs. "Maury's got news for you," he said and grinned.

"About my screenplay?" I asked. *I was in Hollywood now. Where exactly is the Inland Empire again?*

"Oh, no. You're not getting a word out of me. He'll kill me if I say anything."

We walked out to the terrace, where Maki and Maury were seated at the table. Gone was the vase of flowers; there was no only-published-weekly copy of *Variety*, no tattered section of *The New York Times*. The only items on the table were cocktail glasses and a decanter of mint juleps. Maury was consulting the screen of a dark blue HP laptop. He looked over his specs and grinned from ear to ear at me.

"Would you care for a drink, Carol?" he said. "We're celebrating, and you need to catch up."

I nodded. Kimura appeared out of nowhere with an empty glass, and poured me a drink. I told him thanks, he nodded, and disappeared again. I took a chair across from Maury. Alvee sat down next to me.

Maury, still grinning, turned the laptop around.

The site was *FoxNews.com*. There was a still from *Cheyenne Sundown,* where Jody and Reggie are walking down the railroad tracks toward the tottering train. Ryan looked great, as always. Alvee looked great. Both looked perplexed, as befitted the scene. Beneath the picture was the story.

Cheyenne Sundown Rises to Top of Box Office

Los Angeles - When the sun rose on the nation's movie houses on Monday morning, box office receipts for Ryan Gosling's independently released western Cheyenne Sundown proved that fans still enjoy an old-fashioned train heist.

Despite mixed reviews, the movie, starring Gosling and newcomer Alvee Smith-Killem as safe-crackers out for the big score, earned $30 million in North America, and another $70.1 million overseas. The film's opening weekend earnings surpassed the $85 million it cost to make. British ingénue Camellia Swanson also stars.

"It was an incredible opening for an independent film," an industry analyst said. "Ryan Gosling's appeal as a cowboy was not overlooked."

Alvee Smith-Killem's killer blue eyes and smokin' hot body were not overlooked, either, I thought.

I matched Maury's grin. "Congratulations, Mr. Director." I looked at over at Alvee. "Congratulations, *neophyte.*"

"No one will be using that irksome word for him anymore," Maury said. "Not after our little western. I thought about emailing Mr. Stuward with Liberace's immortal words: *What you said hurt me very much. I cried all the way to the bank.*"

Alvee giggled. I looked over at him in surprise. Alvee didn't often *giggle.* "He's been waiting for years to say that to somebody."

"You didn't actually email him?"

Maury smiled smugly. "I didn't have to, now did I? Drink up, Carol. The night is young and so are we – relatively speaking – and it's time to celebrate.

"What d'ya know, Alvee, my darling?" They clinked glasses. "After all these years, I finally made a money-maker."

Maury smiled and drained his drink. Considering the mint leaves in the bottom of the glass, he said, "How can you people drink this stuff? With the little flotsam floating around in there?" He spoke to Maki. Maki looked at his glass, shrugged, smiled. Apparently Kentucky whiskey was okay with Papa-san.

Maury looked over at the pool, where Kimura was lighting the tiki torches. "I'm going to go pick out a nice champagne." He arose and walked unsteadily across the terrace. "We'll talk about your screenplay when I return," he added over his shoulder.

Alvee said something to Maki, and he nodded, held out his glass. Alvee refreshed his julep, and his own. "Carol?" I drained my drink in two quick swallows, and held my glass out, my eyes watering a bit. Kimura was just as good at bartending as he was at cooking – the julep was strong and sweet and minty, just like Ruthie used to make.

I smiled sadly, thinking how happy she would've been at Alvee's success. I liked to believe that she'd also be happy for me, too, here with Alvee, since she couldn't be here herself. What else could I believe?

I drained half my new drink off in one gulp. I had to catch up.

Piano music suddenly, softly rose up from hidden speakers as Maury came back out with four glasses and a bottle of champagne. "In honor of Mr. Showmanship," he said as he set the glasses down. "He was a peach."

"Did you actually meet Liberace, Maury?" I asked.

"Oh, yes," he said. "Unlike myself, he was partial to blondes, after all." He grinned at Alvee. "I was just a kid, really. It was in the early '50s. I had just finished *Miami Moonglow,* and I was over here trying to get Alvee's buddy Patrick Morrison to pick it up for *RKO.*

"Liberace was doing some television in LA – he'd done some work with *RKO,* and Patrick knew him. The three of us all had dinner one night. He was charming, immaculately dressed, hilariously funny." Maury paused, remembering his long-ago dinner with Liberace. "He was a peach."

Maury poured the champagne, and Alvee toasted, "To absent friends."

I liked to believe that my absent friend would be happy for me. But I couldn't brood over things I couldn't do a single thing about.

Maury drained his glass and immediately refilled it. I got the impression that my director aimed to tie one on tonight. That was okay. He deserved it. His film had topped the box office its first weekend out.

"I'm much too smugly basking in the reflected glory of my last project to begin talking in-depth about my next, Carol," he said, sipping his champagne. "But I will tell you that I think I'd like to do *The Eyes of*

335

the Drug Dealer." He frowned. "We're going to have to change the title, of course, and I'd like to shoot it back home, so we'll have to make a few other changes. But I'd like to do it. What do you think?"

Before I could speak, Alvee said, "Maybe Carol doesn't want to change the title, Maury. Maybe she doesn't want to change anything. Maybe she wants to maintain the artistic integrity of her work." He looked at me seriously, but his eyes sparkled. *Oh Alvee,* I thought, *how adorable you are when you're playful.*

"Is that a fact, Carol?" Maury eyed me drunkenly. "You have artistic integrity, do you?"

"None whatsoever, Maury. I can't even spell *artistic integrity.* Change the title, change the location – make them all Eskimos, if you want. I defer to your superior knowledge of the craft of film making, and to your box-office topping draw. I figure you know wherein you speak."

The Kentucky whisky, as it often did, was making me resort to what I thought of as *an elegant turn of phrase.* The phrases would really get to be elegant when I started to slur them.

"I like you very much, Carol," Maury replied. "Your grasp of my directorial skills is astonishingly accurate."

"And if you don't believe him, just ask him," Alvee said.

"It's not my box office draw that we would be counting on, however, if we needed to count on such things." Maury laughed heartily. "It's his." We both looked at Alvee.

"I'm ready for my close-up, Mr. DeMille," Alvee said. "I'm good at being bad. Now we'll finally get it on film."

He smiled slyly at me, that little half a grin. I thought, *I have no trouble whatsoever imagining just how bad you can be, Alvee, my darling.* I grinned back at him, just a little bit slyly my own self. I was sincerely feeling the whisky now.

Alvee's brilliant smile, soon to be known to millions, bloomed. He set his drink down, arose. "Would you like to dance, Carol? It's not often you hear a good piano player these days."

"I don't know how to dance, Alvee," I replied.

"It doesn't matter," he said softly, offering me his hand.

I looked into his eyes and realized that nothing mattered. Nothing at all.

I took his hand. He patiently taught me a few simple steps.

"You know, I dreamed of this once," I told him as we swayed slowly together.

He smiled slightly but didn't say anything. He spun me gently, then brought me back into his arms again.

"It was after Ruthie got me to watch *Manhattan* for the first time. I dreamed that we danced together, in the ballroom, you and me." Alvee just smiled, listening to me talk. "I was a much better dancer in my sleep," I added lamely, mortified that I'd confessed to dreaming about him.

"You're doing okay," he said, and spun me again. I came back a little unsteadily and he put his hands on my waist, drew me close against him. I was enveloped in his smell, could feel his body, warm against mine. I put my arms on his shoulders, then around his neck.

I looked at him, reveled in his beauty. I had resisted it for so long. But when I let myself really look at him, just let myself go, I saw what Maury and Jessika and Lori and Mae and Candace and Ruthanne had known all along.

He *was* Perry Calibri. He was Benedict Arnold and the sad lover in the rain from *Downpour*. He was Jody. He was Franck O'Day. And he was Alvee, and he was holding me in his arms. He was irresistible.

"I'm glad *Cheyenne Sundown* is a hit," he said. "For Maury's sake. It'll be forgotten in a few months, but it's a money-maker. Finally a money-maker for Bobby Ecksmith.

"He's had enough artistic successes, Academy-award nominees, but no blockbusters, no *money-makers*. That's all that matters in this town. Commercial success." Alvee paused. "He doesn't need a dime of the money, of course, but this one put him right smack in the middle of the map. Art will come again later for Maurice Claremount. But a commercial success? It's exactly what he wants right now."

"Here's to getting what you want," I said.

Alvee looked over at the table, but Maury and Maki weren't there. Alvee spun me gently out again, so I could see where they'd gone. They were sitting down at the pool, close together, their feet dangling in the water. They were holding hands.

Alvee put his hands around my waist again, again pulled me close. I put my arms around his neck again. If this was dancing, I was digging it.

Alvee said, "What is it that *you* want, Carol?"

I barked laughter. "What do *I* want? I'm living the American dream, Alvee! Director of blockbusters, of *commercial successes*, Maurice Claremount, is going to make a movie of a story I thought up and jotted down one afternoon after my cousin's wedding. You're going to star in it. How can it not be a hit with that combination? The whole idea – it's . . . it's unbelievable, indescribable. How could I ever want anything more than that?"

"It's a good story. And it'll make a great film. You've got the greatest director I know. But that's all in the future." Alvee looked at me, smiled faintly. "But what is it that you want *right now?*"

I looked up at him and just let it show. I ceased to resist.

One corner of his flawless mouth lifted into that smug, killer smile. "Is that all you want? Why didn't you say something sooner?"

And then Alvee kissed me, slowly, leisurely, just enough passion, just enough tease. Then I felt his breath against my cheek, his incredible voice susurrant in my ear. "Your wish is my command."

He took me by the hand, led me across the terrace. We ran quickly up the stairs, and *this was really happening*, my heart was pounding, the blood was rushing in my ears.

His room was dim but not dark. Moonlight slanted in cinematically, cutting the bed into bars of light and shadow. Alvee moved behind me and kissed the back of my neck – my shiver was immediate, uncontrollable. He put his arms around me, put his hands on my belly. They were hot through the thin material of my blouse. He slid them down slowly and undid my jeans, pushed them off my hips.

The first time, it was all for me, achingly slow and delectably teasing, every pause a delicious agony, an eternity of anticipation. He smiled at my helpless desire, utterly at his command, responsive to his very breath, his slightest touch.

The second time was for him, rough and hard and ardent, as if he meant to devour me, consume me, as if he would obliterate me through the dangerous intensity of his need.

The third time was for both of us, together, watching, learning, catching that faultless synchronicity, riding that perfect rhythm of shared ecstasy.

"Here's to getting what you want," he whispered softly in my ear.

I drifted off to sleep, wrapped in his arms, content beyond imagining.

FIFTY-SIX

I opened my eyes and discovered that I couldn't remember where I was. I took stock. I was in an unfamiliar room, with a strange man's arm around my waist, his body hot and smooth, pressed up against my back. Then I breathed and I could smell Alvee's scrumptious scent, and it all came back to me. It hadn't been a dream at all. I remained motionless, listening to him sleep. His breath was warm, soft and even on the nape of my neck. No. Alvee didn't snore.

I thought that Ruthanne had experienced this, and Jessika, and even, finally, after all those years of waiting, Lori had, too. I thought of all the women, young, old, foreign and domestic, past, present and future, who dreamed of just this wonderful thing. Good for them. Good for all of us.

I considered the sunlight, slanting through the windows, just as the moonlight had done the night before. What time was it? I slid out from under Alvee's embrace, and looked around. The room was lavishly appointed, all dark woods and plush rugs. As I had imagined, there was a walk-in closet, filled with his clothes.

But there was no clock anywhere. What was it that these Hollywood types had against clocks?

I gathered up my clothes and tiptoed into the bathroom, realizing that I had nothing fresh to put on. My suitcase was still in the trunk of the car – my purse was still beside the table on the terrace. Oh, the embarrassment! How Maury was going to grin at me! I was going to have to crawl downstairs, wearing the same clothes I'd had on the night before, when Alvee and I had disappeared together from the terrace like high school kids the moment the chaperone's back is turned.

I peeked into my room. To my astonished relief, my suitcase was on the bed, my purse on the bedside table. Kimura had taken the liberty of fishing my keys out of my purse, and retrieving my suitcase from the car. I wondered dimly when this had occurred, if perhaps he'd heard us. Then I remembered how expensive and well-constructed Jessika's old house was, how adept at keeping secrets. A discreet house and efficient, inconspicuous, discreet servants. More things money could buy.

I reached into my purse and found my phone. It was 10:45. Just enough time to take a quick shower and be right on time for brunch. As if nothing had happened.

I dropped my phone back into my purse, and noticed that there was a fairly thick manila folder underneath it. Inside, I was surprised to find a contract.

It was an agreement between myself and Maury's production company, discussing remuneration for the original work entitled *The Eyes of the Drug Dealer*. It listed a generous salary – in addition to a share of future royalties, I was to be employed as a screenwriter for the duration of the production.

I skimmed the contract. I'd been a legal secretary for quite a while, and the only way I'd kept my sanity was to never read too closely any of the documents I'd typed, some quite similar to this one. And my mind rebelled now, even though that was *my* name there in black and white, *my* name under the blank line where I was to affix my signature. Old habits die hard. It was all too boring, with its *parties of the first parts*, and its *hereafter shall be known as's*.

Comprehension and analysis of these kinds of documents was for lawyers. That's why they made the big bucks – they had the knowledge and the wherewithal and the patience to slog through stuff like this. I was just a typist. I put the contract back inside the folder.

I showered and dressed. I peeked in on Alvee. He was still sound asleep, nose buried in the pillow where my own fortunate head had so recently been. I tiptoed back out of his room, retrieved the contract from the bedside table and went downstairs to face the music.

Brunch had not yet been served – I realized that they were holding it for us. Maury and Maki were seated at the terrace table, as always. Maki was looking at a newspaper lined with strange characters which I assumed were Japanese. Maury was perusing *The Los Angeles Times*, which, unlike *Variety*, was still delivered every day. There were coffee cups and a decanter of coffee. The vase of fresh flowers was back.

Maki looked up and said something to Maury as I approached, and he looked up at me over his specs. "So, Carol," he said, without preamble, as I sat down across from him. "Was it worth it, making him wait?"

Here was a tale Maury had been waiting a lifetime to hear, I realized. Longer than he'd wanted to make a blockbuster movie, longer than he'd waited for his triumphant return to Hollywood's elite. Here was a tale that he'd imagined for nearly sixty years, a tale he'd put on film for the slavering multitudes, for all those hungering fans who couldn't have it any more than he could. But that had only been Maury's imagining of the thing, alluring and fantastically well-lit as it had been.

But I had lived it, was now arriving all rosy-cheeked and fresh-faced from it. Only I could describe it for him, give him the precise details of that one act that he had longed to experience, for all these decades. It was not like he could ever have asked Jessika or Lori. Or Bridget. And he'd never had the chance to meet Ruthanne.

Maury studied my face for another heartbeat, then said, "I'll take that as a resounding yes."

He snapped the paper shut, folded it, and tossed it on the table. Maybe he realized from the look on my face that I'd never be able to tell him. Not that I didn't want to tell him – I would've loved to have told him – nobody would appreciate the description more than Maury.

But maybe Maury, *student of the shameful secrets and perverse foibles of his fellow man* that he was – maybe he knew I couldn't tell him, not because I was shy or ashamed or because I hadn't enjoyed it. Maybe he could tell that I was just not the type that could verbalize such things. Maybe he knew that I couldn't talk about it because I'd enjoyed it *too much* – mere mundane, earth-bound *words* would not be sufficient.

Or maybe Maury was just too sophisticated for such discussions. Maybe he appreciated my inability to talk about it, respected my ability to kiss and not tell.

Regardless, he immediately changed the subject. "I see you found your contract," he said.

"Yes," I said, breaking our unspoken non-discussion of the sublime pleasures of finally getting at Alvee Smith-Killem. "Do you want me to sign it now?"

Maury barked a short laugh. He spoke to Maki, who looked at me in surprise. "Of course you can't sign it now, Carol. Don't you work for an attorney? You must have him look it over, make sure it's all in order, all to your best interest."

"I trust you, Maury."

"Of course you do, my darling. And I trust you. What secrets we all share, eh? But this is business, Carol. Black and white and dollars and cents. Do you have a passport?"

"I do not." I sometimes had a mite of trouble putting gas in the car and food on the table and paying rent, all in the same month. International travel had never been a part of my life plans.

341

"Well, you must apply for one immediately. Jolly old England breathlessly awaits my return. It takes a few weeks to process, and while I'm turning your immortal words into an immortal screenplay, you can have your attorney look over the contract, make any adjustments he sees fit. You can also give him your two weeks' notice and tie up any loose ends you have at home. Then we can all depart for our next great adventure without any tiresome details hanging over our heads."

FIFTY-SEVEN

After brunch, Alvee and Maury and I went shopping. After just one delicious frolic, Alvee and I were a couple now, just like that, for all the world to see. He was as physically possessive as I imagined he got, holding my hand, putting his arm around me, whispering in my ear, kissing me, engaging in all manner of PDA.

The three of us walked around *The Beverly Center*, as if Alvee wasn't starring in a box office smash that was playing all over town. I noticed a few double-takes from a few of the shop girls. Soon this kind of thing would be an impossibility for him, I thought. Soon *TMZ* and the paparazzi would be on Alvee Smith-Killem like ugly on a bulldog.

After the young man behind the cash register at *Chipotle Mexican Grill* shyly, quietly asked for Alvee's autograph, Maury mentioned that filming in England cut down on the paparazzi's numbers a bit. They couldn't all afford the trip over there, he said, and the ones in residence had royalty to pursue.

"We have a better quality of remoras over there," he said. "They're polite and well mannered. They'll only chase you to your death in tunnels."

My director and my leading man had some appointments early Sunday morning, so I left late Saturday night. Something about attorneys and contracts, calling across the pond to speak to agents and actors. Apparently, there was no such thing as business days for Maurice Claremount. The sun shone on Sundays, too, and time was money. No sense burning daylight.

On Saturday night, while I sat at the signal before the entrance to the 101, I remembered that it was the 21st century and I did have an electronic device for communicating with the gray world outside of my bright little Beverly Hills bubble of delight. I turned it on. Doug had called twice. He'd left one text, earlier in the evening: *Call me when you're coming home.*

Oops. That hadn't happened. Too late now, he was probably asleep, worn out from all the thrills of the Happiest Place on Earth.

I hoped he'd been having fun. I hoped he'd been enjoying the heat at Disneyland, with two whiny little kids and his detestable brother. I giggled. I was so sorry I was missing all that. The bright, hot, loud tackiness of the Magic Kingdom, with its legions of people and interminable lines? Or the cool, dim darkness and Tithonus' tender touch? What a decision!

When I showed up at my apartment in the wee hours of Sunday morning, imagine my surprise when I caught Doug in my bed with a woman that was obviously not me. They were not *in flagrante delicto*, but I was still completely gobsmacked. Doug had been living with his parents since his return to town – another thing I'd found annoying about him, and apparently, in the heat of the moment, my place had seemed like a good idea for this little tryst. He was also cheap – something I couldn't stand – and must've figured the risk of getting caught outweighed the cost of a hotel room.

No wonder he'd texted last night: *Call me when you're coming home.* Where he'd supposed I was and how imminent was my return had apparently not stayed him, at least not for too long.

Maybe he was getting tired of my sudden coldness, my every-weekend and sometimes right in the middle of the week absences. Oh, well.

I sat on the couch and waited for him to put some clothes on, to come out and try to explain the unexplainable. I tried to arrange my face in a suitable expression of outraged betrayal, but found I just couldn't do it. I'd been betraying him for weeks, but he was the one who'd gotten caught. That was just funny.

He finally emerged from my room – the least he could've done was used Ruthie's old room, I thought. But there was no bed in there, just the accusing face of Gloria Swanson, glaring down from the wall.

Doug was disheveled, glowing – I'd never noticed him glow after any of our escapades – yet looking just as guilty as he couldn't help but be.

"Carol," he said.

"Who is that?" I inquired brightly.

"That's Meredith. She's Billy's sister-in-law. One of his kids got sick at Disneyland yesterday, so we came home early. Mom doesn't have enough room for all of us. I called, but you didn't answer. Meredith and I came over here. I was going to sleep on the couch, but one thing led to another . . ."

That was the classic expression, was it not? *One thing led to another,* and the part that I was dreading the most, the part involving breaking up with basically nice guy Doug, had been taken care of for me. It was kismet.

"I haven't been completely honest with you, either, Doug," I said.

I've been in Beverly Hills, lazing around the pool, making love with the most desirable man I've ever known. I'm going to England in a few weeks. Richer-than-God director Maurice Claremount is going to produce and direct a movie out of something I wrote. I could not possibly care less about your sleazy little romp with your awful brother's trampy sister-in-law.

"I sold one of my stories. It's the sweetest deal, ever. It's going to be made into a movie . . ." Doug gawped at that, "and they want me to screen write. That's where I've been, talking to the studio." I looked at the contract, on the coffee table where I'd tossed it after walking in on him. I picked it up and flapped it at him.

"I'm going to be leaving for a while." I had no idea for how long, so I just made something up. "For six months or so." Doug just stared at me, open-mouthed. "So, I've got a little deal for you. If you would like to have this apartment as a little love-nest for yourself and . . ." I found I couldn't remember her name. It should've been seared into my brain, the name of the woman I'd caught my boyfriend cheating on me with. But it wasn't. They very idea that I could possibly care who Doug was cheating on me with was ridiculous in and of itself. It was surprising that I could remember *his* name.

"Meredith," he supplied.

"If you and Meredith would like to have this apartment, we'll go see the manager right now. It'll save me the expense of breaking the lease. I'm sure your credit's good enough. I'll even leave you the furniture. The big TV."

What did I need any of this baggage for? I was starting a brand new, exciting life. A dream-come-true life, with my beautiful leading man and my money-making director in glamorous Hollywood. Making movies for fun. Going to premieres. Chatting with *ET*.

Doug and I visited the apartment manager, woke her up. It gave Meredith the opportunity to slink her walk of shame down the steps unobserved.

Arrangements were made. Doug would return with or without his new friend, after I'd packed my stuff and given my two weeks' notice at the firm. I wouldn't even have to pay to have my furniture stored.

I went back up to the apartment that would soon no longer be mine, and gingerly changed the sheets on the bed that would soon no longer be mine either. I plopped down on it and reflected that I should be crying hysterically right now, and maybe I would've been, had I not been where I'd been, doing what I'd been doing, before the awful surprise. If I'd just gone out for a cup of coffee and had returned to find Doug in my bed with some other woman, I might have been sad, indeed.

But I'd been with Alvee, and I remembered his blue eyes gazing into mine. I'd soon be leaving the country with him – even if we did have to fly – traveling to *shoot a movie.*

I just laughed. I hoped Doug and What's-Her-Name would be very happy together.

Everything was working out so unbelievably, so inconceivably *well*.

On Monday morning, I knocked softly on the imposing door to my boss's office. *Uncle Ted,* he'd always been to me, Ruthie's mom's brother. He was tall, and always stood ramrod straight, looking more like the ex-military man he was than the successful, take-no-prisoners trial lawyer that he'd become. But he'd always be Uncle Ted to me.

I told him the same story that I'd told Doug, omitting all mention of Alvee Smith-Killem, as I'd also done with Doug. Alvee's name wasn't anywhere on *my* contract, after all.

Uncle Ted was surprised – his skepticism was plain on his face. He took two days to go over the contract, examining it with the metaphorical fine-toothed comb.

"This looks air-tight, Carolyn," he said at last. "This guy's not trying to cheat you in any way. The salary he's offering is exceedingly generous, and you'll make a good profit off the film." He looked at me with concern. "That is, of course, if the film turns a profit."

I could tell that Uncle Ted thought that I was a babe in the woods. He was suspicious. If something seemed too good to be true, well . . . He had no idea how I'd fallen into such a plum of a deal – he'd had not a clue that I'd ever written a word in my life, and somehow, I could tell that he didn't imagine that his poor dead niece's little friend could write anything that was any good.

So, how *had* I sold something to a movie studio? Even if it was an independent one that he'd never heard of? Was I sleeping with the director, this Claremount guy?

How Maury would laugh at that one, I thought. *'She's not my type, Uncle Ted,' he'd say.*

"There's a possibility that it won't make a dime," Uncle Ted said gravely. "And your contract for paid screenwriting service is only for the length of the project." He paused, allowing the specter of unemployment to creep, all scary and imposing, into the room.

My expression didn't change. I let Uncle Ted see that I was determined. I had a dream. It was all going to work out. He just didn't understand all the facts.

He sighed. "Here's what I'm going to do, Carolyn. You work your last two weeks. But I'm not going to accept your resignation. We're just going to call it a leave of absence. Then, if things don't work out for you as a *Hollywood screenwriter,*" he put the same emphasis on the words as he would've if he'd said *a fairy princess,* "then you can always come back to work for me."

Uncle Ted's magnanimity nearly undid me. How nice of him to see the enticement of such a dream, but also to cushion me when base Reality came back to town, as he was sure it would. I ran around his giant glass and stainless steel desk and gave him a big hug, snuffling back tears. "Thank you, so much, Uncle Ted!"

"It's the least I can do," he said.

It wasn't like I was a partner or anything. They'd hire another girl to take my place, and if I came back with my tail between my legs, begging for my old job back, they'd just move her over and make room for me. But it was the thought that counted, and I was touched by the gesture.

I applied for expedited services when I applied for my passport, and the lady assured me that it would arrive as soon as governmentally possible. I spoke to Maury on the phone, and he told me not to stress about bureaucratic red-tape. We would just wait till it got here. We were not in a hurry. Not yet.

I didn't return to Beverly Hills over the weekend between my last two weeks at work. There were just too many things to do. I packed up my belongings and had them shipped to Alvee's house. I kept back just one suitcase – one suitcase had been enough for Franck O'Day's flight to England in 1967, enough for Lori's to Japan in 1976, and one was enough for me, too. I figured that with my generous new salary, I could just buy anything else I needed once we got there.

I went to the doctor and got a physical, made sure all my immunizations were current. The doctor pronounced me fit as the oft-mentioned fiddle, and told me to enjoy my trip.

I spoke to Alvee frequently on the phone – they were busy, too, with shutting up the house in preparation for an extended absence, and packing, and Maury's writing the screenplay, and stuff like that. I was sad to hear that Kimura wouldn't be accompanying us – he hated to fly as much as Alvee himself did, and there were plenty of adequate cooks in England. And Maki was also staying behind. So Jessika's house wouldn't be standing completely empty, but my director and my leading man still had a lot of stuff to do before bidding Beverly Hills a temporary farewell.

At last the day arrived. I drove to Los Angeles, all aflutter, my one little suitcase on the passenger seat beside me. Everything was glorious expectation, except for the thought of that plane ride. God, how I hate to fly! Perhaps Alvee and I would have the opportunity to get drunk again beforehand.

I parked in the three-car garage beside Kimura's humble Honda. Neither Alvee nor Maury owned a car. They both saw absolutely no need – that's what cabs and limos were for. Ah, the things money could buy!

There was to be no standing in line with the unwashed masses at the United ticket counter, like when I'd last been at an airport, no clandestine drinking out of plastic flasks to steel our nerve. I don't know what I'd been thinking. Maurice Claremount had just directed a box office blockbuster. He had no use for commercial airlines and the unfortunates that were forced to fly on them. The private jet he hired slept four. Alvee and I swallowed a couple of sedatives and cuddled up together. We were asleep before the plane left LAX.

Just like he'd said about his late night escape from Vegas after the fire – we might have changed planes somewhere, but I didn't remember it. We were doped up like rocks stars.

The next thing I remember after crawling into the narrow bed next to Alvee was being jostled by many strange people, strange smells and sounds. I remember being hustled quickly through customs – something about taking the green exit because I didn't have anything to declare.

The sedative had given me a fierce headache. It was just the start of the nightmare.

FIFTY-EIGHT

A limo took us to a very nice hotel. It was near the studio – Alvee and Maury didn't drive over here anymore than they did in the States, where they drove on the other side of the road. I don't remember much of our arrival. Just Alvee and I collapsing in a huge, fluffy, soft bed to sleep off the rest of the sedatives.

The following morning commenced my very first production meeting for the movie version of *The Eyes of the Drug Dealer*.

We sat around in rows, on folding chairs, in a large, dim, cold, drafty room at the studio. Maury stood behind a podium. The first thing I discovered was that the title had been changed to *Kinship*. The second thing I discovered was that my indolent Hollywood playboys were gone.

Maury introduced himself, began speaking to the assembled cast and crew like a general, anticipating a rough battle ahead. There would be casualties.

Alvee sat next to me, but didn't smile, didn't hold my hand. He didn't look at me at all. When Maury introduced him, he stood, gave a little unassuming wave, and sat back down. He was the lead, but he was also the only American in the cast. His little self-effacing wave said, *I know you're all wondering who the hell I am, and that's okay.*

They know who you are, Alvee, I thought. *Cheyenne Sundown did $70.1 million overseas. They all know who you are. They're just not very friendly.*

Sassy Redhead was not a redhead at all but a dark-haired, green-eyed beauty named Melissa Holloway. Her character's name was Cynthia. She eyed Alvee with undisguised interest. I still had a bit of a headache, and some ghetto part of my mind wondered if I was gonna have to cut this bitch if she thought her English actress ass was going to get anywhere near *my* Alvee. But Alvee didn't look at her twice, and the jealous tough girl that I really wasn't subsided.

The role of Basically Good Guy – the character's name was Georgie – was to be played by a thin, unspectacular chap named Jacob Lysander. He smiled and waved and sat immediately back down after his introduction.

Loyal Friend – his character's name was Steven – was to be brought to the screen by Jameson Allen Sanders. Maury mentioned his work in London theater – this was to be his first film role.

Where Alvee was dark-haired and lean, Sanders was blonde and robust, with cheerful tan eyes and a ruddy complexion. They were perfect foils. Maury knew how to pick a cast.

The various other supporting actors and extras were quickly introduced. Then in the moment of silence that followed, as if on cue, the young actress that was to play the Daughter bustled in, dragging a suitcase on a stick, carrying a large purse. Her entrance reminded me of Dora's in *High Times in Manhattan:* all a fluster, in a hurry, harried, seeking to be the center of attention.

"Ah, Miss Rushtin, how nice of you to join us," Maury began, amicably enough. "Take a good look at Miss Rushtin, everybody."

Which is just what she wants you all to do, I thought.

"Because if she ever interrupts one of my meetings again, it will be the last time you see her." Maury was not kidding, not in the least. The playful, deviously off-color gentleman that I knew from poolside at Jessika's house was gone. A sardonic, unimpressed, unamused auteur had taken his place.

He glared mildly at the young actress. "In the future, Miss Rushtin, if you find yourself running late, please wait outside until the meeting has concluded. If you miss anything important . . . well, maybe you should make the extra effort to get here on time."

Miss Rushtin sat down, suitably chastised. But Maury was not quite finished with her. "Stand up, Miss Rushtin, allow me to introduce you. You've already caused disruption enough. My esteemed colleagues, this is Alyson Rushtin. She is set to play the part of Rebecca. That is, if she ceases to be the *late* Miss Rushtin."

Alyson sat back down, embarrassed. She would not pull another ingénue stunt like this again.

But looking at her, I thought that she could arrive as late as she cared to, and Maury wouldn't fire her. He had the upper hand, he had cowed her. But even if that was not the case, I knew that he wouldn't replace Alyson Rushtin. His casting genius was too much embodied in her.

She looked enough like Melissa Holloway – who, beautiful or not, was indeed old enough to be her mother, I now noted with no little satisfaction. She was forty if she was a day.

But Alyson's resemblance to Alvee was uncanny. She was not too much younger than him, probably twenty-two or so, I guessed. They would young her up for the part, just like they were going to old Alvee up to play her father. They wouldn't have to old up Melissa at all, I thought with nasty glee. But I thought Maury would have to use a great deal of industrial light and magic indeed to make her into Alvee and Jacob's peer in the early scenes.

But in street clothes, Alvee and Alyson could be brother and sister. *Twins. Come to think of it, ol' Melissa could pass for mother to both of them*, I thought with a little inward chuckle. Chuckling, even inwardly, made my head pound.

Maury introduced me as the author of *this little story upon which our livelihood depends.* I stood up, waved, sat back down. A paranoia, maybe akin to the little ghetto girl in my head, made me notice a few sly grins among the crew. A grip in the back leaned in and said something to his buddy, who snickered.

It occurred to me that I wasn't so much the author to them, as I was the American lead's on-set squeeze. A trace of the *artistic integrity* that I'd so recently denounced flared up in me. I *had* written the damn thing. Commercially successful director Maurice Claremount had chosen *my* story, said he'd wanted to make a movie out of it, before I was the American lead's squeeze. But they didn't know any of that. Nor did they care.

Did I really need to be here, sitting in on production meetings, watching Maury berate the ingénue? It wasn't like he was going to consult with me, ask my opinion on anything. He'd already changed the title, changed the location, given the characters British-sounding names. I didn't care about any of that. It was still my story.

But this was Maury's show, one hundred and twenty percent, and if anybody didn't think so, then they could just wait outside with Miss Rushtin's ego until the meeting was over.

Couldn't I have just cashed my check and stayed home? Why was I here? Strangely, the idea that I was here because Maury, and more especially, *Alvee*, wanted me here, offered little comfort. I wondered what the grip had said to his buddy, what English cameraman lingo for *the star's girlfriend* might be. I doubted if it was even remotely that nice.

Fuck 'em, I said to myself. Why should I care what they thought? Maybe this headache was making me overly sensitive. *I am the star's girlfriend*, I thought resentfully, *and I did write the damn story*.

Maury mentioned the budget. He said *over-budget* was not a word in his extensive vocabulary.

Then he handed out the shooting schedule. I noted that location shots would be done last. The timeline listed the date, the time, who was in the scene, what props were necessary, which costumes. The period allotted for lunch was seldom more than forty minutes.

Then Maury introduced the film's director of photography, whom he called Mr. 8 Millimeter. "He's says we could shoot the whole thing on a handheld and save millions," Maury said and clapped the man on the shoulder. In other words, *over-budget* was not in the cinematographer's extensive vocabulary, either. "If you have any sort of problems, please complain to him," Maury advised cast and crew. "I'll be busy."

Indeed, I thought. Maury was producer, director, and screenwriter, too. He hadn't asked me to write another word. He'd just taken my little folder and run with it. That was all okay with me.

But the new, brusque, all-business Maury intimidated me more than just a little bit. I didn't want to give him cause to yell at me like he had Miss Rushtin. I knew Maury's sense of humor, had seen a new, almost cruel knife-edge to it. If I got in the way, I could picture him mentioning, before the whole foreign lot of them, that I really *was* nothing but Alvee's squeeze.

Maury dismissed Mr. 8 Millimeter and the crew. They were to reassemble somewhere else and have further discussions. Shooting would start in the morning.

The bit players grumbled when Maury suggested a quick table read, but silence immediately reigned when he looked at them. I realized that I was expected to sit in on it, and I did so. I thought it was brilliant, but no one asked my opinion.

The shoot began. I sat near enough to Maury, but not near enough to be in the way. He didn't have time for me at all, which was okay, because he had become awesome, unapproachable in his director-ness. He was Robert Ecksmith, director of Academy-award nominees – he of the *controversial eroticism*, of the guts and nerve it took to attempt *to canonize a universally reviled traitor*. He was the director of the multi-talents of mega-star Ryan Gosling, the director of international commercial successes. He was everything I thought a director should be, actually – terse, sarcastic, impatient, loud. But I didn't want any of that directed at me.

I was confused by the technical aspects of the production, the chronology of things – scenes were shot out of sequence to the point where I couldn't even follow my own story.

It wasn't like Maury ignored me, he was just busy. He'd offer me a little smile or nod on occasion – but we were not brunch buddies like we were back home. We did not sit around and idly discuss Alvee's beauty. He lunched with Mr. 8 Millimeter, or his actors.

His actors lunched with him, or with each other. Alvee invited me to join them once, but they clearly gave me the impression that they were all embarrassed for me. *These Americans! They think that they can just*

*bring along the piece du jour, call her a screenwriter, and have her sit right down and
conversate like she's just as good as we are.*

Alvee noticed it, and kind of shrugged apologetically to me. *Oh,
well,* his gesture said, *such snubs are all part of the game.*

"They're just jealous because you got to meet Ryan Gosling," he
said to me after they all discovered that *Gee, look at the time! We've got to
get back on-set.* Even though there was still twenty minutes left on lunch.

"I love you, Alvee," I said, and I meant that I loved him for
making fun of his British co-stars, for making me smile.

"I love you, too, Carol," he said, and kissed me right there in front
of all of them, cast and crew.

Something he never did for Miss *Yerdlay,* Aunt Mae's voice said in my
head.

He was Alvee Smith-Killem, American co-star of an international
box-office blockbuster, and I was his girlfriend. The opinions of a
bunch of British unknowns meant less than nothing to him.

Alvee left to return to work, and I thought about what we'd just
said. Did he love me? Did I love him? Is that why'd I'd said it, even
though I hadn't meant it the way he thought I did?

I couldn't dwell on it at the moment. I didn't love anything right
then. Not him, not Maury, not England. Not *Kinship,* not the business
of making movies, neither cast nor crew. I loved myself least of all. I
was miserable. I felt self-conscious and out of place. Unwanted. And it
was only the first week of shooting.

The food was awful, the weather wet and cold and gray, the
production schedule grueling. There was none of that romantic London
fog that I'd heard about, either. Since I was really not needed on the
set, I took a few walks out onto the streets around the studio. These
people spoke English – but it wasn't an English that I could be quite
sure I was comprehending fully. So I quickly gave up on experiencing
an unaccompanied English holiday and went back to the studio and
watched the production. I was neither cast nor crew, so nobody said
anything to me. I took to feeling sorry for myself.

As the shoot proceeded, I discovered that my darling Alvee was
something of a Method actor, at least while the sun was up. If I got a
rare chance to talk to him between takes, he remained in character as
Lawrence – he was cold and distracted, as if he really was tormented by
betrayal and thoughts of revenge.

I would've pouted and thought he was angry with me, or even
tired of me – Alvee was a very good actor – except for the fact that at
night, after the shooting was concluded, after he was done discussing it
with Maury, after he was done with all aspects of *Kinship* for that day,

Alvee would crawl into bed beside me, and smile at me, and tell me he loved me. At night, in bed, he was my Alvee again, all mine, warm and flawless and irresistible. At night, we were a couple again.

There was a power outage at the studio, and we lost almost an entire day's shooting.

Alvee slipped in the mud on location and twisted his ankle. He limped. Maury considered adding the limp in as part of the character, but too much footage of Alvee not limping had already been shot. I thought Maury might fire the continuity supervisor when she gently, bravely pointed this out to him. But the director knew she was right. Alvee hadn't limped for three quarters of the film, and there was no reason he should be limping now, unless they wrote a scene demonstrating how he had acquired the limp. And that might cause us to go *over-budget*. Not to mention that such a scene would be extraneous to the story, would not advance the plot in the least. So it was a trope to which the veteran director would not stoop.

So there was another two day delay while Alvee's ankle healed sufficiently enough that, with the aid of a pain killer or two, he could effectively hide the limp. Then he wasn't even there for me at night, anymore, because he was sleeping off the pain killers.

I became cranky, melancholy, downright bitchy. Maybe this whole movie making thing wasn't for me, after all. I thought about Alvee. He snored a little now – it was because of the pain killers, and I laid there beside him in our over-soft English hotel bed and I tossed and turned, and I thought about him.

He said he loved me. Ever since I'd said it first, he said it all the time now. But did I love him in return? I always said it back, but was I really thinking that egotistical reply he'd used to tell Jessika?

I love you, Franck!

I know you do, Jessika.

No, I wasn't thinking that, because I didn't know for sure if he did love me. I wasn't feeling too loved at all.

I knew I loved to *love* Alvee. He was the pluperfect, archetypal *best*. Of any man I'd ever even *seen*, nonetheless known – I'd never choose anyone else for a lover over Alvee, not even Ryan Gosling. But was that love?

I thought about Lori, and the almost unbearable yearning she'd had for him. But long after he'd *put their sordid little congress to the sword*, as Maury had so eloquently phrased it, I'd observed the interaction between Lori and her still-desired lust object. Once the physical aspect was gone, it hadn't seemed as if Lori had liked Franck O'Day all that much, and it had seemed as if he had barely tolerated her.

Was I like Lori? Was it just Alvee's body, his consummate skill, that I loved?

I knew that I *liked* Alvee very much. I also liked Maury, except that I found them both entirely too different, too alien and unfamiliar, while they were filming. They had become unsympathetic, professional strangers to me. Maury was too busy, and Alvee was cold and distant, when he wasn't snoring in my ear. When he was awake, when he was on-set, he'd become the character I'd written, angry and betrayed. I imagined that he might behave in a similar manner if I let him discover that I was doubting our so recently declared love.

Sure, I liked them both, my wealthy and talented Hollywood friends. But if you took away the incredible sexual aspect, the physical chemistry between Alvee and me, I began to think that the way I felt about them was pretty much the same.

That one little part of my mind, that part that had never quite believed that the fire in Vegas had all been an accident, the part that trusted in the power of dreams, came alive in England. It liked the climate, enjoyed the food, was amused by the people. It spoke to me frequently, most often when I couldn't sleep.

Yeah, sure you like Alvee and Maury, it whispered. *Truth be told, you might actually even like Maury a little bit more than sweet, sexy Alvee, eh? You certainly trust him a little bit more. He did not, after all, miraculously escape a fire that killed seventy-five people. You did not dream that he'd started the fire in the first place, while robbing those people of their very life-energy, in order to make himself young again. Maury didn't say to you in that dream that he was sorry that he'd had to take Ruthanne. That had all been the pretty boy. He's got the bluest eyes, and perhaps – just perhaps – the blackest heart imaginable.*

But Maury's in possession of the same Eastern secret, is he not? Maybe you can't trust him too much, either. He surely doesn't look ninety, does he? And he has never mentioned what happened in Vegas, has he? Not once.

Just when I thought I couldn't feel any more depressed, I and most of the crew caught a nasty stomach flu - probably from the food on set. I thought it may have been from the food in general. The skeleton crew of those not spending all day in the loo crawled forward as best they could.

At the same time, Alvee's ankle stopped bothering him. He stopped taking the pain pills, stopped snoring. The limp was gone, the spring returned to his step.

I laid in bed for two days, my stomach feeling like it was being wrung out by unseen hands, like a soppy dishrag.

By the afternoon of the second day, I was feeling a little better. I was still tired, homesick. But I couldn't just lie around my English hotel room, feeling sorry for myself. They were *making my story into a movie*, right down the street. The least I could do was go and experience it, even if cast, crew, and director made me feel like an unnecessary outsider.

I got up and took a nice, hot, restorative shower, got out, wrapped a towel around myself. I stood in front of the bathroom mirror for a long time, taking stock of my naked face. I looked ashen, drawn, exhausted. I caught a tiny glint in the mirror – to my horror, it was a gray hair.

I was in the process of plucking it out when Alvee came in. He kissed me lightly on the cheek, observed me with the gray hair extended between my fingers.

"Don't pull it out, Carol," he said and grinned. "Three more will grow back in its place."

I yanked the gray out, then turned around and looked at him. "Am I getting old, Alvee?" I asked. A terrible thought had occurred to me.

"Never regret growing old, Carol," he said seriously. "It's a privilege denied to many."

I barked laughter. "That's easy for you to say."

Are you making me old, Alvee? I thought. *Are you siphoning off all my boundless sexual energy, to keep yourself young, to heal your foot? Are you using me up like you used up Lori, making her old before her time, because you realized that she didn't really love you? Do you think I don't love you, Alvee?*

Do I love you, Alvee?

Alvee smiled at me, took both my hands in his. He closed his eyes, and I felt his hands grow warm in mine. Then the warmth expanded, becoming agreeably hot. Then my arms started to tingle and the pleasant heat traveled up and dispersed throughout my whole body in the most surprising, most delightful way.

Alvee opened his eyes. "Do you feel a little better now, Carol? My little American girl lost?"

I did feel better. He had done the energy trick again, and I felt better enough to know that he was making fun of me. He knew I'd been feeling sorry for myself, that it hadn't just been the stomach flu that had kept me in bed for the last two days. I'd been living in my own little Pity City, population, me.

And Tithonus was chiding me about it.

Alvee drew me to him, hugged me tightly, kissed me on the forehead. "You know, Carol, I've been thinking about you a lot lately. I know we haven't spent a lot of quality time together during this shoot –"

"You snore, Alvee, do you know that?" I said, hugging him back. I felt invigorated, lighter than air. My mood had changed, like flipping on a light switch. That was one neat trick he did. "You're too much in character, *neophyte*. You snore like you really are a coke dealer, like you have a deviated septum from years of self-abuse."

"I never engage in self-abuse," he said, smiling slyly at me. "And I don't snore."

"Whatever you say." I kissed him quickly.

Alvee looked at me, his grin fading to seriousness. "Look, Carol. I've been thinking about you and me a lot. I've been thinking a lot about *us*. I was wondering, if you think that we might have it in us. To make a go of it, like –"

There was a sharp rap at the door. Alvee stopped talking, looked toward it. What had he been saying? My life really was like a movie sometimes – were there ever interruptions like this IRL? At such critical junctures? What had he been saying? That we could make a go of it? What was that, Hollywood-speak for *marriage*?

"Open the door, Carol," Maury's voice said. "I know you're in there."

Alvee smiled, kissed me quickly. "Your director beckons," he said. "We'll talk about this again on the plane."

"The plane?" I asked.

Maury pounded on the door again.

"Can I let him in? Are you decent enough?"

I looked down at myself, all wrapped up in the big, fluffy, English-hotel towel. I was decent enough.

Alvee opened the door and Maury stalked in. He looked at me with a mixture of anger and concern. It was strange, one of his formidable auteur expressions. Then he smiled, almost like the old Maury. "What *are* you people doing? In the middle of my shooting schedule?"

Alvee held up his hands in a little warding-off gesture. "I'm innocent, boss."

"What are you doing here, Maury?" I asked. "Both of you? In the middle of your shooting schedule?"

"It is, as they say, a wrap," Maury said and grinned. He and Alvee high-fived. I blinked in surprise at the gesture, at his words.

"And oh, my Christ, it's about time," Alvee said. "This is the absolute worst shoot I've ever been on. If collective pains in the ass equate to Oscar contention, then we're a shoo-in."

"Do you mind if I have a word with your woman alone, Alvee, my darling?" It was the first time he'd called Alvee his darling since we'd left the States. "I promise not to de-towel her."

Alvee smiled, shrugged. "It's a woman's prerogative to change her mind. And you are a sexy beast."

"It's not too late to call Ryan and reshoot the whole thing, you know. If he's not too busy counting his money from *Cheyenne Sundown*." Maury smiled smugly.

"I'll be in the bar," Alvee said.

FIFTY-NINE

Maury and I sat down at the obligatory little hotel room table. I was reminded of Lori's story about her room in Japan, of the little table from which she'd leapt up and attacked Franck. I thought about the little table in her room in Las Vegas, from which she'd told me the story about the other one. I wondered if all hotel rooms, world-wide, have little tables, set up for life-changing vignettes.

Maury took both my hands in his. "I come here on bended knee, Carol, to beg forgiveness for the terrible treatment you've received here. My countrymen, especially the actors, can be a bunch of cliquish assholes sometimes. Especially Melissa.

"Alvee's watch was set to LA time, *your time*, you see, so he just couldn't give *her* the time of day." Maury grinned. My friend was back. "She didn't take that well at all, and I'm afraid she took it out on you. And the rest of them . . . I've worked with them before. They know I wrote the screenplay. They refused to understand that it's still your story. That's why you deserve to be here.

"And Alvee and myself – we are professionals, my dear. It only would've been worse for you if we would've taken time out to hold your hand."

"I don't know, Maury," I said, stung by his gentle derision. "I've been miserable here."

"You can't let this one shoot dissuade you from the business, Carol. It was a miserable shoot. The weather, the equipment, the food. The rude crew, the stuck-up cast. The bitchy director and the snotty leading man." He squeezed my hands. "You've got it in you, Carol, I know you do. *He* knows you do. This is the life for you. You're a trouper, if you'll just get over yourself a little bit." He grinned.

"You can't let one lousy shoot and a bunch of condescending English actors get you down. You've got to hold your head up high. You've got to remember that we're all only here because of *your story*.

"And besides – you're going home, to hot, sunny Southern California, to the Mecca of the entertainment industry. *Home*, Carol. They're stuck here in the shire."

I smiled at the thought of Melissa Holloway milking cows.

"Let me tell you a little story. I promise I'll be brief. We don't want to leave Alvee too long alone in the bar, now do we?" Maury winked.

"I'd only been in the States for a short time. It was in the '50s, like I said. I was shopping around for a studio to pick up *Miami Moonglow*. The only person I really knew here was Patrick Morrison. He said he'd see about trying to get *RKO* to pick up the picture, but it really wasn't their sort of thing. I doubted his ability to talk them into it – I started to doubt my own abilities. It was a dumb picture, I was a dumb director. My ambition had outpaced my youth. I was going to spend my whole career in places like this," he gestured at the room.

"I'd been in LA for a few months, had a little apartment. Some big film director I was. There was a little market around the corner from where I lived. I used to go in there, every day. The young man that worked there, he was adorable, and friendly. He asked me what I did – you know me, I told him all my grandiose plans for taking Hollywood by storm.

"There was always a little old lady in the market. She sat in a rocking chair, just to one side of the counter, like something out of a Ma and Pa Kettle movie."

I shook my head, not getting the reference.

Maury shook his head back. It wasn't important.

"I'd go into the market and talk to the young man – his name was Pablo – and the old lady – she was his grandmother, his *Nana* – she would ask him what I said. He would translate, back and forth, and we'd have little conversations that way, mostly about the weather.

"So one day, I go in there, and I'm depressed. I'd just talked to a guy from *Paramount*. He hadn't even been polite when he turned down *Miami Moonglow*. Morrison wasn't returning my calls. Things were looking grim. I was facing the possibility of coming back here, to all of this." He smiled. "Or giving up directing all together, taking some screenwriting job that was below me.

"I went into the market, said hello to Pablo and Nana.

"*'Por qué estás tan triste, Rubio?'* Nana asked me. 'Why you look so sad, Blondie?'

"I told Pablo that it didn't look like any of the studios were going to pick up my picture for distribution. I told him I only had one prospect left.

"Nana asked what I'd said, and Pablo translated. Nana closed one eye and squinted at me appraisingly, then said something to Pablo. My Spanish wasn't very good at the time, and I waited for him to translate.

"'She says that you have to walk as if you're going *to* a battle, not coming from it, Bobby. If you look like you've already lost when you walk in, then you've already lost.'

"And that has been my philosophy on life ever since, Carol. Walk as if you're on your way *to* the battle – and you'll win most of them. Walk as if you've already been defeated, and you'll lose every time." Maury paused.

"Did *RKO* pick up *Miami Moonglow?*" I asked.

Maury shook his head. "It wasn't their kind of film. But there were other films and other studios. Until, after an unnaturally long life, here I am in this dreary hotel room, asking you to forgive me for this horrible shoot.

"What do you say, Carol? Will you walk into the wrap party on my arm, as if you're still on your way *to* the battle? Because the battle has only just begun. There's still post-production. And your subject matter might raise a few eyebrows, Stateside, especially the way I shot it." He grinned evilly. "You're going to miss Melissa's aristocratically catty snubs once the vulgar peasant reviews come out."

Maury paused, smiled kindly at me. "You know, a lifetime of this kind of three-ring circus awaits you, if you want it."

"I wouldn't miss it for the world, Maury." I leaned across the table and kissed him on the cheek. "I only have one question – when are we going home?"

Maury took my face in both hands and kissed me on the forehead. "I miss home, too Carol, more than you know. I miss Papa-san."

Of course he did, I thought. *The other half to his whole.* In my self-pity, I'd forgotten all about Maki, all about their youth-preserving shared energy.

"We should be out of this vale of tears in about two days, if you can pack quickly enough. Tonight, I take my favorite writer and her ugly boyfriend out on the town. Tomorrow, we suffer through the wrap party. The morning after that, we are homeward bound."

He arose. "I'd send Alvee back up, but I fear he might delay you getting dressed. Put on your dancing shoes, Carol. London swings like a pendulum do."

The next two days were a happy whirlwind of dressing-up and drinking and dancing and back-slapping congratulations. If my life really was like a movie, then Jacob and Jameson and Alyson would've all taken the time, either individually or as a group, to congratulate me, too, to tell me how much they'd enjoyed bringing the tale I'd told to life. Melissa would've told me how lucky I was to have Alvee, perhaps admitted that I was obviously the better woman, therefore.

None of that happened. And I didn't care, because Maury and Alvee were back to being my buddies again, and that was all that mattered. I entered the wrap party with one of them on each arm. If anything, the English cast of *Kinship* blanked me even more at the party than they had during the shoot.

I found that the puny disapprobation of this cadre of English unknowns bothered me not at all. The movie was in the can – *my movie* – I dared to think of it. I was going home tomorrow, back to sun and surf and a big, fat bank account.

I hoped, sincerely, that they all enjoyed the shire.

SIXTY

When we boarded the private jet to fly back to no place like home, I resisted the sedatives Alvee offered. All they did was make me want to sleep for the entire next day. I felt bad about losing the time.

"It's a twelve hour flight, Carol," Alvee said. "Twelve hours of turbulence and engine drone – what was that noise?" He grinned. "And twelve hours of *him.*" He nodded at our director.

Maury was reading a tabloid called *The Daily Mirror*. He looked at me over his specs, then went back to reading. Plane crash survivor or not, flying was not a problem for Maury.

I wouldn't mind talking to Maury for twelve hours, but I had to admit that Alvee was right about the rest of it. The stress of thinking that I might die at any moment, and that there wasn't a damn thing I could do about it, would make me tired enough to sleep for the whole next day, too, just like the sedatives.

I swallowed the pills and climbed into the narrow bed with Alvee.

"When we get home, there's something I want to talk to you about, Carol," he whispered, his breath soft and damp in my ear. "I have big plans for us."

"Whatever you say, *neophyte,*" I replied. I'd worry about all that if I made it home alive.

SIXTY-ONE

In *Titus Andronicus*, Aaron brags of his own evilness to his enemy's son:

> *Oft have I digg'd up dead men from their graves,*
> *And set them upright at their dear friends' doors,*
> *Even when their sorrows almost were forgot;*
> *And on their skins, as on the bark of trees,*
> *Have with my knife carved in Roman letters,*
> *'Let not your sorrow die, though I am dead.'*

I dreamed that I was back in Las Vegas. VFW Post 864 was ablaze all around me. I stood in a flameless patch of the ugly floor. Ruthanne and Lori and Candace and Mae and Penny stood in a semi-circle around me, burning, kept back by the magical circle of the fact that it was all just a dream.

Like Aaron, my subconscious mind was come to chide me. I'd forgotten them. In all my happily-ever-after bliss, I'd forgotten that these people, now lost forever, had once been my friends. *How could I have forgotten them? Why did I no longer mourn for them?*

Ruthanne looked as if she had prepared for some undercover night ops mission. Her face was black, interspersed with streaks of dark gray. Her hair was on fire. Her green eyes blazed out at me. "Be careful, Carol," she said.

Half of Mae's face had melted, was sliding onto her shoulder. She said, "If you wanna know, if he loves you so, it's in his kiss."

Candace, a ring of flames haloing her vacant eyes, added, "That's where it is."

Lori said, "Beware those gray hairs, Carol." Then her ancient face was obscured by a sheet of fire.

Penny's skin bubbled, just above the eyebrows. She said, "It's really *him*, Carol! It's really Franck O'Day!"

I tried to wake up, tried to scream. But the sedatives held me down, like an iron hand on the back of my head, keeping me drowning in this sea of fire and horror.

The emotion that came from the ghosts of my friends was not resentment, however. They were not here to accuse me of forgetting them, of letting my sorrow die. Mourning has a season, just like all other epochs of life, they seemed to say. It isn't meant to last forever. It was okay with them that I'd moved on.

Neither did they resent my happiness. They understood that Alvee was irresistible and they did not begrudge me my enjoyment of him. They all would've gladly changed places with me, if the opportunity had been granted to them. My taking advantage of his charms was not the issue. *His charms themselves were not the issue.* Even from beyond the grave, even though they were telling me that he had sent them there, they still understood Alvee's appeal.

The vibe that I got from my burning friends was simply one of worry, of anxiety for my safety, of concern that this stunning, tantalizing, ageless creature might – just might – do to me what he'd done to them.

"Be careful, Carol," they said in unison, as the flames rose and the ceiling collapsed. "Stay watchful."

I at last shook off the sedative and snapped awake. The plane was dim. Its engines droned in a mechanical monotone, supplying the illusion of safety. Maury dozed in his seat. Alvee slept silently beside me, a little smile on his lips. Alvee wasn't having nightmares.

I closed my eyes and hugged him to me.

It was just a dream. He was reality. Supernatural, perhaps dangerous. But real and alive and beautiful. The sedatives started to reclaim my mind, dulling everything but the sound of Alvee's breathing, his intoxicating scent. I relaxed, letting them do their job, letting them take me back to dreamland.

There would be no more nightmares, but that one part, that part that remained watchful, stubbornly fought the sedatives right up to the last moment. That part of my mind would always be marching *to* the battle.

SIXTY-TWO

The joyful reunion with Maki and Kimura at Jessika's house was a brief one. Just like after the flight over to England, I had a headache from the sedatives. All I wanted to do was sleep. Alvee and I went upstairs, and after a quick, glad-we-made-it-home-alive celebration, we passed out together.

I awoke around one o'clock the following afternoon. I was alone. I got up and got dressed, found Alvee at the terrace table, enjoying lunch. Maki was swimming his dog-paddle laps in the pool. Maury was nowhere in sight.

"The task is all on him now," Alvee said, when I looked at him questioningly at Maury's absence. "He and Mr. 8 Millimeter and the post-production guys. We won't see him much for the next couple of months." Alvee smiled. "But he loves this part, even more than the shooting, I think. Fewer egos to deal with."

Kimura materialized, stood silently beside the table. "He wants to know if you want something to eat," Alvee said.

I shook my head. Kimura nodded and dissolved back into the house.

I put my purse on the table and began rummaging around in it. I wanted to put my hair back, and had left the tie in Alvee's room. I knew there was another one in there somewhere. I took out my wallet and my sunglasses and a small make-up bag. My keys.

"Whatcha got there, Carol?" Alvee asked, gesturing at my keys.

I picked them up. I still had the little California license plate with my name on it that Ruthie had given me. I'd given the key to my old apartment to Doug, but I still had a key to Uncle Ted's office. My car keys.

I still had the two little green keys that symbolized my membership in the now defunct Franck O'Day Fan Club. They were what Alvee had meant when he said, *Whatcha got there?*

I held my key ring out to him, and he took it from me, held the two green keys between his thumb and forefingers, studied them.

"What was the movie about, Alvee?"

Alvee looked up at me blankly.

"Two Green Keys. The movie. What was it about?"

He shrugged. "I don't much remember. I only read the script once – we only shot a couple of reels. It was a romance, but there was also some mysterious element to it. Something about the keys opening some kind of secret box or room or something, somehow revealing some earth-shattering secret. For the life of me, I can't remember what the secret was supposed to be."

He paused, looked again at the keys between his fingers. "I remember I didn't get much of an impression of you from the ones you sent in," he said. "There's a little spark of you in these – they're definitely *your* keys, now. But the ones you sent in originally – I got nothing."

"Ruthie told me to mediate on them before I sent them in."

"Did you?"

"I most certainly did not. I thought it was all bullshit."

Alvee smiled. "Do you think it's all bullshit now?"

I barked a little laugh. "Oh, no. I don't know if there's any energy stored in keys. But you've definitely tapped into one of the secrets of the universe, Alvee. You're proof of its existence."

How dangerous it might be to me, I still don't know, I thought.

"Inanimate objects retain some of our energy, Carol," he said. "Favorite teddy bears, good luck charms – they all hold a little spark of the people that hold them and touch them and wish on them. Lori asked people to send well wishes and love to me with their keys. They did. Sometimes I could feel their . . . *well wishes* very clearly.

"I always sent a little generic energy thanks with the ones Lori sent back. I don't know how many of the fans got anything out of the keys she returned to them, though."

I shrugged. "I'm sure they did. They were good luck charms to Ruthie."

Alvee smiled. "But I don't know if she ever *really* got any returned energy out of them, or if she just imagined that she did. It takes a little practice to feel it – but some people are a little more naturally adept than others."

Alvee indicated for me to hold out my hand. I did so, and he dropped the keyring into my palm. The green ones felt warm from where he'd had been holding them between his fingers. A vision of him naked, in a deliciously compromising position, flashed across my mind, completely unbidden. I blinked in surprise.

"See?" Alvee grinned. "You're more adept at feeling the energy of good wishes than you might've thought."

I smiled at him and dropped the keys back into my purse.

Alvee took both my hands in his. Now he looked solemnly at me. *Here it comes,* I thought. *Whatever he'd been trying to say to me in our dreary English hotel room – marriage, probably.* I was unsure. Did I really love Alvee enough to marry him?

He started out traditionally enough.

"I love you, Carol," he said, "and I'm pretty sure you love me."

I nodded. I loved him enough.

"I think that we have the capability – I think that we love each other enough, and you seem to have a natural inclination for it. I think that we could obtain the kind of equilibrium of energy that Maury and Maki have."

"Do you love me that much, Alvee?" I asked. *Do I love you that much? More importantly, do I trust you that much?*

"I can think of no other," he said and kissed my hands.

Did that mean he thought of no one but me, or did it mean that he couldn't think up anyone else that might fit the bill?

"It won't happen overnight, of course," he said. "It takes years to perfect the process. But the reward is in the journey."

Alvee wasn't asking me to marry him. He was asking me to stay young with him.

Be careful, Carol! Ruthanne's voice said in my head.

"You once said that it takes a damn near superhuman melding of love and respect and understanding to accomplish what they have, Alvee." I said. "I'm not superhuman. Sometimes, like when we were overseas, I feel subhuman. Bitchy. Small."

"You're the one I want, Carol." He squeezed my hands. "Don't you want me, too?"

Alvee endeavored a pout of rejection, something he'd never actually experienced IRL. Who had ever rejected Alvee? It was an emotion that he wasn't actually experiencing now, either, yet after a moment, he pulled it off, looking like he truly believed I was going to refuse him. He was a great actor, after all.

"Want you, Alvee? All I'll *ever* want is you," I said.

The pout vanished. He knew it.

"Maury and I, we're your biggest fans. He told me one time that he could imagine you as anything – saint, sinner, good guy, bad guy. You're his muse, he said. I feel the same way."

I realized all at once that it was true. I'd never thought about it till just then – I hadn't been thinking about writing at all during the Black Hole of Calcutta that'd been my sojourn in jolly old England.

But now I ran a little test in my mind – I tried to quickly dream up a few scenarios. This guy's a bank robber . . . I saw Alvee. This guy's married to this woman who has mental problems. He loves her, but . . . the guy was Alvee. Clones and robots are trapped on this satellite orbiting Earth. It's gonna crash and kill us all. One of the clones must save the day . . . *OMG, clones* – more than one Alvee!

I realized that, just like Maury, I'd never write another character that wasn't him, in some way. He was just that charismatic, just that gorgeous, just that fascinating, and I was in just that deep. Too deep. There was no other man to compare to him in my mind – the rest of the other half of the population were all just stuffed into the backseat behind Alvee. He was himself – delicious, heavenly smelling Alvee that I slept next to each night – and he was also anyone I could imagine him to be. Ryan who?

"Maury and I can go on making Alvee Smith-Killem pictures forever," I said. "That is, if he still wants my collaboration."

Alvee smiled. "He loves your stuff, Carol. Even *The Winds of Desire.*"

I hung my head in embarrassment.

"You just can't be scared of him when he's in Fellini mode," Alvee said. "If you feel strongly about something he's doing, you just have to stand up to him. But make sure it's something you do feel strongly about. Pick your battles. Don't quibble with Maurice Claremount.

"He'll either agree and see things your way, or he'll sarcastically shout you down . . . or he'll fire you. It's in everybody's contract somewhere, that Maury can fire them. Summarily. Even mine. But there will always be a next time, another project. All will have been forgiven, if not forgotten, and he'll call you back."

Alvee grinned, then his smile sobered again. "I'd like to keep making movies that you write, Carol. I'd like for you and me to be together, to be halves to the same whole, like Maury and Maki. I'd like to make that kind of commitment. I'd like to share all this," he gestured around us, "with you. We could be one of those Hollywood success stories."

Be careful, Carol! Ruthanne's voice said in my head again. But I ignored her – I knew that there was that one part of my mind that would always be careful, would always be suspicious, would never quite trust him.

But what choice did I really have? What was I going to say? *Gee, Alvee, I dunno. I've been getting a little homesick again. I've discovered that I miss my boring, mindless job, miss endlessly typing up briefs and writs that I can't even bother to take the time to understand. I miss my bank account, that one that never had a comma in it. I miss my dusty little apartment with its community pool. I miss Doug.*

How ya gonna keep em down on the farm, after they've seen Paree?

"What do you say, Carol?"

I realized that Alvee was *asking*. Alvee never asked. Alvee never had to ask.

What else could I possibly do? I nodded.

Now Alvee smiled his smug little grin, just for me. He said softly, in that smooth, dark voice that I liked so much, "Let me show you what else I learned in Japan."

We went up to his room, and what had before been phenomenal became transcendental. There were all the gloriously sublime sensations of being one with him, but now there was an additional suffusion of light and heat and energy. He showed me how to give, to receive – he showed me how we could make the energy travel back and forth between us like the poles of a magnet. It was like a flood for me, a confluence of satiety and contentment.

"So it *is* a sex thing," I said, once I'd caught my breath, once I'd come down from these incredible new heights.

"It doesn't have to be, but it can be," Alvee replied. "When there is a mutual feeling between two people."

Now that we'd decided to undertake this convergence together, Alvee said, whenever we chose to blend our universal energies (which would be whenever we were in bed together, or so I hoped), the effects of the slings and arrows of the years would cease, or at least slow exponentially. We wouldn't live forever, or course, and we wouldn't even stay young forever. But who would want to be thirty forever, even twice? We would age very slowly, he said.

For me, the mundane, every day, simplest aspect of this miraculous secret was the best part. For someone that lives in the here and now, like myself, the most obvious fact of the arrangement was better than promises of youth almost eternal: Alvee Smith-Killem was mine. I didn't have to marry him – he'd decided that we were soul mates, partners in the Yin and Yang of the universe. That partnership would keep us young.

But all the great philosophical possibilities of this singular phenomenon came down to one uncomplicated idea in my mind: Alvee was mine, exclusively. It meant that I'd never have to worry about him considering any little meaningless romps with slutty tourists from Wichita, with adoring fan-girls, with any of the Jessika Yerdlays and Melissa Holloways that he'd be co-starring with in the long future of his successful career.

He'd chosen me to be his one and only, the other half to his whole, in a way that only he and I, and Maury and Maki could understand. The allure of a momentary dalliance could never top that.

The incomparable Alvee Smith-Killem was mine. Eternal youth? That was just gravy.

SIXTY-THREE

Five months later, I was again walking up the red carpet at the *Cinerama Dome*, this time for the premiere of *Kinship*. The lady from *Entertainment Tonight* was there again, but this time I didn't hang back out of frame. This time she wanted to interview me, too.

Maury had not given me screenwriting credit – I'd not had anything to do with his brilliant screenplay, after all. But he had inserted *from a story by Carolyn Adyon* in the opening credits, and that was good enough for me, good enough for the lady from *ET*.

"*Kinship* addresses an uncomfortable subject, that of father-daughter incest," she said. "What influences did you draw on to speak to such a forbidden topic?"

Ha! I thought. *There was once this teenage girl who was desperately in love with her bitchy mother's beautiful boyfriend . . .* But that hadn't been my inspiration for *Kinship*, now had it?

Maury had warned me that the public would not be able to see the forest for the trees regarding *Kinship*. "They're going to call it *The Incest Movie,*" he'd said.

"The story is about evil," I told the lady from *ET*. "It's about the lengths to which a person will go to fight back against betrayal. It's about revenge. The incest is just a small aspect of that revenge." I paused. "If you want to talk about how that aspect was visualized, you'll have to talk to the director."

Perfect shift to Maurice Claremount, standing right there next to me, prepared to discuss his controversial treatment of *such a forbidden topic*. Even the lady from *ET* was impressed by my segue.

After the provocative film's haughty director, she next spoke to its star. Alvee said that Lawrence had been a difficult, challenging role to play. "So much hatred," he said. Then he echoed what I'd said, that the incestuous interactions between Lawrence and Rebecca were not the point of the film. "The monstrosity of his drive for revenge – that's the point of the film," he said.

Next to be interviewed was the rest of the cast, Jacob and Jameson and Alyson and Melissa. They were all unknowns here, and the *ET* watching public has a short attention span for unknown foreigners, so the *ET* lady interviewed them all together, giving them a chance to say a few words each.

They'd had to fly in from the shire, of course, and boy, I hoped their arms were tired.

The film was not to everyone's taste, as Maury had warned me that it would not be. Cary Stuward was one of the first to pan it, but only after it opened nationwide. He hadn't been at the premiere, even though, Maury assured me, he'd been sent an engraved invitation to it.

"Cary Stuward would pan *Citizen Kane* if Alvee was in it," Maury said. "The man didn't get to hold anything else, so now he holds a grudge."

Kinship received a 77% on *rottentomatoes.com,* with 65% of the audience liking it. *Variety* gave it a good review, and *Time Magazine* gave it a rave review, even though they, too, concentrated on the incest aspect more than the revenge aspect. It turned a small profit, but was not a blockbuster, not a runaway money-maker as *Cheyenne Sundown* had been.

We were again sitting on the terrace, having brunch, a week or so after *Kinship* opened. Maury was reading *The Los Angeles Times.* Alvee pretended to complain about the meager take at the box office.

"Welcome to art, Alvee, my darling," Maury said, not looking up from *The Times.*

"*Paramount* called," he replied. "They want to know if I'd like to do another western." He nodded at me, grinned, indicating for me to watch Maury's reaction. "Am I still under contract?"

"*Mr. Killem's performance will be long remembered in the annals of the anti-hero,*" Maury read from a review of *Kinship* in *The Times.* "*Never before has malevolent, unrepentant evil been so convincingly portrayed by such a pretty face.*" He looked mildly at Alvee. "I was thinking more along the lines of an updating of *The Picture of Dorian Gray.*" Maury chuckled. "Unrepentant evil, indeed."

"Or how about *Richard III?*" Alvee suggested.

"I'd like to make another profitable picture in this decade, Alvee. You are definitely unrepentantly evil enough, but you're too young, too pretty for that role.

"*Deformed, unfinish'd, sent before my time into this breathing world, scarce half made up* – nobody's going to buy you as Richard, Alvee. No one's more *finished* than you. Besides, I don't think Carol's ready to go back to England just yet."

When I blanched, he added, "You can't do Shakespeare properly anywhere but the *auld sod.*"

"Or how about *Macbeth?*" Alvee grinned gleefully. "*By the pricking of my thumbs . . .*"

"*Something wicked this way comes!*" Maury and I said in unison.

Ah, Alvee, the ever watchful part of my mind whispered, *just how wicked are you, really?*

SIXTY-FOUR

It's been almost a year since Alvee and I entered into our mystical union of energy-sharing. It's too soon to tell if it's working, if I'm going to stay young with him.

He still looks like a million bucks, tax free. But I found another gray hair the other day, and like I said in my letter to *Trident,* I've been feeling a little tired lately. Maybe it'll pass, but the fatigue has brought on a little paranoia about the whole deal, so I thought it might be best to write it all down. If something seems to be too good to be true, then it usually is. So I thought that it might be prudent to leave behind this record of events.

Maury's been making me actually contribute to the new screenplay this time. *To earn my keep around here,* he says, *to be part of the team.* We're working on an update to *The Picture of Dorian Gray* as a vehicle for his muse, just as he'd suggested.

Alvee enjoyed the praises he'd received as the antagonist in *Kinship* so much that his director is going to star him as the bad guy once again, just to please his whim. And what a bad guy! Maury is seeking to combine the sophistication and bon vivant of Perry Calibri with the darkness of innocence corrupted – there can be no more quintessential part for a pretty face who wants to explore evil than the black-hearted, eternal youth that is Dorian Gray.

Alvee is *Dorian Gray,* that little watchful part of my mind whispered. *And he doesn't even need a painting in the attic.*

Maury says it's about time that I learned the screenplay formatting that I'm so afraid of, and there's no better way to do it than by adapting someone else's story.

"Look at it this way, Carol," he said. "You want to already know how to drive, before you learn to drive a stick-shift."

"You know how to drive?"

"Of course I know how to drive. I just choose not to. It's one of those privileges of rank." He grinned. "There's no sense in learning to drive – coming up with the story – while at the very same time trying to learn the nuances of a stick-shift – trying to learn to format your story into a screenplay. Some of our little tiny minds just can't handle both things at the same time." He winked.

"So you and I are going to adapt the great Oscar Wilde. We're chauffeuring a master. He's already written the immortal words – we just have to make them understandable to the Facebook generation. And throw in some camera direction. I know you can do it."

So maybe it's just Maury's slave driving on this script that's making me tired. I'm still not that great at the whole process – apparently I want to describe things too much. Scenery and emotions and locations. He gets frustrated with me a lot.

"It's a *movie*, Carol! We're going to *see* what's going on! You don't have to *describe* it!"

But he says that I seem to be catching on a little bit, and a word of praise from Maurice Claremount is worth the world to me. It makes all the long hours rewarding.

So maybe it's just the work that's been making me feel exhausted lately.

Or maybe the energy thing doesn't travel between Alvee and me as efficiently as it could, due to that one part of my mind that, like the cheese, stands alone, refusing to trust him.

Maybe Alvee, skilled as he is in this obscure Eastern talent, senses that little part. Maybe he knows that, try as I might, I'm unable to give him my complete all. Maybe he's taking more than I'm able to give. Maybe I'm not getting enough back.

So, I've written it all down. I'm going to leave instructions for Uncle Ted, going to leave him a sealed envelope, with *Open in the event of Carolyn Adyon's death or incapacity* or something similarly cinematic written across it. If anything happens to me, if I fall into a coma or drop dead from congestive heart failure before the ripe old age of thirty-five, he'll open it. Inside will be a safe-deposit box key, just like in the movies. Inside the safe-deposit box will be this true Hollywood story, with instructions for Uncle Ted to send it to *Trident*, the literary agent.

Because I know I'll never leave Alvee, despite all those brave words in my letter to *Trident*. Alvee is like a drug, like insulin, like air. Even if one small part of me will never completely trust him, him and his supernatural winning of the battle over Mother Nature, something that might perhaps have come to him at the expense of the lives of seventy-five people, something that he might be maintaining at my expense – I could never leave Alvee or Maury or this lifestyle. For the first time in my life, I feel like I'm accomplishing something, even if it is just entertainment.

When Maury filmed *Kinship*, he made my story, my characters, my words, and by extension, *me*, immortal. No matter what happens to me, it'll always be there. I want to create more words, more characters, and have Maury and Alvee make them immortal, too. The appeal of that, like Alvee's voice, is infinitely inviting, the risk be damned.

Maybe I'm just tired. Maybe I do love Alvee with enough of me that we'll both stay young for a very long time.

Or maybe not. Maybe I'll end up like Lori, shriveled and wizened. Maybe that's the penalty for not loving Alvee Smith-Killem with the entirety of one's being. It's not something that Ruthanne would've had to worry about. Ruthanne doubted Franck not at all.

Maybe Alvee is slowly killing me. Maybe he killed all those people in Vegas. Maybe not. Maybe everything is going to work out just like he promises it will.

After all, he said that I wouldn't age, not that I'd never feel tired or suspicious. Alvee never promised that I'd never find another gray hair.

But just like Franck's thoughts on Jessika and Roger – he could never, ever know if Jessika had had a hand in Bridget's death – *not so much because it wasn't possible – anything is possible when a person is obsessed,* he'd said. *But I refused to believe it because there was no way I could ever know for sure.*

So, the most part of my mind refuses to believe anything bad about Alvee, because I can never, ever know for sure. In this brave new world that encompasses the reality of an energy-based fountain of youth – I can never, ever know if he used it to kill all those people, to make himself young again, or if he's using me up the same way. It's just too early to tell.

I can never know if the seemingly beneficent secret also has a dark side, when wielded by a dark master with selfish intentions.

Could Alvee be a dark master? Oh, yes. Alvee is a great actor. He can be anything he wants to be.

So, since I can never know, I'm not going to destroy what we have with doubt and suspicion. I'm going to enjoy myself to the fullest. I might never be able to completely trust him, but I'm not going to destroy what we have over it.

I think that I do love him with the entirety of my soul. He's funny, smart, devious, beautiful. I know he can be cruel. He's old Hollywood, not a man to be trifled with. He is my other half, and I do believe in him with my whole being.

Except for that one little part.

Maury recently told me the story of how Thetis dipped Achilles in the river Styx, to make him immortal. But she held him by the heel, and that part, untouched by the holy waters, became his weakness. Alvee has dipped me in the river of fantasy – the promise of immortality for my words, my characters, as well as the astonishment of staying young with him. But the tiny part of me that refuses to just let go and trust him completely, that's my Achilles' heel. It stubbornly remains, even through my inundation in the warm waters of the good life.

Damn it.

But it's all still too early to tell.

Either way, I'll never give him up, at least not until I know for sure that the dream isn't working. And then it'll be too late.

Maybe I'll end up like Tithonus, in a way – my words immortal, myself growing old before my time.

Maybe not. But it's a risk I'm certainly willing to take.

Well, *almost* certainly.

There is this story, after all.

If something happens to me, and some publisher exposes Alvee for the impossible thing that he really is . . .

On the other hand, there's no such thing as bad publicity.

****

Also by LM Foster

A Passing Resemblance
Contrariwise – A Tale of Twins
Corvino
Crypsis
Duck Feet
Peter's Sisters

Two Green Keys:
Two Green Keys
Adapted for the Screen

One Wilde Ride Trilogy:
Part One: It Might Have Been
Part Two: An Exceptional Boy
Part Three: What Should Never Be

Stars and Guitars:
Talk To a Movie Star
Where The Guitars Play

Tom and Wiley:
This Carnival of Strange
Wiley Royce
Generally Recognized as Safe
Wiley Royce Versus The Martians

www.ingramcontent.com/pod-product-compliance
Lightning Source LLC
Chambersburg PA
CBHW061304170626
46817CB00001B/46